Celestial

Hannah Mae

Published by Hannah Mae, 2022.

This is a work of fiction. Similarities to real people, places, or events are entirely coincidental.

CELESTIAL

First edition. May 12, 2022.

Copyright © 2022 Hannah Mae.

ISBN: 979-8201421977

Written by Hannah Mae.

Dedicated in loving memory to my grandfathers, Kenneth and Robert, and to my Aunt Patsy.

Also dedicated with great reverence and love to Jesus, who made all of this possible. I'd be nothing without Him.

Special Thanks Goes To:

My Cover Artist - Adrianna Colvin

My Copy Editor - Patrick E. Craig

My Close Writing Friends - Crystal Grant, Jason McCoy, Kristi Cain, and Linore Rose Burkard

All my Beta Readers

And most especially, my Friends and Family who supported me through it all. I wouldn't have begun if not for them.

A Word from the Author

WHAT YOU'RE ABOUT TO read is the direct result of a three month expository Bible study and an eight year writing journey. Mankind has depicted angels for centuries, but seldom have these works and stories been built on a Biblical foundation. The sad fact is, we're so indoctrinated to see angels a certain way, we've subconsciously accepted our human traditions as fact. We often think angels are serene, perfect beings; stoic, unflappable guardians; or the subject of figurines and trinkets. However, when we tune into what the Maker of angels revealed about them in His recorded Word—the Bible—, we'll find that the truth about angels is stranger and far better than any of the culture's fictions could dream.

When my eighteen year old self set out to create an angel story, I didn't want to write it as the world would. I desired to honor the Lord by respecting the truths He already revealed to us. It meant ignoring manmade assumptions and regarding only the Scriptures for my creative decisions. It was an intense process. I expected to dispel some misconceptions. What I didn't expect was my entire view of the heavenly hosts to be so drastically redefined and my intimacy with God to be so dramatically increased. Angels are not infallible, robotic creatures who question nothing. They're created beings that were effected by sin's curse same as us, and they too have failings, limits, and longings that also cry out for a new heaven and earth. Two worlds are broken: the visible and the invisible. God's plan leads to both sides mended and healed through the power of the blood of His Son, Jesus Christ.

This has been my prayer for the past eight years. That *Celestial* will entertain, bless, and challenge others to rethink—to expand their understanding of God's ways and His plans in accordance with His Word. For while my story is Biblically informed, Biblically complimentary, and highly plausible thanks to the information the Bible had given, this is still a fictional angel story. I encourage others to seek the Bible for ultimate answers on these matters for themselves. After all, *Celestial* is not really about the angels anyway. It's about God and His gift of salvation, which He uniquely offers to mankind. Angels are the main characters, but it's God's character that's meant to be on ultimate display.

So to those of you who don't know Christ personally, I welcome you. I hope this book will be an enjoyable experience and perhaps give you a view of God that maybe you've never seen before. And to my brothers and sisters in Christ who are opening these pages, it is my sincerest wish that by 'The End' you'll walk away with an enriched spiritual perspective and deepened appreciation for the gift of salvation you have. May *Celestial* encourage everyone to draw nearer and nearer to Jesus. Thank you.

- Hannah Mae

Prologue

HEAVY DARKNESS LAID upon the hospital. Grief and pain tramped along to the beat of heart monitors, and IVs dripped their concoctions into blood veins. Tired nurses held to their dutiful if dreary routine as their work hours trudged on, but for the lone hooded figure they could not see, his work had just begun.

The song he hummed danced down the hall. It issued from his lips like a gentle creek over polished stones, but no mortal ears could hear. Walking in the swirling mist, he searched the rooms. Passing a mirror, he caught sight of the glowing wells of holy fire within his eyes. Alive with that celestial spark, they illuminated his face beneath the shroud. He shook his head at the reflection and continued on.

Doctors shivered as he passed. They pulled their jackets tighter and checked thermostats, but the invisible being paid no mind to their discomfort. Such reactions weren't surprising. He floated through more personnel, sending extra waves of unnatural cold through their core.

The being turned a corner. A distant glow peeked beneath a scuffed door at the corridor's end. It called to him. The misty veil under his command gathered behind him, forming two wings that spread as a canopy above, then carried him in a quick rush of air. He landed and dismissed the mists. They again swept the floor, obscuring his tall stature.

Though unreliant upon mortal needs, the angel drew a reflective breath. His steady hands fiddled with his robes. The grey fabric rippled glimmering silver as he smoothed it. Content with appearances, he straightened. The heat and brilliance within his eyes intensified, and he dissolved into a stardust that sifted through the door. On the other side, the diamond shards reassembled in pieces until his form completed itself. The warmth from the glory in his eyes subsided, revealing their crystalline, emerald hues.

The angel often pondered how the human populace would react if they caught visual evidence of him. He imagined himself being an awe-inspiring spectacle, but for all the mortal admiration in the world, it wasn't one tenth the amount of respect he had for the soul laying before him.

An elderly man gripped his sheet against the cold. His lungs wheezed, no doubt burning for precious oxygen, but the Mark of the Trinity, embedded upon his chest, stole the angel's attention from anything else. Its unfathomable light beat back the spiritual world's shadows with its beauty.

High tones rang out from the Mark.

In obedience, the angel drew near, and his face basked in its light. He nestled a tender hand upon the man's feverish brow. The rapid pulse in his veins subsided beneath it.

The mortal sighed, as if accepting newfound peace. His body ceased its fight and sank into rest.

Assured of his comfort, the angel dissipated his hand and let it flow into the man's mouth. He reached for the breath of life, seated at the heart. Then, taking hold of the man's literal last moment, he pulled. It snapped like a thread. The Mark of the Trinity brightened, and the angel withdrew his hand. "Come forth, Image Bearer," he whispered. "Arise." The symbol extended its reach, engulfing the man in its brilliance.

Untethered from his physical shell, the man's soul opened a new pair of eyes for the first time. He blinked and gave a soft laugh, full of good cheer, but then his eyes widened. His jaw slacked. He lurched back and hid his face in his hands.

The angel sighed to himself. He knew that terrified reaction from a million missions before. His appearance radiated remnants of God's Shekinah glory, after all. No human could withstand its holiness at the start, but determined to reassure him, the angel smiled. He dismissed his hood, letting loose a rush of dark hair interwoven with silver. It swayed and flowed like waves upon the shore. He then rested his strong hand on the man's shoulder.

By that one simple touch, the fear and tension in the human's fresher, younger form melted away. He peeked through his fingers.

"Fear not, God's beloved," the angel said. "The Lord your God invites you into His courts tonight." He released the man's shoulder and offered a hand as smooth as carved alabaster. "I, His servant, have come to bring you home."

The man lowered his hands and stared with eyes so wide the angel could almost see himself in them.

Sympathetic to his hesitance, the angel scooped up his quivering hand and resumed his song. He led his charge into the hall. The mists went ahead of him as if with a mind of its own. It crept along and carpeted the tile floor to honor the man's first taste of immortality.

A joyous smile broke out across the Christian's now youthful face, and despite not knowing the tune beforehand, he took up the angel's song. All thoughts of earth were behind him.

The angel of death smiled, thrilled as always to escort one of God's adopted sons, yet an old dread loomed over him—one that never seemed to go away. The angel shied from select doors and mentally constrained his fog as though to keep a monster on a leash. He quickened his pace toward the end of the hall, then spread his arms apart. A sharp rip cut between dimensions. The gateway led to a fair, green country just beyond. Soon, the Image Bearer and his angelic guide departed far from the second realm and into the third—Home.

Chapter 1

ANCHORED BENEATH THE heavenly realms yet set a dimension apart from the physical realm, the Abyss rested. This vast cave, large enough to harbor a city, served as a prison. Demons were locked here without hope for return. Pools dark as tar pits dotted the floor. The walls and pathways were carved out of the red and beige stone, but stalactites and stalagmites preserved the cavern's natural, warbled beauty. Embers popped from mounted torches, flickering their light upon the glossed pillars, providing some comfort to an otherwise foreboding place.

A few echoes bounced across the cave. Angelic soldiers stood in rigid lines beside a cleared arena. In their valiant red uniforms, they appeared as they intended to be seen, united as one body and one mind. Two of their own sparred while they spectated in interest.

Jediah watched one of his troops, an angel of small stature named Laszio, barrel roll to a stand. His weapon, two silver sticks, chinked far out of reach.

Laszio brushed his tousled sandy hair off his face. He spun around, and his single braid flipped against his cheek. His two wings, meek as a sparrow's, fanned out. Their crystal quills burned brighter.

His opponent, a slightly taller angel, gave a competitive smirk. With a gold whip in his hand, he flicked his wrist, and the end tassel cracked sparks.

The smaller angel's brow furrowed. He balled his fists and charged.

Jediah frowned. In his agitation, his wings, which then coated his shoulders, back, and sides with their diamond feathers, twitched. The sword strapped to his back grew heavier the longer the match continued. He couldn't mistake the strain on Laszio. The inevitable wouldn't be delayed for long. Jediah heard Laszio's best friend, Eran, murmur encouragements from behind. It wouldn't change the outcome.

The taller angel, named Chrioni, swung his arm. Glowing like a fire strand, the whip bit into Laszio's torso. The smaller opponent clutched the cut and tumbled forward. Seizing the moment, Chrioni flung his chord. It wrapped around Laszio's wrists. Chrioni's wings emitted bright energy as they flapped the ground in a swift take off. He flew overhead, dragging the small angel up with him into a flip. Slack from his shining whip coiled around Laszio. The winner achieved a safe landing. The loser flopped onto his back, bound and tied.

Jediah bottled a resigned sigh. It went just as he thought it would. He relaxed his crossed arms and nodded at the victor.

Chrioni bent down to help his sparring partner up. They mumbled mutual compliments as he untangled Laszio. Then, setting the gold whip aside, they stood at attention. They kept their focused stares ahead as their captain planted himself in front of them.

Jediah smiled with approval. "Well done, Sergeant Chrioni. Your progress is unmistakable."

"Thank you, sir." Chrioni bowed his neck and put a hand over his chest.

Jediah paused as he noted a subtle sag in Laszio's shoulders. "Of course, there's always room for improvement. Your determination was admirable as well, Private Laszio."

Pursing his lips, Laszio straightened. "Thank you, sir."

Jediah nodded and turned around to face the rest of his division. "We'll pick this up later. Back to your posts."

"Sir, yes, sir!" Flying off, they dispersed in pairs. Their wings brightened the caverns.

Eran stayed behind. He brushed aside a braid similar to Laszio's that hung from his short, black hair.

Jediah looked over his shoulder to see Laszio standing behind. He sighed and adjusted his stance so both soldiers could be in his view. "Yes, Private Laszio? Something the matter?"

"It's nothing, sir." Laszio's head lowered.

Eran rubbed the ends of his hair along his neck. "Well. Look at it this way, Laszio. You lasted longer this time."

"I know." Laszio rolled his shoulder and walked aside to retrieve his metal sticks. They glinted in his hand. A long silver string, a delicate yet sturdy chord, connected the two bars together. Laszio's fingertips stroked it up and down, seeking knots—if there were any.

Jediah prayed God would break this cycle. For as long as he's known Laszio and Eran, they were the most driven soldiers in his faction. That quality blessed them as much as it prompted them to attempt far more than their capabilities allowed. How often they overtaxed themselves. Jediah didn't care to count, but God bless them. They had gumption.

Jediah rubbed his forehead. His commanding tone softened. "Brother Laszio, it's what I always keep telling you. You and Eran both. You're magnificent fighters, but you need to pick your opponents wisely. Consider your options—"

"Then do what's workable," Laszio recited. "I know, Captain. I know."

Agitated, Jediah arched an eyebrow.

Laszio groaned and rubbed his eyes. "I'm sorry. I'm sorry. I shouldn't have said that."

"I'm glad we agree," Jediah admonished. He crossed his arms. "Words are like arrows, Private. Let a careless one fly, and it's too late."

"Yes, sir." Laszio bowed with a hand pressed to his chest. "My apologies. I do not wish to dishonor you or our King."

Gazing aside, Jediah shrugged. "It's all right. I know you're frustrated."

Eran drew to Laszio's side and patted his back.

Giving them space, Jediah let them commune in silent support. Ever since he paired the two, the arrangement had turned out better than expected. Eran's resourcefulness with Laszio's tenacity balanced the differences and at least granted them a decent shot at winning their sparring matches. Little did Jediah know that their dependence on each other would turn out reaching far past their needs. They were all but attached at the hip.

Eran looked to Jediah. "We'll just be heading back to our posts now, Captain." The two turned away, and the glorious light in their wings heightened.

Jediah sighed. He hated to see them upset over failure all over again. His usual inner battle restarted. Be the stiff commander or the brother?

He rubbed the back of his neck, then called after them. "How about another session? Just the two of you with me."

Their wings lowered and dimmed. Laszio faced Jediah with eyebrows raised. "When?"

"Right now." Jediah crouched. His fingertips touched the floor while his other hand reached over his shoulder to wrap around the hilt of his sword.

Eran made a wry smile. "I don't think another practice is going to change much, Captain."

"A little can go a long way. Light your weapons."

Laszio and Eran shared a look. Each pulled out his pair of sticks. They were carved with complex divots etched into the silver and connected by a sturdy length of chord. The two angels stretched their wings. A couple of lighted feathers touched their weapons, and golden drops leaked forth from the barbules. Light filled the carved patterns, and its glow bled into the strands.

"Now," Jediah instructed, "Focus on the energy within the base of your wings. Let it flow naturally. Don't fight for control. The fight should be out here. Not in there."

Laszio and Eran nodded. "Yes, sir." They sidestepped in separate directions.

Jediah watched them encircle him. Then he scraped his blade against the hardened leather as he pulled it out from its scabbard.

In one sharp motion, Laszio and Eran took their paired sticks in each hand and spread them apart, causing the strings to twang tight. The vibration alone shook a smidge of light off the string. Those same wisps folded in on themselves into a ball of pure energy. Sparks flew as soon as the manifested spheres spun along their lines.

Softening his hardened feathers, Jediah's wing armor unfolded. He allowed a single quill to ignite his sword. Gold and orange embers glinted along the razor's edge. Jediah turned his wings back into armor again and stood up. Repositioning his stance, he twirled the blade, and with the press of a secret button along the hilt, the short sword extended to its full length.

"Whenever you're ready." Jediah's energy, his lifeblood, the very essence by which all angelic beings thrive, surged within. For they were mere empty vessels — empty vessels for God's empowerment to fill.

CELESTIAL

Spring's eve swept over an isolated country village in the United Kingdom, and a ministry angel sat alone atop the local church roof. The skies were cloudless. Dressed in his kind's customary blue, Nechum hummed an ancient prayer while staring into the starry seas above him. Though created without wings, he flew in his mind into the black expanse and soared among its white flickers.

Nechum likened the stars to the angels themselves. They were just as old and just as vigilant over the earth. Their power fended off the darkness, yet were small and meek so as not to steal glory from the moon. Just as God's mightiness reigned supreme, so did the moon remain the rightful centerpiece in the dark spaces.

His legs swung as they dangled off the roof's edge, and Nechum rubbed his hands on the scratchy shingles. To his left, the white church steeple speared the jeweled heavens with the cross at its top. It looked old-fashioned, but it matched the rest of the town. Nechum gazed over the village rooftops. Antiquated buildings, potholed streets, worn sidewalks—its age gave it charm. The fast-paced generation might call this place behind the times, but Nechum preferred it that way. God had blessed his past ten years of guardianship there, and he valued every second of relative peace apart from the major conflicts at large. Thousands of troubles over a thousand lands, yet the significant quiet of a countryside suited him best.

Nechum closed his eyes. His empathic sense, God's secret gift to all ministry angels, reached out. Its passive perception granted him divine awareness of the emotions of all things. Matters of the heart couldn't evade it. Nechum could feel the town and its citizens. Their happiness. Their longings. Their pains. This midnight, he found most residents at peace in restful sleep. Only the usual few remained awake.

Smiling for the normalcy, Nechum re-opened his eyes. He continued his hymn, but then stopped short. A new stirring aroused his senses. He peered to the right. A shooting star streaked from the horizon and banked at an odd curve, rocketing straight over the wheat field. It enlarged and brightened.

Alerted, Nechum jumped to his feet. He pressed both hands over his chest, and his energy activated. His arms spread apart. A shield of rippling azure light stretched out before him. Whatever spiritual attack it might be, it would ricochet off the barrier like a ping pong ball to a paddle.

The speeding object still didn't seem to be stopping. Nechum tensed, expecting impact, but then he caught the glint of gold. Nechum gasped in recognition. He dropped the shield.

A gust blew in Nechum's face from the messenger angel's sudden stop. Gold sparks flickered off the ends of his scrawny wings as they beat the air like a hummingbird. The messenger batted the mess of curls out of his eyes. "Pleh. Pleh." His tongue shoved stray hairs out of his mouth. "Got a little carried away there, didn't I? Almost overshot it by a few miles." He brushed yellow specks off the leather padding that protected his shoulders and chest. The rest of his gold uniform glowed underneath it.

Nechum peered at this strange brother, who at the moment was looking every direction except him. He sensed an innocent curiosity in him, almost childlike, yet Nechum sought to see his eyes. The coloration of the eyes coincided with an angel's mood and would often change color according to disposition.

This messenger's eyes were a deep cobalt blue with a silver sheen as merry as a summer month bathed in sunshine. The brightness they sustained unveiled a spirit that brimmed with the joy of the Lord.

Nechum gave a courteous bow with a hand over his chest. "Evening, brother. Are you new here? Where's Malach?"

"Huh?" The messenger broke out of his distraction. As he spoke, his active hands gestured as if to help explain. "Oh, Malach. Yeah, yeah, right. Malach. The thing is, Malach had to replace an officer's courier. There was some battle or something recently. His messenger lost a wing... and a leg... You know how it is. Very last minute. So Archangel Gabriel asked me to finish Malach's route for him tonight."

Nechum managed a single sad nod. "I see." He hated news from the war they had been locked into since Adam's Fall. "Well, please tell Malach I'm praying for his protection and for the courier's swift recovery. Did he suffer much? The courier? Was he in a lot of pain?"

The messenger shrugged. "He'll be fine. It's not like any of us can die or anything."

"Yes, but... that doesn't make it hurt any less."

Tipping his head, the messenger gave a sad smile. "Well, um, he's okay. He'll regenerate and be up and at 'em in no time."

Nechum put up a blank front. His empathic sense read the insecurity behind the messenger's gaiety. "You have yet to tell me your name, friend."

Without warning, the messenger snatched Nechum's hand in an over-enthused handshake. "Akela. Messenger Akela. At yours and our God's service."

"And I at yours." Nechum cringed a grin as he pondered the appropriate time to pull his hand back. "Nice to meet you."

Akela kept shaking. "Thanks. And your name is?"

Nechum tried to keep his voice steady from all the gyrating. "Nechum. It's Nechum."

"Ah! Nechum! I like it. Got a nice ring to it too—Oh!" Akela dropped Nechum's reddening hand. "Sorry."

Nechum rubbed his fingers, yet tried not to make his discomfort too obvious. "No. No. It's fine. You're fine."

Akela smashed his hand into his topmost curls. "I went and did it again. I'm so sorry. I just get really excited when meeting unknown faces. I see one, and whoop, I forget myself."

"That's okay." Nechum massaged another cramped knot. "Lively greetings don't hurt. Usually."

Akela's wings kept stirring the air as he continued to hover.

Nechum laughed to himself. "Are you going or are you staying?"

"Yeah, I should go. I'm supposed to deliver a message to a recipient—" Akela balked. "Oh, Right! You *are* the recipient. Pfft, there I go forgetting again. Honestly, why else am I here?" He pulled at a leather strap that wrapped crosswise over his chest, and his satchel moved from his side to his front. He clicked the polished clasp and flipped open the flap. "Okay. Let's see." He reached in with the eagerness of a child invading his mother's purse for candy. "Nope. Nope. Nope. Ah-ha."

His entire arm disappeared inside before it returned with the letter. The envelope reflected moonlight like mother-of-pearl. "This should be it." Akela's eyes read the sender and addressee's names. "From a certain Heber to a certain Nechum. Does the name ring any bells?"

Nechum accepted the letter. "Heber's the head of our province." He thumbed a corner. "Must be my daily summons."

"Sounds good. Though, I've really got no say in what you get. I just deliver stuff. That's my job."

Nechum stopped himself from rolling his eyes and chuckled. "I wouldn't have guessed."

A sudden tone pierced the air—a music that trumpeted from dimensions away. Its echo rang loud and long across all creation. Angels near and far, beneath the depths, among the clouds, in the cities, and beyond the hemisphere, could hear it.

Akela's giddiness doubled. He turned to Nechum. "Ready to go?"

Nechum grinned. With one hand over his chest, he reached toward the heavens. Multiple shields appeared and assembled into a set of shimmering stairs as clear as blown glass. Their steps stacked so vertical it resembled a ladder. Nechum climbed, eager to enter his Creator's presence once more. Akela, though more than capable of speeding past him, flew at a polite pace.

Nechum thought it a beautiful thing. Though he didn't fully know Akela, a common loyalty bound them. They couldn't be more different, but they were family.

Laszio's ball of light whizzed close to Jediah's ear, and its passing heat brushed his cheek. His eyes followed the sphere's path into Eran's receiving string. It bounced off the taught cord, but Jediah predicted its coming. Awaiting the right moment, he angled his sword before it could hit his face. It pinged off the blade and exploded inches from Eran's feet.

Jediah spun back around. He nabbed Laszio by the scruff of his neck and threw him forward. Then with a round-house kick, Jediah nailed him in the back. Both Privates collided into a jumbled heap. They groaned and made sluggish work getting off each other.

Jediah rubbed his mouth to stifle the disrespectful laugh lifting the corners of his lips. "Better. You're both getting better." Sword in hand, he brought it close to his face, pointed it upward and offered a small bow.

Laszio and Eran managed tired nods in return.

Jediah pressed the hilt's button. The sword's clicking mechanisms retracted the blade, and he slipped it back into its scabbard. "I think a break is in order. We'll continue training later."

Laszio cast a defeated look yet gave a thumbs up.

The ethereal trumpet called. Its ring poured and filled the Abyss, beckoning them to God's halls. Already, Jediah's troops sang as they headed out with great rejoicing. Even Eran and Laszio's moods lightened.

Jediah too welcomed the splendid shivers those sweet notes stirred within him. He unfurled his wings.

Coming, Lord. We're coming.

Chapter 2

NECHUM SURMISED HE and Akela must have arrived early, for many of their brethren weren't there yet. Just ahead, Jubal, a seraph, had neither lowered his gilded horn nor silenced his herald, and Neryia, the Archangel of Worship, seemed to be attending to the final details.

"Guess we'll have front row seats, eh?" Akela joked.

Nechum nodded, but had no desire to speak. All his attention stayed near the throne.

Archangel Neryia adjusted the shimmering circlet that graced his brow, the symbol of his appointed status, and straightened his attire. The purple velvet robe and cream-colored tunic God had gifted him matched his six luminous wings. All of which splayed themselves behind him as a train. Neryia brushed back his snow white hair, yet ever always, Nechum sensed the uneasiness behind his violet eyes.

Nechum sighed to himself, wishing he could ease that Archangel's self-consciousness. His meticulous nature was indeed ideal, but not for all circumstances. Nechum pondered if striking a pleasant conversation with him after the assembly just might give him the relaxing distraction he'd need. Until then, Nechum opted to meditate on His Lord while he waited.

Just one faint vision of God's throne room made the heart yearn for more. A gentle, pale smoke rose from the dancing flames of a jeweled altar. It collected in the ceiling, leaving a pleasant, purifying aroma. The thickest portions of those curling plumes beget streaks that colored the air in which they hovered—sometimes in colors never imagined.

Crystal waters covered the golden floors. They floated elegantly through pearled pillars and gathered into a deep pool surrounding the Throne. The Great Throne itself stood on a dais of golden stairs. A river of white tumbled down the steps on all sides. It intermixed with the pool below, causing an overflow into a wide inlet. The River of Life it was called, and it never ceased to fill the halls with its tender sounds.

Nechum watched Neryia and the other seraphs bow their heads. They approached the Throne's steps. Their feet walked atop the waters yet remained completely dry. Tiny ripples shimmered and multiplied with every touch of foot and wing, and the closer the angels neared God, the brighter they glowed. By the first step they set on the first golden stair, they overflowed with their Master's glory, the light of which focused and refracted in small circles all over their beings; as though they were covered in brilliant, sacred eyes.

Neryia's violet clothes turned white, and gold embroidery suddenly traced along its hems.

Even Nechum, who wasn't as close to the throne as the worship angels, trembled with the Almighty's power surging and building up inside him. It began filling him to bursting. He hurried forward with an equally eager Akela to their God and King, the Alpha and the Omega, the Beginning and the End, indescribable and unfathomable. As their Creator, all angels couldn't see Him as anything less than their Ruler. The only One truly worthy of their respect.

Archangel Neryia raised his hands toward the Almighty. His contained energy unleashed in a dazzling display of purple fire that engulfed him. His fellow seraphs also ignited in similar holy flames. Their many wings outstretched and danced in synch. Their feathers tingled as wind chimes as they swayed. Lifting off, they floated and twirled like falling cherry blossoms riding the ever-changing winds, and their blazing hands and feet traced graceful circles, alighting patterns that reflected off the clear waters below.

Cherubs joined their numbers, and each climbed the air on four wings. They were less graceful than the seraphs, yet were twice as powerful and exuded enormous strength. Their beings constantly shifted into that of animals to represent all of nature in God's presence. Sometimes they were lions, sometimes they were eagles, or anything in between, and ribboned violet fire from the seraphs shone upon many a shimmering scale and feather.

Nechum heard new voices singing and turned. Angels from every corner of existence now crowded in by the thousands and multitudes of thousands. Nothing in the earth, skies, seas, or galaxies could compare. Ministry angels. Messenger angels. Angels of Death, the Army and Nature angels. All of their clothes shifted to a gold embroidered white that matched the purified worship angels. All of them now bathed in God's Shekinah glory. Their footsteps brushed more golden ripples atop the water's surface in shining strips that reflected off the pillars, and Nechum joined their choir. Their voices lifted to higher harmonies impossible for humans to find.

The last two Archangels, Micheal and Gabriel, emerged from the crowd. Nechum nodded in respect as they passed by to present themselves.

Neryia, who noticed their arrival, slowed into a descent. He landed between them, and it was plain to Nechum that he lifted his head high to make up the difference in his comparably small height. Neither Gabriel nor Michael spoke or sang. However, they gave their smallest Archangel a brief smile of reassurance. Amidst unimaginable lights, colors, and music, they each removed their glimmering circlet, knelt, and placed them upon the lowest step of the Throne before bending to a full bow.

Nechum, Akela, and the whole throng hushed as they followed suit. They lowered to their knees and pressed their foreheads against the waters. Wishing moments like these would last forever, Nechum sensed the warmth in his Master's smile. No angel dared break meditation by looking up. The observed silence was far more profound, far more comforting, and far more beautiful than any song. All was still. All was at peace. All was right in the universe.

After a time, Neryia addressed the crowd. "My brothers!" his voice echoed. "We have gathered once again to present ourselves before our Lord! For this is the day that the Lord hath made..."

"LET US REJOICE AND BE GLAD IN IT!" replied the multitude, as they rose to attention.

The voice of God the Father, loud yet comforting, spoke. "Well done, my good and faithful servants. But before you each begin, a visitor has come forth to speak."

"Must You insist on spoiling my surprises?"

Just like that, all joy died. Nechum shuddered. He'd be a fool to mistake *that* voice.

"Oy-vey," Akela mumbled. "*Now* what does he want?"

After considerable effort, Nechum mustered enough will to look upon the visitor as he came forth.

Self-proclaimed Prince Lucifer, the only rebel brave or stupid enough to set foot in God's presence, strutted atop the River of Life right up to the Great Throne. This corrupted cherub, the strongest of his kind, was well built and gifted with winning charms to equal the most cultured of nobility—whenever he had a mind to use them.

Nechum grimaced at his pallor. Though finely chiseled in appearance, like all demons, Lucifer's luster had paled to a sick grey after being starved from God's presence for so long. The eyes of demons—the eyes of traitors—either yellowed, went red, or were reduced to a black blank. Their wings dulled with grime, and instead of the golden energy that gave angels power and life, their energy resembled blood—hellish and red.

Lucifer leered at the two angelic soldiers who blocked his path. "Move." His four wings wrapped around himself into a black sheer cape. "Or *be* moved."

"Let him come," the Lord commanded.

The angels backed off, and Lucifer elbowed one as he passed.

Archangel Michael unsheathed his sword; his huge wings poised to strike.

"Fear not, Michael," God commanded. "Put away your sword."

The General of the Lord's army obeyed, but his eyes still flared white with fiery energy.

"Yes, we wouldn't want to chip our nails, would we?" Lucifer taunted, as he gave a smug smirk.

Micheal looked ready to pummel him for such blatant disrespect, and Nechum couldn't blame him despite his apprehension for violence. He'd do it himself, too.

Lucifer's head circled from side to side. His wings twitched in agitation at the disapproving company. "Oh come, now," he chided. "Is this any way to treat an Archangel?"

God's voice bore down on the devil. "You gave up that title the day you forsook me."

"Yes, then You picked a new favorite." Lucifer eyed Neryia with acute distaste.

Neryia's throat tensed.

"And here he is," Lucifer continued. "Cowering beneath you like a twittering chick. And how has my former assistant been?"

Neryia averted his gaze, and Nechum's empathic sense registered the oncoming depression that threatened the seraph's sinking heart.

"Doing well, I presume?" Lucifer pestered.

Nechum's hand wrung the end of his tasseled shawl. *Must that devil dig into him at every opportunity? Withstanding his presence was foul enough.*

Lucifer cast a dismissive glance at Neryia's circlet left on the lower step. "You know, you look better without that on. Never did fit you."

"SILENCE, SATAN!" God's voice boomed like the crack of thunder.

The demon choked, his own words rammed back down his throat.

"THIS IS THE ONE TO WHOM I WILL LOOK: HE WHO IS HUMBLE AND CONTRITE IN SPIRIT AND TREMBLES AT MY WORD!"

All around, the angels murmured their agreement like birds communing in a crowded tree.

Lucifer coughed. Scrounging for his dignity, he tried to stand taller and adjusted his collar. "Touchy. Touchy," he mumbled.

"Where have you come from?" God asked.

"You're all knowing. You tell me," Lucifer scoffed. "I've come to complain about *Your* troops once again attacking *my* troops and stifling *my* good work."

"*Your* good work?" Archangel Michael crossed his arms. No doubt he'd cast Lucifer right out with a boot to his backside for good measure.

Neryia touched Michael's shoulder, and the General's tense arms loosened. This was *the* sanctuary, after all. Violence had no place there.

Lucifer smirked. "Yes, General Redundant, *my* good work. Perhaps you'd like to convene with Captain Obvious and Sergeant Pansy." He nodded toward Gabriel and Neryia. "Anyway, before I was so *rudely* interrupted. Was I not exacting long due punishment upon unworthy sinners?"

"You overstepped your bounds, Lucifer," Gabriel corrected. "God would never grant you the right to take those people's lives."

"Overstep my bounds? Were they not to be handed over to me?"

"They were never yours, Lucifer," Michael reminded, not bothering to withhold his disgust. "Those Image Bearers bore the Mark of the Trinity. They are God's people. Your attempt to keep their souls from Him was doomed to fail."

"And soon they'll live in eternal, *undeserved* bliss." The demon batted his eyes as he chirped with false sincerity. He glared at God. "Where is this justice you speak of? Was it not You who declared, 'The wages of sin is death'? You Yourself demand purity. Why is it then that You contradict Your statutes? These 'saved ones' or 'Christians' are no better, if not worse, than the average mortal. They're hypocrites. They wag their tongues, preaching holy living, yet wallow in their own mud—like pigs in their slop. Your salvation is nothing more than a scapegoat for loose living. A 'get-out-of-jail-free' pass for their lusts. So tell me, Holy Judge, where is Your justice?"

"What would you have me do?" God questioned.

"Let me punish them. They deserve it. I can reduce their pride to ash. Your 'consistent' nature demands it be so. Or is it true that hypocrites follow a hypocritical God?"

Nechum, along with his brethren, waited for God's answer.

"Oh, how you have fallen from heaven, morning star, son of the dawn!" God declared. "You prowl around like a roaring lion, looking for someone to devour." His voice rose. "I will repay each person according to what they have done... Yet... while they were still sinners... *I died for them*."

Those four simple words echoed deeply in Nechum's mind. His Lord spoke them with such firm sincerity; they were love incarnate, overflowing with a quiet joy for the heart to marvel to.

"For I so loved the world that I gave my one and only Son, that whoever believes in Him shall not perish but have eternal life." Their glorious King's words flowed as a honeyed balm. Life issued in their utterance, sending rapturous chills in all who listened.

Lucifer grimaced as quiet 'hallelujahs' filled the halls.

God's voice darkened, "But for those who are self-seeking and who reject the truth and follow evil, there will be wrath and anger. For I do not show favoritism."

Once again, Lucifer opened his mouth in protest, but his words seemed caught in his throat.

"I judge the thoughts and intentions of the heart," God continued. "*You said in your heart, 'I will ascend to the heavens; I will raise my throne above the stars of God; I will make myself like the Most High.' But you are brought down to the realm of the dead, to the depths of the pit.*"

Lucifer rolled his yellowed eyes. It was only the umpteenth time he heard his impending sentence. "You could have just said 'no.'" He showed God his backside and strolled out. "It matters not. I'll have my way. Mark my words."

Though relieved he had left, Nechum remained stiff. He didn't fear the Devil. He wouldn't win, but he had a knack for havoc.

Chapter 3

"PUSH THEM BACK! PUSH them back!" Jediah hollered.

The jail break turned the whole Abyss into a madhouse. Demonic prisoners scratched the walls. Angelic soldiers scattered here and there in hot pursuit, and the waves of light from their swishing and clapping wings blasted several demons to the ground.

The demons screamed louder, and their frenzy broke to a fever pitch as they tore into anyone within reach.

Jediah scowled. They were supposed to remain trembling shadows in their captivity. They were supposed to await final sentencing until the End was to begin, but the centuries they spent imprisoned one step away from the hellfires had driven them mad. Suffering a fraction of the heat to come reminded them they were to be fed to the hungry furnace. No regeneration. No healing. Always their outer shells would peel. Forever their wings would blister and char to ash. It's no surprise they'd act like wild animals at the first chance of escape. To make matters worse, they were cherubs, and they were Apollyon's. The power to mutate into any horrible creature, real or imagined, was theirs.

Jediah distanced himself from the frontline. Sizing up the dark masses, he clenched his fist as he searched for their loathsome leader. The monster he sought loomed large behind his teaming pawns.

Lord Apollyon dwarfed them all and possessed an energy capacity tenfold the average. He salivated and foamed at the mouth as he screamed orders for Jediah's head. Five thousand years after the Scorpion Wars and his craving for revenge against the angel who bested him never withered.

Jediah grunted. He wasn't about to falter to the disgraceful riff-raff under his watch. Several of his soldiers regrouped as a batch of demons turned into scorpions and assembled for a charge.

Jediah ordered his first battalion forward. "Archers at the ready!"

Angelic troops knelt before increasing numbers of scorpions and lit up their bows. They harnessed lengths of white to the string.

"Fire!"

Shafts rained like meteors and pierced many eyes, but some demons ignored the blinding stings.

Jediah kept his wings armored. Their opponents were too close for his comfort. The hardened feathers on his shoulders clinked tight together like metal plates, and his scarf that bore the symbols of his rank stayed secure beneath them.

Running towards danger with swift agility, Jediah alighted his sword and carved a path through the thickest of the horde for his troops to follow. He aimed for arms and legs and each demon he maimed he entangled in the Holy Chains—God's exclusive gift to him for such times. Its hot links seared themselves to their victims and sapped whatever energy was left. To Jediah, the chains were weightless, but if he went by how his enemies groaned, they seemed to crush whomever they pinned to the floor.

Two energy spheres whizzed over Jediah's head. They blasted open a clearing, and Laszio and Eran dove right into the thick of it like cannonballs in an ink pool. The intensity flaring from their shining wings forced more demons to back away.

Jediah clenched his teeth. *What are those two doing?*

Laszio and Eran stood back to back. Sparks sputtered from the new spheres spinning on their strands. Back and forth, right and left, they whipped and ricocheted the energy balls against all sides. They added more spheres to their bombardment. Soon they juggled four to six at a time, passing them underarm or overarm like a cycle of sunrises and sunsets.

Jediah hastened his strikes as more demons surrounded the Privates. For he knew they couldn't keep up their barrage for long. He slipped between clashing weapons to reach them faster.

Laszio's voice rose above the noise. "I think we might have bitten off more than we can chew, Eran!"

"You think?!?" Eran shouted. "I followed you in! Remember?"

Distracted by what he heard, Jediah barely noticed the glint of sharp talons. He ducked. The claw missed his neck but sliced his brow. He backed up and fingered the thick energy that seeped from the fresh scar.

The demon responsible smirked and puffed his chest.

Jediah shortened his sword and threw it.

The demon caught the blade by the crossguard, its tip almost nicking his chest. "Is that it?" the demon scoffed. His fingers moved. The button triggered, and the extending blade plunged into his abdomen.

Not wasting a second, Jediah rushed the screaming demon and chained him down. Then, planting his boot on his shoulder and gripping the hilt, he kicked, yanking the sword out.

An earsplitting bang shook the cave. Jediah jolted and stared at a glowing mushroom cloud that expanded to the ceiling. Laszio and Eran were spat from its plumes and sailed several yards before crashing into a safe clearing.

Jediah rolled his eyes. *They attempted an energy bomb... again. They almost collapsed a tunnel last time.* Then he noticed the resulting damage. Several demons, most missing half their limbs, limped and crawled away, and there laid a cleared path to Apollyon. Jediah reconsidered his thoughts. Despite their recklessness, Laszio and Eran had given him an opening. Apollyon now raged just a few feet away.

Jediah walked forward and bound his wound with his scarf. Chaining demons one by one took too long, he realized. There was only one way to finish this fight quickly, and he'd need every drop of energy he could spare.

Apollyon, the strong and proud, locked eyes with Jediah and glared.

Jediah likewise glared back. He fanned his wings, then smacked the ground again and again in challenge. Their drumming rhythm generated small bursts of ringing light.

Apollyon opened his wings and answered in kind.

At the sound, angels and demons both silenced before their leaders. Right of single combat was initiated. The crowd backed away from their champion's war path as they walked closer towards each other and waited for the coming storm to break.

The demon lord's shadow towered over Jediah. Apollyon extended his massive sword. "You're free to bow out now, little captain. Surely, we can negotiate my troop's peaceful dispersion."

Jediah scowled. "You assume too much of yourself. God used us to defeat you once. We'll do it again. There is *nothing* to negotiate."

Apollyon sneered. "So be it." His sword swung down with thunderous wake.

Jediah sidestepped. Apollyon rushed another flurry of attacks, but none touched him. For his practiced mind digested the seconds. He read every little motion in Apollyon's arms, and his own blade, though a mere toothpick in comparison, proved sturdier than its meager size. Both their edges screeched sparks as Jediah deflected the blows, yet his sword never chipped.

Mounting cheers and jeers rang from the crowd.

Frustrated, Apollyon changed form. Jediah soon found himself evading pinchers, a stinger, and the multi-jointed legs of a great black scorpion.

Jediah unfurled his wings and flew up. He straddled the hideous arachnid's back and struck, but the blade failed to scratch the oiled exoskeleton. With an air-cutting hiss, a poison tipped stinger whipped and tore his sleeve. Fearing the next strike, Jediah jumped off and clapped his wings behind himself, but Apollyon's foreleg breezed right through the light waves and pinned him down.

The angels hushed.

In the corner of his eye, Jediah spotted the stinger aimed for his neck. Desperate, he reversed his sword grip and swung above his head. The blade found soft tissue and shored the sinews connecting Apollyon's knee joint.

Apollyon howled. Vibrant red spurted from the lacerated leg.

This time, the demons hushed.

Returned to his normal form, Apollyon clutched the severed stump while the amputated arm fizzled out of existence. Apollyon's eyes burned red. He hammered his blade into the floor. Broken rocks hurtled everywhere, but Jediah avoided them with ease.

The demon paled as his fleeting energy bled out. More glowing red gel dripped from the gaping wound, and with ragged panting, he crumbled to his knees.

Jediah lengthened his back. Focusing his energy, he let his eyes ignite white, and the Holy Chains sparked link by link in his hand. He rocketed forward.

Apollyon scrambled too late. Jediah strapped his arms and legs together, then strangled his neck with a final yard. Then he shouted in a terrifying, righteous tone. "By right of single combat, you, Apollyon, forfeit yourself and your armies! And in the name of God the Father, God the Son, and God the Holy Ghost, I lock you and your hoards away until the end of the age! And you're never getting out!"

Jediah opened his wings to full span and stretched them upward. He could feel the energy climbing up their roots. Prismed colors filtered out each feather in dazzling splendor, and just as his wingtips touched, the intensifying light merged into a piercing star.

The chains brightened. The dark pools dotted throughout the Abyss stirred, and their waters flowed upward, filling the ceiling.

Apollyon and all his demons squirmed and squealed as gold crept up their feet, consuming their legs and then their torsos. Then, as soon as it engulfed their faces, they dissolved into particles that were sucked into the opened pits. Apollyon's remains were banished behind two immense doors that slammed shut. His roars rumbled behind them, but the clanks of heavy locks soundly defied his threat.

Jediah relinquished the fire in his eyes. His troops erupted in shouts of praise and 'Hallelujahs', but he couldn't shake off the wariness that lingered in his mind. *How'd he get out in the first place?*

Laszio fumbled to his feet, too dizzy and exhilarated to stand straight. He grabbed a stalagmite to steady himself. "Well, *that* was a rush, wouldn't you say, Eran?" After no reply, Laszio turned to see his partner purposely staring at the opposite wall. Laszio sighed. He could practically hear Eran's thoughts scrutinizing. He always scrutinized during his sour moods. Laszio nudged Eran. "Hey."

Eran jerked away, refusing to look at his smile.

Rolling his eyes, Laszio gave him a good-natured swat to the arm. "Oh, come on."

"No, I'm not 'coming on,'" Eran argued.

Laszio shrugged. "It didn't go that bad."

"You nearly blew us up." Eran snapped around. His eyes churned a darker grey. "I theorized a long time ago that no energy bomb was controllable enough for close combat. But you went and did it anyway."

Laszio cringed. "Well, now we don't have to guess. Now we know."

Eran shook his head. "Next time, please let me do the thinking. All right?"

"Oh, ye of little faith."

"Oh, ye of little sense."

Shaking his head, Laszio leaned into Eran. "Hey, I'm sorry I messed up the plan, but you gotta admit. That was an impressive explosion, which technically means it worked, and do you recall who thought it up?"

Eran gave a pointed look. "Stop."

"You."

"Please, stop."

"For what? Giving you credit for succeeding?"

The corners of Eran's lips lifted slightly, but he covered it under his hand. "I don't think Captain Jediah was pleased with it."

Laszio waved a dismissive hand. "You mean for inventing a crowd clearing blast? Oh, yes. He's hopping mad now."

Eran released a light chuckle.

"Ah-ha! There you are. It's about time." Laszio folded his arms and relaxed his wings. Their softened plumes caressed his sore back. "What would you do without me, brother?"

"Find a parrot. I hear you've got a lot in common."

"Hardy-har-har." Laszio bumped Eran as his best friend laughed, but then he caught sight of their captain.

Jediah's hardened eyes narrowed ahead as he passed. The scarf wrapped around his brow showed a damp gold splotch that expanded.

The two quieted and stood at attention. "Well," Laszio muttered. "I guess Captain might be a *little* ticked."

Jediah marched toward Apollyon's prison doors, where its chief gatekeeper, Kikeona, fidgeted. "Sergeant," he addressed.

The soldier jerked himself into a stiff posture. "Yes, sir?"

"What happened? How did they get out?"

Laszio cringed for Kikeona, who mumbled a few words before answering. "I don't know, sir."

"What do you mean you don't know?" Jediah pressed.

"Well, sir. I was standing here. Then somebody must have knocked me out, because... I don't know..."

Jediah rubbed his eyes and planted a hand on his hip. "Did no one else see what happened?"

"No, sir," everyone replied.

Jediah snapped around. "Sounds like a lot of eyes doing nothing!"

Laszio's heart sickened for disappointing his captain.

After a few silent seconds, Jediah's glare softened. He sighed and shook his head. "Well, sounds like we might have an infiltrator on our hands. Those of you still able, I want a wide sweep of the area and a new patrol to guard the exit tunnel. Nobody leaves the Abyss until we figure this out. Understood?"

"Yes, sir." A dozen angels spread out.

Letting out a sigh, Laszio rubbed his neck and turned to Eran. "There now. He wasn't upset about the bomb, so this could have gone worse."

Boom!

A huge dust cloud kicked up at the entrance.

"Figures," Eran muttered.

Laszio raised his hands in defense. "Hey, it wasn't us this time."

Jediah ran towards the source of the ruckus. "Secure the entrance!"

Laszio and Eran joined the ranks closest to the dirt cloud that concealed the exit tunnel. A silhouette hacked and coughed behind the dust curtain.

Jediah stepped closer, brandishing his sword. "Who are you? State your name and business."

"Wow," the stranger sputtered. "You all could use a duster in here."

"Answer the question!" Jediah pressed.

A messenger angel stumbled out. Brown powder coated his blonde curls. He batted dirt off his uniform and didn't notice Jediah's sword until its point jutted under his chin. "Whoa. Whoa." He raised his hands in surrender. "Easy there, Sampson. I'm on your side."

Laszio cocked an eyebrow. This odd angel didn't seem so much terrified as mildly surprised.

With sword still poised, Jediah balked at this messenger's behavior. "Uh... It's not Sampson. It's Jediah."

"Okay, perfect!" the messenger replied. "Just the angel I wanted to see." His large eyes soaked in the surroundings. "So, this is the Abyss, huh? It's bigger than I imagined. Very roomy."

Upon hearing Jediah sigh and sheath his weapon, Laszio lowered his sticks and fastened them to his belt.

Jediah folded his wings. "You, um, came to deliver a message then?" he said in a softer tone.

"Yes." The messenger nabbed the satchel fastened to his side and dug into it. "And might I just say, it is a real honor and pleasure meeting you, Captain. God's work through you during the Scorpion Wars was really inspiring."

Laszio never before saw his captain's cheeks go so pink. He chuckled under his breath as Jediah shifted on his feet and cleared his throat. "Um... well... thanks."

The messenger paused his search to bow. "I'm Akela, by the way. At yours and the Almighty's service."

Now in control of himself, Jediah's expression went blank. "Wonderful. Do or don't you have a message for me?"

Akela cringed. "It's in here somewhere. It's just...somewhere."

Laszio whispered in Eran's ear. "Do you think he's always this clueless or only after he crashes?"

Jediah shot him a warning look.

Laszio's throat tightened. Further ashamed, he clamped his mouth shut.

Shaking his head and turning back to Akela, Jediah pinched the bridge of his nose. "Did you, by any chance, lose it?"

"Don't be silly," Akela replied with sudden vehemence. "It's in here. I know it." His skinny wings vibrated. "Drat. It's too easy to lose things in here."

Jediah sighed, but this time he smiled. Stepping forward, he patted Akela's shoulder. "How about you come with me? I can offer you a place to sit while you look."

Akela's eyebrows raised. "Oh, that'd be wonderful. Much obliged."

Nodding, Jediah pressed a hand to Akela's back, ushering him onward. "I also should apologize for our less than cordial greeting. You caught us at a bad time."

"A bad time?" Akela's eyes circled the crowd in concern. "What sort of bad time?"

"A bad time." Eran answered in his usual matter-of-fact way.

Jediah aimed another glare at Eran, and Eran bowed his head in apology. Relaxing his furrowed brow, Jediah spoke to Akela. "Won't you come with me, please?" He gestured for him to follow. "Show's over, everyone! I want that half resting and that half scouting."

The soldiers saluted and dispersed.

Laszio watched Jediah lead Akela on the graveled path; the smallest one that curved around the far wall to the captain's quarters. He almost laughed again at how Akela followed close like a puppy seeking attention. *Quite the character, that one.*

Chapter 4

JEDIAH LED AKELA AROUND the bend into a tunnel. The path climbed to his place of solitude, which nested on a higher vantage point. Dislodged rocks from the recent skirmish cluttered the narrow space. Jediah weaved around the wreckage and regarded the scattered boulders with tired eyes. "Watch your step, please. It's kind of a mess."

"Meh, it's not so bad," Akela said. "I've seen bigger disasters in bedrooms."

Jediah turned to check on Akela. The messenger stared at the broken stones with interest as he passed. Jediah pressed onward. "You, uh, journey through earth often?"

"Sometimes. I recently tried a lemonade someone threw away. Just to see what it tastes like."

"Lemonade?"

"It's some kind of juice—except there's sugar, seeds, and these stringy clearish bits floating around in it."

Grimacing, Jediah shook his head. "Yick. Sounds tempting."

"It wasn't half bad, actually." Akela's footsteps hastened as if hurrying to catch up.

Jediah undid his scarf and fingered his forehead. Moist energy still seeped from the gash.

Akela caught up to him and winced. "Ooo." He hissed through his teeth.

Jediah smiled and waved him off. "It's just a scratch. It'll heal in fifteen minutes, I'd wager."

They entered a corridor to a spacious room lined with dark geodes. Their glazed minerals hid colors in the black like spilt oil under sunlight. Water trickled down the walls in sweet, therapeutic tones.

Jediah stared out through a wide opening in the left wall that overlooked the cave. Attentiveness was one habit he never had to break, and he relaxed further to see his troops accounted for and following orders. He motioned to a smooth boulder that protruded from the floor. "Here. Rest yourself."

Akela hesitated. "Are you sure?"

"Be my guest."

Akela grinned and plopped himself down. He stretched his legs and rotated his ankles before once again investigating his bag for that elusive letter.

Jediah unbuckled the scabbard straps while he waited. His aching shoulders happily shrugged off the sword's weight, but he nestled it in his hands and propped it up on the floor with care. Releasing a tired breath, he permitted his hardened wings to soften and stretch.

He turned to find Akela still fiddling with the bag.

Akela grunted and set the satchel aside. "I don't understand it. I just got this message a minute ago." Propping his elbow on his knee, he laid his chin in his hand. "Oh, wait!" He bopped himself on the forehead, then reached behind the leather guard that protected his chest. "I put it here for safekeeping." Pulling out the letter, he immediately handed it to Jediah.

Jediah peered at the parchment in his hands with even greater interest. "Safe keeping? Who sent it?"

"The Almighty," Akela said with a twinkle in his eye.

Stunned, Jediah ripped it open. His eyes darted over the sparkling ink. His rust brown hair filtered his vision, and he flicked it back.

Akela inched forward. "May I know what it said?"

"Lucifer is planning an attack." Jediah paused. "Our Lord wants two of his best warriors captured before that happens." He read further, ensuring there was nothing confidential. "It says… this shall be a secret mission… no one must know, and you, Akela,… are to come along with me."

Akela bolted up. "Really? What else?" He reached for the letter as though to take it right out of Jediah's hand.

Jediah jerked the letter back. "I'm getting there. I'm getting there." His mouth mumbled more of the written words under his breath. "The other members of this company: Laszio, Eran, Nechum, Alameth." Then, reading the mission's primary locations, Jediah straightened his back, his mouth slightly ajar.

Earth. We are going to earth.

Jediah's eyes wandered to stare at a corner in recess while a hurricane of thoughts swirled in his mind. He paced around the room in silence. His hands brushed the wall's jagged edges, not minding the minor cuts they added to his fingertips.

"Captain?" Akela said. "You don't look so good. Are you okay?"

Jediah was locked in a trance filled with wonder and aching fear.

Akela approached him, waving a hand in his slanted view.

Jediah blinked, breaking out of his daze. "Huh? Oh, yes. Yes, I'm fine." His cheeks flushed.

"Well, okay then!" Akela said. "So I'm your assigned messenger now. Can't wait to work with you!" He offered a handshake, which Jediah accepted.

"And same to you."

With a big nod, Akela turned toward the exit.

"Wait, where are you going?" Jediah asked.

"I've got a few more messages to deliver. Don't worry. This should only take a minute or two." Akela stretched his arms and wings.

Jediah smiled in understanding. "Alright. Do what you need to do, but come back, and by all means, tell no one about this."

"Oh Captain, my Captain. My lips are sealed." Akela zipped out the door, then right back in. "I promise."

Jediah cocked an eyebrow. *He doesn't even know when or where our team is meeting yet.* Jediah sauntered closer to the door.

Sure enough, Akela returned quicker than a Yo-Yo. "I just remembered... if I need to finish more last-minute routes before we embark, at what time and where is our group rendezvousing? Did the message tell you?"

Jediah chuckled. "I have all the information. I'll brief you once you get back, but right now, you've got work to do."

"Right... right... okay, then. Bye!" Akela disappeared in a flash and a gust of wind.

Jediah pushed out a long breath. Keeping that angel focused was bound to take some doing. He returned to his window, relishing his privacy. Times of solitude helped him think best, and much was on his mind.

Something panged inside. Something incomplete and broken. Something he never could fix. *"I'm going to earth,"* his thoughts repeated. *I'm going to earth.* He pondered his life and fully realized he had watched the Abyss with such unbroken dedication for so long, he couldn't tell how many millennia must have passed since he last saw anything from the first realm—the mortals' realm.

Thrilling anxiety pressed his chest. His hands tingled from warmth and cold.

He took off his scarf and wetted it against the damp walls. Sitting down, he dabbed his wounds. The cuts stung but just as quickly eased in the cool, but that horrible panging deep inside refused to leave him alone.

How long have I been trying to distract myself from this?

His inner being cried out, yearning for relief, but only one word echoed in his soul that seemed to give it any respite: Salvation—the most wonderful word every angel understood but could never experience. Once again, Jediah imagined how freeing that gift must feel. That undeserved, crisp sensation of your filth reeked soul being washed clean and pure... God on the inside... your body His temple... sin's curse and all its guilts undone... to bear the blessed Mark of the Trinity.

For a moment, Jediah's emotional sickness lifted. "For God so loved the world," he recited to himself. His mind filled in the blanks before he jumped to a separate Bible passage. "For the grace of God has appeared, bringing salvation for all people." His emotional sickness returned, and he swallowed as he added, "For all *men*."

Jediah couldn't count how many times he reminded himself of that fact. Angels knew God as Creator, Friend, Master, and King, but to know Him as Savior—that sounded so wonderfully different yet beyond their farthest reach.

All angels knew renouncing their loyalty meant to walk the demon's path. It was a one-way road. No return. Yet God saw fit to grant sin-cursed men, lost at birth, a means of escape from eternal death and expulsion from guilt. *They* could return.

But why can't we? Shaking his head, Jediah berated himself for daring to ask that question again, and yet it was all he could think about. *What if this mission is my chance to learn what being redeemed is like? What it means? How it feels?*

His curiosity boiled, taunted, and even frightened him. "Too many risks," Jediah told himself. "Too many risks." He'd be spotted easily if he fraternized with humans while trying to find his answers. He was the Keeper of the Abyss. Demons would swarm him and steal the Abyss's key on sight. He shuddered to think of Apollyon rampaging again, especially now. No wonder God called this to be an undercover mission.

Jediah shook his head. *I can't partake in redemption anyway. So why bother? I probably wouldn't understand a thing.*

Wringing out his scarf, he ordered himself not to entertain the idea any further, but that lingering malaise in his being continued to haunt him. It wouldn't leave him alone, and it never had for five thousand years.

The demon huffed and puffed. Paranoia spurned his tiring wings to keep stroking. Overcome with wariness, he glanced behind himself as often as he dared. Already he forgot how he managed to sneak in and break open Apollyon's gates undetected. Not that he cared to remember it. Jediah was that close to entrapping him with the rest.

Night covered the Romanian landscape. The city lights of Cluj-Napoca drifted beneath him. White headlights and red taillights trailed each other as cars wound between buildings like beetles. Even as high up as he was, the demon could hear the hustle and bustle of the metropolitan zoo, yet his sights were on the blackened forest just beyond the suburbs.

Reaching the tree line, the demon clamped his wings together and dropped between the leafed clusters. He then re-opened his wings, parachuting for a soft landing.

Hoia-Baciu Forest's trees didn't grow straight. They were twisted and gnarled as though they had grown in pain, writhing in their infancy. The atmosphere, thick and heavy, stifled breath and smelled of terror. Even the full moon had not the power to lessen the gloom. For fog choked out its silver sheen.

Hearing the voices of his kindred, the demon followed them to their source. They came from a clearing the locals called the Devil's Heart. Most humans feared to come near it. A longstanding demonic presence had forever stained its soil. Only stubbled grass could live. All else, whether tree or bush, couldn't even set root there, for the discordant music of worship demons had forbidden life. It furthered the Sin Curse for miles, and though some fools attempted planting sprouts, they'd only find them shriveled and dead in weeks.

Nearing the clearing, the demon swallowed. He knew Lucifer waited for him along with his Captains and their messengers. Distracted, he bumped into a guard.

The soldier promptly throttled him. "What are you doing, angel scum?"

"Wait! Wait! Wait! I'm not an angel!" Realizing he forgot to remove his disguise, the demon wiped the fake face off, and his bright red soldier's uniform faded into an aged maroon.

"Let him pass," Lucifer chided, as he glared from a distance. "We were expecting him."

The guard bowed low in piety. "Apologies, sire."

The demon got up and brushed his clothes, tidying them up. He passed all the Commanders at present to throw himself before the Devil's feet.

"Well?" Lucifer growled. "Was your mission successful?"

"Yes, great one. I infiltrated the angelic ranks during their assembly, penetrated Apollyon's cell, and incited the jailbreak. Just as you commanded."

"And?"

"And-"

"Stand up, for fool's sake!"

The demon flushed cold and leaped to his feet.

"I can't hear you with all that groveling." Lucifer folded his arms and cocked his eyebrow. "Now tell me. Is it true what they say about Jediah's key?"

"Yes. The rumors are true. His wings control the cells and bars. I saw it in action myself."

Lucifer's eyebrow rose higher in mild interest. "Interesting. And how many guards are there?"

"About a hundred."

One captain pounded his fist in triumph. "That's hardly a legion. We can lay siege on the Abyss tonight. Let us strip Jediah of his wings and free our brothers!"

Lucifer backhanded the officer's cheek. "Fool. It's not that simple. Jediah would chain and lock you and your troops up before you reached the doorstep, Captain Zivel."

The small demon chuckled at the officer's embarrassment, but lowered his eyes. "And it's about to get harder." The whole counsel suddenly leered at him. He had spoken out of turn. "I-I'm sorry."

"You *will* be," Captain Zivel threatened.

Lucifer waved a hand, silencing him. He squinted his eyes. "I will overlook your offense, imp. *If* your information is worth something."

The demon shuffled his feet. "Jediah won't be there. He's been assigned to a covert operation on earth."

Murmurs spread throughout the council.

Lucifer's wings draped his shoulders as he folded his hands in a thinking position.

Zivel stepped forward to address the assembly. "So he'll disappear, and the key will disappear right along with him to who know's where!" he declared. "We must act now!"

Once again, Lucifer silenced Zivel and ordered him back to his place with one gesture. He pointed at the demon. "You."

Feeling extra small, the demon shrunk back.

"Do you know anything more? What *is* Jediah's mission?"

"He's been tasked with arresting two of our key warriors, sire. But I know not whom."

"You don't know?" Lucifer's neck sprouted scales beneath his collar. His teeth sharpened, and his irises shrunk to slits.

Falling backwards, the demon shielded his face. "But- but I *do* know one who's going with him."

"And I should care why?"

"It's Akela."

The demon peeked through his fingers. Lucifer's being returned to normal, but his biting eyes still dug into him. "Akela you say?"

Grasping that glimmer of hope that he might escape the Devil's wrath, the demon nodded. "Yes. Still ever the flying circus, that one."

Lucifer said nothing. He instead folded his hands behind his back and paced around the group in a circle. "Moriel," he called.

A tall and lean messenger stepped forward. "Yes, sire."

"Has your master, Yakum, finished his work yet?"

"Almost, my prince. Malkior is still gathering data for him from the world's hospitals as we speak."

Lucifer nodded. He rubbed his chin. "Our gift to mankind is almost prepared, but we're too few yet to unleash it at large without Apollyon's troops. We need that key." The level of perceptive thought could be clearly seen churning in Lucifer's furrowed brow that dipped deeper and deeper.

Raising large, impressive wings, Captain Zivel brandished his sword. "Then let's take the key now before it's too late." He licked his lips with hunger. "I'll make Jediah squeal."

"No," Lucifer countered. "We discussed this. I need *him*."

Captain Zivel's eyes narrowed, displeased with his master's answer. "No. No, I refuse to work with him again."

"You can, and you will!"

"We've tried recruiting him for centuries," Zivel argued. "He's refused to see me since the age of gods. He never listened to you before, sire, and I highly doubt that's changed."

Lucifer laughed to himself. "Everything changes, Zivel. Besides, I've got a feeling your old partner will find this job a bit more... agreeable to his personal tastes." Straightening himself, Lucifer raised his raven wings. They fanned and crowned his head like the back of a high throne. "Head for Mexico immediately, Captain. High time you paid your old accomplice a visit."

Chapter 5

NECHUM PASSED VERY few humans during the late hours, and the sidewalks were all the lonelier for it. London's dim street lamps lit the evening fog. Their orange glow tinted the floating droplets and blanketed the street shadows in its warmth. Spring showers had purified the air. Little streams trickled down storm drains.

Nechum adjusted his makeshift hood. Usually, his shawl would be wrapped about his shoulders, but the cryptic letter he received from Akela insisted he come in secret. Not knowing why put him in a terrible unease already, but the urgency behind the sender's heavy handwriting he found even more disturbing.

A single car zoomed by and sprayed water tracks, as Nechum stopped at the crosswalk. On the street corner stood the opulent Church of London. If this were a normal meeting, teams of ministry angels would crowd inside. His kind were vast in number, and without a distinct Archangel as leader, they worked in smaller collectives encamped all across the globe. Tonight, however, Heber, the overseer of the Britain province, summoned him and him alone.

Swallowing down a nervous lump, Nechum hurried. He focused on the massive oaken doors and phased right through. His boots padded against the glossed tile floor. The chapel bells chimed the hour, each dong reverberating through the high arched ceilings. Nighttime suppressed the usual vibrancy from the stained glass windows.

As he passed pew rows, Nechum focused his attention on the ministry angel kneeling in prayer. Candles for the midnight mass illumined his blue linens so that they shimmered in the flickering light.

Nechum stopped and listened. He wished not to disturb Heber's worship.

Oh Lord God, no matter the time or the place,
You're the master of angel, man, and space.
Grant to us, your servants, wisdom in every case,
When to be silent, when to speak, and when to show grace.
Amen.

Heber lifted his head.

"Amen," Nechum repeated. "Brother Heber, you sent for me?" Nechum pulled the shawl off his head and re-pinned it to his shoulders.

"Yes, Nechum." Heber stood up and gave a kind smile. "Thank you for coming on such short notice."

Nechum's fingers wrung together. "Is anything wrong?"

"No, I wouldn't say that." Heber motioned Nechum to follow him. They sat on a pew side by side. "What I'm about to tell you must stay with you. Do not speak of it to anyone."

Mind racing, Nechum nodded. "No one. I promise."

Heber looked him deep in the eyes. Nechum could see the sincere concern stirring within them. "The Lord has spoken to me regarding you. He asks that you disappear on a military mission with Captain Jediah."

Nechum's jaw gaped. The urge to refuse outright arrived first, but he bit his tongue. He would not dishonor God by disobeying. Still, a million questions burned. He put his head in his hands and cupped his face.

"I know," Heber said. "This is a strange command even to me."

Nechum straightened. "Uh," his voice trembled. "W-what does the Lord expect me to do?"

"For Jediah's team, you'll be their guide and their teacher in human affairs."

Searching Heber's face, Nechum squinted and dipped his chin down. "And what *else* am I to be?"

Heber drew closer. His voice brought down to a near inaudible whisper. "That's the part not even your comrades must know."

Nechum shook his head. "I don't understand."

Pursing his lips, Heber stared at his hands resting on his lap. "Nechum, we all know how far the Sin Curse has spread. It sickens not only the soil beneath us. It permeates the farthest spaces, both visible and invisible."

"Yes, I know it well." Nechum lowered his eyes, as a regretful sadness for an innocence long lost welled up inside.

"There is one in your group who has grown very ill from it."

An urgent concern struck a chord within Nechum. "Who?"

Heber shook his head. "The Lord would not tell me, perhaps out of courtesy for our hurting brother." He turned to Nechum, a hopeful smile on his face. "But He asks that you be His hand and help put in motion the events God has planned for our brother's healing. This mission isn't just for the world. It's for him and all of you."

Bewildered, Nechum stared up at the jeweled cross on the altar. "But who am I? That the Lord should consider me?"

"One of His chosen," Heber answered. He wrapped a comforting arm around Nechum's shoulders. "And that, my friend, comes with a promise."

The sudden weight of responsibility and all its gravitas coursed through Nechum. Fear gripped him by the chest, but the thought of a brother in suffering overpowered his initial hesitance. He was needed.

Uncomfortable quiet covered Mexico's swamps in the late dusk. A few frogs, hidden among the unruly reeds, silenced their croaks as a puny boat passed. Two boys rowed with the weak current, and the point of their canoe cut through the algae. Julio steered the stern, careful to watch their boat's sides. The churning of liquid could be from their oars or the thick body of a crocodile slipping below the water's surface.

Julio ducked to avoid the moss curtains that draped from low limbs. He searched the sky behind them. Just above the treetops, orange tinted the night clouds. Mexico City's lights were a good reference point should they get lost. The bank of Isla de las Muñecas—the Island of Dolls—should come into sight soon.

His little brother, Roberto, leaned over the bow.

"Ay!" Julio yanked him back by the shirt. "Dónde está tu cabeza?" he hissed. "There could be crocs."

"I wanted to see the island."

"And get your head munched on the way? Just sit still and keep quiet. We're here." A shoreline emerged from the dark.

The boat's bottom rubbed the riverbed as the water became shallow. Their canoe slowed to a stop. The wooden hull smushed the muck, disturbing the gnats. A stench wafted from the upturned mush.

Julio whipped out his flashlight. He clicked it on and pointed it into the trees. Countless dolls were strung up by the neck, swinging like carcasses neglected to rot on the gallows. More dolls were tied to the tree trunks and others were strewn on the ground. Caked in mud, the toys from the newest to the oldest mimicked stages of decay. Green and sun-bleached splotches spoiled once smooth plastic. Several had their hair missing in patches. The most ancient of these couldn't be distinguished at all, save for their empty eye sockets.

Julio couldn't stop staring back at the glass eyes. They seemed to bore into him. He straddled one leg over the boat's rim, and his foot planted a print into the mud. "Do you have Anita's dolls?"

"Right here," Roberto replied. In one hand, he clutched the stolen toys.

"Okay then. Let's go." Julio moved one step, then stopped.

Roberto stayed frozen in the boat as if someone had nailed him there. "Hey, Julio. Do you think those tales about that drowned girl are really true? That her ghost drove the island's caretaker mad, then drowned him?"

Visions of corpses multiplied in Julio's mind. The stench of bogs raised the tiniest hairs along his arms to a stand. "Well, he collected these dolls to appease her, didn't he?"

Roberto shuddered. "M-maybe we should go." He bent down and bumped the boat with the oar.

Julio grabbed his brother's shoulder. "Don't chicken out now, hermano."

Roberto shot a scathing glare out of wounded pride. "I'm not chicken!"

"Then man up. You wanted to come with me."

"But I didn't believe in ghosts then."

"Roberto." Julio pulled him close to his face by the collar. "We planned this prank for months. Papa's not going to be home for hours and Anita's at her friend's. It has to be tonight. Now, come on." He yanked Roberto to his feet, then marched into the woods.

He could hear Roberto's quickened pace and muttered complaints.

Farther into the trees, Julio grew far less confident and wary. Dolls, dolls, and more dolls surrounded him. His heart fluttered. The air seemed to thicken, and he heaved quiet breaths.

"Julio?" Roberto's voice quivered.

"They're...they're just dolls, amigo," Julio gulped. He sensed a million faces scrutinizing him. As though weights were strapped to his ankles, his steps grew heavy, slowing to a shuffle.

A dreadful change altered the atmosphere. No fog covered the path, but clouds screened the moonlight into an eerie dimness. Julio's heart quickened. His body heat tingled up his arms and circled beneath his cheeks. Fear stole his will. He felt as though a monstrosity stalked him, and whether or not he moved made the difference between life and death. Terror incarnate pressed inside his chest.

Then came that breath: a sickening, warm breath that moistened on his skin. The sensation spread down his neck, making him more uncomfortably hot than before.

Roberto huddled closer to him. His shoulders hunched as he hugged Anita's dolls. "Let's go back. P-please?"

Julio's tongue stuck to the floor of his mouth. He nodded and forced his legs to twist around towards the beach and their boat. Then a voice tickled his ear. His eyebrows raised, and he stopped.

"What?" Roberto hushed his own gasp. "What is it?"

"Did you hear that?"

"What are you talkin' about, you loco?" Roberto rambled. "I don't wanna hear nothin'. I wanna go home—alive!"

Julio batted his hysterical brother aside. "Shut up, hermano."

Roberto crouched lower, as though sinking into a panic. "D-do you think it's h-her? The ghost girl?"

For once, Julio didn't have an answer. That strange, innocent giggle seemed to flit side to side, yet Julio dared not fidget.

"That thing! Over there!" Roberto shook a pointed finger.

Julio's eyes darted toward the item in question. "What thing?"

"I swear, Julio, that doll opened its eyes." Roberto's tanned finger quaked at a bound doll; its dress long soaked by the tree trunk's moss.

Julio crept closer to the sorry looking thing. Webs covered its shorn head. The lace fringe had rotted off the mildewed satin, and an old spider sack sat anchored on its neck. But those unnatural glass eyes were indeed open. They were clean too—seemingly untouched by the elements, and its lips were cracked open, as if caught mid-speech.

That same giggle escaped its mouth. Julio jolted backwards into Roberto. "It's nothing," he stuttered, feigning bravery. "Just a voice string."

"I...see...you," it whispered, like a tiny girl at play.

Julio could feel his eyes bugging out.

"I...see...you," it chanted again. Its eyes turned directly at them. "I...see...you."

Julio hustled away from the accursed thing and dragged Roberto along with him.

Then another voice behind them repeated, "I...see...you." They whipped around to see another hanging doll open its eyes. "I...see...you," said one to their left. More and more voices joined.

Taunting laughter surrounded the boys, and they took off like a shot for their canoe. Loose leaves slipped around under Julio's sneakers. A splat from behind forced him to turn back.

Roberto struggled to lift himself up from the foul mud where he fell.

"Come on! Come on!" Julio hoisted Roberto by the pants. He threw Anita's dolls and screamed in case the phantoms could hear. "Here! Take them!"

They made another break for it, and the dolls fell silent as their oars splashed back down the bayou. What they didn't hear was the whispered acceptance of their offering.

Chapter 6

THE BRITISH FIELDS were waking to the refreshing cool of a crisp spring morning. Nocturnal creatures turned to sleep, yet the rest of creation had not yet stirred. It couldn't be quieter. Early sunlight grew in strength, chasing night's last shadows. Before long, the barest bit of sun peeked over the horizon. Dewdrops atop the highest hill captured the first rays, and grass blades held the shining droplets like tiny mirrors. A brief rose hue first painted the sky, heralding the gold to follow. Then the colors all threw their arms over the plain.

Nechum stood atop the church steeple to greet every dawn and to bask in its glory as a faint reminder of God's greater glory. He closed his eyes. His empathic sense felt the earliest risers on the move. They'd be cupping their coffee mugs, drinking in the scented steam while breakfast sizzled in their pans. Others, still under sleep's spell, would curse the day for showing up, then burrow themselves under the sheets.

Feeling the sun's heat fully emerge, Nechum bowed his head, folded his hands, and sang the same hymn as he had done each morn:

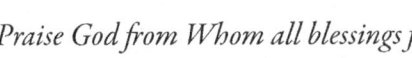

Praise God from Whom all blessings flow.
Praise Him all creatures here below.
Praise Him above, ye heavenly hosts.
Praise Father, Son, and Holy Ghost.

After a final "Amen," Nechum pulled out the notes he scribbled the night before and re-scanned their contents.

"*Captain Jediah,*" he mentally read to himself "*Two of his wingmen, a messenger and a Destroyer. That's six angels, including myself.*"

Jediah...long had he heard of him. What angel hadn't? He secured a long-celebrated victory. Conquering a beast like Apollyon—surely this Jediah had to be one of those mighty, no nonsense commanders that Nechum envisioned—as confident as soldiers come.

Akela he had met a day ago. Nechum smiled, happy to have an optimistic brother to lighten this dangerous enterprise, but the last three team members were an enigma to him. Nechum guessed Laszio and Eran's role easy enough. Jediah would need wingmen, but this Alameth, an angel of death, seemed more out of place than even himself.

Nechum withheld a worried sigh. A Destroyer in their midst rarely bode well. They were God's judgment arm as much as the personal escorts of God's adopted children. Pain and sorrow followed them often.

Refolding his paper, Nechum stared into the sky as its intense colors softened to common blue. "I know Your timing is perfect, Lord, but I wish You granted me more time to prepare."

Despite lacking wings, Nechum dove headfirst off his perch. He concentrated on the shingles and phased through both them and the attic into the sanctuary. After a somersault, his graceful feet landed with less force than a feather, and his knees bent in one fluid motion, absorbing the velocity. He straightened, then took a seat by the pulpit. His company would arrive soon.

Though pitiful by comparison, Nechum liked the sanctuary. It mimicked home. Rich light streamed through colored glass, staining the whitewashed walls in its spectrum. A wooden cross stood tall in the center—right where the Great Throne would be. Brass candelabras copied the fiery seraphs when lit during evening services, and though no incense burned nor were coals stoked on an altar, the spiritual aroma of the worshipers' prayers and songs lingered there for days at a time.

Nechum flinched at the sound of footsteps. Over his shoulder, he saw three figures approach the aisle way. Their heads were covered with blue cloaks, but Nechum didn't need his empathic sense to know they weren't actual ministry angels. Most telling was the sword hilt poking out from behind the leader's back.

Nechum stood to receive the three as they removed their coverings and bowed his head. "Welcome, brothers."

The one with the sword, whom he guessed had to be Jediah, bent his head in turn. "Thank you. Are you Nechum?"

"At yours and our Lord's service," Nechum replied. Placing a hand over his figurative heart, he made an even deeper bow. His eyes were drawn to the slight glint of their golden, armored wings that peeked from under their loosened disguises. "Forgive me for saying so, sir, and I mean no disrespect, but you may want to hide your wings and sword a little better."

The leader drew the fabric closer to himself and loosened the scabbard straps. The sword slipped further down his back under his cloak. He regarded Nechum with a kind tone. "No. Please speak. We need your judgment."

Nechum peered closer. Jediah wasn't the hardened officer he expected. Even as he commanded his wingmen to rest as they waited for the others, there was no demanding tone. No impression of a domineering spirit. His brown hair hid red highlights that only revealed themselves in direct sunlight. His brown eyes glowed like lacquered wood, and gold lines, translucent as amber, mixed with those warm, earthy tones. To Nechum, they captured the fleeting majesty of a sunset—as well as its sadness. There laid strength and courage but also potent sorrow.

Is he the one?

Nechum turned his attention to his wingmen, Laszio and Eran. They spent a while examining the porcelain angel statues and frowning at their misinformed feminine image. Already, Nechum sensed a close bond between the two. Their braided locks matched, right down to the length and the polished silver beads that tied them. Their grey eyes showed tints of pale greens and blues, and were as tumultuous as the restless sea. They itched to test others' strength and character, as well as their own.

A yellow blur dropped through the ceiling and landed between the pews like a meteor.

Before Nechum could raise a shield, Jediah had pulled him behind himself and drew his sword. Laszio and Eran had also armed themselves.

"Ow." A hand grabbed the pew's back. A second hand did the same. Then Akela's curls emerged, followed by the rest of him. He swayed back and forth to a stand. "Ow."

Nerves shot, Nechum released an exasperated breath.

"Akela?" Laszio's face soured with annoyance. "What are you doing?"

Akela stumbled around the pew bench. "Crashing, apparently." He rubbed his scalp and rolled his neck. "Misjudged my distance again." After wiping the bleariness from his eyes, he beamed. "Oh, hi, Nechum. How're you doing?"

"Fine, but are *you* okay?"

"Yeah. Yeah," Akela said with a wince. "Happens a lot." He shook his head, then whipped his gaze around, surveying the group. "So is this everyone?"

Jediah sheathed his sword. "Almost."

A light tapping echoed from the sanctuary doors. The faintest grey wisps leaked through the middle crack. Clouds then billowed beneath the door. It crept along the carpet, then churned into a pillar that gained height and form. The cloud peeled away. Shrouded in his fogs and his sliver grey robe, the angel of death chosen to accompany them stood. His long hood hid most of his face, but as his head tipped up, Nechum could see a pair of emerald eyes just beneath the fabric.

Respectful, Nechum kept a slight distance and bowed. "Welcome, brother Alameth."

The angel of death returned Nechum's bow; his expression more blank than a sheet of paper.

Nechum invested all his empathic power to find what scraps of emotion were in Alameth only to come up dry. The greens of his eyes teetered between darkness and light—a delicate balance between joy and despair, and Nechum dreaded what it might imply. It looked barely stable, with only a practiced discipline preventing utter chaos.

Now it seemed to Nechum that two were in desperate emotional need.

Night had not yet ended in Mexico after the two foolish boys scrammed from Isla de las Muñecas. Hanging doll trinkets swung as the chilled wind whistled between thin twigs, and Elazar fingered the two dolls the intruding boys abandoned. *"More trophies,"* he thought sarcastically. *"Great."* Such meager offerings were a pittance compared to the lavish sacrifices he once received from the ancient peoples. Still, scaring the two youths witless was a pleasant diversion to the demon.

Elazar stepped over the last demon messenger who dared bother him. He stopped a moment to admire his handiwork. The imp laid unconscious with his chest ripped open and his energy pooling like blood. Elazar smirked. It wouldn't be till noon tomorrow before the whelp could move again.

The cluttered path of toys and sticks took him over thicker roots and into thicker brush. Moonlight peeked through the rustling canopy above. After dropping off the dolls in a rotted shack, Elazar reached a still pool. Setting himself down on the sandbank, he stared into the waters. His blue ministry garb had long darkened. His pitch-black hair reflected the unfeeling light he basked in, but his one good eye locked onto the reflected scar that carved the other.

His empathic sense stirred to a presence behind him.

"Look at you. The great Elazar. How does one go from ruling kingdoms to conjuring ghost stories and cheap tricks?" scoffed Zivel.

Elazar smiled ruefully at the sound of his name on Zivel's tongue. "Ran out of messengers, I see. And how've you been all this time, *Xipe Totec*?"

"Get with the times, Elazar," Zivel huffed. "The age of gods is long over. That old moniker is dead and buried along with the Aztecs and their tombs."

Not caring to give that so much as a response, Elazar pulled out the medallion he stole from the demon messenger's pocket. His thumb stroked the engraved dragon. "So what does Lucifer want from me now? What new carrot has he got to dangle in front of my nose today?" His senses resonated to Zivel's jealous fury.

"He wants someone 'taken care of', and apparently..." Zivel's voice lowered to a rumbling grumble, "he thinks only you can handle him."

Elazar flipped the medallion like a coin repeatedly in his fingers. "Name him."

"He wants Captain Jediah."

At that, Elazar stilled. "Jediah?" he mumbled. Lowering himself to loom over the water's surface, he stared once more at his wavering reflection and his jagged scar. Jediah's name passed his lips again but in a low growl that vibrated against the waters like a curse.

Elazar breathed deep. His energy glowed as a red aura compounded within his chest. He concentrated to shift it from his shoulder, down his arm and into his hand. His fingers tensed. A translucent crimson shield surrounded the medallion in his grip and levitated it above his palm. Then, with little thought but mountains of repressed rage, Elazar tightened the force-field like he was splitting a skull. The brittle medallion cracked. It wrenched into a crumpled ball, then splintered to shards, and by a flick of his fingers, the force-field vanished, releasing shrapnel that sprinkled the ground. "I accept."

Chapter 7

THE TOWN GLOWED UNDER the afternoon sky. Crisp winter air had not quite left, but flower buds peeped their sleepy eyes.

Jediah held his breath. For the first time in ages, humans—God's Image Bearers—walked before him. They were most sacred of all life. Made up of a body, soul, and spirit, three in one, they echoed the Triune God Himself. Yet as he surveyed the crowds, Jediah frowned. Most of them wore broken fragments of His Mark on their chests. Without His Holy Spirit, their symbols were incomplete, as if partly erased. They were meant to bear a bold, completed sigil.

As he leaned from his perch on the rooftop, Jediah's energy heated, pounding and thirsting to cross the dimensional divide from the second realm to the first for the first time.

"So, is everyone ready?" Nechum asked.

Jediah stood up and nodded, careful not to look too eager.

"Very well." Nechum stroked the caramel color out of his hair. The locks smoothed straight under his palms as he painted them into a dark brunette with each swipe. He then lengthened it, pulling it down the nape of his neck. By the flicking of his wrist, it twisted into a neat braid. Nechum then rubbed the aquamarine out of his eyes and replaced it with hazel. Soon his entire form turned feminine and petite, and with a final shake of his clothes, he swapped his blue uniform for a T-shirt, shorts, and flat shoes.

After they all altered their appearances, Jediah and the others followed Nechum down from the roof and into the cramped alley.

Nechum stared at the sidewalk, then signaled everyone to step further back. "Okay, I know some of you have never entered the physical plain before. Crossing over might, well, feel a bit weird, but don't be alarmed. Whatever sensations you're about to experience are normal. You'll be fine." Nechum's form dimmed, losing its heavenly luster.

Jediah followed suit, suppressing his energy and forsaking its essence. He gasped. It didn't hurt. Rather, it put him in shock. The second he cut himself off from the spiritual realm, every instinct in him wanted to go back. A weight dropped in his newly forming gut. His internal energy scrunched itself into a dot, and weird, heavy insides filled the newly emptied spaces within him. Then he felt something hard, like sticks sprout and branch out in every joint, and soon a flesh coat vacuum sealed itself to the firming bones.

Trembling, Jediah sucked air into lungs for the first time. His unaccustomed angelic senses ran wild. The tiniest sound banged in his eardrums. His fresh knit skin tickled to air molecules and shivered from cold and cooked from heat.

"It's okay," Nechum assured. "It's okay. Give yourselves time. The strangeness will lessen in a minute."

Jediah raised and flexed a hand and felt every delicate tissue and muscle stretching. Looking around to check on the others, Jediah saw Laszio sucking in heavy breaths and Eran pinching his arm, testing how skin folds and springs back into place. Only Akela and Alameth stood by, unfazed and clearly well practiced.

Jediah strolled down the sidewalk, more conscientious of himself than he had been in his life. He admired Nechum, who weaved through masses to and fro with ease. *How long did it take him to gain the confidence to pass humans so effortlessly?* Jediah feared his true angelic strength might come out and harm whomever he bumped into.

Aiming to act natural, Jediah focused on the streets instead. Stores were strung along both sides of the road. Scented wood chips scattered from the carpentry shop's open air workbench. A bakery unleashed smells of buttered rolls and cinnamon with every swing of its doors, and several windows displayed products meant to catch the wandering eye.

Nechum led them to the shady street corner by the crosswalk, where fewer people traveled. He signaled them to wait, and Jediah, as well as all five of them, stopped in a perfect row.

Nechum looked back and shook his head. "Um," he whispered. "Maybe, try to make it look a little less intentional."

Everyone shuffled, turning their line into a less definable shape.

Giving an assuring smile, Nechum nodded, "Better."

"So, where are you taking us?" Laszio asked.

Nechum pointed. "We are going to have some practice in this shop."

Jediah beheld a glass door with a sign that blinked "Open". It appeared innocent enough, yet he stared at it like it intended to eat him alive.

Reaching the door, Nechum grabbed the handle, ready to open it for them. "I'm thinking going in and just making pleasant conversation is a good way to get everyone's feet wet."

"What do people talk about?" Eran asked, as he folded his arms and sized the entire building up.

Nechum shrugged. "The weather. The store. Easiest way to start a conversation, though, is to ask them about themselves. Don't ask anything invasive. Just stick to the basics."

"Okay then," Akela chirped. "Let's go."

Nodding, Nechum opened the door but froze with it half ajar. "Oh, one moment." He cringed. "I'm sorry. I should have mentioned this before. There are a few things to keep in mind. Not to make any of you nervous or anything, and I don't mean to overwhelm anyone, but try to remember not to break anything. Don't buy anything either. Don't ask about politics, and most important of all, don't forget to blink."

"To blink?" Laszio approached Nechum. "What's to blink?"

Nechum's feet shuffled a moment. "Um, well, it's, uh, this." He shut and open his eyes.

Laszio squinted, then fluttered his eyes.

By the uncomfortable expression on Nechum's face, Jediah guessed Laszio's attempt wasn't convincing.

"Um, close," Nechum said. "Try it again but a tad slower."

Laszio's second 'blink' made him look sluggish and sleepy.

Dead silence fell between them until Nechum nodded. "Doing better."

The angels clustered close together as they passed rows of nicknacks. Jediah peeked over the shelves at humans lined up before a beeping device. A young lady, burdened with shopping bags, left the seller's desk and bumped against the door. She grunted, trying to push it open.

"Hang on." Akela ran to her aid and opened the door.

"Thank you." She nodded without so much as looking him in the face.

Akela placed a hand on his chest and bowed. "Tis an honor, milady. Would you like me to carry your bags for you? Where are you headed?"

A strange, disturbed look crossed her face. "Um, no. Thanks but no."

"Are you sure? It's no trouble, really. I insist. Let me help-" Akela reached for a bag.

She lurched back. "Pervert." Her shoes scraped the sidewalk as the heavy door shut in Akela's face.

Akela's eyebrows dipped as he turned to Jediah. "Was it something I said?"

Nechum drew to Akela's side, patting his shoulder. "No. You're fine. It's just the times. There's a lot of suspicion going around these days. Just keep personal space in mind."

Jediah winced. This would be much harder than he thought. He watched Alameth pass several customers, but the Destroyer didn't bother to say anything. He stuck to head nods and courteous bows. Jediah considered adopting his example. It seemed the safest option.

A man crossed paths with Laszio and dropped a pair of tagged sunglasses. Laszio dipped down to retrieve it.

Snap!

The glasses laid in two pieces in Laszio's hand. His cheeks reddened as he offered the broken object. "I'm terribly sorry."

After considerable staring at the glasses and Laszio, the man scowled. "Are you jossin' me? I just paid for those."

Poor Laszio could only mumble more apologies as the man continued berating him.

At a loss, Jediah racked his brain to rescue him from such awful embarrassment.

Before he could come up with something, Nechum stepped between them and picked up the pieces. "Terrible, isn't it? The cheapness of plastic. They don't make things to last anymore, do they?" The man's anger subsided as Nechum continued. "We're so very sorry, sir. We'd be happy to pay for the damages, if it'll help."

Laszio's eyes widened. "I don't have money."

Nechum gently ushered Laszio aside. "It's okay. I do."

Jediah then noticed him pull a brown leather square from his pocket. "How much was it?" Nechum asked.

"Seventeen."

"Hmm." Nechum leafed through pale colored strips. "I've only got twenties... here." The man accepted the flimsy paper. "Keep the change."

As soon as the guy left, Jediah whispered in Nechum's ear. "How'd you get money? Did God give you that?"

"I earned it from scattered jobs here and there." Nechum stuffed the pouch back into his pocket. "Can you imagine what would happen to the world's economy if God just *manifested* money for every ministry angel on the planet?"

Jediah never felt so stupid. Despite thinking through what Nechum said, he couldn't grasp the concept.

Nechum smiled. "Never mind. It's not that important." He paused. "Uh-oh."

Jediah turned to see Eran fumbling through his words to find a conversation piece. The mother he spoke to inched away and gripped her daughter's hand. Jediah couldn't figure out why until he noticed how Eran stared into her. He wasn't, as Nechum put it, 'blinking'.

Jediah stepped behind her. Gesturing for Eran's attention, he pointed at his eyes and demonstrated a blink.

Eran squinted back.

Jediah blinked harder and faster, but then the woman turned around and saw him. She gave the same put-off look the first lady gave Akela.

Suppressing his rising panic, Jediah waved. "Hi. Sorry, my brother and I need to...um...go. Come on."

Eran took the hint and followed him into another aisle.

Jediah released a breath. "Blink, Eran. Don't forget to blink."

"I'm sorry, sir. This whole thing feels so odd."

"I know, but it'll be okay. We can only improve from here."

Later that day, Jediah returned to the safety of his angelic form and pulled the hood of his blue cloak low. They were leaving by plane in the morning, but if he wanted to see more of the town Nechum so loved, he couldn't risk being recognized by anyone—angel or demon.

As he strolled the village outskirts, he lost himself in the sunset. He couldn't even remember the last time he saw one. The horizon traded blue for crimson and crimson for violet. Crickets, hidden in the wheat field, chirped between the stalks. Then the last speck of sunlight ducked behind a hill, and thus coronated the moon and its starry courts to govern the world.

"Enjoying the view, Captain?"

Startled, Jediah turned around to see Nechum raise his hands in apology. "I'm sorry. Didn't mean to startle you."

Disappointed that Nechum saw right through his disguise again, Jediah shook his head. "I'm that bad at hiding, huh?"

Nechum pursed his lips and wrung his hands. "Well, um, kind of."

Jamming his hands into his pockets, Jediah laughed at his own pathetic-ness. "I expected as much."

Nechum scuffed his heel against the gravel. "You're not that bad an actor. I can't imagine how hard it must be for you—coming to earth after all these years. It's a far-cry from the days of Eden you might have remembered."

"But what about you?" Jediah asked. "Training hopeless cases like me and leaving all these humans you care about?"

Closing his eyes, Nechum dipped his chin down and nodded. "My stand-in will watch them in my stead. Besides, it wouldn't be the first time I've had to say goodbye. I've said goodbye a hundred times to thousands of people who never even met me. Most of which I'll never see again." His shoulders sagged, and he bit his lip. "But yes. It never gets any easier."

After a moment of silence, Jediah gestured toward the road. "Care to join me? I thought about taking a walk, and I'm liable to get lost anyway."

"Oh, this place is small," Nechum laughed. "You couldn't if you tried."

As they walked, Jediah felt no need to speak. There was something in the way Nechum carried himself that seemed so un-rushed; like he demanded nothing of you nor expected anything from you. Not at all like the troops Jediah directed from day to day, and yet Jediah couldn't shake the feeling that Nechum kept glancing at him. He knew ministry angels possessed an empathic sense. How much of himself was Nechum reading? "Is something wrong, brother?"

Nechum averted his gaze. "Sorry, sir. I'm making you uncomfortable."

Hearing the shame in Nechum's voice, Jediah took his shoulder. "Hey, enough apologies, and I'm your brother right now. Not your captain."

Still, Nechum's chuckle quaked. "Right...right..."

They took a right into a residential area. The houses were past their heyday, but appeared able to keep their owners warm and dry.

Nechum halted and stared ahead.

On instinct, Jediah reached for his concealed sword. "What is it?" He followed Nechum's line of sight. A young girl sat on a porch with her knees drawn to her chin. A purple spot splotched her face, and her eyes were red-rimmed. Jediah clenched a fist when he noticed the bruises. *What senseless coward dared hurt a child?*

Nechum left Jediah's side and crouched in front of her. She could not see him, but her heaving sobs calmed at his touch. Then, to Jediah's surprise, Nechum's clothes turned white. It seemed a mystery at first, but then the girl put her legs down. The Mark of the Trinity pulsed with the Holy Spirit of God inside her. As Jediah gazed upon it, those longings he repressed earlier deepened against his will.

Nearby, a stray cat, light on its paws, slinked along the wall and sat just behind the girl. It looked at her with half-opened eyes as it wrapped its tail over its front paws. Something sparked in Nechum's face when he noticed the calico. He approached the feline, and upon placing a hand on its tiny head, he dissolved and merged inside it.

The cat gained a silver glint in its eye. Jediah marveled as Nechum steered the little creature he possessed, making it rub its whiskered cheek against the girl's back.

The girl snapped her head around to a squeaky "mew". "Oh," she sniffled. "Hello." She stroked its fur as it contentedly pushed against her palm.

With distinctive feline grace, the cat helped itself to her lap and gave that secret grin all cats seemed to have when they're happy. Its velveteen paws pushed and pressed on her knee and purred. The girl opened her legs wider. Then the little calico plopped on its side. Its exposed, pillowy white underbelly prompted the girl to let out a cheery laugh.

Without thinking, Jediah inched closer to the scene. He reached out a hand to touch the girl's shoulder but retracted it. His whole being trembled. Then, building up the courage, he touched her shoulder. Shekinah glory from his Lord filled him, turning his clothes white and sending shivers through his soul. Christ's Spirit felt like...*home*.

Chapter 8

NECHUM TRIED TO REST on the plane, but his restless ears wandered around without him. He drank in the hypnotizing hum of the turbine engines as they sped across the English Channel, but knowing their destination, Paris, was a mere hour away meant the start of their first actual mission. Rolling his shoulders, Nechum attempted to settle his nerves.

Akela's feet thudded on nearby suitcases. Stacks of them varied in height like rock pillars in the baggage hold, and the messenger amused himself by hopping from stack to stack. His thumping almost annoyed Nechum. He began wishing he could bring himself to ask Akela if he wouldn't mind just picking a suitcase and sitting down like everyone else but let him be. *"Everyone deals with stress in their own way,"* he reasoned.

Nechum's next recourse was not to think of Akela or their mission, but he only ended up obsessing about his own mission. In an instant, his thoughts careened down that fast track they had been on since yesterday. Five brothers, each harboring a different brokenness, and he had no idea who God wanted him to help. *Lord, why are you so cryptic sometimes?*

"Attention, please."

Eran and Laszio shot up from where they sat as Jediah returned with his newly formed plans.

Not wishing to be disrespectful, Nechum rose too and tried to mimic their rigid postures. Akela and Alameth stood tall as well.

"Thank you." Jediah nodded, giving them permission to sit. He lifted a golden paper, and a grave seriousness shadowed his face. "Remember the stakes, brothers. The Lord has tasked us with this purpose, and if any word spreads about it, we may very well lose our two primary targets. We can't be seen by anyone. We speak of this to no one."

Nechum echoed Laszio and Eran's instant 'yes, sir'. Jediah's commander persona seemed such a far-cry from the reserved angel he strolled with the previous night.

Jediah pursed his lips and pushed out a breath through his nose. "I won't sugarcoat it, brothers. This mission requires all that we have. Our primary target? Yakum of Beijing."

Cold shot through Nechum. Laszio and Eran's mouths dropped, and even the unflappable Alameth looked the slightest bit uncomfortable.

"Who?" Akela asked.

Laszio leaned forward and cocked an eyebrow at Akela. "Yakum of Beijing? As in Lucifer's leading authority over the Chinese principalities?"

Akela blinked.

Eran frowned. "You never heard of him?"

"Can't say that I have. But he couldn't be that hard to handle, could he?" Akela cringed. He patted his hands together to appear upbeat, but by the way Nechum's empathic sense resonated, it seemed more out of jitters than optimism.

Eran rubbed his face. "Yakum is a Destroyer like Alameth and controls demon legions throughout the Chinese province."

Licking moisture back to his lips, Nechum turned to Akela, placed a hand on his knee, and mustered as compassionate a tone as he could offer. "Akela, God had stripped the power to take life from Yakum, but he's a disease experimenter. He likes to make toxins and unleash them on human victims." Nechum swallowed before continuing. "You, um, probably heard of the Black Plague?"

Akela's weak smile evaporated, and his cobalt eyes flashed with hints of black. His stare fixed on Alameth.

Alameth, however, said nothing, but he folded his hands, confirming all that Nechum shared.

"Okay," Akela said at length. "That's pretty bad."

Jediah lengthened his back. "It is, and God has revealed to us that Yakum is close to perfecting a virus for Lucifer that will decimate the seven continents."

"Lord, no. Not again," Nechum whispered as he covered his mouth.

"What does Yakum think he's trying to pull?" Laszio snapped. "God won't let him win. Not by a long shot."

Jediah pointed to them. "Which is precisely why God sent us to Paris."

"Yakum is in Paris?" Eran asked. "I thought Beijing was his base."

Nodding his head, Jediah unfolded the paper. "It is, but we're getting his informant first." He panned a picture around for everyone to see. The colored sketch appeared vivid enough to be real. A powerful jaw. Red hair that had browned like dried blood. "His name is Malkior. He stands at six foot, ten. He's an accomplished archer, and I'm told he's been infiltrating hospitals and collecting medical data for Yakum."

Jediah's eyebrows raised in caution. "Malkior was a nature angel: fire class. He's also a notorious coward and potentially destructive if panicked."

Laszio and Eran drew in a sharp breath and clenched their teeth. The nature angels were elementals, gifted with powers that effected both physical and spiritual realms.

Nechum shuddered too, imagining the massive catastrophes such an enemy could inflict on the human population.

Jediah gave a knowing look. "Clearly, you all realize the delicacy of the situation. The only way to do this without causing citywide havoc is to chain down Malkior before he even thinks he's in trouble."

"And what level of threat does he possess, Captain?" Alameth asked.

Nechum's ears pricked. He hadn't heard Alameth speak before.

"He's developed a new way to convert energy into arrows," Jediah answered. "These arrows are highly combustible, capable of blasts that can harm hundreds at a time."

"So, we're after a twitchy sniper with a knack for explosions," Eran dryly commented. "Fun."

Jediah pulled a map from his pocket and set it on the suitcase in the center of their circle. He ushered everyone closer. "Malkior is here at Austral Région Hospital. I've been going over the layout, and I believe I have a pretty good grasp of the area." His finger pressed on a tiny dot surrounded by yellow lines and white patches. "Now, since Malkior has been hacking human devices and peeking in locked medicine cabinets, it's safe to assume he won't be in human disguise. Therefore, some of us will comb the place in human disguise to lower suspicions while the others take care to block his escape routes."

"Okay," Akela piped up. "How are we going in?"

"There are four levels to this building," Jediah explained. "I'm assigning four of us, including myself, to go in and check the rooms. The last two will keep watch in the trees surrounding the building." He faced his wingmen. "Laszio. Eran."

"Yes, sir."

"You two will secure the perimeter. I want you both in your ministry angel cloaks and positioned in these corners. You should have a clear visual of the hospital walls from there. Keep yourselves hidden in the trees should there be any trouble. If not, find a car or a trash can to hide in. Should Malkior make a break for it, chase him down. I'll get there as soon as possible. Understood?"

Laszio's eyes sparked with anticipation. "One hundred percent."

"That will leave the rest of *us* to search the rooms." Jediah's finger circled over Akela, Alameth, and Nechum. "Alameth, you and I will go in as regular visitors. Act normal, normal but be vigilant. Nechum, I understand what I'm about to ask you goes against usual protocol, but you're the most experienced of all of us. I want you to impersonate an actual worker."

Nechum lurched back, horrified. "What?"

Jediah remained resolute, yet he stepped closer and patted Nechum's shoulder. "I'm sorry, but someone needs to search the staff areas, and it's unlikely the other employees would accept just anybody in a uniform. It's less compromising if one of us looks like someone they know."

"But what about the actual person?" Nechum cried. "Unless they've got a twin, I'll be caught anyway."

"Not so long as the actual person isn't there." Jediah's eyes trailed to Alameth.

A weakness fell over Nechum, and his knees trembled. "You don't mean-"

"Worry not, brother Nechum." Alameth turned toward him. "I swear whomever you choose shall not die." The angel of death placed a hand over his chest and bowed. Then his green eyes closed in thought. "The trick will be to ensure no one is aware of his or her absence until we're done."

"Which also means you'll have cut off his or her means of communication, Nechum," Jediah added. "Before Alameth does his... thing."

Nechum rubbed his temples, almost wishing to be sent into combat instead. "Yes sir, but I'll need to study the victi—I mean, the person first."

"What about me?" Akela interjected. "What do I do?"

Jediah smiled. "You, Akela, will get basement duty."

The messenger brightened. "Okay. Neat. What's basement duty?"

Jediah leaned in toward Akela with a glint in his eye. "Can I trust you, Akela?"

Akela bent forward, meeting Jediah's face. "I live to serve."

"The building relies on a boiler to keep it heated. The day before we move in, you break that boiler. The hospital staff should then try to call repair service, but as soon as they dial the number, I want you to hijack the phone line, intercept that call, and pass yourself off as the repairman. Then you're clear the next day to access the basement."

Akela grinned. "Oooh. I like this plan."

"But you've got to stay there," Jediah emphasized. "If one of us besides me finds Malkior, I want them to alert you. Then you *discretely* alert me. Then alert everyone else. Got it?"

Akela winked. "Got it."

Jediah locked eyes with him. "I'm trusting you here, Akela. So please, for goodness' sake, don't socialize when you can."

"Why?" Akela waited, but after a few seconds of Jediah's dry expression, his smile disappeared. "Point taken," he moaned. He leaned back and crossed his arms. "Sheesh. Mess up once and you're convicted for life."

Jediah relaxed. "Thanks for understanding. Don't fix that boiler until we find Malkior. Make excuses if you have to." Straightening his posture, Jediah looked around. "Any questions?"

The silence was unanimous.

"And if anything goes wrong-" Jediah motioned to Alameth. "Alameth? Care to demonstrate?"

Alameth stood and opened a hand. A stream of ribboned mist collected above his palm, forming a smooth ball. He then clamped it in his fist and compressed it. Wisps popped between his fingers. Then in his reopened hand laid a grey pellet. He first held it between his finger and thumb before he smacked it on the ground. It burst near Laszio's toes, and a thick cloud plumed in his face. Laszio coughed and rubbed his tearing eyes in the smoke screen. "My apologies." Alameth said, as he handed Laszio a bagful of pellets. "Don't swallow."

Nechum bit his lip. The Austral Région Hospital buzzed with activity. Narrow hallways were cramped with stretchers that either ferried patients from one room to the other or were left parked by the walls like boats at a dock. No matter where he went, constant stimulus flooded Nechum's senses. A mother screeched in labor. A family sobbed for a loved one. Life and death danced under the same roof.

Pretending to be a random young man, Nechum tried not to look too pensive around the doctors, nurses, and clerks. *Someone with free access.* He spotted a doctor reading a clipboard and surrounded by nurses. *No, their schedules were too tight.* Clerks tapped on computers. *Too stationary.* A surgeon dashed to the emergency wing. *Definitely not!*

Nechum pressed his head in his hands as worry set in. *I'm gonna get somebody fired.* Standing there, he caught sight of a subtle yellow glow that crept along the floor. Then Akela's head poked through the ground like a dolphin's dorsal fin. Akela spotted him, and winked as if to say, 'You got this.'

Nechum smiled back, but only briefly.

Akela crept up to the front desk just as a loud nurse groaned to the desk clerk. "The boiler broke again. That stupid rust bucket needs to be replaced."

The clerk sighed. His fingers made a medley of clicks on his keyboard. "Alright. Alright. I'll call them." He picked the phone off the receiver.

From his position, Nechum watched Akela dive under the clerk's chair and reach for the phone line. Upon clutching the cord, his whole being zipped into the wire, and the electrical currents swept him right into the receiver.

"He's going to feel utterly drained after doing that," Nechum thought. He himself experienced the sharp tingling of cyber-travel before. It was as tiring as it was disorienting.

The clerk stopped drumming his fingers. "Hello plumbing service?"

Nechum made a rueful smile and wandered toward the elevator. *Well, at least Akela has a handle on this. Maybe I'll get a clue of who to choose upstairs.*

The doors dinged, and a cart full of mops, brooms, and cleaners blocked Nechum's way. The disengaged janitor grabbed its handles. "Pardon me, sir."

"Oh, sorry." Nechum stepped aside, but before the janitor could clear the elevator, the doors pinned the cart on both sides. He grunted something inaudible. Unfortunately, Nechum had a good guess at what crass word was said.

Nechum took hold of the cart. "Sorry. Let me help you with that."

"It's fine." The sullen man, who was well into his thirties, pushed it as the doors separated and wheeled it along. "Thanks anyway."

Nechum peered at the ID tag that hung from his shirt pocket.

That evening, Nechum scoured the janitor's apartment. For someone who's job *is* to clean, he didn't seem bothered by his personal landfill of a residence.

The man slurped his ramen noodle supper and paid no attention to anything else. The curled pasta flipped broth all around his bowl, greasing the table.

Nechum stuck his hand into the cellphone beside his elbow. The screen displayed: "battery—forty percent". He twitched his fingers. A weak jolt pricked him, and the screen went dead.

As the janitor got down to the last spoonfuls of creamy broth, Nechum looked toward the city lights beyond the slightly ajar window. Alameth still waited for him, peeking through the leaves of a distant tree.

Shuddering, Nechum stalled to at least give the poor man the chance to finish his meal in peace. Just then, the janitor raised the bowl to his lips and drank the last drops. Resigned, Nechum sighed. He bent his knees. His heels lightly bounced on the hardwood floor, then charged the window. Jumping right through, he nabbed a telephone wire, swung twice around to gain momentum, then let go. His somersault sent him across the street in a perfect arch. He extended a foot and landed atop an upper branch. After balancing a few seconds, he climbed down.

Alameth gave a slight smile. "So, wingless angels really do fly." His comment came with such a stoic tone, Nechum wasn't sure if it was a compliment or a joke.

"Um, thank you?"

Alameth rolled his shoulders, straightened his back, and held out his bow to Nechum. "Hold this for me, please." With his arms freed, the Destroyer raised a hand. A pillar of mist rolled up before him. He clapped over it with both hands and rubbed vigorously. The grey wisps rolled and lengthened until it hardened into a long shaft.

Grasping it, Alameth squinted. His hands traveled its length up to the tip to mold a sharper point. Pricking his finger, he nodded in satisfaction, then reached for his bow. "Thank you."

Nechum hesitated but told himself, *"This was all for the best,"* and handed the weapon back.

Alameth anchored the glowing shaft to the arrow rest. White particles dusted off the arrow as he pulled the drawstring back. The bow curved slightly as the string touched the right corner of Alameth's mouth.

Nechum counted the breaths Alameth took and sensed a faint nervousness. He looked back into the apartment. The janitor stood up, about to carry his bowl to the kitchen.

Alameth's arrow cut the air. The man walked toward the left, almost disappearing from view, but the shaft slipped right through the window glass and into his stomach. The man paused. He patted his chest, releasing a burp.

A subtle gasp drew Nechum's attention back to Alameth, whose shoulders seemed a little less rigid. Alameth, upon noticing Nechum's concern, offered a faint smile. "Give him a couple days. He'll be fine." Riding on gentle mists, he floated down to the sidewalk.

Nechum lingered a moment before joining him. The edges of the leaves Alameth touched withered. Nechum's gaze then turned to the window, only to watch the poor man clutch his abdomen and dash for the bathroom.

Chapter 9

JEDIAH FIXED HIS SLIPPING collar and pulled it back up to his neck. His plaid shirt had him swimming in fabric, and his thick denim jeans were hot on his legs. Why anyone would enjoy baggy clothes too cumbersome to move in bewildered him.

He had been wandering the hospital for over an hour. The sickly sweet smell of medicine and floor detergent nauseated his unaccustomed stomach. *And here I thought people came to hospitals to get well.*

Repressing a gag, Jediah peeked into the next doorway. Much to his consternation, it looked the same as the last hundred rooms he checked. Hooped fabric hung on rails. Two railed beds. A few chairs and some devices. He couldn't tell one room apart from another and wished something would break the monotony — anything to get him out of this deja vu.

Jediah peeked under the curtain that cut the room in half, subjecting his nose to the pungent chlorine wafting off the tiles. Frustrated, he got up and made for the next room. Every lost second was another second Malkior remained free.

Noticing his rising impatience, Jediah sucked in a soothing breath, shoved his hands deep into his pockets, and turned left into the next hallway.

A nurse, sporting a messy bun and a loudly patterned smock, exited the closest room. By her wrinkled brow and her glum eyes, she seemed trapped in downcast thoughts. She shook her head at her clipboard as she passed him. "The poor thing," she mumbled.

Jediah couldn't help watching her disappear around the bend and contemplating what she meant. He turned toward the door. Not knowing what else to do, he lightly rapped his knuckles on the metal frame. "Hello?" He leaned in. "Someone here?"

A bedridden little girl stared back; her frail form nearly drowned in an ocean of messy, white sheets.

Jediah froze. A stone dropped from his throat to his gut.

Her hair was missing. Her arms were thin as reeds, and the pallor of her Caucasian skin almost blended too perfectly with the bedding. In fact, Jediah realized if she weren't sitting up, he might not have noticed her at all. The one strength in her he could see was a subtle vibrance in those brown eyes.

The girl's head cocked to one side, and for a moment, rain pinged the window like piano keys as the child and the angel stared at each other.

Jediah noticed her left hand fingering some plastic tubes protruding from her flesh. Unsure what they're for but guessing they were important, he broke from his trance and hurried to her bedside to stop her. His hand took hers in a gentle firmness. "Ah, I don't think you're supposed to do that."

Her hand resisted him, and her innocent gaze locked onto him, uncertain yet not quite afraid.

"It's okay," Jediah cooed as he slowly worked her fingers off. "It's okay. I'm a friend."

Jediah looked up and almost jumped out of his skin. Hidden behind the curtain sat a ministry angel, one who started to cast suspicious looks. Swallowing a lump, Jediah averted his eyes, fearing he already blew his cover to the other angel.

The girl picked at the tubes again.

In an instant, Jediah forgot the ministry angel and pulled her hand off. "No. No. No. You mustn't do that," he said in soft tones.

Yanking her hand from his, she whined and thumped it against the mattress.

Jediah then noticed her Mark, and the worst possible dread pained him. It was incomplete. The Spirit wasn't inside to comfort her. The Son wasn't there to cleanse her. The Father wasn't there to hold her. Then her horrid and sudden hacking pulled Jediah from his thoughts. Her eyes screwed shut, and her body convulsed, inflicting Jediah with a debilitating helplessness, the likes of which he never experienced before.

The girl clutched his sleeve and bunched the cloth between her fingers, as if begging him to make the coughs stop.

Powerless to do anything more, Jediah rubbed her back, and as soon as his fingers stroked those knobbed bones that formed her spine, his heart broke. *Had she been starved too?*

She buried her head into his torso. Jediah hugged her close and patted her shoulder. "Shh. Easy now. Easy." Her coughs died down into thick swallows.

After she pulled back, he watched her thin lips form a strained smile, but her eyes watered.

Jediah's mind raced to deduce what she needed. *Water! She needs water.* "Uh, just a moment." He walked around, trying to recall what water containers today looked like. He grabbed a plastic cup from a tray, sniffed it for contaminants, then slipped into the bathroom.

Jediah leaned over the rimmed bowl, ready to dip the cup, but halted. Something inside nagged him. *This wasn't right.* Turning his gaze, he spotted a higher bowl with a tiny spout attached and a mirror hanging over it. His eyes danced between the two bowls, until realization dawned on him, and he turned away from the lower bowl. "Not a well. Not a well." He twisted the blue marked handle and caught the water in the cup.

Upon returning, he saw her hand rubbing her chest. Her guardian angel peered at him and his cup as he rushed past. "Here we go." Supporting her back with one hand, Jediah knelt to her eye-level and brought the cup to her lips.

She grimaced, but kept gulping.

"Not too fast," Jediah cautioned. "Drink slower." He pulled the cup away and watched for any sign of relief. Wiping her mouth, she released a weaker cough that rumbled wet in her throat.

Jediah cast a sympathetic look at her bald scalp and imagined a crop of healthy hair where it should be. No one was meant to live like this — clinging to life, hooked up to unfeeling machines. The Sin Curse the humans' ancestor Adam incurred so long ago had grown far worse than Jediah ever expected, and a sudden desire to see her smile overtook him. "So what's your name, sweetheart?"

Her cheeks blushed, and she hid her face behind her sheets.

"Mine is," Jediah paused, catching himself almost saying his real name. "Jack. I'm Jack." His hand brushed a distinct bump from under the covers. Reaching in, he pulled out a stuffed lion. Its mane had been braided in so many clumps, it looked like bundled crops of wheat, and twisted strings entwined the fiber hairs.

"Is this yours?" Jediah asked.

She said nothing.

Jediah then read the name written on the plushie's tag "Chloe. Is your name Chloe?"

She nodded.

Jediah set the lion's paws atop the bed. The legs dance as he bounced it up and down, as he made a playful growl. Chloe giggled. He then made the lion climb her sloped sheets, and her giggles grew louder. Then, in a quick motion, he pressed the lion's muzzle into her cheek while he faked silly "nom nom" noises. Her bright laughter erupted and grew louder as Jediah repeated the same puppetry twice more.

Chloe grabbed the lion and hugged it close. "Stop it," she said, with a twinkle in her eye.

Jediah wished to keep that smile forever, but reality set in. Without salvation, she remained destined for final and complete death, and by the state she was in, she might not last long. The wheels in his head turned. His human neck beaded sweat. Yes, he needed to find Malkior, but precious, sacred life was on the line. He couldn't leave her. Not yet.

Nerves skittered in his arms and legs as he looked around for what he worried he would not find. His eyes landed on a Bible sitting by the windowsill. *Miracle of miracles!* Jediah stood up and used both hands to retrieve the Sacred Text in as respectful a manner as possible. He opened its gold and black cover. Just inside, three words were scribbled: 'With love, Grandpa.'

Jediah turned to her with a smile. "Would you like me to read this to you for a bit?"

Chloe's eyes drifted to a corner.

"Just a few chapters?" he pleaded.

Chloe shrugged, though she looked disinterested.

Jediah's spirits sank. Reading all the Scripture in the world wouldn't do her any good if her mind wandered. She needed to do something to keep her in the present. He stared at the lion's matted and braided main and observed how her hands automatically twisted another lock of its fur. "Did you do all those braids?"

Chloe's eyes sparked, and she gave an enlivened smile.

"Do you want to be a hairdresser someday?"

She blushed, looking ever shyer.

Jediah drew up a chair. "How about this then? You can braid my hair while I read a little to you. Sound good?"

Chloe beamed.

Setting the nearby chair back against the bed rail, Jediah settled down and leafed through the yellowed pages. "Did you ever hear the parable of the loving Father?" His memory guided him to the New Testament. "I think you'll like it."

Alameth lingered close to the walls and kept his arms to himself. He didn't like crowds, especially in hospitals, so to him, the sooner they found Malkior, the better. A rushing girl bumped into him. He flinched, but after watching her run off without incident, he released a breath and ran a hand through his hair. *No harm done.*

The tension in his shoulders slacked as he entered a gift shop. Fewer people bustled amongst the plush bears and blown glass figurines. He scanned the ceilings, walls, and corners. No Malkior.

After several fruitless minutes, Alameth turned toward the exit, but a muffled weeping stopped him in his tracks. He looked behind himself and waited. Another bitty sniffle reached his ears. Following the sound, he searched behind a shirt rack.

A young boy, curled up in the corner, choked on his sobs. His face looked ready to burst, only he seemed too embarrassed to let it out, or at least not in full.

Without a second thought, Alameth knelt beside him. "Something wrong, little one?"

"I—I can't f-find my mom."

Softening his eyes and allowing a smile, Alameth reached for the boy's hand. His palms trembled, careful not to hurt those tinier fingers. "Then how about we find her together?"

Chloe's bed bumped Jediah's back as she wiggled. Her scrawny fingers fished through his hair. He winced at the pinching as she tugged a patch behind his left ear.

"So why did the father forgive the son?"

Jediah grunted as Chloe pulled a tenth batch of hair. "Because he never stopped loving his wayward son, even after he squandered his life." Nestling the Bible in his lap, he could feel his skin burn around the tight roots of each braid. He glanced up at the ministry angel who sat on the windowsill. That brother never ceased to watch his every move, but time passed. His mood lightened, and by his few winks and nods, Jediah got the sense that he figured the real him out. Thank goodness the ministry angel felt no need to draw attention to it.

The ministry angel cupped his mouth, muffling several loud chuckles.

Jediah smirked back. He could only imagine how ridiculous his hair looked.

"Will you come back?" Chloe's voice came in a mumbled whisper. "After you go?"

Jediah sighed. He had indeed tarried long enough, but every protective instinct in him pleaded not to go, not in her current condition. Then he remembered Nechum's words from two days before. There were countless people Nechum said he loved that he never saw again. What if the same thing happened between himself and her? She'd never see God. All creation would soon return to the purity of its infancy, like the days of Eden... but she wouldn't be there. Not even a memory.

Jediah squeezed his eyes closed, demanding himself to come up with a solution. "Chloe, to tell you the truth, I am—" He took a moment to reconsider his words. "I am traveling very far away soon, and it is unlikely I'll see you for a while. Maybe never again." Standing up, he turned and spoke to her with a firm promise. "But I will return, if I can."

Footsteps entered the room. "Chloe? Is someone with you?" An elderly man, whose hair color mimicked salt and pepper, examined Jediah up and down. His face turned harsh. "Oh. Hello, and who are you?"

Jediah noticed the full Mark imprinted on his chest. Though pleased to see a Christian here to keep Chloe company, he realized what his actions might look like and backed away from the girl, praying he looked less threatening. "Jack. I'm Jack. Just a friend. I was about to leave."

"He let me braid his hair, Grandpa!" Chloe said.

Her grandfather's frown deepened. "Yes, I can see that."

Chloe sat up higher on wobbling arms. "He read to me from your Bible too!"

This time the man's eyebrows raised. "Really. Well, that's very nice of him." Tucking jingling keys in his coat pocket, the grandfather leaned in as if to tell Jediah a secret. "You know that's how she runs her little slave chain, right? Let her braid your hair, you're hers for life."

Setting the Bible on the bedside table, Jediah stiffened, wondering if braids truly implicated a slave.

The gentleman waved a hand. The wrinkles in his face disappeared from his cheeks as he chuckled. "Kidding. Kidding. I'm just kidding."

"Oh," Jediah said, relieved. "Funny. Real funny."

Walking up to Chloe's bedside, the man lowered his voice. "Did your friends send you letters yet?"

In that one instance, all the cheer Jediah tried so hard to instill in Chloe fled from her face. She hugged her lion and fiddled with its tail.

Her grandfather frowned. "I'm so sorry, sweetheart. I'm sure they'll send you some soon."

Jediah took this as his sign to leave, but stalled at the door. He walked back. "Chloe."

The little girl stared up at him as he took her hand in his. "Jesus loves you... and so do I. Never forget that." Jediah bowed to her, then approached the door. He froze and turned to face her one last time. "I won't forget you. I promise."

Her pale face regained some color as she squeezed her lion closer and rocked it.

Just behind her, the ministry angel waved goodbye in silent approval.

"Goodbye, Chloe."

Chapter 10

WALKING DOWN THE HALLWAY, Jediah tugged a string out of his hair. One braid loosened, and he wasted no time unraveling it.

A figure came into view.

Jediah's hands froze.

The dark being wore a green robe. His eyes trailed a woman as she entered the lady's room, and to Jediah's disgust, the demon licked his lips and followed her right in.

Malkior.

Jediah's energy roiled. Heat filled his face, but he ignored the urge to ambush the bathroom outright. Taking a silent breath, he slipped into the neighboring men's room. Keeping his eyes down, so as not to encroach anyone's privacy, he checked the stalls, pushing lightly on all doors one at a time. None were occupied.

Jediah hurried to the door and locked it from the inside. "Alright, Malkior. Game time." One glimpse in the mirror made him jump, and he grimaced. Knotted locks stuck out all sides of his head like some bizarre pin cushion. "Good grief, Chloe. What did you do?"

Jediah relished being in angelic form again, free to move anyway he wished. Trailing the hospital's pipelines, he stuck his head through the basement ceiling.

Akela, in human form and wearing a ball cap and overalls, whistled a high-pitched tune below.

"You've tampered with that boiler for two hours," a voice shouted. "I think we might have to trash the whole thing at this point."

Akela grunted and threw his head back, revealing smeared rust powder all over his cheeks. "Oy," he muttered to himself. "Could this guy leave me alone for a lousy ten minutes?" He picked up the wrench Nechum borrowed for him from the janitor's closet and rapped it on some metal plates, pretending to work. "Patience, my friend. Patience. It'll be up and kicking soon." Akela leaned to one side. "You won't remember you ever had a problem soon enough."

"You better not be paid by the hour," yelled the voice as it faded.

With Akela less occupied, Jediah climbed down and perched above his head. "Akela."

"Gah!" Akela jerked upright and banged his head into a pipe. Jediah winced as the messenger rubbed his temple.

"Hey! Are you okay?" the voice again called.

Akela gasped. "F-fine. I just... um..." Cringing, he let the wrench fall and flinched as it hit his foot. "I... dropped... a wrench... on my toe."

"Is it swelling? You need an ice pack?"

"Uh, no." Akela cleared his husked throat. "No, it's barely doing anything. Actually, it's doing nothing. My toes are fine. Got toes of iron. I'm... iron-toed." He passed an apologetic shrug to Jediah, who could only shake his head and roll his eyes.

"Oookaaay." Footsteps faded again down the corridor.

Jediah raised his eyebrows. "Smooth."

"Got rid of him, didn't it?" Akela argued.

Jediah jumped down and retrieved his sword from underneath the boiler. "I've spotted Malkior on the third floor." Slipping the leather strap under his blue cloak and over his shoulder, he buckled it tight. "You know what to do. Alert the others." Pulling his hood down, he grabbed the ducts to climb back up.

"I can't leave right away," Akela whispered. "They expect me to sign papers."

"Then sign fast. We're on the clock," Jediah ordered.

Akela saluted with his wrench. "Roger. Roger."

Jediah emerged through the bathroom floor and found the automatic lights had already switched off. He crept through the dark to the door and pressed an ear against the wood. Low humming from the air conditioners made eavesdropping trickier than usual, but he still caught the distinct squeak of hinges from the neighboring door.

Jediah's brow furrowed. Manipulating objects in the first realm while still in the second took significant concentration, but his turning palm felt the doorknob's inner workings move. He gave it a stronger twist. Its tumblers clicked so slowly, each clink tickled his ear. Then a single strip of light shone through the door crack, and inch by inch, he coaxed it further ajar.

Malkior, the demon they were looking for, leaned against the wall. His ashen appearance sucked in light like some black-hole. A bow, hewn from onyx, hung from his wingless back. The green, nature angel's garb he wore was stained with soot, and its fringes had hot embers for tassels—customary for a fire type like himself. Their hellish glow gave Malkior the look of a dormant volcano, liable to erupt, given any arbitrary reason.

Jediah's instincts screamed to pounce on him now, but Malkior scratched his chin and walked farther down the hall.

Jediah crouched low and passed through the door, and after Malkior showed no wariness, he rose to his feet. Each step he took, he synched with Malkior's, nullifying any chance for noise. Lengthening his stride, Jediah summoned the chains, then looped the links into a noose.

Nechum hummed to the elevator's soft speakers and tapped his hand on the cart. So far, so good. No one suspected him. He was the custodian everyone saw nine hours a day, six days a week. Of course, it helped that so few people even bothered to interact with or greet him. Sighing, Nechum pitied the real custodian. The poor fellow's social circles were so tragically small.

The elevator dinged. Nechum gripped the cart handle, ready to push on, but his nerves jittered and startled him. He didn't know why until...

The double doors opened, unveiling an ugly smirk and red eyes.

Nechum's human heart thumped against his rib cage.

Malkior.

For an eternal minute, Nechum forgot everything. His mind went blank. He didn't remember the plan. He didn't remember what Jediah told him to do. He remembered nothing, but noticed somebody gesturing to him.

Jediah stood right behind Malkior, signaling him to come forward, but Nechum found his own two feet stuck in place. Malkior's eyes narrowed. He leaned into his face. Nechum turned his eyes away, pretending not to notice, but then Malkior puffed air from his nose. Nechum flinched.

Jediah lunged for Malkior, but it was too late. The demon dashed through the left wall.

"No!" Jediah slammed his wings against the floor and took off. His blue cloak fell to the floor.

Nechum jolted back to his senses. "I'm sorry! I'm sorry! I'm so sorry!" He slapped his forehead, aghast at such a costly mistake.

Jediah leaped through the wall Malkior ducked through and dove headfirst after him into the parking lot. Malkior disappeared through the asphalt without slowing, but before Jediah could think about it, he fell through the pavement too, not expecting the tunnel just beneath it. His head banged on eroded cement. His neck burned furiously, and shooting pain coursed through a broken right arm.

Jediah grunted as he tried to sit up. His injuries bled gold streaks, but he saw Malkior's cloak turn the corner at the far end of the tunnel. Jediah couldn't bother binding wounds this time. He scrambled to his feet and tucked in his wings. With the tunnel too tight for flying, he had no choice but to pursue on foot. He prayed Laszio and Eran wouldn't take too long to provide backup.

Stupid! Stupid! How could I be so stupid!

Nechum sped with the cleaning cart, desperate to get rid of it. It rolled too fast from his hand right into the utility closet, and a mighty crash of brooms and 'wet floor' signs spilled out. Worried someone might notice, he tossed the mess back inside and slammed the door before it fell out again.

Ducking into another room, he eschewed his human guise, then sprinted for the emergency door but forgot the stairs. His fumbling feet skidded, and he tumbled down the first flight.

Jediah's running jostled his broken arm, but he couldn't afford to lose Malkior in that network of catacombs. This underground maze seemed endless, and it grew apparent that even if his wingmen followed him in, Laszio and Eran had no chance of navigating its dark twists and turns. They were likely scrambling to find their way already.

Jediah sucked in through his teeth and sprinted faster, more aware that he was on his own.

They reached a straight stretch of tunnel. Finding a wide enough space, Jediah alighted his wings, flapped, and shot a light wave meant to knock Malkior off his feet.

Malkior peeked over his shoulder and yelped. He phased through another wall before the light could connect.

Letting his empathic sense guide him, Nechum descended through the basement into the underground tunnels. It smelled old and putrid. Then, after looking down, he reeled into a corner. Centuries-old skulls and bones littered the floor.

A grey figure slipped in behind him, startling Nechum. "Oh! Alameth, it's you. How'd you follow me here?"

"I heard you fall." Drawing his hood over his face, Alameth hovered upon his mists over the long-dried corpses.

"Jediah and Malkior are somewhere in these burial sites," Nechum explained. "I think we should split up to find them." He pointed toward two branching tunnels. "I'll let you pick. Which do you prefer? Right or left?"

Jediah flicked off his sharpened quills.

Malkior ducked, and the feather darts speared the walls. Panting, he squeezed himself into a tighter space and shook from panic as he slid along. "Stop chasing me!" He kicked at Jediah, and a stream of fire erupted from his boot. Their flames bloomed into teeth that engulfed the ceiling and floor.

Undaunted, Jediah sped up. He armored his wounded arm and long-jumped straight through the inferno. The fiery maw brushed his clothes, but their flames did not catch. The orange rings surrounding him died out. His boots then landed amidst the scattered sparks without missing a step.

Red flashed to Alameth's right. He peered at the entryway where it came from, for its whiffs of toasted clay were unmistakable. Looking in, he caught sight of two silhouettes just beyond the dying embers that disappeared around the bend.

Alameth pressed his lips together and furrowed his brow. Planting one foot back, he focused his energy. His eyes went white. Spreading his arms out, he commanded his mist to tighten around him in a close circle. It compacted against his chest, then churned and thickened, and once the pressure grew too uncomfortable, he unleashed it all. Fog exploded in one burst, filling the intersecting tunnels like water in a trough.

A faint breeze from behind brushed Nechum's hair and gave him the funniest feeling.

Uh, oh.

Nechum raised a protective shield. Fog erupted, blowing him down.

Jediah had pursued Malkior into a four-way intersection when a sudden chilling force shoved him from behind. Smoke swallowed everything. Jediah's toes gripped within his boots as they strained for footing, but he fell forward.

He couldn't see two inches in front of himself. His eyes watered as the mist's vapor invaded his nose. The scrapes on his face and broken arm burned as if they were being nibbled on by parasites, and he felt more energy bleeding from his arm as if the fog siphoned it right out.

Jediah covered his mouth and nose with his good arm and stared ahead into the weakening fog.

Malkior's silhouette scrambled up. He hacked around, but managed to turn on Jediah and pulled out his bow. Two thick arrows made of embers sparked in his fist.

Jediah scrambled back and grabbed for the nearest wall.

The drawstring twanged. The sparking arrow struck, and Jediah barely had enough time to protect his front with hardened wings. A chunk of wall blasted apart. Stone shards struck his feathers in front, as his exposed back slammed into the opposite wall. His right shoulder crunched and dislocated. His numb wings hummed as he slid to the floor.

Letting out a gasp, Jediah tested his good arm. It didn't seem to be broken. His mind screamed at him to get up. He lifted to his knees but froze at the sound of another arrow nocked to its bow.

Arms twitching, Malkior aimed for his head. The fire arrow trembled in place like a stick of dynamite in the hands of a drunk. A crazed glint sat in Malkior's eye as he laughed in hysterics. "Didn't count on that, did ya? Put your wings behind your back."

Jediah glared.

Malkior again drew the drawstring to his cheek. The fire coals that embellished his green tunic pulsed red. "Do it! Else I blow the entire block!"

Jediah drew his wings back one inch at a time.

Malkior chuckled and relaxed his arms.

Hoping to throw him off, Jediah pulsed energy through his eyes. They flashed, startling the demon, but Malkior hyperventilated a laugh. "Ha. Ha. Ha. You think that's funny, do ya?" His pupils dilated unevenly, and he swayed so much, Jediah guessed the fog must have further warped his insanity.

Malkior yanked the drawstring back again as he backed away. The arrow flared. Then, after he glanced twice to the left corridor, he released.

The seconds slowed. Malkior's arrow ignited as it flew toward Jediah's head.

"Captain!" Nechum jumped into the arrow's path. He cupped a blue disk that he stretched out to an arm's length. The arrow slipped in, but popped before Nechum could enclose it, and the explosion chucked him right into Jediah.

Fresh pain racked Jediah's throbbing arm and shoulder as he laid there, pinned under Nechum. He willed himself to wriggle out, but his excruciation spiked. Jediah groaned and pounded a fist against the floor. *Malkior got away.*

Nechum panted, shell shocked and frozen in place.

Suddenly, Jediah's thoughts turned from himself to his shaken brother. "Nechum?" he croaked. He coughed the rasp from his throat. "Nechum. Are you okay?"

Nodding, Nechum shimmied off. The movement bumped Jediah's arm, causing Jediah to cry out. Nechum snapped around. His eyes widened, and his hand cupped his mouth. He drew to Jediah's side and cast an agonized gaze over his ruined arm as though he blamed himself for it.

Touched by his concern, Jediah strained to turn his wincing into a smile, but he hissed the second Nechum fingered the wound to examine it.

Nechum's eyebrows dipped, and darker shades chased the usually soothing aquamarine colors from his eyes. "Never again, Captain. Never again. I swear I won't ever freeze like that again."

Jediah forced himself to sit up, feigning good health. "It's okay, Nechum. It's okay."

Nechum pressed a gentle hand against Jediah's chest. "Wait. Don't move." After helping Jediah lean against the wall, he unclasped the silver pin that held his shawl in place. "This is the least I can do." The fabric fell from Nechum's shoulders, revealing a water skin he had slung under his arm. Setting the shawl aside, Nechum took the skin and unscrewed the cap. He tipped it over the shawl. Crystal drops from the River of Life itself trickled out and dampened the cloth till it shimmered.

Nechum's hands showed practiced skill as he then wrapped Jediah's arm with the damp shawl. Jediah hissed. His arm stung terribly, but soon the herbed waters from the make-shift sling started their work. The moist fibers cooled his wounds. Jediah smiled to Nechum and mouthed a soft 'thank you.'

Akela passed through the intersection in a golden flash, then double backed. He panted, leaning with one hand against the wall. Scratches peppered his face. "Finally. I found somebody. Yay." He raised a fist in weak triumph. "Sorry for being late. Navigating this tangled mess is a nightmare."

Jediah closed his eyes and thudded his head against the wall. He did *not* want to hear about it.

Chapter 11

LUCIFER'S ATTENTION snapped to the messenger, who darted in and bowed low. He dismissed his attendants and broadened his shoulders. "Rise and report."

"Captain Zivel sends word. Elazar will do it."

Such a potent sense of triumph swelled in Lucifer that he felt victory was already achieved. "Perfect."

"But not for you." The messenger shook his head. "Zivel ordered me to make it clear that Elazar won't do it for you."

Lucifer raised an eyebrow and rolled his eyes in annoyance. Zivel had always harbored a terrible jealousy for Elazar. That stupid oaf never could reconcile the fact that a wingless ministry rogue outclassed an average soldier like himself. "Well, you can tell your captain that I don't care *who* Elazar does it for so long as he just *does* it."

A second messenger dropped in from the east and threw himself before the Devil face down. "Pardon, my liege. Urgent news from Malkior."

Surprise curtailed Lucifer's agitation. Malkior usually communicated only with his master, lord Yakum. He didn't expect to hear from either Malkior or Yakum until their plague was truly ready. "Then speak," Lucifer commanded.

"Malkior says they attacked him," the messenger answered. "Jediah, and a ministry angel with him."

A cold jolt ruined Lucifer's original self-confidence. He lifted the demon up by the throat. "A ministry angel? Who was it? Who!"

The demon's feeble hands pulled against Lucifer's wrist. "He doesn't know," he half-choked. "Malkior doesn't know! He never saw him before, but he was there, and he aided Jediah. That's all! That's all!"

Noting the defeated look in the messenger's eyes, Lucifer realized he'd get nothing more from him. He relented his grip, letting the demon drop hard to hack around in the grass.

"Begging your pardon, sire," Zivel's messenger approached with lowered eyes. "It's just a ministry angel. He's practically harmless."

Lucifer rushed into his face, ready to break his neck. "Has this war, after six thousand years, taught you nothing? I've underestimated God's pathetic scrap heaps one too many times. No one He throws in is *ever* just a harmless *anything!*"

Brushing the wrinkles off of his robe, Lucifer pointed at the other messenger. "You! Tell your master, Malkior, to disappear and find a hole to cower in. He's good at that. And you." He turned back to the other and adjusted the loosened edges of his collar. "Send word to Elazar and Zivel. Tell them to ready Zivel's legion and put my plans into motion." The messenger's neck tensed and arched back as Lucifer continued to speak. "I may not know this meddlesome ministry angel, but I know Akela. He's obsessed with his relationships. Once I set my trap, he'll seek that nature angel friend of his, and provide exactly the bait we need. If God is withholding Jediah—His ace—then I guess I'll start with His joker."

This kind of waiting tested Jediah's patience most. Every lost second meant another step behind Malkior, but until Akela returned from scouting, it meant he could do nothing. None of them could. They were stuck in the Paris catacombs, surrounded by pieces of the city's darker histories.

Jediah looked down at Nechum's makeshift arm sling. Gold stained the fabric. He frowned and determined to clean it out before returning it. Nechum deserved better than a splotched shawl for his kindness.

Testing his broken arm, Jediah moved it but a few inches before the stings bit back. Pain and frustration forced him to lie back again, anxious and bored.

Seeking some way to relax, Jediah ran his hand through his hair. The cool strands soothed his roughed fingers until they met a single bump. He paused and fingered the thicker locks at the nape of his neck. It was a braid. He had missed one.

Thoughts of Chloe flooded his mind and stopped his initial urge to undo it.

No, I mustn't undo this. It mattered so much to her, and I mustn't forget her.

But then he wondered if he should forget. Her illness had her mortal life hanging by a thread, and her unsaved soul teetered on the edge of absolute death, ready to plunge into darkness. Cutting the braid and cutting his ties to her sounded easiest to rid himself of potential grief.

Still, Jediah shook his head. *But she had her grandfather who loves her and gave her that Bible. There still may be a chance... for her, that is.* Once more, dreams of salvation and its mysteries returned to him, and Jediah saddened at the irony. He wanted it, but couldn't have it. She needed it, but didn't reach for it.

He pinched the bridge of his nose. *But I can't abandon her while she's unsaved and dying.*

Releasing a sigh, his inner commonsense criticized the new plan forming in his head. It sounded crazy. Absolutely nuts. He didn't know what it's fully like to carry the Spirit inside, but he knew God. His understanding of salvation was limited, but he knew some things. His quiet debate went on until the arguments for the plan slowly gained the majority.

"You know what humans need to do to be saved," he reasoned. "That should be enough, right? Besides, she loved letters. Surely, I can spare enough time for one."

Frowning, Eran watched the pained look on Jediah's face. If their captain was disappointed in them, he had every reason to be. Eran hated to admit it, but once again, he and Laszio's usefulness struck a dead end.

They spotted Jediah when he chased Malkior underground. They leaped into action as instructed, but instead of helping, they wound up lost in the labyrinth, choking on fog, and shooting light at harmless shadows. Malkior might not have gotten away if they moved faster. True, their prestigious captain never berated them for their slipshod performance, but what was there to be said other than they embarrassed themselves? Jediah never shied from giving criticism, but he never attacked anyone's personal worth.

Eran released a breath. That was one of the many character qualities he so admired about his captain. Eran often asked himself why he couldn't be as morally balanced. Why couldn't he be as resourceful? Jediah was forthright, forgiving, and knew what to do. He *always* knew what to do.

Trying to keep his frustrations from his face, Eran rubbed the back of his neck. *Jediah shouldn't have to pick up our slack.* Eran heard a grunt from Laszio, who paced in tight circles. He released a light chuckle. It never ceased to amaze him how his best friend always displayed on the outside how he himself felt on the inside.

Laszio cast suspicious glances at Alameth, who prayed in the distant corner with his hood so low it touched the tip of his nose.

Eran shuffled in his seat. He didn't feel comfortable around Alameth either, for he didn't know what to make of him. He constantly seemed aloof, like he wanted to be cut off from everything and too well practiced at it. Not to mention, it was *his* fog they suffocated on not but a couple hours ago.

Eran leaned over to Nechum, who hadn't yet spoken a word since the incident. "Hey, Nechum," he whispered. "You ministry types have this empathic sense, don't you?"

Nechum squinted. "Yes?"

"What can you tell us about him?" Eran nodded toward Alameth.

Twisting in his seat, Nechum stared at Alameth, then faced Eran head on. "Forgive me if this sounds harsh, but I hardly believe that's your business."

"But do you sense anything strange? Perhaps a bit off?"

An indiscernible expression crossed Nechum's face. Eran couldn't put his finger on it, but the way Nechum's head tipped sideways made it appear he wanted to retreat from the conversation—a telltale sign when an honest person couldn't lie but hated to share the truth.

Nechum pursed his lips. "You mistake my gift for clairvoyance, brother. I cannot read minds or sense what all is *in* a person or being. Only what they feel."

Laszio, who apparently eavesdropped, knelt next to them. "Then what *is* Alameth feeling? What emotions do you sense in him right now?"

Folding his hands in his lap, Nechum's face fell, and Eran tried to piece together what that meant. "Are you saying that Alameth isn't feeling much at all?" Eran asked.

Nechum closed his eyes but didn't deny it.

Eran traded looks with Laszio. "Should we be concerned about that?"

For a moment, Nechum didn't move. "Yes," he breathed. "And no." His aquamarine eyes deep with pity, he stared at Eran and Laszio. "I don't know all that Alameth or others of his kind have seen or been through. He's probably seen things, wretched things, you and I can only imagine *for six thousand years*. So I ask you, which would be worse for Alameth? For him to emotionally detach himself from the grim side of his work? Or to like it too much?"

Terrible scenarios played out in Eran's mind, and he grimaced.

Laszio drew in close and spoke in a soft voice. "So do you think Alameth needs help, Nechum?"

Nechum stared into his wringing hands that rested on his lap. "Everyone needs help, brother Laszio. Including you and including me."

Akela's head poked in through the ceiling. "Hey, everyone. I'm back." He jumped down, and a burnt scent wafted off his steaming wings. He rolled his shoulder. "Boy, that flight was a workout."

Jediah wobbled to get up while only using one arm, but he rose to a stand. "How'd it go, Akela? Did you find Malkior?"

Akela swayed back and forth. His hands fiddled with his satchel. "Sorry, but no. I checked every building, street, sewage pipe, doghouse, and potted plant. Everything. Came up with zip."

"Great. We wasted an hour," Jediah said.

Akela grinned. "But it's not over, sir. Far from it."

Surprised by his comment, Eran stood up in interest. "How?"

Akela's wings hummed. "While I was searching, I hatched an idea."

Laszio raised his eyebrows. "A plan? You?"

"Hey, I'm not the smartest messenger, but I have my moments," Akela returned.

"We're listening, Akela," Jediah said as he nailed Laszio with that familiar warning look.

Feeling sorry for his friend, yet agreeing that his interjection came rather rude, Eran bumped Laszio in the shoulder.

Akela, unbothered, clapped his hands together. "Okay. So. Malkior is a nature angel, right? They're wingless, so he had to flee on foot. But he's not anywhere in the city or the outskirts, so it's safe to assume he jumped ship into the third realm."

"So now we're really stuck. He could be anywhere," Eran said, then crossed his arms.

"Ho, ho, ho. You'd think so," Akela said. "Well, little did he know, he left traces of this!" He opened his hand. Two black specks the size of poppy seeds rolled in the center of his palm.

Laszio frowned at the flecks. "Dirt. You found dirt."

"Yes!" Akela responded with increasing jubilance. "But it's not just any dirt."

Nechum cupped Akela's hand in his own and leaned over the specks. "It's ash."

Eran peered at Nechum. "Which means what?"

"Physical matter isn't readily susceptible to spiritual influence, but see how Akela can hold these so easily?" Nechum nudged a speck. "This ash must have come off of Malkior when he escaped. This could lead us right to him!"

Eran peered closer. "How?"

Closing his hand, Akela drew the ash close to himself. "After the Sin Curse, God appointed nature angels to help delay the earth's rapid decay. They keep it from tearing itself apart. Thus, it's only natural that they interact with the physical realm on a near constant basis, and it just so happens that after a time, their beings 'imprint' or 'acclimate' to the place they manipulate most. They mimic their surroundings kinda like a copy machine, and praise the Lord that He made volcanic sediment as individual as the stench of a camel!"

Before Eran could even question what on earth a copy machine was, Akela dug into his satchel. "Now where did I put that—Ah, here it is." He pulled out a tiny bottle. After carefully containing the ash and corking its top, he buried the bottle back into the bag.

Eran's hope dawned. "So you're saying that we use this ash to identify Malkior's volcano, swoop in, then flush him out."

"Bingo!" Akela winked. "and I know just the brother who can help us."

"Who?" Jediah inquired.

"Jedd. He's my best friend and a nature angel of the wind class. He'd be more than happy to identify this soot for us."

Shaking his head, Laszio frowned. "No, he can't. This is a stealth mission, Akela. No one's supposed to know we're even here."

Akela hand-waved at Laszio. "Who says I have to tell him what it's for? He and I are tight like that." He crossed his fingers, then turned to Jediah.

Jediah looked pensive and more than a little wary, a rare thing for him by Eran's recollection. He wondered if his captain was more concerned that Akela would blab too much or if Jedd would deduce too much.

After a minute, Jediah nodded.

Akela grinned. "I won't let you down, sir! I promise. I'll talk to no one but him. You'll see."

Jediah lifted an eyebrow. "Do you know where Jedd is right now?"

"Mexico. El Puente de Dios to be precise. They'll be pushing the warm front to the north. They do that every spring season this time of year."

Jediah covered his mouth in thought, then straightened his posture. "Fly to Mexico, get his advice, then come straight back. Understand? No detours."

"No detours, got it," Akela affirmed.

"And no socializing."

"Of course. Of course." Akela's thin wings raised. Gold lightning sparked from their tips. "Be back soon!" He shot out of the tunnel.

Eran rubbed his brow and found a spot to make himself comfortable for prayer. As far as he knew, this could be a disaster.

Chapter 12

NECHUM NEVER THOUGHT it would take Akela so long, and his imagination filled to bursting with all the ways things could have gone wrong. He sighed and rose from the floor. Worrying around wasn't helping things. He needed to take a walk and clear his head.

Alameth still sat in prayer. So still had he been through the hours, he could well have been an alabaster statue—flawless and regal yet distant and cold.

Nechum's countenance saddened. For the same reason he knew a man cannot live on an island alone, he desired to draw Alameth, the real Alameth, out. He was in there, somewhere behind that stoic exterior. Nechum reached for his shoulder, eager to hear if he was okay from his own mouth, but Nechum drew back. A supernatural instinct, one from God, informed him it wasn't the time. He relented. *Alameth still needed his space.*

Walking on, Nechum passed Laszio and Eran, who sat on their knees. They concentrated hard on their training regiment. Their wings were wide open, and the edges of their feathers transitioned between forms. One second their barbules softened to the point of splitting apart, then just as quickly sharpened to knives.

"Pardon me for interrupting," Nechum said. "But what sort of training is this?"

Releasing a breath, Ean let his wings lax. He regarded Nechum over his shoulder. "Feather drills. For flight techniques."

"Oh. And how many flight techniques are there?" Nechum asked.

Laszio twisted around. "As many as there are birds."

The thought reeled in Nechum's head. "How do you keep them all straight?"

Laszio shrugged. "I don't know. It just became second nature at this point."

After a silent moment, Eran cupped his chin. "Nechum, how do you think Akela learned so much about that ash?"

Nechum sensed a deeper reason behind Eran's question and reflected longer than usual on Akela. *Chipper, inquisitive; as cheerful and lively yet as unpredictably spastic as a firecracker.* Nechum smiled. "I think Akela enjoys God's creation so much, he simply loves to learn about everything anytime and anywhere he is. Which probably explains why he's so distracted most of the time."

Eran looked aside. "I guess that makes sense."

Nechum's empathic sense picked up on Eran's frustration, but not one that was aimed outward but inward, and he read in both of them the hallmarks of hearts burdened by inadequacy.

The two Privates begged their pardon and resumed training.

As he watched, it became all the clearer to Nechum. Their fears of failure drove them. He wished to continue their conversation, but just like with Alameth, Nechum held his tongue. He didn't know their story yet. His relationship with them hadn't time to grow either, and any encouraging words he may have said would carry little weight.

Caught up in thought, Nechum walked on. The group dynamic had again changed on him. Now, with more and more issues cropping up from each of his brethren, figuring out whom God expected him to help became more perplexing than ever. Anxiety churned Nechum's energy to the point where his neck and face flushed. "*It could be any of them, Lord,*" he prayed. "*Who is it?*"

Nechum paused, ordering his thoughts to freeze their frenzy. *Or maybe not knowing so I'd help everyone is the point.* Pondering where this conclusion led to, Nechum took another minute to let the idea unfold. *In which case, I must look out for everybody. Is that correct, Lord? While their focus is on the enemy, I focus on them?*

Overwhelmed by the responsibility of such a revelation, Nechum turned the corner.

Jediah, who was seated, rushed to hide something. Nechum squinted. Whatever he had, he tucked into his belt under his ministry cloak. Jediah acted unaware of him, but Nechum recognized the nervous gaze of a pretender.

Despite suspicions, Nechum decided confronting his captain wouldn't be wise. Still, his mind committed it to memory. He folded his hands. "Oh. Hello, Captain, I didn't know you were resting here."

"It's just 'Jediah' right now, brother Nechum." Jediah gave the kindest smile, yet Nechum noticed his golden brown eyes lost their luster.

Nechum examined Jediah's arm, which now laid free from the sling. "How are you feeling?" he asked.

"Fine. Thank you," Jediah handed Nechum his now perfectly folded and freshly cleaned shawl. Glinting flakes shed off the dried fabric as it traded hands. Wrapping it about his shoulders, Nechum refastened the silver pin. He then noticed how Jediah gazed at the pin's shape, almost with longing. The adornment glinted with a cross in its center, and three unbroken circles crowned its arms. It was the angelic crest and bore a striking resemblance to the Mark of the Trinity. Every angel wore it. Jediah's fingers traced the same design at the center of the captain's crest sewn into his scarf.

Jediah's jaw trembled. "Nechum?" He licked his lips. "Have you ever... do you... uh."

Confused, Nechum sat down beside him.

"What is it like to..." Jediah's voice petered out in a sigh.

Nechum placed a gentle hand on his shoulder. "Go on."

For a moment, Jediah fell into a lost stare. He closed his eyes and released a chuckle from deep in his chest. "It must be amazing for you to get to watch God enter an Image Bearer's heart. It must be the most wonderful part in your role."

A wistfulness overcame Nechum as a flood of memories rushed by. "Yes. The most wonderful of all."

"W—what is that like for them?" Jediah asked. "What happens?"

Nechum's eyebrows dipped. For the second time that day, he sensed a veiled motive behind a question. "Well," Nechum started. "They ask Jesus into their life and pardon for sin, but it's not as simple as walking an aisle, or praying a prayer."

Jediah nodded. "I know. I know. There's gotta be more to it."

"There is."

"And it's not salvation by works."

"Absolutely not."

"So there's a core to redemption that stays with them afterwards. What do you think it is?"

Jediah's eyes rekindled the more he inquired. Puzzle pieces fell in place, and a sudden concern seized Nechum as he saw where this led. "Captain, we can't—"

"Captain! Captain!" Laszio called.

Jediah shot to his feet. "Laszio? What is it?"

They followed Laszio's voice around the corner, and standing in the tunnel stood Akela, huffing and puffing and holding a weary nature angel up by the arm. Instinctively, Nechum rushed to help Akela lower his companion to the ground. The nature angel's tunic had been ripped. The white wisp embellishments, marks of a wind angel, flipped in weak angles, and a terrible exhaustion covered the angel's face as if he was just salvaged from a war front.

"Akela!" Jediah shouted. He marched into his face. "What are you doing bringing him here?"

"I'm sorry, Captain," Akela panted. His hands seized Jediah's arms in a death grip. "I had to get Jedd out of there. I just had to. And we need to go back!"

"Go back? What do you mean, go back?" Jediah coaxed Akela's hands to loosen. "Calm down. Tell me what happened."

"Jedd and his clan were attacked on route to America. We barely escaped."

"By whom?" Jediah asked.

"Soldiers. Demon soldiers."

Laszio scowled and gripped the sticks on his belt. "Why would they attack wind class nature angels?"

Lifting on his elbows, Jedd sat straight up. "To hijack the warm front."

"By the way, this is Jedd," Akela interjected. His hands motioned introductions. "Jedd. Everybody. Everybody. Jedd."

Eran rolled his eyes. "We figured that, Akela."

Jedd swayed, and Nechum drew him closer. His half-shut eyes closed for a moment as he leaned heavily against Nechum's arm. "My clan was maintaining the south wind," he wheezed. "It's supposed to reach America in two days, but now it'll be there in one."

Jediah shook his head in confusion. "And is that bad?"

Jedd's eyes popped open to the size of saucers. "Is that bad? The warm front is moving too fast! It'll inevitably smack head on into the cold front. Don't you understand? It's an oncoming, unsanctioned natural disaster! We're talking a massive supercell that'll generate the most devastating tornado strike in history!"

Nechum swallowed down his personal dread.

Kneeling, Jediah met Jedd at eye level. "Where are the other wind angels now?"

"In Mexico," Akela answered. "They were let go, but they're in worse shape than he is." With pleading eyes, Akela stepped forward, his hands folded and shaking. "Sir? Please? I know we're on a mission. I know it's secret, and it's a bit of a detour. I promised no detours, but we—we have to do something. Please? *Brother?*"

"But what can we do, Akela?" Jediah said, quiet and regretful. "None of us can bend the winds."

"We can't, but *he* can." Akela motioned to Jedd. "He'll be able to do it. I know he will, but he can't go back alone. Those same demons are tailing that warm front and will slaughter him on sight, but if he had some protection..." He gestured toward Jediah, then everyone else.

Nechum bit his lip, awaiting Jediah's answer.

Jediah planted his hands on his hips and stared at the ground.

"Sir." Eran stepped forward. "If I may suggest, we can fight and still hide our identities."

Laszio nodded in agreement. Passion lit the grey in his eyes to a lightning azure.

Jediah's brow wrinkled, but Nechum could barely hear him mumble in a quiet breath, "Do not withhold good, when it's in your power to act." Then, taking hold of his blue cloak, Jediah wrapped the looser folds to cover his lower face.

"Uh, is this really necessary?" Nechum's hands trembled as he fashioned a translucent shield into a waterboard big enough for him and Jedd to stand on. He listened to the crashing waves of an angry sea as it smacked the Normandy beaches in fury. Nechum shook his head with increasing vigor. "Maybe Jedd should fly with Akela and the rest of you go ahead without me. I can catch up."

Laszio slapped a hand on Nechum's shoulder and pointed toward the black horizon. "You want to run to the Mexican Gulf through *that*? Be my guest."

Winds howled and threw blinding sea spray into the clouds. *"Who knew storms were brewing both here and there?"* Nechum thought.

"No one's leaving anybody," Jediah emphasized. "Are you about done, Eran?"

"Just a sec." Eran knotted his and Laszio's strings together, then screwed one stick from each pair into the other, creating a handlebar. "That should do it."

Jediah examined Eran's handiwork and nodded. "And you're sure this'll work."

"It should, sir."

Jediah patted Eran on the back and handed the handlebar back to him. "Let's hope so."

Nechum molded four footholds into his waterboard and set it upon the water's edge. Balancing on first, he slipped his feet into the straps. Jedd wrapped his arms around his waist and fitted his feet in as well. "Are you sure you're okay with this, Jedd?" Nechum asked.

"Of course. It looks pretty fun actually."

Nechum nodded to himself. He should have expected this level of optimism from Akela's closest friend.

Laszio handed Nechum the makeshift handlebar. "Don't let go." Laszio tied one of the long ends around his wrist. Eran similarly tethered himself to the other cord.

Alameth, who had been gazing into the foul distance, turned to Nechum. "Are you gonna be okay?"

Touched by Alameth's sudden show of concern, Nechum hesitated, then answered. "Yeah." He adjusted his hold. "Yeah."

Akela bounced foot to foot and shook out his arms. "Captain, we gotta leave now!"

"Akela," Jediah ordered. "Stay close to Laszio and Eran and keep watch for surprises."

"Like demon sharks?"

Jediah rolled his eyes at the lame joke. "Sure, Akela. *Demon* sharks."

"Aye, aye," Akela saluted, then joined Laszio and Eran, who stood atop the smaller crests.

Jediah gestured to Alameth. "You watch our backs." He took Nechum and Jedd by the shoulders. "You two ready?"

"Um, yeah." Nechum cringed at himself. His voice sounded more anxious than he wanted it to. "Just in case I fall—"

Jedd nudged his back. "You're not gonna fall. You're gonna do great."

Nechum looked over his shoulder. "You do realize you're the one hanging on to *me*, right?"

"You're going to be fine. I'm right behind you." Jediah unwrapped his wings. They spread far out the sides of his blue cloak. "Laszio! Eran! Start slow, then pick up speed!"

"Sir, yes, sir!" Lifting off, the two rose with the slipstream. The lengthened cords tied to their wrists dragged behind them length by length.

Nechum double checked his grip on the handlebar. "So I do nothing, right?"

"Mostly." Jedd hugged tighter.

"Mostly?"

"Well, prior experience says lean back and don't let go."

"Prior experience? Then why aren't you the one hanging—" The rope yanked him forward.

Chapter 13

FOR LEAGUES, THE FOAMING waves towered high, building and falling all around Nechum and threatening to collapse on his and Jedd's heads. Laszio and Eran, who tugged them along the currents, circumvented the Florida peninsula towards an Alabama coast that was under siege by a black, growling sky. If not for the angels' spiritual nature, the torrents of rain would have stung their faces.

Lightning clapped at the rising, watery peaks. The resulting flash startled Nechum, making him and Jedd wobble as they scaled the next wavering mountain.

Jediah flew down and steadied their shoulders. "Hang on! We're almost there!"

Akela, who left his place in the front, slipped back to fly by their side and pointed ahead. "It's the supercell!"

Nechum felt Jedd rise on his tiptoes to see. Then, jumping off their board, he surrendered himself to the winds that carried him toward the violent coast.

Taking the lead, Jediah seemed to charge the rolling clouds as their increasing mass sped inland. "Privates!" he called. "Hard right!"

Laszio and Eran raised their left wings and caught a heavier gust. The waterboard skidded in the sharp turn, and Nechum leaned so far to compensate, his ear almost scraped the water's surface. Alameth, who had trailed behind the whole trek, tipped Nechum up straight.

A half molded dock trembled under the ocean's beating. Upon reaching the last league, Nechum released the handlebar, coasted a crest, then leaped, kicking off the board and landing on the first rotted planks. His ears rang, for the tempest squalled louder on land than at sea. Flashes tore through the clouds every few seconds. Thunder rumbled, hungry for destruction, and a sticky, humid breeze clawed through the grass.

"Wow, that thing looks mean." Laszio said, as he unscrewed his stick from Eran's.

"And moving fast." Jediah adjusted his hood and face covering. "Jedd, how do we stop a storm this size?"

Staring at the clouds, Jedd frowned. "We technically can't. Not unless God alters the earth's rotational pull, but I can slow it down if I smother the storm's supply of warm air."

"Are there any other wind angels around here we can rally?" Eran asked.

"No." Jedd said. "My kind are too few."

Jediah pursed his lips. "Okay then. Akela, you and Jedd pair up. Take him wherever he needs to go as fast as you can. Laszio, Eran, you and I keep attackers off Jedd and Akela's tail. Got it?"

"Yes, sir."

Laszio and Eran pulled their blue hoods to cover their faces. The carvings etched in their sticks glowed to life.

Nervous and at a loss, Nechum was taken aback when Jediah pointed toward him and Alameth. "You two pair up. You're emergency support."

Clinging to a car-roof, Nechum kept a lookout at ground level. The grumbling cloud plumed blacker and blacker as it billowed into the hemisphere. Electrical streams threw themselves in countless branches, and sleet plinked one at a time on the vehicle seconds before their numbers teamed.

Nechum squinted. Jediah, Laszio, and Eran's silhouettes followed Akela and Jedd's to cloudier heights above, making them harder to keep track of. "Do you still see them?" he asked Alameth.

Alameth shrugged and shook his head.

Nechum searched the rotating sky again. Once in a while, he thought he counted only five figures umbrella'd by the storm's shadows, but the shapes the lightning cast planted doubts in his mind. He could almost swear there were more silhouettes up there.

Wind blasted the windshield. Rubber tires screeched the blacktop in a swerving skid and sent Nechum sliding off to the right. Nechum's fingers cramped as they clenched the roof edge, but Alameth grabbed his sides and hoisted him back up. "Thank you!" Nechum yelled, as he fixed his footing.

Jediah suppressed the sickened sensation rising in his throat as the air pressure shifted. Already a few twisters had latched themselves to the ground. Like leeches sucking blood dry, they consumed all they touched and writhed in chaotic directions.

He and the others overtook the cumulonimbus at a gradual pace and ascended into the frigid cold. Ice chunks floated up and down, gathering water and gaining weight. Farther in, the cloud's unmistakable slow swirl gained speed. Another new cyclone was about to be born.

Jediah watched Akela's golden trail as he and Jedd cut through the flying ice-field. Akela let his friend drop into the burgeoning tornado's center. White flashed from Jedd's eyes as he plummeted in free fall. Dry cool air followed his descent, poured into the growing funnel, and choked the moist humidity right out. Then, as the swirling cloud slowed to a stop, Akela swooped and caught Jedd from the cyclone's dwindling end.

"Looks like it's working!" Laszio shouted, as they all exited the first cloud.

But Jediah frowned. Four more funnels waved their gnarled fingers over the taller trees. Knowing they mustn't fall behind, he directed his wingmen on a lower angle for a swifter glide. Akela and Jedd just evacuated another funnel they dismantled when his warrior instincts kicked in. Four to five unidentified shadows tailed Akela and Jedd from behind.

"Rise!" Jediah ordered. He, Laszio and Eran rode a swift updraft. Flaming energy flicked off Jediah's wings, and the flying fire alighted on his blade. The demons he targeted spotted them first and dove to greet them with swords.

Jediah feigned an attack, dodged to the side, and gave Laszio and Eran their window to shoot. The two Private's spheres blinded them. Then Jediah swooped around and sliced their wings clean off.

"Gah!" Another pair of demons had jumped Akela. He fumbled his grip, dropping Jedd into the arms of two more.

Jediah reached them in two flaps. His sword slew the ones assaulting Jedd, spattering their red energy all over him while Laszio and Eran freed Akela and dragged the attackers into a downward spiral.

A strong gale held Jedd aloft, but his arms quaked in shock as he stared at the fresh wet specks.

Jediah wiped a splotch off Jedd's face. "Never mind it. Get to Akela and get out of here."

After a dazed nod, Jedd curved around to his friend.

More demonic soldiers lunged for Jedd, but Jediah clapped his wings, smacking light into their sides. Akela and Jedd rejoined, then charged for the storm's heart.

Jediah checked on Laszio and Eran below. They were bombarding five more renegades with their light balls, but red from a demon's light wave filled the corner of his eye, and his breath hitched. The surprise attack missed Eran, but hit Laszio.

Laszio cried out and gripped his side. Eran flew to his aide, oblivious to the whole enemy legion that assembled beneath them, and clapped their wings in unison.

Nosediving towards the incoming volley, Jediah dragged his wingmen with him to fall straight through the barrage. So much red filled the air, there seemed hardly two inches of clearance between. Battered, they all spun out of control.

The street pavement below enlarged. Jediah twisted himself around and flailed his wings, but couldn't straighten up. Realizing he had no time, he retracted his wings, covering himself with as many quills as possible. The outer feathers he hardened into diamonds. The inner feathers he softened to a plush.

A crunched "*Pow!*" hit his ears, and his armored shell absorbed the impact but cracked terribly. Jediah rolled to his hands and knees. His quills shivered from the painful tingling. He tried shaking them out. Broken feather pieces flicked off his wings and clinked onto the pavement. Shards from Laszio and Eran's wings scattered like shattered glass close by.

Laszio clutched his side. Gold seeped thick between his fingers as he collapsed on the street and curled in. Eran gripped Laszio's shoulder as he checked the gash.

Before Jediah could get up, the tip of an enemy's sword pricked his cheek, and his peripheral vision caught sight of plated boots.

"Fancy meeting you here," the demon said. The sharp point of his sword cut a scratch down Jediah's face, then pulled down his mask.

Angered panic set off within Jediah. His scarf was exposed. The captain's crest laid bare.

"Hello, Captain." The demon's blade popped a single thread.

Jediah snapped his wings. Leftover shards from the crash flew, and the demon reeled as the hot pieces burrowed into and smelted his face. Jumping up, Jediah reverse-gripped the demon's arm and broke it over his shoulder. His opponent's sword clanged to the ground.

Throwing him over, Jediah straddled the demon and yanked him up by the collar. "How'd you know about me? Answers! Now!"

The demon grinned despite his sweltered face.

Jediah heard beating wings from behind. He barrel-rolled off, seconds before red waves chopped his attacker to ribbons. Jediah hurried to Eran, who hoisted Laszio up. Grabbing Laszio's free arm, he pulled them both into a sprint with a demonic onslaught hot on their heels.

Jediah studied the demon ambush behind them. Their leader, the tallest and biggest one, leered with a thirst. Then Jediah realized... his greedy eyes lingered on him—and only him.

Restraining a sense of panic, Jediah reeled. *This whole thing was a setup, and we walked right into it!* He fired two retaliatory shots. "You two reach Nechum and Alameth and get out of here. I'll draw them away."

Laszio's head snapped up. "But—"

"No buts!" Jediah shouted. He flew westward, and as predicted, the wings of his pursuers swished not far behind and stayed close.

The last dim remnants of daylight were snuffed out. Night joined the storm. Spastic lightning alone now lit the countryside, and trees creaked in agony as their roots were torn from their precious soil.

Nechum clapped a hand over his mouth, unable to believe Jediah would abandon Laszio and Eran, wounded as they were. That is, unless something went horribly wrong. He watched Jediah soar in the opposite direction. A swarm of demons chasing him, yet neither Laszio nor Eran attempted to follow. "Alameth?" Nechum asked, "Should we be concerned?"

Alameth, who now hung from the car's back hatch, said nothing, but his gaze stayed glued with acute attentiveness toward the two wingmen.

With the car speeding past and further away from them, Nechum built the resolve to go back. Sliding, then clinging to a side window, he judged the distance between his spot and the blurred roadside, but then rough hands had him by the tunic. His feet left the car in a rush of wind. Alameth yelled his name. With the ground getting further and further away, Nechum fumbled for his smoke pellets. The demon shook him in response and threatened to drop him. A spurt of panic spurned Nechum's energy, and a large shield expanded and shoved his assailant off.

Nechum's shoulder scuffed the asphalt first, and he tumbled off-road into the gravel. Trapped in a dazed stupor, he covered his head. His face buried into the dirt as if that would hide him from the situation.

"Get up!" Alameth barked.

Nechum jolted, stunned both at the angel of death's booming command and the intense, dark fury churning in his emerald eyes.

Alameth stooped and offered Nechum a hand, but then a demon war-cry rang out. Alameth snapped around. Fog burst from his palm, grabbed the assailant, and slammed him into a street sign. He then pointed Nechum eastward toward a roadside hotel. "More are coming! Go now!"

Still not quite put together yet, Nechum obeyed on instinct. The weather's growling intensified a thousand decibels and drew his attention to the right. A cracking flash unveiled an ugly funnel. It touched down, ripped up a patch of cornfield, then retracted and bore back down again. Reading the flow of the clouds it came from, Nechum predicted its traction. This 'jumper' was heading left, straight for the very hotel he was sprinting to.

Nechum's empathic sense triggered. He picked up signs of human refugees under its foundations and gasped. *Come on, legs! You can run faster!*

Telephone posts swayed, pulling their cables apart until they showered spitting sparks. Leaves stripped from their branches, and Nechum dodged mangled balls of wrenched metal that whizzed past. Upon reaching the parking lot, he balked and ducked fence posts as they speared parked cars. A bus barreled over his head and cannonballed a truck, but this time he wouldn't flinch. Not this time.

He phased through the hotel's doors just as dust and dirt kicked up into a smog.

Jediah's wings shuddered during heftier strokes. Too many flight feathers were broken by his earlier fall to keep him stable. Hopes of outpacing his pursuers were dead. Thus, Jediah committed himself to pin turns, somersaults, and aerial tricks of the highest caliber to out-maneuver. Most fell behind, except one. Their leader, the large one, matched him one-to-one.

Jediah flicked what sharp feathers he could spare, but missed.

"Nowhere to hide, Jediah!" the demon taunted as he shortened the distance.

Jediah searched for defendable cover, but saw only exposed, flat farmland. That is, except for an oncoming patch of silver spires. As he got closer, it morphed into distinction. Tall metal poles were anchored within a square surrounded by a clattering link fence. Cables swung above graveled rocks from pagoda-like mounts, and several large lettered signs read, "High Voltage."

Jediah blanched, realizing he was leading a demon straight toward what Nechum called a power grid. Still, he unsheathed his sword. No time to change course now. He pitched his wings hard right and barrel rolled to a stand behind the first wood post. The demon followed too eagerly, and Jediah swung. His blade sliced the passing demon's arm.

The demon sprawled, shooting feather darts as he fell, but Jediah's blade blurred and parried the black barbs. Flipping back to his feet, the demon avoided Jediah's follow-up thrust and swiped with a sharp wing. Undaunted, Jediah angled his sword, deflecting the wild strike. The demon toppled off balance, and Jediah drove his blade deep in his side. His enemy thudded to the ground.

"Who are you?" Jediah demanded.

The wounded creature groped for the clattering fence and dragged himself up, but Jediah's patience long dried. He seized the scruff of the brute's neck, slammed his face into the voltage sign, and rammed his elbow square in the middle of his back. "This storm was an ambush scheme, huh? Just to get at me?" After no response, Jediah rammed him into the fence again.

The demon sneered. "Afraid, Captain?"

Jediah stuck the point of his sword under his chin. "I'm not taking any lip from you. Who informed you about me, and how did you know I'd be here?" He pressed the blade in. Red dripped down its edge. "Answer! I won't ask again!"

Wind blasted through the fence and dislodged a cable. It swung into the chain links, sparking and twitching. The demon's eyes glowed crimson. He wrenched himself from Jediah's grip, took a slash to the chin, and seized the active wire's exposed end.

Jediah ducked from the freakish snapping and cracking that popped from the demon's fist. Electrical currents vined down his arm. Power units blasted apart, as the currents were sucked into the demon's every opened wound.

Nechum flinched at the sudden blackout. The huddled people around him in the hotel cellar screamed.

Amidst the smoke, Jediah watched the demon rise tall. The wire he once held now hung quiet. His low laughter rose to megalomania as his electrified feathers jerked about. "I am Captain Zivel," he announced. He stretched a hand toward Jediah. "And *I* am your better."

Zivel's fingers tremored. Jediah sensed a sudden change under his feet; a sharp tingling that traveled up his legs. His hair stood on end, and he barely dodged Zivel's lightning bolt by a hair. Zivel thrust his hand again, casting a new net of blue from his fingertips.

Nechum listened to the light click of popping human eardrums. The basement's air pressure changed. The foundations moaned. Plaster above crumbled, and mothers hugged their wailing children, pressing their little heads close. Hail beat the squatty windows, and Nechum held a breath as jagged lines webbed the glass.

The windows burst inward. Debris flew in like ballistic missiles, and no one besides Nechum could hear the ceiling vibrate and sag in the deafening rumble. It dropped. Nechum raised his hands, investing every ounce of his focus to catch the falling roof. His arms, shoulders, and back burned. His legs were forced into a deeper bend. He grunted, dropping to one knee, until three stories of wood, glass and cement ground to a halt with a droned crunch against his back.

Jediah leaped through clustered trees. After landing on a thicker branch, his fingers sensed the sap inside super-heat to a boil. The expanding bark exploded into splinters at Zivel's lightning blast. Swept by the smoke and wood, Jediah crashed into a barrel roll. He shook the dizziness off. There rested thicker brush not but a few feet away. He sprinted for it, but skidded to a halt. Zivel had beaten him to it.

The power drunk lunatic scoffed. "You're mine!" Static sparked from his flicking fingers. Crinkled ultra-violet streaks sprang forth.

Jediah's reflexes overruled him, and he raised his sword. The blade buzzed. His feathers accidentally touched the hilt, and the violent jolts raced through his right wing, into his left wing, then zapped right back out, biting into their initiator's feet.

Zivel screeched and collapsed in a writhing heap.

Jediah's whole being vibrated from excess energy. He lost his grip. His head throbbed and the stings in his arms continued to prick even after the initial shock.

Re-piecing what just happened, Jediah stared at his weapon. Steam wafted off the hissing metal.

Zivel moaned as he retreated into the brush.

Expecting a counter-attack, Jediah grabbed his sword, soared up the closest pine, and perched on its top. Rigorous gales bent the tree so far it seemed only the bark kept it glued together.

Jediah pointed his blade toward the skies. Fully encasing his arm in feathers, he ensured a single quill touched the crossguard. The other wing he straightened outwards, and he scanned it back and forth over the tree line. "Come on. Come on," he mumbled. "Show yourself. I dare you."

Jediah panned his head around. For a moment, only the storm spoke. He squeezed his eyes closed. *Lord, Master of skies, disperse Your holy wrath on those who dare defy You.*

Jediah's hair stood up.

Zivel burst from the clapping leaves a few feet away.

Positive charges hummed up Jediah's legs, and a negative charge stepped down, igniting on contact. Lightning traveled the blade once more. Its might leaped from Jediah's quills and consumed the demon in its roar.

The flash subsided.

Thunder rolled for miles.

Jediah gasped. His wings jittered from a frightening amount of invigoration. He wobbled to steady himself and rubbed his brow against another burgeoning headache. Shaking his head, he forced his vision to clear.

Captain Zivel, crippled, one-armed, and missing half his face, limped into a barn a short distance off.

Rolling the tingling out of his shoulders, Jediah glided after him. Even if Zivel's mouth was missing, he'd get that villain to talk, even if it took all night.

Jediah coasted low to a stop. The aged barn creaked from neglect. Chipped wood sported jagged splinters. Its scarlet paint had long dulled to a sick brown, and its rickety foundations swayed so much a house of cards would be considered more stable.

Jediah approached the huge open door and peeked through the doorway. Darkness shadowed the withered straw and filthy planking. He saw no one.

Refolding his wings into armor, Jediah raised his sword and stepped inside. The sweltering orange glow from his blade dimmed.

"Still playing hero I see."

Jediah flushed cold. *That voice.*

The heavy door rattled over the exit.

Those old pangs of guilt struck Jediah's core. His weakened arms let his sword point stick the ground. He wished not to turn around. It pained him to.

"Isn't it interesting how the centuries can change an angel?" the voice chided. "Last I saw you, you resembled a lion. My empathic sense, however, reads the presence of a frightened sheep."

Jediah shuddered and pursed his chapped lips. "Yes, much has changed, Elazar." With what will he had left, he turned around.

A figure, silhouetted by the scant flashes between the wall boards, cocked his head. "Much indeed." He stepped into the sparse light emanating off Jediah's feathers.

A scarred, dead eye came first into view, and the sight of it cut Jediah's heart open, bare and vulnerable.

"Hello, *old friend*."

Chapter 14

BEFORE JEDIAH STOOD a living nightmare. Its gaze bore into him, accusing and bitter, but the most haunting thing about this monster was its familiarity. Jediah knew those eyes, that face, that hair but not the grey phantom who wore them.

Elazar scowled. His irises, originally of water-colored amethyst, were spoiled. The left eye was an empty pit. A ravenous crimson scar that stretched from his brow to his chin vandalized the other. "So," Elazar said, as he crossed his arms. "Here we are."

"Elazar." Jediah's lips faltered. "You don't know how I—"

"Wish you never saw me? *Brother*?" Elazar cocked his unbroken eyebrow.

"Elazar, listen—"

Elazar turned his back on Jediah and folded his hands. "I'm listening."

Jediah's neck heated. He swallowed a lump. Thousands of years rehearsing the words he'd say, yet not a one could satisfy. Anxiety twisted his insides.

"If this is an apology, you're very poor at it," Elazar remarked. "Not that I expected any sort of apology from you. What would an apology fix, anyway?" He eyed Jediah over his left shoulder. "Nothing. Absolutely. *Nothing.*"

Anger replaced Jediah's initial fear. "I *am* sorry, Elazar."

Elazar dipped his head. His laughter came out pained and rueful. "Oh, Jediah. Are you familiar with the phrase 'too little too late'?"

Nechum gasped under the hotel wreckage. A corner of ceiling crumbled and nearly hit a young lady. His legs quivered as his energy levels fell fast. "Alameth?" he called. He knew it seemed silly to think the angel of death would hear him from outside, but he had to try. "Alameth! I could use some help, please!"

A demon scrambled through the wrecked ceiling and landed hard on his chest.

Nechum sucked in a breath. *Not that kind of help!* He closed his eyes and steeled himself for fanged jaws or a hacking blade.

One second. Two seconds. Three seconds.

Nechum peeked one eye.

The demon had dragged himself into the farthest corner and curled into a fetal position, whimpering.

Bewildered, Nechum almost considered asking his mortal enemy what lurked outside. What could reduce a hardened warrior like him to tears? What could—

Grey fog phased through the wall and plucked the demon off the floor. The demon screamed. The mist slammed him into the wall, smashing his face in repeatedly. Nechum chilled as the hits grew rapid. More visceral. Then, pulling the demon against the wall, it squeezed his head, eliciting shrill shrieks.

Nechum looked away, but the wetted cracking sounds put an all too vivid picture in his head. He hesitated to look again. The second he dared to, he immediately regretted it.

The retched being laid unconscious. His energy painted the wall and stained the crags.

Nechum paled.

Alameth,... What were you thinking?

Laboring not to crumble under the weight of his emotions, Jediah locked his jaw.

Elazar's good eye calculated him for a moment before becoming disinterested. "Drop the tough act, will you? You can't hide what you're actually feeling from me. Besides, I know."

"You know what?"

"I know what plagues you." Elazar leered closer. "Even as you're standing there right now."

Jediah averted his gaze, but knew Elazar's empathic sense was unstoppable.

"The thing that ails you? That thing that breaks you down and never leaves you alone?" Elazar inched closer and whispered, "Guilt."

Jediah's feathers bristled. His breaths came in huffs, and his neck tensed.

"You want someone to heal you, but you know no one will. You seek forgiveness but there's none." Elazar stepped back and raised his hands. "No cure. No resolution."

Jediah raised his sword. "You're wrong."

"Am I now?"

"Our Lord is good and kind. Surely there is hope for me."

"Do you hear yourself?" Elazar continued to circle him. "Your God doesn't care about you. He'd rather redeem undeserving worms than you. You as well as the rest of your fellow loyalists are just the stick He uses to pen up His favorite lambs—destined for menial use, then forgotten in a corner. The ones who don't suit His whims He just burns."

Jediah's anger burst from his mouth. "Who are you to judge God?"

"His better," came Elazar's calm reply. "He lets witless murderers, molesters, and thieves go free. Silences anyone who questions Him and recruits hypocrites and failures like yourself under threat of banishment. Lucifer may be the father of lies, but your King is the god of them."

"And now your madness reveals itself," Jediah interjected. "Would you then play god in His stead after all He did for you? You who once knew His mercy and compassion?"

Elazar stopped in his tracks. "Compassion?" His laugh was quiet and mocking. "Compassion." He loomed closer. "Look me in the eye, Jediah." Elazar's scarred eye stared with the eery blankness of a dead corpse. "I already got a good taste of *His* compassion thanks to you."

Jediah's throat tightened.

Elazar huffed a smile, then cocked his head. "Guess I was wrong. The years haven't changed you. You're every bit the self-righteous zealot I remember."

The back of Nechum's head ached from bracing the thousand tons threatening to crush the survivors, yet his thoughts remained with Alameth. He needed to get out of there, but how? His neck and shoulders flushed cold as his energy waned, and a wooziness narrowed his vision.

"Lord," he grunted. "Grant Your servant courage. Lend me the strength to see this through."

Dust sprayed to the sounds of loud chipping. Nechum clamped his eyes shut. His foot slipped out an inch, and he strained to pull it back... yet found it easy to do. His burden lightened. Nechum's eyes fluttered open, and he dropped his numb hands.

Two Christians—vessels of the Holy Ghost—were praying. Their folded hands, speckled by dirt and tears, pressed into their lips as they uttered petitions of thankfulness in faint whispers.

Their Marks of the Trinity beamed. Streams of color covered the ceiling as the Holy Spirit Himself lifted the mass on His adopted children's behalf. One of these spectral bands brushed Nechum's clothes, staining them white, and thousands of faceted prisms shimmered above him like an aurora borealis over arctic snow.

Elazar observed the barn's rumbling walls. "Well. Our little get together has been fun, but the storm won't wait, and I'm on a tight schedule." He rolled back his sleeves. "My superior wants something from you."

Jediah pulled his armored wings tighter in. "So Lucifer's your master now?"

"Don't insult me," Elazar snapped. "I care nothing for that blowhard. He's obsessed with his prestige and nothing else."

"And what are you obsessed with?" Jediah asked.

Elazar ignored his question. He looked him up and down, but then his eye locked onto something. A mocking smile lifted the corner of his mouth as he reached behind Jediah's ear and pulled Chloe's braid out into the open. "Is that new?"

Jediah swatted Elazar's hand away.

The wooden planks around them thundered on their rusted nails. A steel panel peeled off the roof.

Elazar grinned with a chuckling sneer. "Whoever did that, she must be adorable."

Jediah rammed his shoulder into Elazar's chest and bolted for the battering door, but a force pulled his feet out from under him.

"Did I say you could leave?"

Jediah attempted to stand, but couldn't. A heavy weight had shackled his ankles then dragged him back over the dung littered straw. "Lucifer promised you to me," Elazar said. "It's only fair that I honor our agreement."

The rough force flipped Jediah over like a pancake. Elazar's eye pulsed a dark red that was but a few shades short of black. He extended an arm. A red aura, like crimson fireflies, gloved his hand, and shields—normally used by ministry angels for defense—shot out, pulled Jediah's legs, and squeezed. Their edges like thick, sharp glass cut into Jediah's boot leather.

Desperate, Jediah beat at them with his sword, but the blade skidded off. Elazar kicked the sword out of his hand. The force-fields expanded, consuming Jediah's calves, thighs, and everything else from the neck down. He couldn't move.

As the shields forced him upright, Jediah hyper-ventilated. All of his years' combat experience was driven right out of his head.

Elazar gripped his jaw. He pulled out an obsidian knife from his outer coat. "One key for one, captain," he droned. "A fair deal. And you know how meticulous I am about keeping my deals." Slipping the knife's tip under the edge of one of Jediah's quills, Elazar pried one feather up and let it slap back. "Give up the key willfully. Or this'll be as painful as *I'd* like it to be."

Jediah resisted a groan as the shields started wrenching his joints in all the wrong directions. A wicked grin punctuated the malice in Elazar's voice. Shields slipped under Jediah's armored wings and slowly thickened, prying them like a peel off an apple. Jediah resisted, but could feel his feathers begin to crack.

The whole barn rattled to the shrieking wind. Rusted farm machinery clattered.

Elazar threw Jediah down and stomped on his neck. "Cough it up already!"

Two explosions of light popped beside them, and Jediah took the opportunity to barrel roll away. He coughed and gagged.

Laszio and Eran dropped in like meteors and flanked Elazar on both sides. The green and blue tints of their eyes consumed their usual gray coloring with rich color.

Jediah scrambled to get up. His wingmen knew not whom they challenged, and he cursed his tired self for not recovering faster. He shouted at them against the tempest to retreat, but his commands went unheeded.

Elazar, eyes hot with ravenous fury, dodged their shots. He targeted Laszio's wounded side, implanted a force-field, and stretched the gash wider. Laszio crumbled to the ground, screaming. Eran charged, but Elazar raised a wall. Eran veered to avoid the collision, but Elazar anticipated such reflexes. With the flick of his fingers, two shields ensnared Eran's wrists and snapped them. The sticks clattered out of Eran's limp hands.

"Elazar!" Jediah retrieved his sword and swung sideways. Elazar blocked with a shielded forearm. Jediah's blade screeched off, but the force Jediah put behind it disrupted Elazar's balance. Jediah then kicked him in the hip, sending Elazar sideways and banging his head into rusted farm equipment.

A funnel ripped open the hay loft—their best escape. "Get up! Now!" Jediah shouted. He yanked Eran to his feet.

Laszio wobbled and retrieved Eran's weapon, but glared at Elazar.

"Leave him!" Jediah ordered. "Let's go!"

A powerful updraft pulled them into its current as wood cracked to toothpicks and metal wrenched in high-pitched squeals.

Nechum steadied himself as he tripped into the outside. Red, blue, white, and yellow flashes bounced off the hotel's shambled remains. Police boomed instructions as emergency crews dug the survivors out of the rubble. They were all covered in varying degrees of wood, dirt, bruises, and blood. A few people clambered about, isolated in their own incoherent babbling or trapped in a silent cage, but Nechum breathed a thankful sigh of relief. Everyone made it out safely.

Alameth, however, was nowhere to be seen.

Nechum weaved around the jumbled mess into an upturned country. The plains were tattered. Unrecognizable junk littered the roads. What few trees still stood were naked, and grass patches were spoiled to muddy sludge pits. The thick, humid air soaked up their stench and reeked of gas and sewage.

Though sickened, Nechum hurried down the road. He had only gone the first few feet to find the first pool of glowing red that was once a demon fifteen minutes ago. A few feet more and there was another and another. The carnage was everywhere. The sight of it all filled Nechum with nausea, as the sounds of the earlier demon's head splitting open echoed in his ears.

Sitting nearby, in a soft patch of grass, was the bowed figure of Alameth. His arms wrapped tight around himself like a child after a night terror, and he had buried himself deep in feverish prayer.

A deep sorrowful empathy washed away Nechum's initial horror; for Alameth's overtaxed heart cried out to him. He set a tender hand on his shoulder and rubbed soothing circles. "Alameth? Alameth? Are you okay?"

Alameth quivered. His head turned. Just under the bottom edge of his hood, Nechum could make out a dark blue tint replacing the dark portions of his green eyes and a moist glimmer that welled in their corners. Alameth's trembling voice rumbled low as he spoke. "They had *no* respect for life."

With tears of his own, Nechum knelt to draw Alameth close. "I know, brother... I know."

Chapter 15

ERAN, LASZIO, AND JEDIAH coasted low to the ground when a thud and a groan prompted Eran to stop. Laszio's wings had given out. "Captain, wait," Eran called.

Down on his hands and knees, Laszio clutched his abdomen and coughed up gold between scratchy rasps. Eran pushed past his wrist sprains to lift Laszio up by the shoulders. Laszio leaned into him, limp and delirious. "Sir," Eran said. "He can't go any farther. Not like this."

Jediah hurried back. Though his face was once again covered by the cloak, his exposed eyes showed concern and agitation.

Laszio jerked himself awake. "Nonsense, I can—" He lifted on one knee but promptly fell. He curled in, and his hand attempted to pinch the gash closed.

Jediah shook his head. "We have to keep moving or he'll catch up to us."

Eran thought back to their encounter with the scarred demon. Despite hailing from the ministry kind, he was fast, efficient, cruel. "Captain," Eran realized, "You called him Elazar... by an angel's name."

Jediah's eyebrows dipped.

Eran hesitated to ask. "Did you know him?"

"Why do you ask me this now?"

Eran flinched, startled by the sudden sharpness in Jediah's voice.

Jediah's gaze darted about before falling back on him. "This is not the time," he said in a much quieter tone.

Eran nodded, accepting the answer, but in an unsettled, intimidated silence. He never knew this side of his leader existed. It stung like a slap to the cheek.

Jediah's eyes softened. His hand rubbed his scabbard buckle as if to ease some underlying stress. "I'm sorry, Eran. I'm sorry." Kneeling down, he gripped him by the shoulder. "Take our brother straight to the third realm while I get the others. We'll meet you by the Crystal Sea."

Noting the regret in his apology, Eran took his captain's hand and gave him a smile. "Yes, brother."

Jediah shook both his shoulders. "Stay safe." He took off without another word, but what had transpired between them lingered behind.

Eran looked to Laszio and found him sharing the same concerned look.

Rain drizzled softly around Nechum and Alameth. The two rested in the silence after they had talked a while. To Nechum's comfort, the angel of death had calmed, seeming much more at ease around him than anyone else. The coloration of his eyes returned to normal, and Nechum now understood the full message they were speaking.

"Prepare for landing!"

Nechum twisted around to see Akela skid, then tumble onto the road. Jedd, who rode his back, had jumped into a gentle breeze, and landed with all the grace Akela lacked. The two friends laughed as one helped the other off the wet ground.

Nechum laughed with them. "Are you both okay?"

Akela and Jedd grinned and stood shoulder to shoulder. "We're fine." Akela said as he waved an arm.

"Fit as a fiddle," Jedd added with a thumbs up.

Jediah curved in from the sky. "There you all are," he breathed.

Nechum's empathic sense lurched, and he clutched his breast against the potent anguish that seized it. Searching Jediah's eyes, he discovered they were haggard. The golds were snuffed out, and the lacquered browns were spotted black.

Jediah's words were rushed. "Our mission's been compromised. We have to leave now."

Akela balked. "Compromised? How? What does that mean?"

Jediah gripped Alameth's shoulders and lifted him to his feet. "It *means*, our enemies know we're here." He then got into Akela's face. "Which means, we have to go." Jediah turned to Jedd. "Sorry, I wish we could have met under better circumstances. Truly. But before we leave, we need you to analyze something for us." He snapped his fingers and opened his palm to Akela, who promptly gave him the vial. Jediah handed the bottled ash to Jedd. "Akela says you can identify it. We need to know where it came from."

Jedd squinted as he rolled the vial between his fingers.

Nechum watched Jediah anxiously scan the fields and wanted to shrink into himself. He seemed to expect some vicious animal.

Jedd's mood brightened. "Ah, ha. I got it."

"Knew you would," Akela said, as he nudged Jedd's arm.

"Good," Jediah said, "So where'd it come from? Which country?"

"It's from no country," Jedd replied.

"Then where on earth?"

Grinning, Jedd shook his head. "It's not from earth." He held the bottle in front of his nose and peered closer at the specks. "This ash has the sedimental makeup of a moon from the outer rims of this solar system. The humans called it Io, and it's one of ninety-seven moons that orbit the planet Jupiter. Volcanically active."

"Volcanically active?" Jediah's posture stiffened. "Wait. Do you mean to tell me it's covered in volcanos?"

Jedd chuckled. "The *entire* moon."

"But do you know which exact volcano this is from?" Jediah pressed.

Jedd frowned, and his eyebrows slanted upward. "Eruptions, earthquakes, lava flows, avalanches; Io's landscape is in a constant state of flux. It literally never sleeps. I'm sorry to tell you this, Captain, but navigating a place like that is near impossible. Few landmarks last more than a day."

Nechum felt woozy just thinking about such a writhing hell-bed.

Jediah rubbed his chin. "So. Malkior has become a needle hiding in the biggest haystack."

"Well," Akela said. "At least we know which haystack he's hiding in."

Powdered sand under Eran's boot padded his weary feet. Eran breathed in the cleansing, scented air. The Image Bearers called it heaven. Angels called it home.

Time did not exist in the third realm, yet the sky had its phases. Human minds may not comprehend a day jeweled in midnight's elegance nor a night as radiant as an afternoon, but it was so. For it was God's glorious light, not a sun nor a moon, that lit the land in unending splendor. Tonight the sky hinged in a twilight unlike earth's. Indigo, melded with velveteen violet, clothed the sky in night's royal garb, yet no true darkness lingered. Gradient patches of dawn's rosy yellows and baby blues swirled in pastel clouds.

Laszio clung heavily to Eran's shoulders, but Eran didn't mind it much. They both were below-average in height for soldiers anyway. His wings cradled him easily, but he'd carry him to Hell and back on a busted knee without wings if it came down to it. Eran didn't want to be anywhere without him. Honestly, he didn't even know where he'd be without Laszio's gumption. He never seemed able to get beyond the thinking stage whenever he strategized on his own. It always took someone as small as himself, yet twice as rambunctious to spurn the confidence he so lacked for action.

Eran heard Laszio sigh—the first contented sigh he heard from him in weeks. These last few days were rough on them both, after all. Carrying him to the nearest stone, he used his wings to lower Laszio onto a comfortable spot.

He checked Laszio's gash. Around the wound's edges, the faintest golden flickers worked in slow repair. They plinked with a light tinkling sound like chips of broken glass fixing themselves in reverse. The gash indeed had shrunk a bit, unassisted, but now that Laszio was home, the process would surely hasten.

Eran sat down beside Laszio to take in the view while he rested. The Crystal Sea lapped the pearled shores in lulling tones. With starlight in every drop, its tiny waves peaked with diamond crests that sprayed glittering colors whenever they clashed against the beach, yet the main body of water itself laid still, smooth as a silken mirror.

Eran attempted to unwrap his wrist straps. He tried picking at the first fastener knot, but to even loosen one loop fired up his sprains. He bit down on his lip, determined to continue tugging the tie inches at a time.

Laszio's hands cupped his. With a light touch, he pinched the leather ties and pulled the ends apart. Eran hissed through his teeth but relaxed the second the stiff wrist brace no longer pressured the cramps. Laszio then uncoiled the second wrap.

"Thanks," Eran replied. He stood up and walked to the water.

"Don't mention it," Laszio said.

Eran's knees sank into sand as white as a fresh blanket of snow. A few grains slipped into his boots and massaged his shins. He dipped his wrists into the cool waters as they rose and fell. Their healing purity seeped into his soaking hands.

Eran gazed left, up the highest hill to the golden city. Long had the Trinitarian God prepared it. New Jerusalem, the soon to be capital of a new heaven and earth, was the first fruits of the Saved's inheritance. This perfect jewel, fastened atop a gardened mountain, gleamed with a gold so purified it was transparent as glass. It outsized a continent, with its dazzling towers pointed high like hands of praise. The River of Life, which fed the Crystal Sea, flowed along the paths into its twelve gates, and the highest Citadel, God's Temple, crowned it with His richest glory. Even from that distance, Eran could hear the multitudes in song that rejoiced within. The city yet waited for the full number of its citizens to come.

Eran drew his wrists from the lapping waves. They were dry and quite restored, save for a stubborn kink that had yet to sort out. Memory of the injury linked back to the scarred demon and Jediah's troubling behavior. Eran frowned. Anger, worry, confusion all tugged him around till he was lost, not knowing what to think or how to feel about it.

Determined to clear his mind, Eran cupped the jeweled waters and took a drink. He then splashed his face. The water shimmered particles that moisturized his cheeks. Then he combed his wetted fingers through his black hair.

"Got some leftover for me?" Laszio asked in good humor.

Eran chuckled. "One second." Opening his wings, he flew inland to the closest tree. Its silver bark reflected its fluttering, orange leaves that were forever caught in the painted fires of Fall. Eran's eyes traced an emerald ivy vine that rose to the highest branches. There, he spotted the tree's largest lilies. Their petals of mother-of-pearl cast pale hints of blue, pink, and green. Selecting one, Eran flew back to the shore and dipped it into the sea.

He walked it back to Laszio, careful not to spill, then trickled drops out of the cupped petals into Laszio's open wound. Laszio winced, but the final space in the shrinking gash zipped closed.

Eran offered him the flower cup. "Here." As Laszio took the first gentle sips, Eran returned to the sea to soak his wrists again. After considerable silence, Eran still obsessed over the events from less than an hour before.

"I'm worried about Jediah, too," Laszio finally said.

Eran froze but then acted unaware of his friend as he tended to his hands.

"We need to do something," Laszio persisted.

Eran sighed in frustration. "Laszio, don't."

"What?"

"You know 'what.'" Eran shot him a warning look over his shoulder. "Your invasive meddling."

"It's not meddling It's an intervention."

"An intervention Jediah doesn't want." Eran twisted around to better face Laszio.

"Interventions aren't *wanted*. They're *needed*," Laszio argued. "You saw that look on his face, Eran. He's hurt and scared. More than he's ever been in his life. I know you feel it as I do." Laszio rubbed a hand over his chest where a human heart would be.

Eran shook his head. "Whatever Elazar is or was to Jediah is none of our business."

"That demon has blown our cover, Eran. As far as I see it, he's *made* himself very much our business."

Eran stood up but failed to find a counter argument.

Laszio tipped his head and cocked his eyebrow. The one braided lock of hair, the one meant to match Eran's as a symbol of their bond, swung freely.

Indignant, Eran crossed his arms. "We don't really know what's going on, Laszio. Elazar might be an exceptionally strong opponent, and nothing more. And even *if* Jediah is locked in an old grudge match with him, what could we possibly do about it?"

Laszio leaned forward with that usual fire in his eyes that so often motivated Eran to do anything. "Keep Elazar as far from our captain as possible. Put an end to his menace."

"You know perfectly well we can't kill him, Laszio. What we are cannot be vanquished but by God alone. He'll just keep coming back."

"Then we don't let up!" Laszio retorted. "We just keep knocking Elazar down as many times as it takes. We can't let this go, Eran. Lucifer hired that demon on purpose."

"What makes you think that?"

Laszio huffed. "Are you seriously telling me that Jediah and Elazar's confrontation was a coincidence?"

Eran couldn't respond.

Irritated, Laszio rolled his head. "Oh, come on, Eran! Read the signs! It was a set up! All of it! You don't expect me to believe someone as smart as you didn't figure *that* out."

Eran's eyes closed. He suspected it, but didn't want to admit it—especially when he was the one who convinced Jediah into helping Jedd fight that storm. "Yes," he sighed. "Yes, we were baited."

Laszio gave a solemn nod. "Exactly, and this Elazar? Lucifer called him in for one reason and one alone: to destroy our captain, and I hate to admit this, Eran, but… I think he possibly could." Wings drooped, Laszio turned his gaze toward the alabaster pebbles by his feet, and for a moment, only the tender surf had a voice. "Jediah has done so much for us, Eran… so much. So stopping Elazar isn't something I feel we should try. It's something we must *do*… or at least… that's what *I* must do."

Struck by the sincerity in his best friend's words, Eran stared at his wrists and re-lived the battle. Elazar, this new enemy, was practiced, swift, and powerful. He had Jediah at his mercy and decommissioned both of them in seconds. What else was such an enemy capable of?

"Besides." Laszio's tone dipped dark and deep. "I don't think we'll have much choice in the matter."

Eran's energy pounded in his chest.

"Elazar is hunting us," Laszio pointed out. "And he's going to haunt our every step until he gets Jediah, whether we like it or not."

Eran scowled and balled his hands into fists. "Then by God's grace, he won't get far."

Elazar stood on a fallen maple covered in wood chips. He chuckled at Captain Zivel, who limped up from behind. "You look gorgeous."

Despite missing a quarter of his face, Zivel had recovered enough of his mouth to manage a grotesque snarl. "Need I remind you that you failed too?" he slurred.

Elazar fingered the hilt of his dagger. "And yet neither you nor your troops could stomp two of Jediah's boot lickers as I instructed." He turned to him. Rage narrowed his working eye. "What part of 'lead Jediah to me' meant blast him out of the sky?"

Zivel lengthened his back and puffed his splintered chest to emphasize his superior height. "You know full well I was more than capable of handling him myself."

"All evidence to the contrary." Elazar motioned a hand over the carnage Jediah's lightning inflicted on Zivel. He then laughed and shook his head. "Zivel, your blinding ego is twice as comical as I remembered. You always were the most unbearably pompous of my associates when we ruled the southern regions. Now that inflated, entitlement of yours turned you from a big ham to a meat-headed dullard."

"Why you!" Zivel threw a punch.

Elazar leaned. Still missing most of his right side, Zivel hit the ground face first, and Elazar shook his head at such a disgraceful, sloppy effort. "And to think I actually helped you become a god those bloodthirsty Aztecs could worship."

Zivel roared, jumped up, and charged again. This time, Elazar dodged and slashed with his knife twice. His skill sheared off Zivel's nose yet spared the eye.

Crumbling, Zivel screamed foul curses and covered his face. He then spun around, and with his crimson energy dripping down his mouth and chin like magma, he sputtered drops as he spat. "Our Master, Lucifer, shall hear of your insolence!"

Rolling his eye, Elazar made a miffed chortle. He shifted his focal energy from his chest to his hands, and he launched shields to strap Zivel down. They arched his back over a fallen tree trunk like a human sacrifice tied to a pagan altar.

Leaning into his face, Elazar's empathic sense trembled with excitement at the raw panic it drank in. He forced Zivel to stare into his ruined eye. "Now get this straight," he growled. "Lucifer is *not* my master. *No one* is. And you? You're just a loudmouth bug."

Elazar plunged his knife in deep. Zivel's opened mouth stayed silent, unable to elicit any scream to justify. Going off ancient memory, Elazar pictured the demon as a mortal, one the likes of which those puny, sinful humans once sacrificed to him ages before. He carved a sizable cavity where the human heart would be. Warm liquid stained the knife's hilt and seeped between his fingers as he submerged the dagger further. He yanked it out. Red speckled his face, and a thick drop hit the corner of his lip.

Elazar licked it. The hot, crisp flavor of energy hummed down his throat. He imagined Jediah's taste upon his tongue next.

Jediah sought immediate solitude. The only trouble in heaven for an angel were the troubles they brought with them, and he didn't want his plaguing the others—not after such a harrowing experience. He needed time alone. In prayer. Just him and his King. He must sort this out... for everyone's sake.

Jediah hid himself beneath the orange dome of a towering tree. Rich light filtered through the leaves like stained glass in his sanctuary. Preparing himself to speak to the Lord from a genuine place, Jediah finally let the grief in. He unbuckled his sword. It fell several feet, clattering down the limbs. His shoulders drooped under the weight of his own feathers—each quill a stone. He had his unfurled wings wrap himself in a blanket of soft down and lay back to nestle his head against the trunk.

"My Lord and my God," he began. Jediah swallowed. His chin quivered, and he covered his eyes as they began to sting.

He didn't know what to say.

Chapter 16

THEIR SEARCH ON IO, Jupiter's volcanic moon, took hours. Eran climbed with Laszio along the eastern canyon wall. Their red uniforms blended perfectly with the radiated rock. They could ask for no better camouflage, yet Io's 'living' terrain still kept Eran on edge. Constant quakes hummed under his fingers. His ears twitched at every rumbling decibel. For any noise could either be the moon itself or Malkior.

Eran wished they weren't searching on foot, but as usual, their captain made the right call. Malkior could snipe from anywhere, and flying out in the open couldn't put them in a more vulnerable situation. Eran noticed another cave above them and frowned. Tunnels speckled both sides of the canyon. To him, they were an endless system of enemy foxholes and escape routes.

After they regrouped in the heavenly plain, Eran could already see that, while less on edge, Jediah was twice as sullen. He had hoped their excursion through Io might put Jediah at ease; get his mind off the previous night, but every time he looked into Jediah's dulled eyes, Eran could see Elazar's menace lingering, threatening him. The Jediah Eran knew hadn't returned yet. His honorable qualities may have never left, but the vigor behind them had been stomped out.

Eran shook his head. Thoughts of defeating Elazar and making things right possessed him, but he recognized such notions were just that: notions. They couldn't outweigh facts. Ministry barriers were unbreakable. The empathic sense was acute, and Elazar had honed both powers to their zenith. Thus, no matter how hard he and Laszio might train, Elazar could counter their every move without trying. Attempting any lengthy skirmish with him was out of the question. They needed one hit—one foolproof hit.

Suddenly, their upcoming battle with Malkior wasn't just their mission to Eran. It was his test. If he and Laszio could decommission Malkior in a single decisive blow, there'd be a chance; one slim, small chance they could stand against Elazar. If not...

Tiny streams of dirt dusted off the quaking wall. Over his shoulder, Eran watched a mass of sediment a mile to their right break.

Bang!

Jediah clung to the vertical crag he squeezed into. The eruption blasted the distant cliff-side and unleashed sulphuric dioxide that recolored the landscape in white powder. Dislodged boulders soared, slowed, then floated in the moon's weak gravity. Flaming bombs rocketed miles into space, and an entire mountain peak caved in as a magma pocket emptied beneath it. Lava bled thickly from the remains.

Jediah prayed his crag wouldn't be next as he climbed higher. It amazed him how God kept such a violent place in one piece. The rugged slopes below cascaded into a geyser valley that cupped rivers of splashing light. Steam rose from rock spouts like smoke stacks. Golden rain fluttered from earthen cavities on high, and the drops cooled from creamy orange to ruby red, then back to yellow before solidifying into the sleek, black pebbles that carpeted the lava bed below.

Anxious for the others, Jediah searched for his team. Laszio and Eran should be patrolling the opposite side. Alameth was to survey from within the rising smoke. Nechum and Akela were combing the valley, but Jediah couldn't see any of them from his vantage point. It worried him at first, but thought better of it. If he couldn't spot them, there was little chance Malkior could either. They stood a better chance at finding him with little trouble.

Jediah began moving on, but then his fingers seized up. Guilt struck again. Jediah clamped his eyes shut, pressed his brow into the stone, and took deep breaths. Elazar's scathing words may have dulled since the day before, but they had stricken him with a recurring illness of heart. Emotional pangs squeezed his insides. It numbed his hands.

God, why can't I be redeemed? Please, tell me. Is it that my kind isn't worth it?

Jediah scolded himself. He mustn't ever think that way again. God's ways weren't his. He had a good reason to save whom He saved. He had to.

Then Jediah remembered the braid—that little braid hidden in his hair. He once more regained composure. Hope may or may not exist for himself, but it existed for Chloe, and he had yet to finish his letter to her. He must before she dies, and it's all too late. In his long, measured pause, thoughts of saving her eternity restored power to Jediah's limbs. He'd finish this business with Malkior, then send his letter to her, without fail.

Jediah craned his neck. His wall arched above his head and jutted over the ravine. With careful movements, he clambered upside-down. The sword scabbard strapped to his back dangled from its leathers as he scurried up the overhang's edge and slipped inside a cave. He locked his jaw, expecting anything.

A peaceful second passed. Letting his shoulders relax, Jediah inched toward the cave's mouth.

A click caught his ear.

He froze.

A red dart whizzed in.

Bang!

Jediah leaped out seconds before the angry sparks could do more than sting his neck. His wings stretched out as he glided on a downward right angle. A second explosion struck just behind him. A third blasted the rocks in front, and floating broken boulders spread in all directions, fencing Jediah in.

Jediah armored his wings to shrink his targetable size and clung behind a rock in that hovering complex. He heard the whistle of another arrow and leaped as his prior perch was obliterated. On and on it continued. With each successive shot, more rocks broke into a dense swarm of sharp chips.

Nechum pulled Akela by the shirt behind a mound at the first explosion. Daring a peek, he watched Jediah dodging relentless fire and brimstone. Endless rounds of Malkior's plasma arrows shot from a tunnel halfway up the eastern cliff face. Squinting, Nechum spotted two figures. Laszio and Eran were zeroing in on Malkior's position. He cringed, expecting either of them to get blown to bits.

Akela pounced on Nechum. "Hit the deck!"

Pressure from the shockwave rang in Nechum's ears as flashing heat detonated above their heads.

A second after, Akela hopped about in hysterics. "Fire! Fire! I'm on fire!"

Nechum bolted up. "Lay flat!" He tore off his shawl, almost breaking the pin, and wrapped Akela's back. Smoke leaked as he batted out the flames.

Trembling, Akela peeked at the damage over his shoulder. "Is it bad?" His charred wings withered to charcoal powder.

Jediah's jaw tightened as he sheltered behind the last remaining boulder. Floating pumice, rough as sandpaper, corralled him in. He knew Malkior would have another arrow nocked and ready for him already. Options were running thin.

Eran and Laszio planted themselves just below Malkior's perch.

Eran lit his sticks. The light bled into the chord that connected them, ready to generate an energy sphere. "You ready for this? It'll be all or nothing."

Laszio, who already lit his sticks, nodded. "One punch. One shot. We can do this."

"*Okay, Lord,*" Eran prayed. "*Let this work.*"

Rising on a rush of air, they clapped their wings. Their light waves struck Malkior's feet. Malkior stumbled back, giving Eran and Laszio time to land and flank him on both sides.

Prepping his wings for an instant getaway, Jediah dared to peek around his boulder—his last means of protection from Malkior, but gasped in surprise to see Laszio and Eran already cornering Malkior in his hole.

They got him!

His wings wasted no time taking off.

Eran circled behind Malkior while Laszio strung a sphere. Laszio glared at the demon. "Your move, sunshine."

Malkior attempted another arrow, but Laszio twanged his string tight, shooting his sphere and knocking the bow out of Malkior's hands. Eran rushed in, coating his arm in diamond feathers.

Just one hit!

Eran threw a punch at Malkior's head.

Malkior ducked, tripped Eran into tumbling close to the cliff, then scrambled for his bow.

"No you don't!" Laszio intervened, grappling Malkior in a headlock.

Screaming, Malkior's eyes shone red, and the embers adorning his green tunic flared, scalding Laszio's arms. The angel had no choice but to let go.

Eran, who tried to get back on his feet, dropped back to the floor, as Malkior shot a fire plume inches above his head. By the time the flame died out, Malkior had a fully armed bow aimed right in his face. "To Hell with you!"

"Eran!"

Pow! Laszio's feather-encrusted fist blindsided the demon. Both the bow and Laszio's feathers shattered to pieces.

For a moment, Eran laid, stunned with elation. *It worked! It actually worked!*

Then the moment turned ugly. Malkior foamed at the mouth, screaming curses at them.

"Clear the way!" Jediah shouted.

The two Privates evacuated the cave just as Jediah cast a handful of smoke pellets. The resulting smoke spilled from the cave's mouth like a warm breath in a subzero morn.

Despite its pungent vapor, Eran flew closer to the smoke, ready to subdue Malkior for Jediah to put in chains. The demon should have stumbled out, disoriented and defenseless, but instead, Eran caught sight of a single spark.

He lurched.

The smoke ignited like methane gas.

White consumed Eran... Ears ringing... A burnt stench... Someone yelled his name.

Gold sprayed the air. Jediah's heart dropped as two figures smeared the rock wall. Laszio and Eran, one maimed, the other a broken lump, hit the lava-bed below. Jediah regulated his breaths, commanding himself not to react on an emotional level, but as he bombarded Malkior with light, he found his strikes becoming faster and near effortless.

Malkior scuttled his way up the cliff for the nearest volcanic spout. His flames, now pigmented blue, punched the air in chaotic, defensive arcs as he pulled himself to the top.

Soaring on a curve, Jediah swooped in and cut off his escape. "You're not running from me this time," he declared.

"Who said I was running *from* you?" Malkior countered. He stomped the ground. A brand new lava spout erupted, and Jediah was thrown to the side amidst spurting magma. The tasseled embers of Malkior's tunic spit flickers in rapid pops. "Didn't I warn you in Paris *not* to follow me?"

Eyes bright crimson, Malkior slammed his hands into the ground. His fingers pierced its crust. Stone broke, and orange veins spread, cracking and consuming the area.

Jediah then realized what Malkior had done. He fully unleashed Io's inner beast and condemned it all to immediate and total hell.

Surrounding volcanos awoke, and their booming voices reverberated loud in the canyon, throwing Nechum off his feet. Superheated stones were upturned. Chasms jutted and gutted the ground, and sloshing lava poured out into a network of sizzling rivers on all sides.

Nechum clenched his teeth. Eran and Laszio were still unconscious on the opposite side of the lava flow. Its current churned into a torrent, and its width expanded, overflowing its banks.

Nechum gripped Akela's shoulder. "We must get them out of there! They'll be swept off for sure!" He bolted after them, but before he could run much further, additional fissures broke out in the hundreds. Poison clouds jet-streamed, choking the air with their toxins.

The chunk of stone Nechum stood on snapped in half. It tossed him backwards. He flailed his arms, desperate for a hold as the feeble slab tipped, sliding him right toward the lava torrent.

"Nechum!" Rock broke under Akela's feet as he snatched Nechum, sprinted up the cliff, and sped far past the mountain range entirely.

Nechum couldn't catch his breath or his wits. Everything around them was an unrecognizable blur. "What in the—?" Putting two and two together, Nechum gasped. "Akela, wait! You're running too far! Stop! Stop! BRAKE!"

Akela's boots screeched. He skidded, dropped Nechum, and stomped on his chest as he careened forward and plopped face-first. "Ow," he groaned. Taking a second, he dragged himself up and smiled. His cheeks ripened to an embarrassed red. "Heh. Sorry about that. You're okay, though, right?"

Nechum fingered the new tender bruised spot on his chest. "Mostly," he wheezed.

Akela brushed off his shoulder pads and offered a hand. "We better get back there. Come on."

Nechum's eyes widened, and he shook his head. "No. No. Go ahead. Pick me up later."

"And strand you here?"

"Yep."

"You sure?"

"I insist."

Malkior's magma fountains spewed a canopy of suns. Searing drops bit Jediah through his clothes, but his mind had long reached the numbing point. He paid no attention to the pain. Jediah charged the cataclysm head on. For he knew if he just got close enough, he could end it all in two moves.

Sword blazing, Jediah slipped under a lava spray that singed his hair. He swung, but to his surprise, Malkior produced a sword of his own out of violet plasma. The blades connected with a flash of purple and white. The combatants clashed again and colored fire spilt from both blades onto the ground until a terrible inferno hemmed them in.

Malkior swung on a downstroke. Jediah blocked, slid his sword down the opposing edge, and cocked his wrist inward. His blade cut his intended mark: the neck. Red liquid energy bled from Malkior, but Malkior reached and latched onto Jediah's neck. Those searing fingers smelt of sulphuric acid, and Jediah screamed as they branded him. He tore himself away, falling backwards.

Using one hand to press his neck wound, Malkior raised the other. The surrounding purple and white fires gathered to him and accumulated into an army of insurmountable columns. A crazed glint gleamed in Malkior's eyes. "Goodbye, Captain—"

A grey force strangled a gurgle from Malkior's throat. The fires dimmed. The fog then dragged Malkior backwards over his own coals. His nails chipped as they carved claw marks, but an army of similar tendrils then coiled Malkior's whole being.

Jediah watched petrified as the rest of this nightmare seeped out of the ground along with its master: Alameth.

Fog twisted Malkior around to meet the angel of death's glowing eyes—cold and calloused eyes, ones that raged yet shed a deathly cold. The longer Malkior stared into them, the shriller his cries grew. Alameth's hair billowed beneath his hood, and by some silent command, the mists subjected Malkior to the most brutal beating no one could forget. It pounded him, wrung him like a dishcloth, and invaded his insides, doing God knows what else.

Jediah felt the urge to run in terror. This psychotic instinct; this senseless mutilation; it wasn't righteous action. It was senseless torture. Jediah had witnessed brutality before, but nothing so frightening as this. For it came not from the usual demonic sadism. It came from a fellow brother—one of their own. Alameth, the quiet Destroyer, had either lost his temper or had at last gone insane.

As Alameth continued to bury Malkior's pleas under pounds of fog, Jediah's rising fear for Alameth's sanity mounted. Alameth hoisted Malkior up and leered as their faces drew together. Mists wrapped around each of the demon's limbs.

Jediah went cold. *He's going to dismember him!* "Alameth, stop this!" he cried.

Alameth froze seconds before committing the grisly act.

Jediah stood up and called forth the Holy Chains. "He's had quite enough! Now put Malkior down!"

The unfeeling white fled from Alameth's eyes. His face ashened. His eyebrows dipped. A shortness of breath robbed him of his fighting spirit, and he gawked at his trembling hands in a trance-like state.

The mists evaporated. Malkior flopped, reduced to a traumatized, miserable wreck. Alameth too dropped to his knees. His shaking hands clamped together as if clinging for dear life. A devastated shell compared to the monster he was moments ago, Alameth cast a sorrowful look at Jediah. He turned and fled.

Jediah called to him, but Alameth disappeared beyond a mound. He would have chased after him if not for their new prisoner.

Looping chains about Malkior's wrists and ankles, Jediah strapped him tight. The demon couldn't do much to resist besides twitch and babble incoherent words. Jediah doubted if Malkior could even register what was happening in his shell-shocked state.

The raging lava streams around Jediah slowed to a sluggish goo. The surrounding volcanos quieted to sleep, and smoldering flames dwindled to flickers incapable of lighting a candle.

Malkior, by some surge of awareness, spasmed against the restraints.

Jediah glowered at him at first. The loathsome demon had this coming, but a tragic thought softened Jediah. This defiant being once graced heaven's courts. God granted Malkior dominion over fire, the lifeblood of planets and stars. Now he laid in disgrace, lower than the wrangled calf he had become. Love, purpose, family were his. He sold it all—all that was good—to pursue godless ambition. Just like Elazar.

Jediah shook the thought off. He couldn't dwell on that now. He raised his wings, and Malkior's being dissipated. His golden shards flew to the cell of God's choosing, and the fleeting glittering remnants blended amongst the stars. Picking up his sword, Jediah pressed his brow to the flat side of the blade. "To Your glory and honor goes the victory, my Lord."

Then, sheathing his sword, Jediah slumped to the ground. He settled himself and criss-crossed his legs, thankful for the freedom to do so. Io still rumbled, but the relative quiet had become as pleasant to him as a flowered meadow. Still, there yet lingered four loose ends.

Yakum, Chloe, Elazar, and now Alameth.

Chapter 17

ERAN AWOKE IN DARKNESS. Muffled sounds hummed. An orange flicker, tiny as a needle point, appeared, then vanished in his vision. Then came another flicker and another.

Eran moaned and tried to move, but everything ached. A humming pain hammered his head. After rubbing the bleariness from his dry eyes, he squinted and searched around to regain his bearings.

A tiny volcanic mound, demure as a campfire, released gentle sparks that danced and lit the jeweled cave. The slightest glimmers from the gem encrusted ceilings were drawn by the dim, wavering light. Topaz and rubies captured the beauty of flame. Rainbows peeked from diamond veins, and the cloudier amethysts and sapphires contrasted the other jewels with their cool visage. No amount of human wealth could buy such a trove.

Turning toward his opposite side, Eran looked out the cave's round opening that framed Io's vast landscape. It seemed a curiosity how he had missed Io's transient beauty until then. The subtle glow of its golden rivers illuminated the now darkened mountains. Splotches of red, black, yellow and white painted the region with their color swatches, and all of this was begat in the aftermath of what would surely be known as the Battle of Io—at least, once their mission was completely over.

Eran remembered. Malkior, the fire demon, was captured. Yakum, demon lord of Beijing, was next.

Those muffled hums Eran heard a minute ago clarified, and he noticed Akela, who sat nearby, singing. The notes of his song ebbed and flowed in pure tones equal to the skills of the Poet King, David, himself.

Could we with ink the ocean fill, and were the skies of parchment made,
Were every stalk on earth a quill, and every man a scribe by trade;
To write the love of God above would drain the ocean dry;
Nor could the scroll contain the whole. Tho' stretched from sky to sky.
Oh love of God, how rich and pure. How measureless and strong.
It shall forevermore endure. The saint's and angel's song.

Recognizing Akela's hymn, Eran smiled. "That's one of my favorites."

Akela twisted around. His cobalt eyes shone a richer blue than the seven oceans. "God bless you, brother. You're awake!"

Eran rolled his pinching neck, and his kinked wings cramped.

Akela fidgeted as Eran worked through the pain. "Oof. That Malkior really packed a wallop, didn't he?"

Eran paused. The memory of it flooded back to him. Their brief victory. The explosion. His falling. "Where's Laszio?"

"Behind you," a raspy voice answered.

Laszio rested on a sandier patch of rocks. He had stumps that were once his left arm and leg, but he still had that spunky smirk as if he dared Malkior to return from the Abyss and dish out some more.

Eran tried using his hands to turn himself around.

"Don't do that!" Akela cried.

Eran crumpled to the shooting pain that racked his legs. He reached down to reposition them but touched air. They were missing.

Shaking his head, Akela stood up. "I tried to warn you." After walking over, he bent down and wrapped his arms underneath Eran's. "Okay. Hang tight." He interlocked his fingers, forming a two-handed fist over Eran's chest. "One. Two. Three." Akela hoisted him up.

"Agh!" Two gold smears trailed behind as Akela dragged Eran closer to Laszio, but he set him down much slower and steadier than Eran ever expected from him. Everything still stung, though, and Eran shoved his agony out in a sharp push of breath.

Akela patted Eran's shoulder. "Sorry," he said. "I wish I could've made it hurt less, but, gotta be honest, I'm not the gentlest angel." Akela plopped down to a sitting position but winced the second he did so. He hissed and strained to rub the dark spot centered on his back.

It was then Eran noticed Akela's scorched wings with their flaked, blackened quills. Eran reached out. Certain not to rub too hard or too soft, he massaged the area Akela reached for. Akela's back went straight like a rod, but soon melted under Eran's practiced touch. After centuries of battle, therapeutic skill came in handy once in a while.

"Oh, that's the spot," Akela remarked. "A tad lower. That's it. That's it." He let out a dozed sigh. "Ahh, that's the ticket. Thank you, brother."

"Don't mention it," Eran said.

Sinking into deeper thought, Eran recounted their skirmish against Malkior, and his heart leaped. *"God blessed our effort!"* he thought. *"The new move worked! Using wings as punching gauntlets was a high risk, high reward option, but still. It worked! Nail Elazar with that much striking force the next time he comes poking around, he'd be left recovering for half a day. It was perfect!"*

Eran reigned in his excitement. *Perfect? Nothing apart from God is perfect.* He recalculated the facts. The move was not perfect. Far from perfect. There were too many variables, too many ways it could go wrong. What if instead of Elazar they punched one of his impenetrable shields? How could they possibly get close enough? Mounting negatives threw his positivity into a downward spiral.

Eran stopped his careening assumptions. He reminded himself that he asked God for proof that there was a chance. God answered, and a slim chance didn't mean 'no' chance. He just had to go with it.

"You know?" Akela said, interrupting Eran's thoughts. "You two are pretty incredible."

Laszio stirred and arched an eyebrow. "What makes you say that?"

Facing them, Akela smiled. "You're unstoppable, and I'd daresay, you carry more inspirational power than even Jediah does. And he's *already* pretty inspirational."

Touched but skeptical, Eran asked, "But how does that work?"

Akela chuckled. "If even God's 'little guys' can make the major plays, it says a lot about what He can do with anyone and everyone."

The compliment was delivered with such sincerity and kindness, a powerful vigor coursed through Eran. "Thanks. And you are faithfulness personified, Akela. You may be scatterbrained, but you don't lose sight of the Big Picture—just like your smile."

Akela bowed his sheepish, beaming face. "... thank you."

After a moment, Eran squinted. Three faces were missing. "Akela? Where are the others?"

Akela cleared his throat. "Oh, um. The captain and Nechum went looking for Alameth. He went missing shortly before Malkior's capture."

Instant irritation flipped Eran's joy on a dime. "Alameth bailed?" he asked in disgust. Exasperated, he let the back of his head hit the rock. "Well, that's a fine thing to do. What's wrong with him?"

"Wrong with him?" Akela asked with a perplexed look.

Laszio huffed. "Alameth seldom speaks. He doesn't smile. He smoked up the catacombs—*while* we were in them, which aided Malkior's escape no less. Nechum already admitted he's emotionally dead, and now he's a deserter. How can there *not* be something wrong?"

Lowering his eyes, Akela fiddled with the fringe of his satchel.

Eran sighed. "We're not saying Alameth's gone rogue, Akela."

The corner of Akela's lip lifted in a wry, lopsided smile. "It sure sounds that way." His eyes then stared at them with an uncharacteristic seriousness. "Mind a word of advice?"

Stunned, yet impressed by Akela's sudden sobriety, Eran nodded.

Akela shook his head and sighed. "Don't assume the worst in your brothers. Especially the ones you know little about. And just to let you know," Akela added. "It wasn't Jediah, Nechum, or I who saved you two from the lava bed."

Nechum loved the sky there. Io's non-existent atmosphere didn't dim the stars. They glistened twice as bright as on earth, and their bountiful clusters were jewels of frosted blue that overlaid their neighbors, forming galactic sapphire bands outlined in violet.

"Any sign of him?" Jediah asked. He hadn't yet stopped eyeing the mountain ranges.

"It's difficult to say," Nechum replied. "Alameth is a tough one to sense." He saddened to once again see Jediah's burns. The scabbed handprint Malkior branded on his face stretched from his chin, over the cheek, across the nose and around the eyes. Similar burns etched his neck and hands. He appeared barbaric, like the violent, ancient Highland tribes Nechum once knew. But Jediah wasn't anything like them. Painted handprints were the Celt's intimidation practice—a ritual to celebrate bloodlust. Not Jediah. His peeling sores and scars were a testament to his zeal, and Nechum loved and respected him all the more for it.

Nechum patted the waterskin under his shawl. It flattened empty against his side, with its last drops having been spent resuscitating Laszio and Eran.

Jediah stepped on a higher rock. "Do you detect his distress anywhere?" he asked.

Nechum rechecked his empathic sense, but the only distress he felt came from Jediah. Its potency overpowered anything else. "No, sir," he answered. "Just yours."

Jediah's strong countenance dwindled, and whether it was the less rigid posture or the exposed tiredness in his face, his inner weariness suddenly made his youthful appearance match his ancient age.

Nechum folded his hands and spoke quietly. "Brother, I know you must always be there looking out for the others, but please, stop pretending you're all right. If for no one else, then for me." Nechum's neck tensed as he drew near. "Jediah? What are you afraid of?"

Hesitant, Jediah pursed his lips. "Of... messing up what I'm about to do."

Nechum tipped his head. He sensed more than doubts on Jediah's mind. "Are you referring to the situation with Alameth? Or something else entirely?"

Before he could respond, Jediah's eyes focused on something. They widened in interest, but not with joy.

Nechum turned and also spotted a familiar, hooded gray speck that wandered along a rugged ridge.

Jediah walked ahead. His rapt attention on Alameth seemed equal parts sad, agitated, and fearful. Alameth too stopped where he stood. For it seemed even from a mile away, their eyes had connected and locked as if drawn to each other.

Jediah's armored wings softened, and the feathers lifted off his shoulders and sides. "Mind giving us a minute, Nechum? I must speak with him alone."

Nechum gathered the courage to counter his superior's request. "With all due respect, sir. I'd like to be there for the both of you, but I promise I won't interfere."

Jediah stood silent, as if waiting for Nechum to fortify his point.

"Alameth and I have talked regarding *this* before," Nechum explained.

Jediah looked toward Alameth, then back to Nechum. "Very well."

Alameth didn't move an inch as they approached him. Nechum reached out with his empathic sense. A miserable depression burdened the angel of death, but he had calmly surrendered to it as if it were a normal thing. After patting Alameth's shoulder, Nechum selected a spot to sit and listen.

Alameth bowed in respect, as Jediah flattened his wings behind himself, giving a non-confrontational demeanor. "We're glad to have found you, Alameth. Care to explain what happened?"

A careworn pallor aged Alameth's expressionless face. He stared at the ground as he spoke. "You saw what happened, sir. What's there to explain?"

"I *saw* what happened," Jediah said as he stepped closer. "But I'm more interested in why. Why did it happen?"

Alameth cast uncomfortable glances. "Is it a crime to defend my brothers? To desire their well-being?"

Jediah folded his hands behind his back. "No. No, it isn't, but your methods concern me. I've fought in more battles than I care to recall, Alameth. I've watched fellow soldiers go to impossible lengths to complete our objectives, but as God's soldiers, we take care in how we do it."

Jediah scraped his sword out of the scabbard. The polished blade captured the infinite heavens in watered silver. As he laid it in his palms, Jediah seemed to cup the galaxy in his hands. "When I wield this blade, Alameth, it's a reminder to enemy and ally alike that I am not my own. For I am to God what this sword is to me. A sword does not slay for its own glory, nor does it grasp revenge on its own accord. It acts by its master's will and his alone." Jediah tipped it upward and stared into its mirror. "It's a tool, and a tool apart from its master is nothing." He swung it around in skilled twirls, casting its starlight. A flurry of colors shone off the dull rocks. Lowering it, Jediah set its point into the ground, then slid the weapon back into its scabbard. "We reflect God to everyone, Alameth, so if we fight mercilessly, what image of Him will others see?"

Alameth seemed unmoved, but Nechum sensed Jediah's words sinking into him.

"Alameth," Jediah continued. "I've seen soldiers take the fight too far and relent in seconds, but you... you carried on for a solid minute."

Alameth didn't argue, as he sat on a smoothed mound. A distant eruption cascaded light off his clothes in a mournful sheer. His shoulders sagged, and he fingered the intricate clasp that pinned his hood to his collar. Its delicate silver cross gleamed. "I'm tired. So tired," he said in a murmur soft as morning haze.

Squinting, Jediah crossed his arms. "Tired of what?" he asked.

"Of this," Alameth responded. "All of this. Sin, death, the curse, this war, every wrongful act that traps me in a role I never wanted... I wish God ended it all now."

Nechum flinched as he sensed Alameth's irritation stir the mists. Even Jediah inched away. But in one drawn breath, Alameth calmed, and his restless fog settled to a standstill. A demure glint betrayed the steadiness in his eyes. Alameth's voice gained strength. "I delight to bring God's people home, Captain. It's my greatest joy, but I can hardly bear condemning the lost." His hand combed rigorously through his hair. "So why? Why must there be such beings like Malkior who brutalize others and treat life with such contempt?" Alameth then rubbed his eyes and buried them into his forearm sleeve.

Nechum couldn't take it anymore. He got up and rubbed gentle circles into Alameth's quivering back.

After a while, Alameth collected himself and lowered his arm. "I can't stop sin's destructive consequences. No matter how much I ache to," he said. "But just when I thought for once... just once... I could protect someone... all I end up doing is... becoming just like *them*." Alameth's voice cracked and broke into silence. He bent his neck, hiding his face from them.

Nechum hated it, making Alameth rehash his torments to another all over again. In the beginning, Alameth's powers begat beauty and life. To have to endure the centuries, wading neck deep in a marred creation's filth pits... Nechum could hardly endure the world's ugliness himself. For Alameth's kind to withstand what they have, it required nothing less than the most remarkable fortitude that only God could sustain. Nechum sighed and kept soothing Alameth with a compassionate hand. The renewed heaven and earth couldn't come sooner.

Jediah knelt to Alameth's eye-level and gripped his shoulder. "You are *nothing* like them, Alameth," he said in a firm, uncompromising tone. "And I'll have words with *anyone* who says otherwise."

Nechum's spirits lightened, as the brighter colors in Alameth's eyes overtook most of its darkness, but then they lowered. Alameth swallowed. "I have one request, Captain—if I may ask it."

"Yes, name it," Jediah said.

A portion of darkness returned to shade Alameth's eyes, destroying the peace they just regained. "Once we find Yakum, don't involve me."

Chapter 18

ELAZAR QUIETLY CRITICIZED the officers and messengers Lucifer surrounded himself with. Hoia-Baciu Forest buzzed in their uproar. They harped and squabbled, vying to gain their prince's favor. Elazar found better purpose in sharpening his dagger with a flint than participating in such a mindless bedlam.

News had spread quickly, whether by hushed whispers or proclamation throughout the spiritual realms. Malkior was gone, banished forever until the end of the age. The angels reacted with cheers or solemn approval. Demons, on the other hand, accepted it the only way they could: with pompous swears of vengeance. Truth of the matter was, they were more petrified by this development than they had been for a long time. No one had been condemned to the Abyss or any spiritual prison in the past four thousand years. To them, this was a threat message, and to their further discomfort, the military scouts reported that Jediah's chains weren't hung up yet. One more official was slated for capture.

"We should have done as Captain Zivel said," an officer argued. "We should raid the Abyss now, before another one of us is picked off!" His proposal met mixed approval as the other war leaders murmured questions between themselves—not least of which was Captain Zivel's whereabouts.

Elazar smirked to himself. That stupid oaf wouldn't dare show his embarrassed face to Lucifer again, not after his humiliating failure during the storm ambush. Elazar left him split open in Alabama. By the time Zivel would have resuscitated, he had already reported of his disobedience to Lucifer. Slinking off was the smartest thing Zivel ever did.

"Weren't any of you listening?" Lucifer bellowed. Growing in immense size, his shadow menaced all of them. "So long as Jediah has the key, we are at a disadvantage! We're not attacking until we have it and guarantee victory!" The growls in his throat rumbled louder than ten lions.

Everyone in the circle bowed and expressed full fealty by laying their softened wings flat on their backs.

Shrinking to his normal height, Lucifer rolled his shoulders and smoothed his hair. "Until Jediah is crushed and stripped wingless, the Abyss is off the table."

At that, the lot of them threw themselves into another chorus of arguments. Each single voice tried to topple twenty others.

Elazar rolled his eye and picked at his nails with his dagger point. *They're as productive as a coop of headless hens.*

"Quiet!" Lucifer finally roared. "Quit pretending like any of you know what you're talking about. None of you do. Master Elazar, care to join us?"

Unintimidated, Elazar didn't need the use of his empathic sense to feel the demonic counsel's utter disdain for him. Leaving the tree he leaned on, he entered the circle center, gave a small bend of the neck, but did not lower his eyes. "You called, your stupendousness?" He weathered the Devil's narrowed glare.

"*I'm* the one who recruited you, rogue," Lucifer reminded. "What do you make of this? Where might Jediah go next? Who might he be after?"

Elazar grinned but feigned deep thought to rub his superior importance to the rest of the council. He scratched his chin and paced large circles. "Hmm. Tall order there. Figuring out the angel himself, that's easy. To figure out his Master, though, is another matter. What was that the humans like to say again? 'God works in mysterious ways'?"

"Skip to the point, Elazar. Or one scarred eye will be the least of your pains," Lucifer warned.

Elazar raised his hands in as minimal show of respect as he could get away with. "But of course, my liege." He cast looks at the leering crowd. "However, I hold no confidence in your competitive company."

Lucifer scowled.

Elazar queried, "Wasn't it you who promised I would get Jediah? And no one else?"

After turning his slitted eyes towards the others, Lucifer waved them off. A few lingered out of stubbornness, but two seconds under their prince's scrutinizing glare sent them shuffling like children ordered to bed. Lucifer then folded his arms, bunching his long opulent sleeves. "Remember, Elazar, you're no more important to me than any of them."

"Why else do you think I never pledged to you?" Elazar retorted.

Lucifer lifted an eyebrow, somewhat impressed by Elazar's tenacity—if by a little. "Start talking," the Devil growled.

Elazar smiled. "God may work in mysterious ways," he began. "But He works systematically and consistently."

Lucifer rolled his eyes. "Oh. I didn't know that. Really," he huffed.

"God took out Malkior," Elazar continued. "He was a talented informant and a key player for your invasion. It's likely his higher up is next."

"Yakum then," Lucifer concluded.

Elazar smirked. "Yakum." He produced a jet black page as dark as coal from his pocket. "I suppose I should forewarn your chief biochemist, shouldn't I." Elazar approached the nearest tree. After unsheathing his knife, he sliced his palm and smeared a coat of his own ooze over the blade. Then pressing the paper against the trunk, Elazar scribbled sharp, vicious strokes with the flat of the knife's tip. The scarlet ink cut across the parchment's fibers like blood whipped from a slave's back.

Lucifer loomed over him as he wrote. "It's curious," he said. "You had your chance to snap Jediah in half during that storm, except you didn't. You could have won."

Annoyed, Elazar was tempted to rebut him, but decided against it. He didn't have to answer or explain himself to anyone, especially the Great Deceiver.

Lucifer murmured a mocking chuckle as he mused. "I guess wrecking Jediah wouldn't get that angel to hate you to your satisfaction, would it?"

Elazar dotted the last period and pressed his handprint as a signature. He offered it to Lucifer, who tucked it in his robes.

"But I wouldn't fret about Jediah if I were you, imp," Lucifer added. "I'm sure he hates you plenty."

As he turned away, the Devil's condescending grin irked Elazar. He would have loved to strangle him. Rubbing his face, Elazar's fingers stopped over his ruined eye. He traced the scar's inflamed line. Its length had shortened. Grunting, he whipped out his dagger and checked his cloudy reflection in its obsidian mirror. Red particles attempted once more to repair the scar as it always had for five thousand years.

Elazar grumbled. His fingers squeezed, bunching the handle's leather straps. He aligned the razor to his cheek's thinning line but paused. For old memories coupled with Lucifer's words held him in place. At their taunting, he overthrew all hesitancy. His wrist twitched, then came the upward stroke. The swift slash finished the job. Elazar stifled a yell. The new scars always throbbed and burned, but after this long, Elazar found he couldn't live without one.

Jediah hovered over Nechum, who hunched over the buttoned device he had called a computer. The screen blared in the dark library, and Jediah hoped the bookshelf walls hid the brightness from the building's security cameras that Nechum had pointed out earlier.

Glued to the display, Nechum pecked the keys in rapid clicks. It impressed Jediah how easily he manipulated the fragile, squared letters while in angelic form without breaking them. Even Laszio and Akela stood enraptured as his nimble fingers danced.

"I still don't quite understand why travel visas are required for Image Bearers to cross borders," Laszio remarked.

"It is difficult for beings like us to understand, Laszio," Nechum replied. "But right now, I need to concentrate. This isn't as easy as it looks." Garish pictures crowded the screen. Nechum grunted, grabbed the oval device called a 'mouse' that sat next to the lettered grid, and clicked them away.

Readjusting his blue hood, Eran turned to Jediah. "Do you really think it's a good idea to remain as humans during our Beijing operation?"

"I don't see there being much choice," Jediah said. "Word has spread about us, so now everyone's on the lookout for soldiers in ministry clothes. Besides, Nechum informed me that less than two percent of China's people are Marked Christians. I'm expecting we're going to be vastly outnumbered there."

Eran nodded, but stared ahead with eyebrows furrowed. "Sir? Do you think Elazar will track us there?"

Jediah drew an agitated breath, crossed his arms, and kept his eyes glued on Nechum. "He may. Let's pray that he doesn't." This was the third time Eran inquired about Elazar, and he wished he'd drop the subject.

"And what about the others?" Eran asked. "Shouldn't the others know the name of our whistleblower?"

Jediah looked Eran square in the eye. "If we go completely underground for the rest of this operation, Elazar should be a non-issue."

Eran looked away, dissatisfied but compliant.

Nechum clicked the plastic 'mouse' device again. A tiny arrow darted across the screen in sync with his hand. Then he sat still, waiting for the computer's response.

Laszio tapped the display. "How long do these things usually take?" After a minute of nothing, he leaned in and tapped harder. "Did it die?"

Nechum sighed. "No. It's just thinking."

"Pfft. Thinking. Like junk can think. They'd have chips for brains if they did," Laszio said, rolling his eyes.

"Well, you're not too far off there," Nechum chortled. The display cleared, and his fingers set to racing once more.

Laszio nodded. "Oh good. It's alive."

"Technically it's not, but I get your figure of speech," Akela said with a wink and a nudge Laszio seemed to tolerate.

Jediah checked the empty aisle behind him. He pulled his hood down to his eyebrows, half expecting a creeping shadow or a red eye, but there was no one. No Elazar. He then watched Akela, who was investing his interest into everything. Jediah's wheels turned. His letter was finished. This night would be his last to help Chloe before he vanished into obscurity, and flaky Akela was his linch pin. If the messenger refused to help, his hopes were shot.

Anxiety prickled Jediah's tantalized nerves. He rubbed his hands together and became altogether convinced he'd keel over and die right then if he weren't an angel. Disgusted by his behavior, Jediah chastised himself. This was Akela he was pondering about, the friendliest angel he knew, yet he found it tempting to just let tonight's opportunity pass into quiet. Chloe's grandfather is a Christian. Surely, he could handle ministering the Gospel to her himself.

"*No!*" his conscience cried. "*You don't know what she has or hasn't heard. Chloe needs this. Do it for her. Then leave the matter to God.*"

The trick then became choosing the least awkward moment to pull Akela aside. As Jediah raced through his options, he drew to Nechum's side to check his progress, hoping to watch without causing a nuisance.

Nechum glanced up. "If you have a question, sir—"

Jediah shook his head. "No. Just stick to your task."

Apologetic, Nechum replied. "I know this is taking so long. Sorry. It's all just very short notice. You have no idea how far ahead people plan international trips. It can take months' worth of preparation and money. Thankfully, though, I've saved enough to cover expenses."

Nechum clicked, and a company banner popped into existence. He then interacted with two white bars labeled 'ID' and 'password.' "You know what's funny?" Nechum said as he typed. "After all these decades, I finally understand why God asked me to start this bank account. All those hoops I had to jump through..." He pushed out a wistful sigh.

Intrigued, Jediah pressed, "What sorts of hoops?"

"Oh, adopting several identities. Laws I had to abide by. People to convince. Odd jobs I took here and there," Nechum said. He nodded to himself. "I tell you, the whole thing was one of the lengthiest assignments I ever had." He gave a faint smile. "But now, after years of disuse, these savings will finally see purpose."

Words like 'transaction', 'credit cards', and 'forms' flashed by, as Nechum's hands recited innumerable number sequences one after the other. Jediah trusted they all somehow accomplished something.

Nechum let out a satisfied breath. "Okay. Now to print off the Visas, passports, and receipts. God willing, they'll be verified quickly, and that copier isn't out of ink." With two taps of his fingers, another machine whirred. Nechum drummed his hands on the desk. "Okay. Here comes the tricky part." Typing the words 'Beijing Hotels' in a white bar, he scrolled down, reading offers and prices fast enough to rival Akela's flight speed. He paused and rubbed his forehead. "Reserving a hotel room for this weekend will be a miracle, but God will open accommodations for us. I'm sure."

Laszio crossed his arms. "Hotels? Accommodations? Sounds like were going on vacation."

"*We're* not," Nechum said. He twisted in his chair and retrieved the fresh photographic documents from the copier tray. "The *Gershom* family is." He then handed them to Laszio, careful not to smear the warm ink.

Laszio's eye color paled as he counted and perused the six personas. "Oh, boy. And it's only going to get tougher from there. Isn't it?"

Nechum cringed but answered, "Beijing is densely packed, and the Chinese people live under strict scrutiny under their authorities. They're sticklers for security. Everyone from their President to the local bum is strictly monitored."

"And most especially tourists like us," Jediah added. He turned to the others. "Normally, I'd suggest going about our capture mission another way, but in the current circumstance, this is the path of least resistance to Yakum."

Laszio winced as if he knew where this was going. "So..."

Jediah took the papers from Laszio's hands. He leafed through them and pulled out two. "Nechum and I will pass ourselves off as your parents."

Laszio chuckled. "Okay. Which of you is 'mommy'?"

Grimacing, Jediah rolled his eyes. "Me."

"Guess it's, 'Ma'm, yes, ma'm,' from now on then, huh?" Laszio burst out laughing, but his mirth quickly fizzled when he noticed Jediah's returned smirk.

"Close, Private, but not quite." Jediah handed him his ID and picture.

What remained of Laszio's humor soured.

Eran peeked over his shoulder and snorted a laugh. "Oh, my gosh!"

In a stricken daze, Laszio shook his head as he repeated rapid-fire 'no-s', but Jediah could only pat his shoulder. He handed Eran and Akela their copies. "Akela?" he muttered.

"Yes, sir?"

"I'd like you to come with me. I need to talk with you, after I give Alameth his ID."

Quizzical, Akela squinted. "Okay?"

Venturing through the building, columns of used and abused books towered the halls, and the thick dust that coated the coverlets gave a musty smell. Jediah entered the open lounge. Sofas were set in semi-circles before large draped windows, and moonlight filtered through the milky residue that streaked the glass. Alameth lingered close to the window. His hood was up, but Jediah knew by the tip of his head that he was staring into the heavens. "Found the quietest place, huh?" he said.

At first, Alameth didn't respond. Only his raised, then lowered shoulders hinted at a long-drawn breath. "Yes. It's quiet."

"Here are your identification papers. Would you mind if Akela and I have the space?" Jediah asked.

Alameth gave a small bow, accepted the papers, and took his leave.

Jediah waited until he got out of earshot. He pushed out a breath. This was it. "Akela, there's something I want you to do for me."

The pounding in Jediah's chest gained speed the longer Akela sat slack jawed on the sofa cushion. After shaking his head, Akela squeezed his temples and hummed for a second. "Excuse me. What now? Y-you want me to do what now?" he asked in a babbling yet dangerously calm tone.

Licking his lips, Jediah restarted. "Akela, I know it sounds bad."

"You want me to do what?" Akela shouted, shooting up from his seat.

"Shhh!" Jediah shoved him back down. "Akela, please, get a hold of yourself."

Puffing spaced breaths, Akela fanned himself. "But what you're asking is... delivering an unsanctioned letter to a little girl—a human—is... is..."

Akela didn't finish his sentence, but Jediah already filled in the blanks with all the answers he wouldn't have liked. "Unprecedented. I know," he offered.

Standing up, Akela looked him square in the eye. "What you're asking is dangerous."

Jediah swallowed, clearing the rumble in his throat. "I know, but I don't see how I can neglect helping her".

"Captain... it likely won't work."

Jediah's neck heated. "But where is it written that I cannot try? Or that man can no longer have contact with us?"

Akela dropped his head into his hands, rocked on his feet, and pulled his cheeks. "What do you expect me to do?" he demanded. "Zap, bang, boom into her room in the middle of the night? Yeah, that'll turn out swell. She'll be the youngest recorded in medical heart attacks."

Frustrated, Jediah got in Akela's face. "Akela, listen," he whispered sharply in his ear. "Time is short. My chances are running thin and so are hers."

Akela shrank. "Your chances? What do you mean 'your' chances?"

Realizing he slipped up, Jediah conspired to steer the topic away from himself. "Do you remember the Garden, Akela? God walked side by side with Adam in Eden, and so did we. They could see us—talk to us. For those first few days, neither sin nor guilt barred our worlds. Life was innocent."

Akela nodded. A tinge of sadness mingled with the nostalgia in his smile.

"And," Jediah continued, "It's like the original innocence never left you, Akela. In your eyes," Jediah paused, considering his words. "I see Eden."

Sheepish, Akela lowered his eyes. "Thank you for your kind words, sir."

"Then please, Akela," Jediah entreated. "Chloe is sick—dying perhaps. I don't know how many days she has left—if any. But the Spirit is tugging at her sleeve. I know it. He's standing there, waiting for her, but she hasn't reached for Him. If I don't encourage her to, and she dies unsaved, Akela, I'll live the rest of this age knowing my complacency condemned her. But if you help me deliver this letter, I'd be able to rest knowing I did what I could do, no matter if she accepts Christ or not."

Eyes filled with conflicted pity, Akela shook his head. "I don't know, sir. This is unmarked territory."

"Then tell me I'm forbidden from sharing God's message of grace with her," Jediah challenged. "Say it now, and I'll rip this letter apart before you right here." He held out a folded envelope.

Akela reached to take the spotless parchment, but hesitated and drew back.

"Please, Akela," Jediah entreated. "Help me teach her to walk with God. Rekindle Eden in her heart."

Despite the color being driven from his eyes, Akela bit his lip and took the letter.

Jediah shivered a sigh. "Thank you."

Akela examined the letter, then burrowed it under his leather guard instead of his satchel.

"Don't let the others know," Jediah said. "It's best they weren't tangled in this. And Akela? If things go wrong, I swear you will not bear the blame." Jediah placed one hand on his chest and raised an open palm with the other to invoke the gravest of angelic oaths. "May God deal with me be it ever so severely if this act of mine brings her harm."

Akela shuddered, "No pressure, right?" His wings blurred into a hover. "Sir," he said as he turned to leave. "When I called this idea of yours dangerous, I didn't mean it was only dangerous for her."

Chapter 19

CAUGHT IN TRAFFIC OUTSIDE of Beijing, Jediah couldn't help taking another look in the side-view mirror. He frowned at his lipstick. Pastel brushed eyelids, narrowed chin, slim shoulders; he expected he'd end up greeting his reflection by accident, eventually. Pressing his temples, he rehearsed the innumerable reminders Nechum cited for feminine-like behavior. Grasping masculine nuances was tough enough. Females were a far cry.

Nechum tapped a thumb on the leather-stitched steering wheel. His attention couldn't be torn from the hundred car pileup ahead for anything.

"Gootchy-gootchy-goo."

Jediah peeked behind to see a toddler-sized Eran tickle baby Laszio's chubby chin.

Laszio's exasperated grunt grumbled from the booster seat. "Do you have to do that?"

"Sorry," Eran chuckled. "This is too priceless. After all... you make a really cute baby."

"Must you tease?" Laszio huffed.

Akela, who sat opposite to Eran, chimed in. "But he's right, Laszio. You are adorable. Besides, being the family baby is the best human gig ever. No one expects anything of you and they're obligated to wait on you hand and foot!" Akela leaned over Laszio. His ribboned ponytail swung over him, while his preteen girl dimples glowed a rosier pink.

Wriggling, Laszio fumbled his bitty fingers to tug at his restraints. "You wouldn't like this so much if I stuffed you in a diaper. This thing chafes." He waved his arms and legs in random directions. "And I have zero motor control. What's this skin made of? Dough?"

Jediah twisted around, an action that bunched up his skirt. "Gives you a new perspective on God's willingness to become human, doesn't it?" he asked.

After a pointed silence, Laszio calmed. "I suppose it does."

"We know it's hard, Laszio," said Eran. "I'm not too keen on being a four-year-old boy either."

"Or a woman," Jediah added. "But it's best for us to act opposite to our true selves. Less suspicious."

Eran cocked an eyebrow and turned to gaze at Alameth in his young adult charade. His lightened hair was shortened, yet he dressed himself in a black hoodie, complete with headphones resting around his neck. "Less suspicious," Eran mused. "Riiight."

Jediah sighed. Smoothing his skirt, he settled back in his seat.

Nechum adjusted the rear-view mirror and lightly pressed the gas pedal. It was the first few inches the car had crept in the last ten minutes.

Smog shrouded Beijing as though to cover a cultural treasure. Its structures expressed industrial power, yet it intermingled with nature's alluring influence. Modern skyscrapers stood high, while the ancient styling survived in the architectures of hutong allies. A cacophony of car horns persisted alongside ringing bike bells. Hip-hop soundtracks played in the public malls. Traditionalist musicians performed their stringed erhus and dizi flutes in the public squares. Beijing was indeed a city that bridged the centuries. One foot in the past and one in the future.

Millions through the dynasties and presidencies called Beijing's streets home, but Jediah found Nechum didn't exaggerate their numbers enough. No matter where he looked, gobs of people were sandwiched together, and the sidewalks, rooftops, trees, and even the open sky, were populated with demons. The few ministry angels that passed by their car stuck close to their Christian's sides, guarding them at a personal level.

Determined not to draw demonic attention, Jediah stared into his lap. He picked at his polished nails, yet he still couldn't resist risking another peek. A demon heckled a ministry angel at a crosswalk, but, unbothered by such childishness, the angel disregarded the demon's jabs with an almost bored expression. He then shoved the demon aside with a barrier and walked on with his human.

Their car stopped, and Jediah stared at the red light hanging overhead from thick cables. Choosing to lean back and relax, he noticed Nechum's neck tense. His brow glistened damp. "What is it?" Jediah whispered.

He traced Nechum's gaze to a demon who peered uncomfortably close to their windshield. Jediah shifted toward the passenger window to avoid eye contact, but Nechum's heavy breaths increased. A sudden thump on the roof startled Jediah. The demon outside chatted with whoever plopped himself on their vehicle. *"Good. He's distracted,"* Jediah thought. But then the demon paused mid-word and took a particular interest in Nechum. He loomed inches from the glass.

Nechum's fingers drummed the steering wheel, and his eyes pleaded with the traffic light. Desperate to calm him, Jediah patted Nechum's leg.

Green light.

Nechum stamped the gas pedal, and two surprised voices yelled.

Jediah checked the rearview mirror. One demon nursed a squashed foot, and the other was thrown flat on his back. He bowed his head to hide a grin. "Easy, *dear.*"

Nechum released a constricted chuckle. "Yes, hon."

Eran poked his little head between Nechum's and Jediah's seats. "Hey, how exactly are we going to track Yakum in all this hustle and bustle?" he asked.

Jediah gazed out the passenger window. "We'll figure something out."

"Sounds like a plan." Eran went back and clapped his hands together. "You know, Laszio, your baby form might work to our advantage."

"Really. Do tell," came Laszio's flat reply.

"If we need to get out of a jam, just cry."

"Hardy har har."

"No, I'm serious. Go ahead. Try a wail. Or at least a little whimper."

Based on the silence, Jediah imagined Laszio giving Eran a deadpan stare. "Wah. Wah." Somehow his voice ended up even blander.

"Oookay," Eran said. "Let's retry that."

Nechum pulled into a parking spot. "Here we are."

Jediah listened to the shift of the parking gears and the jingling from the keys as their car disengaged. He unbuckled his seatbelt. "Wait for my signal." Unlatching the door, he planted a careful foot on the cobblestones.

His skirt bunched up. Cringing, he stood up and pulled it back down over his thighs. With his first step, his high heel got stuck in a crevice. He attempted to take another step, but this time lost his shoe. Settling his nerves, Jediah dislodged the irksome thing and slipped it back on.

Calm down. Calm down. No one noticed.

Jediah brushed loose curls behind his ears and pulled out blush and a tiny mirror. He powdered the pink dust over his cheeks, but his attention was on the circled glass that he tilted in every direction. No demons stalked behind or above him. Clamping the pocket mirror, he turned to the vehicle and gave a nod, signaling the 'all clear'.

Akela sprang out and sniffed the air. "Mmm, something smells good," he exclaimed.

"I should hope so." Nechum said, as he checked his watch. "The hotel restaurant should be open for dinner soon."

"They serve dinner too?" Akela asked.

"With a fee," Nechum explained. "But breakfast is complementary."

"Sounds perfect," Akela said. He strutted toward the open street, humming.

"Ahem." Alameth glared at Akela. He hunched forward, and his baggy shirt hung loose from his lean chest.

Akela frowned, but nodded back. "I get it. I get it," he conceded. "Less talking."

Jediah smiled to Akela and said, "But humming is fine."

With a piece of his former eagerness restored, Akela resumed his tune with a high-stepping gait.

"Captain, aren't you concerned about his... reputation?" Alameth asked.

Jediah patted Alameth's shoulder. "Sometimes the most noticeable things are the most readily dismissed."

"Ugh." Eran's hands picked at Laszio's car seat buckles. A few seconds and pinched fingers later, he grumbled, "Who invented these? A sadist?"

They followed Nechum along a quaint street beside a small stretch of connected buildings. Trees lined the sidewalk, casting their cool shade on the dusted road. The distinctive, rippled roofs curved downward according to old Chinese customs. More striking, however, was this miraculous quiet. The very heart of Beijing felt remote. Fewer people milled about. The noisy metropolis no longer drowned out the birds, and the rustling of leaves from their pruned branches went unhindered.

Nechum led them to a building with rounded lanterns that lined its roof. "Here we are."

A painted gateway greeted them. Its conglomeration of reds, blues, and greens were woven harmoniously in tight patterns and framed a sunbathed garden. Bronze tables and chairs were meticulously set according to the pavement's patterns of decorated stone. More swaying lanterns with golden tassels displayed Chinese calligraphy all around them. Sculpted lions guarded the path inside, and beyond the garden, stone dragons flanked the golden knobbed doors.

"Whoa," Akela uttered. "It's lovely. Like in a storybook." He patted Nechum's arm. "Great pick. I expected some mega skyscraper suite or something, but this is way more charming. Very nice."

Nechum smiled and gestured them forward. "Shall we?"

The reception room's restrained opulence did not swamp the eyes. Hand-carved furniture, dark as cocoa, lined every available wall. Silk cushions adorned the couches, and octagonal windows were framed with intersecting scarlet squares that formed styled edges and corners.

Alameth settled into an armchair.

Jediah, who cradled baby Laszio, searched for a particular furnishing Nechum described to him earlier. Spotting the one that fit the description, he pointed Eran and Akela to a tower of shelves stacked with folded pictures. "Fetch a few pamphlets there. We'll need *prospects*."

Nechum and Jediah approached the main desk, and a young Chinese lady with a wispy ponytail and combed bangs smiled. Though her English diction slurred, she spoke confidently. "Hello. Welcome to Courtyard Hotel. I am Miss Xia Ju. You have reservation?"

Nechum responded in fluent Mandarin. "Yes, we are the Gershom family."

Gasping, the lady glowed. "You speak very well, sir! Just a moment, while I check your room status." She turned to the desk computer and jiggled that 'mouse' device Jediah became somewhat amused by. It looked nothing like a mouse to him, no matter which direction it was facing.

"Do you have your visas and passports?" she asked.

"Yes," Nechum responded.

She watched Nechum line up the papers and laughed, "You have a large family?"

"Indeed I do, miss. Although, you should see the size of my extended family." Nechum winked to Jediah.

Jediah choked down a chuckle. Who knew unassuming Nechum possessed a sense of humor?

The clerk continued typing. "How wonderful. We're allowed to have larger families too now," she said.

"Really?" Nechum asked. His eyebrows perked up. "They've abolished the single child policy?"

"Yes, now couples may have two children."

Nechum glanced to Jediah, then back to her. "Well, that's wonderful. Are you married?"

"No," she giggled. "But I will be soon."

"Congratulations," Nechum said. "May God bless you with those two children."

"Thank you," she said, before investigating the documents. "So you are Mr—"

"Neal. Neal Gershom, and this is my wife, Jemima." Nechum pulled Jediah into an awkward side hug. The two feigned affection, then promptly separated. Nechum then pointed to Alameth. "Over there is Alex, and that's Kayla and Aaron." He motioned toward Akela and Eran. "And finally, we have little Leslie." Nechum stroked Laszio's bald head.

Xia waved meekly at the little infant. "She's so adorable."

At that, Laszio wriggled in Jediah's grip. Jediah clenched his jaw as he struggled to keep Laszio from falling. "*Yep*, she's a *doll* all right." He slung Laszio over his shoulder and slapped his back hard, pretending to burp him.

"Oh!" the clerk exclaimed. "You speak Mandarin too?"

Jediah sucked in a breath. He forgot to speak English.

"That's great! Do you visit China often?" she asked.

Jediah fought for composure, both between his mistake and Laszio's squirming. "Actually, I've never been here before. You see, uh, my husband visited Beijing a while back for business. Had a lovely time of it, he did, and his stories of your country really turned my head."

The lady's eyes sparkled. Her cheeks rounded cutely, and she nodded her head in rapid small bows. "Thank you! Thank you!"

Laszio continued to fuss. Frustrated, Jediah gritted his teeth. "Um, *dear*, could you excuse us for a moment?"

Nechum's face tensed, but he managed a calm tone. "Of course. I've got much to take care of here anyway, so you and the kids relax."

"Thanks. Where's the, uh, restroom?" Jediah asked. After receiving directions, he hurried down the hall, darted inside the women's room, and accidentally hit Laszio's head against the swinging door.

"Ow!" Laszio's normal voice burst out.

"Quiet," Jediah shushed. Checking the stalls for occupants, he opened the diaper changing station and plopped the infant hard on his rump. "What was that all about?"

Laszio crossed his arms. "I'm supposed to be a boy."

"You *are* a boy."

"Named, Leslie?"

"That's a boy's name."

"Nechum didn't correct her."

Jediah threw his hands up. "Is this worth griping about?" he asked. "Look, Private, I know you're uncomfortable about this. I am too, but you don't have to *be* a child to *act* like a child." A foul stench caught Jediah off guard. His eyes widened. "Wait a second." He sniffed the air again. "Laszio? Did you?"

Shrinking into himself, Laszio darted his sheepish eyes side to side. "Did I what?"

Jediah ambushed Laszio and peeked into his diaper. A powerful whiff socked him in the eyes. He recoiled and pinched his burning nose. "Agh! You did!"

Laszio bowed his head like a criminal caught in the act. "Okay. Okay. The truth is... Ugh, look. I had to get out of there quick, okay? I didn't want you or anyone to know."

"But—but how? You didn't eat anything, did you?"

Laszio cocked an eyebrow. "You mean besides the gallons of milk from all the practiced bottle feedings? Nope. Not a thing."

Jediah grimaced and rubbed his brow. "Oh, for pity's sake. You couldn't keep it in?"

"I'm stuffed in a pint-sized dumpling with sausages for arms," Laszio complained. "How'd you think the *rest* of me would do?"

Retching at the disgusting thoughts invading his head, Jediah waved his hands. "Okay. Okay. I don't need details."

Laszio smirked. "So, *Mom*... You up to changing diapers?"

Jediah knew no amount of makeup could hide the sick shade of green his cheeks were turning. "Uh, how about you revert to angel form, bypass this... inconvenience, and we never speak of it again? Deal?"

"Deal."

Surrounded by his black mist, the demon of death, Yakum, hunched over his work. He guided tiny black tendrils with minute precision. Their branches multiplied, and chemical reactions fizzed as different portions fused together. Yakum eyed a particular batch. Grasping the concoction, he hardened it into a pellet, then rolled its smooth surface between his fingers. No leaks.

He patted a bagful of his prior babies with fondness. Much had improved since those earlier attempts. He had come to the cusp of his latest magnum opus, but his pestilence had yet to reach total immunity. Yakum long stewed over God's imposed limitations over him. He was a Destroyer stripped of power, and the effectiveness of his conjured illnesses grew tougher each year in this modern world.

Yakum recalled his former glory. His black plague, the hallmark of his career, he had achieved with little effort by harnessing toxins to fleas. Now, humans invent pesticides, vaccines, ventilators. God cheated him of his power. Now they attempt to cheat him, too. It was the last straw, the ultimate insult.

Yakum threw himself right back into his project. He couldn't stop. Not with perfection so near. Those Image Bearers needed to be reminded what real power is. They were feathers beating a mountain to even think they could defy death himself.

A whirring wind brushed his ear, yet Yakum paid little attention to his personal messenger demon, Moriel. He conducted his experiment as he spoke. "What news, Moriel? More data from Malkior? Or is Lucifer still pestering us over deadlines?" Yakum opened another bag and plinked a new pellet inside.

"Malkior is in the Abyss. For good." Moriel answered.

Yakum's mist lost form. He stood up and snapped around. "What? The Abyss? Who dared to—"

Moriel shrugged. "It's keeper, Captain Jediah, of course."

Yakum clenched a fist. "Jediah." He punched the desk with enough spiritual force to topple the physical lamp. It hit the floor, breaking the bulb.

Moriel's skinny wings twitched. "The project is ruined then," he bemoaned.

"No!" Yakum said. "No. It's just a minor setback. Let me think."

"Fine, but before you start," Moriel pulled out black parchment. "You might want to read this."

"Ugh. It's probably another of Lucifer's dreary list of demands along with his superfluous titles," Yakum sneered. "Fine. Hand it over." He marched to Moriel and ripped the letter from the messenger's hand. "Honestly, I'd be done by now if he'd stop micromanaging me."

Moriel shook his head. "It's not Lucifer this time."

"Not Lucifer?" Yakum asked. "Then who—"

"Would you just read the darn thing?" Moriel muttered, exasperated.

Put out yet tolerant of his closest compatriot, Yakum read the glowing crimson text. "High alert. Jediah of the Abyss is at your doorstep. Hide yourself. Look for my arrival. I am coming to incarcerate him. Lucifer sends his regards. Signed: Master Elazar."

Yakum frowned and tossed the black parchment aside. "Hide? Elazar that disloyal, wingless featherweight telling me to hide?"

"Jediah took down Malkior, my lord," Moriel pointed out. "That coward probably squealed your location. We'll have to leave now."

"I'm not going anywhere! Who is this soldier to think he can best a demon of death?"

"The same one named Apollyon's Bane," Moriel said in his trademark dry tone.

Yakum groaned. He hated it when someone besides himself made a valid point. He thought through the message again. "And why Elazar? How did Lucifer even rein him in, anyway?"

Moriel shrugged and grinned. "Our prince must have given him an offer he couldn't refuse."

Yakum splashed black vapor into Moriel's face. "Moriel, your overindulgence in human entertainment concerns me sometimes."

Moriel sputtered. After wiping the spit off his chin, he straightened his posture and brushed black specks off his clothes. "You're no fun at all," he mumbled. "Look. All I know is that Elazar's only in this for revenge."

Yakum crossed his arms. "Revenge, huh? And I'm guessing Lucifer just wants Jediah's wings to control the Abyss, right?"

"That's what I heard." Moriel's sly grin grew. "I know that look, Yakum. What are you thinking?"

"I'm thinking," Yakum droned. "A remarkable specimen for study has just stepped through my door. After all, if Jediah's coming, we aught to welcome him properly." Yakum again picked up Elazar's letter and stared into it. "Okay, Elazar. I'll hide." He turned to Moriel. "Send word across Beijing that we're trading locations and prepare scouting parties. I want every soldier in my province on the hunt."

Moriel bowed. "As you wish, sir."

"Elazar will have Jediah and the wings," Yakum mused. "After I toss him the leftovers."

Chapter 20

ALAMETH PACED CIRCLES. The dawn promised an exquisite day. The golden sphere's radiance trickled in, unhindered by the barrier Nechum set outside to barricade their rooms, but Alameth wished it would retreat behind the horizon where it came from. This morning's hours were leading to the night he dreaded most all year. He didn't want to relive its shadow again... not away from home... Not away from his Lord's presence.

Alameth's hands chilled as if they contracted a fever. A weak malaise within snowballed to a staggering ache in his limbs. He chastised his mind, ashamed of it for even entertaining his traumas again. Flashbacks shouldn't even bother him after this long.

"*Prayer,*" he reasoned. "*I just need prayer.*" Choosing a corner of his bed, Alameth sat and collected his hands.

A soft tapping at his door interrupted. "Alameth?" Nechum called. "Alameth? May I enter?"

Noticing his own stiffness, Alameth released his posture. It didn't have to be so straight. "Yes, brother."

Nechum phased through the solid door, and gazed at him with his usual, wonderful kind intent. "Having trouble again?"

Hesitating to answer but then slowly giving in, Alameth nodded. "I am."

Nechum's eyes darted to the window. "Do you wish to talk about it?"

Alameth resisted the idea. He shared many things with him and Jediah already. It had relieved him in inexplicable ways, but his behavior right then, over something he considered a non-issue, was shameful—immature. But how would Nechum view him after this one?

Then Alameth shook his head. *Pride. This was pride.* "You know what?" he said, as he turned to Nechum. "Yes. Yes, I need to talk about it."

Another knock sounded at the door. Laszio poked his head in. "Good morning. Jediah wants us gathered in the breakfast area."

"Thank you, Laszio," Nechum said. "We'll be there in a few minutes." After Laszio left, Nechum rubbed his hands and stared into them for a while. He released a breath and nodded. "It's because it's Passover, the Night of the Grey, isn't it?"

Alameth's eyebrows raised. The empathic sense of ministry angels was truly a gift. For a third round, talking with Nechum would be easier than ever before. Besides, he found it comforting.

Savory aromas welcomed guests to the hotel's restaurant. Cream-colored tablecloths with embroidered dragons on their corners glowed under a strengthening sun. The breakfast buffet presented a blend of eastern specialties and western staples. Fried egg rolls sat next to sausage links. Cereal dispensers were beside the rice containers, and many a cuisine was spiced, seasoned, or flavored to satisfy every craving. Many a plate was overfilled.

Jediah pressed his back against the lacquered chair. He twirled a toothpick between his fingers as he stared at his herbed potatoes and scrambled eggs. No matter if it were dumpster scraps or the freshest and finest, human food never looked edible to him. His inability to hunger or build any sort of appetite didn't help either. He asked himself again why he even directed them to eat at all. Spiritual beings didn't require sustenance, but Jediah once again reminded himself of their precarious position. He was now both the hunter and the hunted. Yakum could be anywhere. Elazar could be anywhere, and so long as humans ate to live, no detail was too extreme for him and his team not to follow.

"We're an American tourist family," he mentally repeated. *"An American, tourist family consuming a mortal's basic breakfast."*

Baby Laszio sat in his high chair. He cast disgusted glances at his bowl of mush Nechum called 'baby food.'

Jediah suddenly felt a tad more thankful. At least his meal could be identified apart from camel spit.

Akela claimed his spot at the table. Steam wafted off the fifty kinds of rice he sampled and the succulent oils sizzling from his bacon. He took a long, satisfied whiff from his platter. A queasy sensation squeezed Jediah's stomach, but Akela smiled at him. "Sure, it's not heaven's food, but it's really not half bad. I mean, give humans some credit. It's not like they have zero taste."

Jediah nodded yet remained unconvinced. It still looked revolting.

"Of course," Akela added. "If you really really hate your food, you can always wash it down with God's original classic: crisp cold milk." He lifted his beverage as though to toast.

"I'll keep that in mind," Jediah chuckled.

Laszio clutched his belly. "Please. No more talk about milk. It makes me nauseous."

A passing boy, having heard Laszio, paused. He squinted hard at the baby.

Avoiding eye contact with the kid, Jediah covered his mouth. "Baby talk," he rushed between coughs. In an instant, Laszio flailed his arms and gurgled saliva bubbles. The disgusted child hurried off. Laszio, however, had his eyes closed and continued his spasm.

Jediah cleared his throat and kicked Laszio's seat.

Turning a deeper red than before, Laszio stopped and thudded his forehead into his food tray.

"Is the baby misbehaving?" Eran said with a smile. "I recommend spankings." He winked at a glaring Laszio as he passed and claimed a seat. "Are we all here or waiting for someone?"

Akela rolled rice grains in tight circles with his fork. "Just one."

Scooting his seat up to the table, a somber Nechum straightened his knife to be perfectly parallel with the plate. "Just give Ala-Alex a minute."

Jediah spotted 'teenage' Alameth lingering beside the buffet line, unmoved and unmotivated. When he finally joined the stream of hungry customers, he bypassed one nutritional option after another to the point where Jediah doubted he would pick anything. Minutes later, Alameth returned with the last lonely piece of buttered toast.

They prayed, then ate in silence. As Jediah worked through his meal, he couldn't help but think of Chloe again. The letter haunted him all night. He relived the hours of writing and re-writing he spent. How no draft satisfied. How none seemed to hit the mark. It squeezed his head, remembering how he agonized over every teeny little word. What to include. What to omit.

Jediah commanded himself to stop this crazy worry cycle. "*You finished the letter,*" he chastised. "*Akela took it. God brought it to her. What happens happens. End of story.*"

Jediah sighed under his breath. Then why wasn't he more relaxed? What nagged him so? Is it that he feared it wasn't enough? Would the message fly over her head? What hope did he have that an angel like him could write sensibly to a young girl about a subject he had little understanding about?

"Your food not agreeing with you?"

Jediah almost jolted.

Nechum was leaning toward him. He gestured to his plate.

Shaking his head 'no', Jediah took a swift bite of potatoes. Its hints of garlic and basil tasted far better than expected.

Loud thuds and shouts echoed from outside. The angels all froze. With a burst of light and feathers, an army angel tore through the dining hall. Two demonic warriors chased him while a second pair of demons tried to intercept their prey at the front. The angelic soldier fanned his sharpened feathers in defiance.

Eran and Laszio cast expectant glances at Jediah.

Jediah, however, bowed his head over his platter and hoped they'd follow suit. He regretted it, but they couldn't help. Not this time. "So," he asked. "Have you kids decided where you'd like to visit?" He plopped a pile of pamphlets on the table. "You never know what you'll find."

Laszio's legs ached from disuse. Nechum had carried him through the Forbidden City's courtyards for hours. Curved river moats flowed under carved stone bridges. Yards of dull flat stone were accentuated by magnificent palaces that cropped up in every direction. Their scarlet walls glared in the sunlight. Sloped roofs of glazed tiles gleamed pristine golden brown, and tiny metal creatures guarded their four corners in neat rows.

Laszio did not like wandering such exposed spaces. His warrior instincts wanted to find cover. They were too vulnerable standing out there, and what if Yakum—or worse—Elazar were around and spotted them first?

Nechum carried Laszio to another palace called the Hall of Preserving Harmony, and just like so many other key architectures, the opened doors had low bars, permitting tourists like them only a peek inside. Laszio craned as much as his short neck allowed. Crowding spectators did not help, and he ended up seeing little more than the tallest point of an oaken-framed golden screen, the usual backdrop to the third of many thrones this opulent maze possessed. He looked at Nechum and Eran to see if they saw anything, but by their stoic expressions, Laszio guessed they didn't.

After another few minutes and finding another blocked area, Laszio grunted. They couldn't cover a fraction of this city within a city at that rate. They needed to move beyond the public eye.

Recalling the signals they devised before setting out, Laszio winked to 'toddler' Eran.

Eran then tugged Nechum's sleeve like any four-year-old would. He bounced on his heels and pointed at the restricted western gates to the inner courts. "Daddy? Daddy? Can we go explore? Please, can we? Can we? Can we?"

Laszio almost burst out laughing at Eran's pouty lip.

Nechum frowned. He glanced at the security staff nearby. They were busy confiscating a man's phone for taking unauthorized photos. Nechum bent down and gestured toward the stern men. "Okay," he whispered. "But be quick."

Rising on tiptoes, Eran took Laszio in his deceptively powerful arms. "Is daddy coming too?" he whispered.

Nechum watched the occupied guards again. "I'd be spotted. Go on."

Eran adjusted his hold on Laszio. "Meet us at the outer gate."

"Be careful," Nechum implored.

A bigger crowd began passing by. Eran weaved through the throng, slipped past the guards, and behind a secluded lion statue next to the barred gate. He set Laszio down. "Be my lookout, okay?" Kneeling by the gate, he wrapped thin fingers around the metal posts. They squealed as he pulled.

Laszio's heart jumped to his throat. "Shh! They'll hear us."

"It's the only way," Eran argued back. He bent the posts ajar by another centimeter.

Laszio rolled onto his belly for a peek behind. The guards now regarded the squealing gate with confused looks. Laszio scurried backwards. "Hurry!"

"We're in," Eran whispered. "Come on." He pulled Laszio through the gate, then re-shaped the rods. They ducked behind the wall. Two shadows lingered over their previous spot. Frigid moisture beaded Laszio's brow, but in moments, the shadows left.

Laszio hardly had time to loosen up and question why liquid sprouted on his skin before Eran sprinted with him across the garden pavement. He slipped down to his chin in Eran's arms, and the jostling squeezed his throat.

Eran stopped under a bush in the shadiest spot under the thickest tree. "Where to now?" he asked.

Laszio waved his pudgy arms, hitting Eran's cheek. "Let! Go!" he gagged. Eran released him, and Laszio coughed oxygen back through what felt like a collapsed windpipe.

Apologizing, Eran lifted him back to his feet, but the second Eran removed his hands, Laszio's chubby legs buckled. He plopped backwards on his padded diaper just as a figure passed. They froze. For this stranger wasn't mortal.

Eran gazed in uncomfortable silence as the demon soldier walked on. He lifted to his knees for a better view. Laszio also scanned their surroundings through a network of twigs and leaves. Armored demon sentries patrolled sidewalks, trees, and rooms just ahead. "Bingo," Laszio whispered. "A demon lord's entourage if I ever saw one."

In his attempt to stand, Laszio's baby body flopped him forward. "Oh, for pity's sake," he groaned. "I can't move in this."

"Then we'll have to continue as angels." said Eran. He cast fast glances. "No one's around. Change. Quickly."

The Great Wall stretched through the East and Western hills as a towering ribbon of stone. To walk its cobbled paths was akin to walking on air. Jediah thanked God only the sections closest to Beijing mattered. It was massive enough to inspect, let alone its full thirteen thousand one hundred and seventy-one miles.

Jediah stirred to the signs of a raging battle in the northeast distance. Wings electrified the sky as angels were locked in a bitter war with a demonic battalion. He squinted to see the fight but opted to use the old-fashioned camera Nechum bought for them. Peering through its optic lens, he zeroed in on a particularly dark blur, but the demon's movements were too spastic. The second he flew into view, he flew right out of it.

A glint of red caught Jediah's attention. He increased magnification on the direction it came from. A demon was trapped in a chokehold. His newest scar bled a profound amount and dripped into the angel's sleeve. Jediah's human heart bruised against his rib cage. The demon freed himself. Jediah's stomach dropped. Dagger feathers swiped.

"Mom?"

Jediah fumbled the camera. It bounced out of his hand, and he rescued it mere seconds before it dropped over the Wall's side.

Akela cringed. "Oops, sorry," he said.

Hugging the device to himself, Jediah relaxed to find it unbroken. His neck heated, but he subdued his rising anger. "Don't. Do. That," he warned. "What is it?"

"Um, I think we're being followed," Akela said.

A gripping anxiety seized Jediah. He pulled Akela into a corner by the shoulder. "Who? By who?" he demanded.

Akela kept his eyes on him but began gesturing his head to the left.

Jediah peeked over his left shoulder. Two ministry demons walked towards them. They inspected the faces of every person they passed with intense scrutiny.

His eyes wide and unsure, Akela lowered his voice as he spoke. "They've tailed us for the past five minutes. Like they're looking for something."

'Or someone,' Jediah suspected. He released a breath to calm his nerves. "We need to leave."

Akela nodded. "I'll get Alameth." He hurried up the eroded stairs.

A stray white shot struck the pavement a foot away from Jediah. Despite being in human form, his legs registered the energy's heat spray. He turned around. The battle was coming to them.

Laszio and Eran stuck close to the compacted walls of the inner court—the ancestral home of emperors, their wives, and their concubines. They dashed across another section of the imperial gardens and struggled not to get lost amidst hundreds of buildings and their thousands of rooms.

Hearing another patrol coming their way, the two angels vaulted several flights of stairs and hid in the rafters of a pavilion roof. Detailed artistry in the extremes met them inside. Hammered gold crammed every spare inch of the ceiling. Dragons and deities were painted in patterned swirls of white, red, blue, and green, and the dying light of oncoming sunset elongated on the floor to set the ornaments aflame.

Laszio shook his head in disappointment at the poor use of such extravagance. All this focused on a line of mere men who claimed divinity as 'sons of heaven.' How did owning an abundance of colored metal entitle one to worship?

Enemy footsteps quieted below. Laszio released the tension in his shoulders. "Eran," he whispered. "We can't risk this anymore. We have to head back."

"No," Eran rebutted. "Not until we get a clear sighting of Yakum."

Laszio watched the fading sunlight. "But what about Nechum?"

"Shh! I'm thinking!" Eran scrunched his eyes and pinched the bridge of his nose. "Do you think Yakum could be hiding underground?"

"I don't know about Yakum, but *they're* not," Laszio said as two demon guards climbed the stairs. The loose side-platings of their helmets clattered at their slightest move.

Dropping down, then hurrying at a soft run, they jumped and sat behind a low wall on the opposite side of the pavilion. A black-faced cat with white paws was sitting erect beside them. Ever unconcerned, it blinked its sleepy sapphire eyes.

"You sure you saw someone?"

Laszio and Eran stiffened at the heavy, timbred voice.

"I thought so," a second voice answered.

Laszio's fingers twitched as they gripped his sticks. Anticipating discovery, he regulated his breaths and attempted to remap every path and exit. *They had to escape. They had to escape. They had to—*

A shrieking meow and a crazy ball of fur and claws flew over his head. The cat bolted over the wall, hissing. Startled and confused, Laszio turned to Eran. He sat there with a guilty wince. Whatever he did set the spooked feline off. Eran shrugged again at Laszio and mouthed an apology to the poor thing.

"A cat," the first demon droned. "You saw a stupid cat."

"I swear it was bigger than a cat," the second defended.

"You mean bigger than that pigeon you spotted this morning?"

"Don't be stupid."

"I'm *with* stupid."

Sweet relief permitted Laszio to relax his hands. His feathered armor opened and closed in release. Metal chinked again, and he re-stiffened.

"Would you stop?" the first demon called. "The daily tourist convention is over, and lord Yakum expects us at the Hall of Supreme Harmony tonight."

The second demon responded in a comical baritone. "The Haaall of Supreeeme Harmony-y-y-y. Pfft. Could a name be any more pretentious?"

"You mean like yours?"

"Maher-shalal-hash-baz sounds awesome. You're just jealous."

The first demon groaned. "Must you rename yourself every year? Are you that insecure? An exhausting mouthful like that should be a crime."

"Hey," the second defended. "This 'mouthful' strikes fear."

"It strikes tongue cramps," the first countered. "but if Elazar arrives before we do, Yakum will cut *ours* out."

Laszio's ears pricked at Elazar's name. His nervous energy tingled. It couldn't be real. How did Elazar track them? Did he already locate Jediah? Was it all too late? Elazar's menace suddenly morphed into something fearsome and larger than life.

"*No,*' Laszio reasoned. *"This was perfect. If they played this right, they could neutralize Elazar's threat and give Jediah the intel he needed to ambush Yakum."*

Dwelling on the potential benefits of their coming opportunity, Laszio looked to Eran. The grey of his friend's eyes churned in equal determination. He was thinking the same thing. Sharing a nod, they raised and clinked their weapons together.

Chapter 21

DUSK HAD DWINDLED AND expired. Alone in his room and in his true form, Jediah leaned over the desk. The fifth try at his second letter to Chloe stared at him, criticizing him, mocking him. He pivoted his heel in and out on the plush carpet. He set his elbows on the rosewood, but no rest would come. Half of his team was missing. Yakum ruled the streets. Elazar thirsted for revenge, and Jediah's mind again started that subtle climb from worry to hysterics.

Head in his hands, he ran his fingers through his hair. It seemed the only way to console his anxiety was to throw himself into trying to convince her again. Chloe needed salvation. He needed her to need salvation. As his fingers reached Chloe's braid, horrible shame slapped him in the face.

Was all this really for Chloe? Or for myself?

Jediah jerked straight up as if the braid bit him. The motives behind his present actions clarified. "God forgive me," he whispered.

Hands clinging to his disguise cloak, he retreated to the octagonal window in search of God's nightly firmaments. The moon dwelt out of view. Artificial lights choked out the stars. Denied of their comfort, Jediah never felt more distant from his King's presence. He wandered past the dresser, but the mirror gave him pause.

His pasty pallor and sunless eyes seemed more akin to the human's ghostly fictions than a true spiritual entity, and it frightened him. That sinking feeling, the sensation of plummeting a million miles, refused to leave him alone.

Elazar's words still administered their poison in drops, and the venom's concentration doubled with each drip. *"What would an apology fix, anyway? Nothing. Absolutely. Nothing."*

Jediah tried shaking its memory out of his head, yet the old guilt spiked.

You want someone to heal you, but you know no one will. You seek forgiveness, but there's none. No cure. No resolution.

Jediah's own inner voice fought back. *No, there's hope for me. There has to be.*

"There is no hope for you," Elazar's voice answered, as though it gained its owner's sentience. "*Your God doesn't care about you. He'd rather redeem undeserving worms than you.*"

"Enough!" his inner voice commanded. "*The Lord my God declared, 'This is the one to whom I will look: he who is humble and contrite in spirit.*'" Jediah calmed a little. "*Surely, He has extended some mercy to me—an imperfect vessel.*"

Stilling his spirit, Jediah sat down on the edge of the bed. He checked the mirror. His brown eyes still missed their golden pigment.

Then why did it all still hurt?

His heart returned to longing for the blessed mystery. To be joined to the Father. To be guided by the Spirit. To be cleansed by the Son.

Entering the living room, Akela adjusted his leather shoulder pads. It felt good to be back in uniform again. He stretched his wings. "Close call at the Wall, wasn't it, Alameth?" He said. "I sure hope the others will return soon." He stopped and bit his tongue.

Alameth sat cross-legged before the low coffee table. The silver strands of his hair glistened among his ebony locks that freely laid over his shoulders.

Akela glanced at the clock. *Two minutes till midnight.* He watched Alameth, wondering if he worried over their missing teammates, too. Slow and methodical, Alameth hid his hair under his hood in ceremony. His hands folded together.

It hit Akela. It was the Night of the Grey—the annual commemoration of Christ's death on the cross. Akela rubbed his head in embarrassment. Once again, his enjoyment of the adventure had blindsided him to his brother. He reflected on the day, recounting every visible clue that should've been obvious. A new overpowering drive to join Alameth threw Akela's thoughts into a race.

There has to be something I can contribute. Akela wrung his hands. His eyes fell on the dining table centerpiece. He then grabbed for the candlestick, but his hand phased through. Focusing again, he felt the weight of the copper stand and the waxen stick. Then, taking silent steps, he approached Alameth from behind. He cleared his throat. "Um, Alameth?"

The angel of death didn't so much as fidget and said, "Now isn't a good time to talk, brother."

"Actually," Akela walked around him and set the candle on the table. "I wanted to ask if I could observe the Night of the Grey with you." Sitting himself down on the opposite side, he placed his hands on his knees.

Alameth's eyebrows raised, and the severity in his face softened.

Akela suddenly realized he didn't light the candle. "Oops!" he exclaimed as he jumped to his feet. "Just a sec." He hurried to the kitchen counter and retrieved the matches. He then leaped, slid on his knees right back into his spot, and leaned forward with the packet.

Alameth, however, shook his head with a demure chuckle. "Allow me." A sliver of fog attached itself to the wick. Its tip glowed pure white until it kindled a flame right through the dimensions.

Akela tossed the matches and plopped back down. "You could've just told me you could do that," he muttered.

"You didn't ask."

Like the Spirit anchored to a grieving heart, the seedling of light balanced on the feeble wick. Weak orange strengthened to warm gold. The room's shadows lingered close, yet they could not snuff out something so small. The candle lulled Akela into a place of remembrance, and his ever restless mind quieted without the need to be reined in.

Alameth's somber humming began. Its soothing melody issued so quietly it seemed imaginary. Loose and undefined, it lacked conventional rhythm, but like the crooning of the Armenian duduk, the notes mourned the Sacrificial Lamb in fluctuating sobs.

Akela often avoided sorrow. With Christ's greatest victory won, what need was there to dwell on how He suffered? He had listened to the angels of death sing this song countless times, yet sitting there, listening to Alameth begin it with such earnest need, Akela found this kind of sadness to be comforting. Perhaps because it acknowledged past evils without flinching and treaded despair's valley unto dawn. It was accepting, honest, yet unafraid.

Another voice from outside paired with Alameth's. Their harmonies melted together. Akela envisioned the second angel of death standing on their roof. His rolling mists would stream down his long grey coat, dissipating like a vapor on the garden below. His hood would be pulled down, yet he'd behold the sky. More non-projecting voices from other Destroyers merged into a substantial whole.

Alameth's hums turned to words. Soon the whole globe would hear the Night of the Grey once more. No spiritual bystander could ignore or interrupt it. It captivated the earth. It permeated the waters. It beckoned mankind.

Mark your posts.
Paint your doors.
Let not your lintel be bare.
Death visits once.
Death visits all.
Come pour your hearts and be spared.

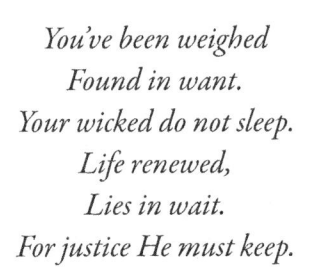

You've been weighed
Found in want.
Your wicked do not sleep.
Life renewed,
Lies in wait.
For justice He must keep.

David's line,
Judah's heir,
Why to you must He go?
You are sin.
Blood your price,

For You He bows so low.

Adam's sons,
Do not sleep.
Your Savior suffers awake.
Sweat like blood,
Wrath's cup poured,
Each drop He still chose to take.

Bloodied robe,
Thorns His crown,
His hair they did shave.
Quiet still,
Voice unheard.
No defense Christ gave.

God's own Son,
What say ye?
For Him what's worthy of trade?
Silver coins,
A criminal man,
Sold. You bartered and paid.

Nails in hands.
Mouth so dry,
The Father turns away.
Severed tie,
No relief,
Forsaken was He that day.

It is done.
Mountains quake.
The curtain's torn in two.
Love unloved,
Love most pure,
This love He meant for you.

Alameth stopped, letting the moment reflect in silence. Under the candle's glow, Akela encountered a peace upon him that defied his former sullenness.

Akela glanced out the glass door. The earlier sunset indeed shed red. He turned back to Alameth. "It's going to be a beautiful morning."

Opening his eyes, Alameth smiled. The corners of his lips reached so high, his cheeks drew up and revealed a shimmering light in his eye.

Touched by the sight of it, Akela tilted his head. "I knew it."

Alameth bent his neck a little lower. "Knew what?"

"That you had the best smile."

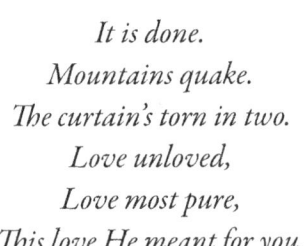

The Night of the Grey's song echoed in Jediah long after it finished. Recounting the cost His King paid for mankind shamed him. Who was he to mistreat the sacrifice of the Son and muddy its message with his personal agenda? And who was he to endanger Chloe with his innumerable enemies seeking more ways to hurt him?

Sitting on the edge of his bed, Jediah gazed in the mirror and at the sword hilt that loomed above his right shoulder. He fingered Chloe's braid, lingering on it as long as he could.

His hand moved from the braid to the hilt. The 'shing' of the blade leaving his scabbard made him feel dead inside. The vacancy in his stare befitted an executioner, but he couldn't afford to register on an emotional level. This he knew, otherwise he could not go through with this. It was for the best.

Jediah pulled the braid upward. It emerged from the thicker hair, and he set the razor's edge beneath it.

A cradled tear escaped from the corner of his eye.

The Lord must increase in her life... and I must decrease.

Upward thrust. He clutched a lump of hair in his hand, and the spot on his head felt bare. Jediah let go. Chloe's braid, string and all, fell lifeless at his side.

Chapter 22

ELAZAR STOOD BEFORE the opened doors of the Forbidden City's Hall of Supreme Harmony. Two sentries tipped their heads, pounded their spears once on the concrete, then stepped aside to let him in. He scoffed under his breath. It seemed *somebody* was compensating for something. More guards in similar helmets lined either side of the rich carpet. Dragon etchings curled around massive golden pillars. Incense urns smoked black, and Yakum himself sat elevated with the splendor flanking him above, behind, and below. His rolling dark mists encircled him.

Yakum extended a hand to Elazar. The opulent patterns hidden in his silken sleeve revealed themselves in a fleeting sheen. "Welcome, Elazar, to my principality."

Elazar cocked an eyebrow. "The pleasure is mine," he droned. "Tell me. When did 'hiding' mean mustering armies and sheltering in the most obvious landmark possible? Hardly subtle."

Yakum's eyes narrowed. "I have my reasons."

"Sure you do. Because Destroyers, as your kind are so aptly called, require backup," Elazar said as he shoved his hands into his pockets.

Cocking his head, Yakum gave a strained faux grin. "Whatever happened to your smashing headdress, Huitzilopochtli? Ran out of chicken feathers?" he asked.

"You know. I actually reserved some level of respect for you," Elazar remarked. "So don't ruin it with cheap-shots."

"Oh?" said Yakum as he raised his chin.

Elazar smirked. "Don't get too excited, smokey. I still don't like you."

Yakum rose to his feet. Mists that billowed from under his robe floated him down. The guards pounded their spears twice in sync, then dispersed to the far corners and the walls.

Elazar inspected Yakum's stance. He honed his empathic sense and sensed Yakum's irritated killer instinct. Elazar shielded his hand and captured the pellet Yakum aimed at his chest in a round shield. The pestilence popped. Ink swirled and filled the sphere, and Elazar threw it at the closest guard. The caged fumes burst, and the unfortunate sod clawed at his throat. He dropped to the floor, writhing and kicking.

"Interesting," Yakum said, smiling at Elazar. "Seems rumors of your talent weren't completely unfounded." He gave a head nod to one of the guards. The dutiful demon nodded back and dragged the convulsing victim out. "So. Have you found Jediah yet?"

Agitated, Elazar crossed his arms. "If I did, I wouldn't have bothered coming to you."

Yakum fingered the platinum buttons of his collar. "I thought you wouldn't, hence why I requested your presence. I hoped you might hear out my proposal."

"Your proposal?" Elazar huffed. "First you insult me; you chuck poison at me, now you want to make deals?"

"You accepted prince Lucifer's deal," Yakum challenged.

"His interests simply suited mine."

"And you're interested in Jediah's humiliation, right? Well, consider this a bonus deal. An extra cherry to throw on top, if you will. How would you like to double Jediah's suffering?"

Intrigued yet cautious, Elazar folded his hands behind his back. "I'm listening."

Yakum gestured toward the vacant spot where the infected guard once stood. "You just witnessed my latest and finest work."

"Yes," Elazar replied. "Lucifer mentioned you were cooking something in your kitchen."

"It's near perfect, but—" Yakum stepped closer. "I need the perfect specimen for a final trial."

Elazar stepped back, minding the distance between himself and Yakum's fog. "And that's what you want Jediah for."

Tilting his head, Yakum spread his lips in a crooked smile. "Exactly. If my plague can utterly wreck a spiritual being like him, the human populace won't stand a chance."

"M-hm," Elazar said. He nodded and rubbed his chin. "And I suppose his wings, the key to the Abyss, doesn't interest you whatsoever."

Yakum shook his head and answered, "None whatsoever."

Elazar's energy boiled as he sensed Yakum's deceiving heart tip its hand. Yakum was lying. No question about it, and he had mustered his armies so he could hog Jediah for himself too. Elazar ground his teeth beneath closed lips. Jediah was his. If Yakum intended to deprive him of his revenge...

But knowing it'd be foolishness to upset a demon lord in the middle of his base, Elazar played along. "And what are your terms for this 'arrangement'?" he asked.

"Simple," Yakum said. "Once Jediah is ours, we'll take him to my caves deep in the western mountains. I finish my experiment. You deliver him to Lucifer. Lucifer gets his key. Everybody wins, and you'll get to enjoy the 'fun' every step of the way."

Elazar stroked a hand through his hair. "Tempting. Very tempting," he replied. "But I'm going to have to decline."

Yakum gave an insulted, bewildered look. "Decline?"

"Lucifer made himself clear when we struck our bargain. Jediah and his key are to be turned over to him immediately. No exceptions." Elazar shot a firm glare. "And I *will* honor our agreement."

"Pfft!" Yakum scoffed. "What's this nonsense I'm hearing? 'Honor your agreement'? I thought you hated Lucifer. You're not loyal to him."

"But I *am* loyal to my word," Elazar growled. "I made a promise, and I am keeping it. Something a backstabber like you could never understand."

"Look who's talking!" Yakum convulsed in a roaring laughter. His face turned red, and he wiped his tearing eyes. "You turned on Jediah, your closest friend, centuries ago, and you wanna talk about backstabbing."

Elazar clenched his fists. Glowing red filled his fingers, lighting the underside of his face. His scar throbbed. "I didn't betray anyone," he insisted. "*He* betrayed me."

Pressing a hand over his chest, Yakum pushed out a breath and stopped chortling. "Oh stop. I heard the stories about your falling out. You might be an independent, Elazar, but you're every bit a demon as I am."

Elazar's hands shook. "I said, 'I betrayed no one,'" he growled. "And I am *nothing* like you." His anger reaching its peak, he relinquished his compounding energy and pivoted around to leave.

"Then who struck first?" Yakum called out. "You? Or Jediah?"

Elazar stopped at the doors. A regretful sorrow, the kind he spent centuries trying to kill, strangled his throat. "My original deal with Lucifer stands," he finally said. "I settle my score against Jediah. Lucifer gets his key. You get to keep your freedom. And you'd best hope it doesn't change."

Elazar stepped into the chilled air, but something was off. The two sentries from before had abandoned their posts. Elazar's chest tingled. His attention turned to two human workers. Faces careworn, they swept and collected the plastic cups and paper scraps close to the inner court's western walls. One wheeled the trash bin. The other collected the junk. Elazar scowled. Whoever attempted this trickery were was an absolute moron. No human cleaned trash at three in the morning.

Elazar tailed them one step at a time. The janitors quickened their gait, and their trash barrel's rumbling wheels curved around a small gateway. Elazar slowed. He bent his knees, deepening his stance. Then he turned into a walled-in pass—likened to a hallway without a ceiling. The janitor's abandoned broom clunked against the lonely trash barrel. Lifting a glowing hand, Elazar walked further in. The two men were nowhere to be seen, but his empathic sense picked up a presence.

Elazar snapped around and caught an airborne spear in his shielded hand. Hot energy coursed through his fingers, and the oaken shaft snapped. His attacker, one of the two guards he met at the palace door, rushed him. Elazar dodged, then strangled him with a force-field. He lifted him higher by the neck. The soldier's pointing feet gyrated in frantic efforts for the ground.

Elazar's limbs buzzed in a euphoric rush. "If you or your master Yakum throws something at me again," he said. "So help me—" Elazar banged the sentry around hard enough to split stone, but then he spotted red and gold colors hiding under the demon's burgundy cloak. Confused, Elazar slammed him on his stomach. His helmet rolled off.

An angel glared back. Gold dripped from his nose, lips, and temples. A braided, sandy lock hung in front of his right eye.

Elazar chewed his lip. It was one of Jediah's wingmen. The smallest one. "Ah. A familiar face," he commented. "It's Laszio isn't it?" He used another shield to pull the stringed sticks off the angel's belt and tossed them out of reach. "Well now, little sparrow, am I a dog that you come at with sticks?"

Though winded, the angel grinned through pained breaths. "Interesting choice of words."

A golden flash came at Elazar from the side. Elazar bent backwards. The second disguised angel's fist brushed the tip of his nose, scorching it with its coat of hardened feathers. Stepping aside, Elazar faced him directly. "Which makes you Eran," he guessed.

Eran leaned to swing another punch, but hesitated. His feather gauntlets were raised, yet an anxiety belied the fighting spirit from his eyes.

Elazar grinned and waved his shielded hands in mocking circles. "Come now," he goaded. "You've thrown your hat into the ring. Now do it!" Noticing Laszio's hand reaching to grab his ankle, Elazar stomped on it. Eran lunged, but Elazar grabbed and twisted Eran's arm until it popped. Eran screamed. He plopped on his side and clutched his mangled shoulder. Elazar then stripped off his helmet. A black braid similar to Laszio's flipped so hard with it, its silver bead hit the pavement. The angels laid there silent.

Battle over, Elazar shook out his hands. "You are those two pests who interrupted my reunion with Jediah," he said. "Honestly, I half-expected more from Jediah's wingmen, but it wouldn't surprise me if you're both from the bottom of his barrel, either. He's always had a soft spot for pet projects."

"Save it," Laszio, the blonde, retorted. He propped himself on one elbow and tried to stand.

Elazar grabbed his knife, and a scream ripped from Laszio's mouth as he stabbed his hand clean through.

"Laszio!" Eran cried. The ferocity in his glower would frighten a bear into her den.

Elazar yanked the blade out, grabbed Eran by the hair, and pressed the wetted edge against his neck. "What're you two doing here? Out breaking curfew?" he interrogated.

Before Eran could answer, Elazar heard hands and knees shuffling behind him. He looked to see Laszio's shoulders shaking in another attempt to get up. Gold dappled the pavement beneath him from the ruined hand he sheltered.

Elazar kicked him in the head. "Stay down or I'll hurt you again."

Laszio laid still, but his right eye opened to a slit. His hoarse voice rasped with harsh intensity, "May God deal with me, be it ever so severely, if I ever willfully stay down to the likes of you."

Elazar peered into Laszio's emotions. Anger, borderline hatred, fueled his stubbornness. This wasn't a mere mission to them. This vendetta of theirs was personal. "All this fury," Elazar commented. "You two must be real desperate to get rid of me."

"We know Lucifer hired you," Eran gasped.

Elazar's eyebrows raised. "Hm, smarter than I thought," he acknowledged.

"S-smarter than y-you'd ever be." Laszio added.

Elazar addressed Eran. "Your buddy isn't looking so good."

Eran lurched, but couldn't free himself from Elazar's grip. "Why do all this?" he demanded. "What has our captain ever done to you?"

"Interesting," Elazar mused. He cocked an eyebrow as he slipped into a strange calm. "So Jediah's never told you about me. Never mentioned me."

Eran's scowl turned to pure disgust and said, "If *I* knew a traitor like you, I wouldn't mention a peep about you either."

Elazar threw the knife aside and shook Eran by the collar. "I'm *not* the traitor," he shouted. "Jediah may pretend like he did nothing, and I don't matter to him. It's just like him to shove his old shames under the rug, but he knows I'm the hatchet he can't bury. The sin he can't wipe. Because I'll always keep coming back." Elazar called upon his force-fields to retrieve the knife and poise it over Eran's face. "And neither of you can fix me for him."

Elazar's knife scraped a dome shaped shield as he struck. The dome then expanded bigger. It shoved Elazar off Eran with such force, he tumbled and hit the left wall. Pain racked his lower back. His stunned arms wouldn't move, and Elazar hungered to rip the angel responsible apart.

Behind the shimmering veil, a copper-haired ministry angel slipped out of the bird he previously possessed. He rushed to Laszio and Eran's sides. His eyes darted back and forth between them, unsure who to help first. Pulling out a waterskin, he unscrewed the cap.

"Won't do you much good, little one," Elazar remarked. He got his bruising self to sit up. He balanced with a hand on the wall. "Shield or no shield, none of you are leaving here."

The ministry angel's eyes snapped to him. Anger tainted by apprehension dimmed his aquamarine eyes near grey. His eyebrows furrowed. His lips pursed tightly, but he unhooked his shawl, poured silver water in the fabric, then dabbed Laszio's wounds.

Elazar rolled his eye at such wasteful sentiments. "There's no point in using up your healing water," he advised. "Don't be an idiot."

"With all due respect, sir," the ministry angel replied, his tone grave. "I'm not the one who made an enemy out of the Alpha and Omega." The angel's eyes regained a luster so vibrant, their former green and blue pigments tripled to include violet.

A sudden loathing for the angel so overwhelmed Elazar, that it shocked even him how quickly it came. Crimson energy burst red sparks from his eye, and his face contorted so tight it split the edges of his mending scar wide open. "You listen, you piece of—"

Waves of black mist socked Elazar in the temple. His head snapped, and a weird, burning twang shot down his neck. He hit the floor. His consciousness wavered, but seconds before he went under, he heard Yakum's voice. "Pardon the interruption, whelp."

Yakum's boot, wreathed in living black, appeared in Elazar's tunneling vision.

"But I'll be needing them more than you," Yakum said. He knelt beside him. "You should have taken my offer."

The tunnel shrank, and all Elazar could do was slur the most repulsive insult that came to mind.

Chapter 23

THE MORNING'S FIFTH hour chimed. The palest blue crept in through Jediah's window, but it escalated his distress. No longer did he hope for Laszio, Eran and Nechum's arrival. He expected a ransom. His unblinking eyes stayed glued to the digital clock. He desperately prayed for the next seconds to tick faster. Each was another inch closer to the humans' normal daytime hours. He'd scour the entire city on foot as a human if he had to.

"Captain! Captain!"

Jediah's hand snapped to his sword.

Akela ran in. His whole being vibrated. "Come quick!"

Jediah dared to hope. "What is it?" he asked.

"Our brothers," Akela panted. "They're back." He sped right back down the hall to the living room.

A rush of relief washed Jediah's spirit. "Thank you, Father God." He dashed for the hall but stopped at the doorframe. In the corner of his eye, Chloe's second letter and braid laid abandoned on the dresser. He had avoided looking at them all night, and now his better judgment chastised him for not destroying them.

"Captain?" Akela called.

Unwilling to leave them lying around, Jediah collected braid and letter into his pocket. He dashed down the hallway and entered a living room dressed in the fledgling dawn's dreary grey.

Jediah's breath caught. Their moans were ragged. Half their feathers were missing, and the exposed sections of their uniforms were soaked in their own energy. Eran was lying on the softer rug. Alameth lingered close to him as he raised and lowered his legs, as if trying to mitigate pain to other areas. Nechum and Akela supported Laszio as he limped to reach the couch. His scraped face looked as though shredded with a board of nails.

They turned Laszio around to lay him on his side, but when Laszio couldn't bend his knees, Akela crouched and lifted Laszio's feet by the ankles. Laszio's good eye widened. "Wait," he mumbled. "Message." He pointed at Jediah and repeated the same word over and over. Each mutter dwindled quieter than the last.

Nechum rushed hushed words to calm him. He turned to Jediah after laying Laszio onto the cushions. "I'm sorry, sir," he said. "It took all the water I could spare just to resuscitate him."

"Captain!" Laszio's head lolled as if raising his voice took considerable effort.

A groggy Eran threw a hand up to grip the couch's side and hoisted himself up. Alameth cautiously tried to support him but recoiled when Eran hissed through his teeth.

Unable to stay professional anymore, Jediah rushed over and dropped to his knees to take both their hands. "Right here, Privates. I'm right here. What happened?"

Laszio's eyes darted to Nechum. "Message," he repeated.

"First, tell me what happened," Jediah commanded. "Who did this to you? Yakum?"

Eran shook his head. His fingers squeezed. "Yakum... *and* Elazar... know you're here."

Jediah's world broke like thin glass. He went numb. His grip failed, and as their hands slipped from his, he rose to his feet and backed away. Those marks they bore weren't random anymore—the scars no longer haphazard. They were a clear and violent message from a violent heart. Elazar's wrath had spilled over to those near him and would continue until they settled their personal war.

Nechum knelt and tended to Laszio's slashed hand. "I'm sorry, Captain," Nechum's voice shuddered. "We split up our search in the Forbidden City. I shouldn't have lingered outside the place for so long. I should have gotten there sooner."

Eran took his shoulder. His chest heaved. "Not... your fault."

Clenching his fist and holding strict posture, Jediah steeled himself for the worst and asked, "What are their terms?"

The dead silence weighed so thick it could crush stone. Nechum released Laszio's hand. He stood up, and the calming nature in his tender eyes was consumed by bitter sorrow. "You," he replied. "Yakum infects the city with his plague or he has you."

Akela squeezed his eyes shut. Laszio and Eran bowed their heads and hid their faces. Not even Alameth's controlled breaths could hide his despair completely.

Jediah's energy flowed cold. "I thought so." He stared out at the growing light. "How long do I have?"

"Daybreak." Laszio slurred. "at the train station."

Jediah dipped his chin. "An hour... That's it then."

"No!" Akela objected. "There's got to be another way. Something we could do. Eran?"

Eran wouldn't look at him. He wouldn't look at anyone. "Captain," he said. "Laszio and I have a confession." His wings propped him up higher. "We... We tried to take on Elazar ourselves. That's how he caught us."

Jediah's neck heated, and a surge of anger changed his tone. "What?" Both Privates locked their jaws as Jediah raised his voice. "How? Why? Why would you do something so stupid?"

Laszio raised his neck. He winced as he said, "He—threatens you."

Both their eyes pleaded with Jediah, begging for forgiveness. Jediah's arms shook. "I expected far better judgment from you both. Do you have any idea—" He stopped the rebuke short. He knew he ought to rail them for such a costly mistake, but once he came to it, he lacked the will to. In as pitiful a state as they were, it seemed far less compared to how they agonized beneath the surface. They did what they did out of love for him.

Jediah released a breath. "What did I do to deserve such reckless loyalty?" he asked.

The corners of their lips lifted an inch.

Nechum touched Jediah's shoulder, but the way he did so made Jediah take pause. The fingers were tense and almost dug in.

Jediah faced him.

Nechum let go and peered close. "Captain?"

Jediah swallowed hard. He could imagine Nechum's empathic sense diving deep into him, and for the first time, he felt like he was the demon wishing for escape.

Nechum's eyes dipped down. They danced as though calculating. Then they froze. He stared at Jediah again, as though expecting an explanation.

"What?" Akela asked with a tremor. "Nechum, what's wrong?"

A tingling chill rippled through Jediah's being. By the realization in Nechum's eyes, he knew he had him figured out.

Nechum's mouth dropped open. "Did you know Elazar?" he asked.

Jediah found his tongue too stiff to speak, but his silence confirmed Nechum's question well enough. Ready to fall apart, Jediah steadied himself against the nearby counter and rubbed his forehead.

"You knew him, didn't you," Nechum said, his gaze unwavering.

Jediah rubbed his eyes but nodded 'yes'.

Akela's head twisted right and left as though unsure how to handle this. Stopping himself, he bent his neck low. His front curls hit his eyebrows. "Captain?" he said. "Does this also relate to that letter you had me deliver too?"

Lord God help me, Jediah prayed.

Now they were all staring at him, perplexed and troubled.

Jediah considered whether to sit. The few precious seconds he had weren't enough to properly select his coming words, but he delayed long enough. He owed it to them. "Elazar didn't leave with Lucifer," he began. "He left because of me."

Jediah cleared his throat. "It was after our victory in the Scorpion Wars. Human society was in its infancy then, and our Lord appointed me the Abyss's keeper." He grimaced. "I remember how impulsive I was. I'm ashamed to say that my wanton desire for justice went unchecked, but I just... I just couldn't stand it. Demons not only betrayed our King. They exploited and hurt the Bearers of His Image. I couldn't... I couldn't leave the judgment seat to God. And Elazar was there beside me through it all."

A wistful smile crossed Jediah's face. The former Elazar regained shape and form in his memory as he spoke. "He was one of the most trusting angels I ever met. He burst with confidence, and though he was a ministry angel, he had a gift for strategy and thirsted for justice just as much as I did."

Jediah released a mournful sigh. "He put so much faith in me. He never doubted our ability to serve God." His face fell further. "That's what led to our downfalls."

Jediah rubbed his dried mouth. "Before the Great Flood, Elazar approached me. He spoke of a new technique he discovered. One so absolute, we couldn't possibly fail, but once he described it to me, I had yet never imagined such a dishonorable and gruesome tactic."

Laszio healed enough to sit up to listen closer.

"Elazar suggested we drink the energy of our fallen foes and double our power," Jediah continued.

Nechum covered his mouth before he could gag. Alameth pulled his hood lower, keeping his reaction well out of view, and the others stared at each other with wide, unbelieving eyes before returning to Jediah.

Jediah clenched his hands together. "Yes. Yes. I know and don't think that I ever considered such wicked practice for a second. I insisted I wanted no part in it, but Elazar persisted. He goaded me again and again, claiming it to be for the greater good, until one day, I couldn't take it anymore."

Jediah's shoulders rolled forward. His chest throbbed. His chin quivered, and by then, he knew he reached the point of no return. One more word, and the dam would break. "We argued," he shuddered. It hurt worse to say it aloud. "We argued... I don't remember what all I said... I don't even remember how loud or rough my tone was, but I know I'd rather have had my tongue cut out than to repeat it... My fury blinded me and..."

Jediah covered his mouth. Tears pricked the corner of his eyes. "I struck him... I struck him, like he was the Devil himself... and the next thing I knew... he was gone." Jediah's weakened knees caved. He sat on the nearby footstool. "Gone."

Doubled over, Jediah's shoulders shook unbidden, and his throat burned from caging the sobs. "In my relentless pursuit of what's right... I committed a greater wrong." He paused. "I killed him... I killed him." Without thinking, Jediah slammed his wings into the carpet. Light flashed, then faded into glittering wisps of smoke.

A hand rested on his shoulder. Nechum spoke, quiet and sincere. "And you've been living with that guilt ever since."

Jediah couldn't bear to talk anymore. He wiped off the streams tracking his face.

"Is that why you asked me those questions? About human salvation?" Nechum asked.

Jediah nodded.

"You wish you could be redeemed."

Jediah nodded again. "I just can't imagine... how wonderful that must be... I hoped if I could just understand what it was like... what it truly meant... But that wasn't the only reason I asked you those questions." From his pocket, he showed the second letter and the braid. "I just now decided not to send this, but Akela helped me deliver one already."

Nechum opened it and read the text aloud. Jediah flinched at every spoken syllable, but knew it was best they all heard it. Everything. As soon as silence returned, part of Jediah feared looking up, but as soon as he found the courage, he raised his head. To his relief, not so much as a cocked eyebrow or a crossed arm met his sight. Rather, they looked at him as if they saw the real him for the first time.

"Captain," Nechum offered. "I don't think less of you for any of this." He handed the letter back, lock of hair and all.

"None of us do." Akela smiled, though his eyes were equal parts hopeful and sad. "God meant what you're going through for a reason. I don't know for what reason, but there's a reason."

Somewhat encouraged, Jediah got himself to stand. "I'm sorry," he apologized. "To all of you for everything. If not for all that I have done, this whole mess could have been avoided."

"Not all of it," Laszio interjected. "This ransom. It happened thanks to us and our idiocy."

Eran said nothing, but nodded in agreement. Wobbling yet able, they both got on their feet.

Jediah shook his head. "What's happened, happened. There's nothing we can do to change it now." He folded his wings around himself, each quill clinked against the other as they hardened one at a time.

"Then sir," Eran slowed to say. "... What will we do?"

Jediah stared outside. Golden light peaked. "I'm out of time." he said. "We give them what they want."

Loud 'nos,' silent objections, and all the strings of suggested options didn't sway him. "Listen, brothers," he began. "I've spent lifetimes tormenting myself for my mistakes and wishing for something I can't have. If offering myself is what ends Elazar's rampage, then so be it. I may never experience redemption. But perhaps by reaping my consequences, I will find redemption somehow and finally put the past behind me." He turned to Eran and Laszio. "If they take my wings, I'm counting on you both to defend the Abyss without me."

Both Privates paled but responded by planting their hands over their chests. "Yes, sir."

Lending a small smile for their comfort, Jediah faced the door. The words of King Solomon came to mind. "Whatever is has already been," he recited. "and what will be has been before; and God will call the past into account." Jediah's energy shifted, and he phased through the door.

Chapter 24

BEIJING WEST RAILWAY Station. Its front decor was a stylized pavilion that teamed with people. The back was a field of tracks, dusty rocks, and warrior demons. A sleek bullet train sat at the loading station as passengers stepped aboard, little knowing that Yakum, a demon of death, and his personal guard would ride along with them.

Alameth tailed Jediah, same as the other angels, as best he could. He wasn't sure which propelled him forward more: the desire to prevent the capture of a brother he loved and respected or to just to be there for him and bid a temporal goodbye. Thinking over Jediah's story, he couldn't stop sensing something deep and personal—an invisible tie linking the two of them together. For so long he questioned his place on this team. Why would God pick an angel as unstable and broken as him? Now it seemed too clear to Alameth he'd been too blinded by his own traumas to realize he wasn't the only broken one. Jediah needed him. He needed all of them.

He found Jediah hiding behind one of the unused train cars. The public boarding platform was not but a yard away. Jediah peeked under the steel wheels and appeared to be counting how many demon sentries there were by counting the pairs of plated boots.

Careful not to attract attention, Alameth drifted on a rush of mist and settled beside him.

Jediah sighed, "Alameth, I'd rather you stayed at the hotel."

"With all due respect, sir," Alameth countered. "A wise friend sticks closer than a brother. And thankfully, you have many." He pointed out the others, as they ducked and bent low behind scattered machinery.

Akela and Nechum kept further back with troubled eyes rapt on Jediah. Their care and compassion continued to trump whatever fears they had. Laszio and Eran positioned themselves nearest to the station, brandishing their sticks as if ready to launch an attack.

"Captain Jediah!" a voice bellowed.

Alameth leaned against the train car and slid to a crouch with Jediah.

"The time is nigh!" the voice shouted again. "Come out or my plague begins!"

Alameth peeked around the train car just enough to see a scrawny messenger demon standing beside Yakum. His wings pulsated energy that cracked red static, and he swung about a drawstring bag that no doubt carried the poison pellets.

Alameth's brow creased. He held Jediah's shoulder and prompted him to look him in the eye. "This isn't the way, Captain. I've witnessed countless ransoms gone wrong. You give yourself up and there's nothing to stop them from breaking their agreement."

"I know," Jediah replied. The slack in his posture revealed a resigned spirit. "But there's no time to think of another way, and all I know is that unless I go now, there's absolutely zero chance they won't poison the city."

Whatever else went on in Jediah's head, Alameth couldn't read, but he had a pretty good idea. "Surrendering to them won't resolve your past either," he commented.

Instead of responding, Jediah plastered a stoic expression on his face. He arose, straightened his red uniform, and arranged his luminous feathers into armor.

"Sir," Alameth started again.

"Two more minutes, Captain!" Yakum's voice boomed.

Letting out a breath, Jediah turned to go, but without thinking, Alameth gripped his arm. "Sir!"

After a silent moment, Jediah gently removed his hand and ordered, "Don't get involved."

Alameth bent his neck, hiding his face under his hood's shroud. "But Jediah—"

"It'll be all right, brother," Jediah responded. "This isn't goodbye for good."

Alameth's eyes lingered on Jediah's sword; its hilt jutting out above its owner's right shoulder. Jediah's words on Io echoed in his memory. *"We reflect God to everyone, Alameth... What image of Him will others see?"*

Pursing his lips, Alameth nodded. *This must happen.* "You're right, Captain. This isn't goodbye."

"My patience wears thin, Jediah! Surrender now!"

Nechum's hands wrung his shawl harder the more he watched and heard from that vile figure. Yakum paced around as if entitled. That malicious gaze hungered for what it wanted and would be abated with nothing else—which right then was Jediah.

Nechum's empathic sense rang from the tension, not just from those around him but himself, and for the first time in his life, he wished he had some menial fighting skill to contribute.

Ear-splitting hisses issued from the train wheels. Yakum scowled and beckoned the messenger demon, who fondled the bag. "Moriel. Do it."

"Stop!"

Nechum's breath hitched.

Jediah stepped out into the open. His uncloaked red uniform stood out with pride among the dull rocks. The ends of his embroidered scarf waved like royal banners, and his armored wings were aglow against the bleak, overcast sky. "I'm here, Yakum," Jediah declared. "As you wanted."

Despite the dauntless vibrato he displayed, Nechum saw right through it. Jediah felt empty inside. *"And yet,"* Nechum thought, *"somewhat relieved?"* But then he remembered. Jediah considered all this recompense for his mistakes. Still, Nechum frowned. It seemed too self-destructive a way to handle one's guilt.

Yakum laughed at Jediah. "I was wondering if the courage of angels failed."

Jediah didn't respond. He just took his time, preserving dignity in each step toward his enemies.

Yakum shared a sidelong glance with Moriel, then motioned for two guards. The demons ran to Jediah, armed with razored lances aimed for Jediah's chest. "Drop your sword," one ordered. "Keep your wings in and put your hands up."

Jediah didn't relent his biting glare yet unfastened the buckle. The scabbard's strap slipped off, and the sword clanged to the ground.

Nechum almost couldn't stand watching. They wrenched Jediah's arms around his back and shackled his wrists so hard the scuffed fetters must have pinched. For gold trickled down the cuffs and the chains. The brutes then grabbed and shoved Jediah along.

Laszio sprang from their hiding spot so fast Eran failed to restrain him. "We have to do something!" he shouted. "They have no right to him!" Eran tackled him, pulling him back.

Moriel, who heard their commotion, snarled. He charged his wings and pulled out a black pellet.

Nechum, at risk of being spotted himself, ran to them, hoping to help calm Laszio down.

"Stop it!" Eran hissed in Laszio's ear. "There's nothing we can do."

"No, there has to be," Laszio argued.

The train's engines roared, and the wheels squealed to life. Yakum yelled at his warriors. "Hurry and get Jediah on this hunk of metal before I pin you under it!" The demons sprinted and threw Jediah inside the last passenger car. Yakum settled himself atop the crawling train. Its speed picked up by the second.

"This was our fault!" Laszio exclaimed. His feathers bristled and sharpened as he squirmed against Eran's grip. "We can't just—"

"Um, brothers?" Akela, who walked up from behind, stared ahead with eyes big as saucers.

Moriel, the demon messenger who stayed behind, saluted Yakum as the train took off. He turned and smirked at the angels, as if waiting for their situation to sink in. A portion of Yakum's legion lined up before him as he swung the pellet bag in a taunt.

Nechum, Eran, Laszio, and Akela stood together in icy silence. "Oh no," Nechum muttered.

Moriel's wings sparked. "Sic 'em."

A battalion of spears and claws charged right for them. Laszio, still too weak yet to fly, knocked down the first five demons with a long distance shot from his emblazoned wing.

Eran shot light spheres, further thinning the crowd, but his attention was on a fading crimson streak that pointed east. "Akela! Stop him!" he ordered.

"On it!"

Pow!

Akela traced Moriel's trail and blinked into the horizon.

Nechum, on the other hand, set his sights on the train track.

Akela entered that familiar realm where his speed could ignite the atmosphere. Everything that moved or breathed seemed trapped in stasis. His surroundings stretched to lengthened strips. Vast oceans, mountain ranges, city specks, and wilderness were reduced to color swatches in his vacuum.

His unsuspecting opponent came in sight, giving him the gumption to speed up. Their chase looped the earth a hundred times over. They were gold and red meteors, clashing neck and neck. Volatile energies reacted on contact in tremendous bursts as they bashed each other's sides. Multicolored lightning tangled and clapped together.

Akela flew underneath Moriel and attempted to snag the bag, but Moriel swerved higher.

"You wanna play, pipsqueak?" Morial took out and threw a black pellet.

Gasping, Akela dove and snatched it, but doing so caused him to fall behind. He grunted and strained his wings to catch up. "Hey! Not funny!"

"On the contrary," Moriel replied. He loosed the drawstring. The bag's mouth opened wide.

"Oh no, you don't!" In a sudden spurt of strength, Akela tackled Moriel, sending them both spiraling in freefall.

The bag spilled a good dozen.

Horrified, Akela relinquished his hold on the demon. His curls whipped his face as he zig-zagged and retrieved all twelve pellets. He stuffed them in his satchel, praying they wouldn't pop inside.

Akela pivoted around, but Moriel was gone. Only the barest telltale red pointed his last direction. Swatting his hair off his eyes, he rolled his shoulders. "Okay. Streak bend to the left. Which means he's curving at a fifteen-degree angle. Estimated flight-speed mach 1,000. If his speed stays constant, his arrival point should be right about..."

Akela angled downward. He phased through miles of stone and crust; rocketed out of the earth; and blindsided Moriel with a square kick to the wing. It shattered on impact, and the demon plummeted amidst the ruby rain.

Akela nosedived. "Come on. Come on," he pleaded. The bag came inches to his fingers.

Boom!

Green sparks exploded, startling Akela. The colors expanded into a dome, then disappeared. Another round of blue light banged in his ear. Then rockets squealed and screamed in squiggled circles.

"*Fireworks,*" Akela realized. "*They're fireworks!*"

Akela looked down. Between purple and white showers, he spotted Moriel twisting himself around and stretching out as he fell towards a rollercoaster track. Akela shot down through a round of fizzling copper. He grabbed Moriel by the tunic, but the demon reached behind and wrested him off his back.

The two clutched each other's uniforms. They flurried punches and kicks, until Moriel clutched Akela's throat, keeping the angel between himself and the incoming ground. He then wedged the bag between them and smiled. Akela cringed as fresh panic set in. If they both crashed, the bag bursts and the plague begins.

"Guess Jediah shouldn't have picked you for his messenger, huh?" mocked Moriel.

Akela growled, "For the record, Jediah did *not* pick me! God did!" As they dropped past the coaster's tallest hill, Akela batted his wings, flipping them both over. He ripped the bag from Moriel's hands, but Moriel twisted just enough for them both to hit the middle of the coaster track on their sides.

The bag fell between the rails. "No!" Akela shouted. He swung down by his legs and caught it, only for Moriel to pull him up and steal it back. He threw Akela backwards, which sprained his right wing.

Moriel loomed over him and flung the bag around like a toy. "A wing for a wing," he mused. "Sounds fair."

"Sure, but whose keeping score?" Akela asked. He back flipped. His boot nailed Moriel in the chin, knocking him off balance. The bag sailed high into the air. Akela leaned to catch it, but slipped. Hanging desperately off the steel track's edge, he stretched out a leg, and the bag landed safely on his foot.

Relieved, Akela released a stiff laugh, but a warm drop landed on his arm. Moriel stood, bleeding over him. Startled, Akela impulsively kicked the bag away. "Oh, pinfeathers," he groaned to himself.

The bag tumbled down a steel support, rolling all the way to the loading station roof. It landed on the edge, dangerously close to falling.

A disgusting series of wet clicks caught Akela's attention as Moriel straightened his crooked jaw. "Can't you stay put?" he asked.

The coaster track shook. "Nope," Akela answered. He let go as a coaster train rammed into Moriel. Sliding down the support beam, he landed on the roof that sheltered the loading station. Garbled words issued instructions to awaiting riders from the speakers below. The bag tipped over as two side-by-side coaster trains departed and dropped into an empty passenger seat.

Akela went slack jawed. "You've gotta be kidding me!" He leaped into the red coaster's backseat.

Nechum sprinted along the train track. He fought back a whimper as the locomotive's hum faded. For as remarkably swift as his feet were, the train kept getting smaller. He gritted his teeth as reality set in. He stopped, and stared after the metallic tail-end, thinking only of his brother being taken further and further away. Shaking his head, he snapped himself out of despairing. There had to be a way.

Nechum leaned to one side. The tracks beyond ran into the forest and snaked around a steep hill. Nechum ran left and bounded uphill. He dodged and phased through the thickets. As the trees thinned out, he ran faster, but skidded over the side of the cliff.

Dangling over a steep incline, he spotted the train track at the slope's foot several feet below. He gasped in relief, happy his guess was right, but then he heard the locomotive coming in his direction.

Nechum assessed the drop. "Okay. Okay. Okay..." He squeezed his eyes shut. Then, planting his feet against the vertical wall, he gave one last cringe and sprang off. As he dropped, he generated a blue strip that spread ahead of him and bent into a gradual slant. A bashing and bruising marathon met his back, shoulders, and knees, as he tumbled down the ramp into the rocky dirt. One final face slam, and he reached the bottom.

Delirium swam in his head, but Nechum's subconscious knew the train wouldn't wait. Its screaming wheels beckoned him to hobble up. It mystified him how he even reached the tracks, yet all he kept hearing in his head was, *"Keep walking. Keep walking."*

Nechum laid flat between rails. The machine boxed him in, and the occasional popping flash lit the undercarriage of the rumbling behemoth. Steeling himself, Nechum grabbed hold of greasy metal. The sudden velocity almost startled him loose, but he clung tighter, as wooden ties blurred and jagged rocks zipped under him.

The red and blue twin rollercoasters rattled loud up the chain lift. Akela vaulted another passenger car. He reached under the seats. Nothing. He climbed into the next car. He peeked around a man's legs. Empty.

Akela looked ahead. Only a few hundred feet remained before the ride's initial drop. He climbed into the next car but halted to the black silhouette that slinked in the corner of his eye.

Moriel was crouched on the opposite coaster, about to leap across. Akela pounced on him first. Both coaster trains careened down the steep hill. The two messengers floated in airtime, then thudded against the opened shoulder harness. G-forces held them down as their ride raced up the next hill for an inverted loop.

Nechum crawled along the undercarriage of the passenger train's baggage car. Honing his empathic sense, he felt the demon guards. Even in their captivity, Jediah still put the fear of God in them. Nechum counted enemy numbers and discovered they teamed around a familiar presence just two inches above his head. It had to be Jediah.

Encouraged, Nechum whispered, "So far. So good," to himself.

Some painstaking minutes later, he met the open air beyond the caboose. Edging himself around the windows, he climbed onto the train's topside. Closing his eyes, he again visualized the demonic presence below. As expected, the baggage cars were being patrolled. There was no way for him to sneak in unnoticed.

Nechum, instead, leaped his way toward the passenger cars. He shortened his hair, slanted his eyes, and traded his uniform for a business suit. As soon as he passed the last detectable demon sentry, he phased through the roof into the bathroom. Nechum peeked through the cracked door. Noting nothing out of the ordinary, he submerged himself into the physical realm and opened the door.

An elderly gentleman stared. He had reached for the restroom door and was obviously perplexed to see someone in a vacant bathroom.

Nechum smiled, stepped out, and widened the door. "I forget to lock the door sometimes," he explained.

An uncomfortable grin crossed the man's face, but he nodded politely and slipped inside.

Pushing out a breath, Nechum walked down the carpeted aisle for the closest unoccupied seat and rubbed his brow. *I hope I brought enough change for a ticket.*

The coasters veered into corkscrews that wrapped around each other. Akela leaped off the blue train, intercepted the bag as it dropped, then clung to the red train as it turned upright. The tracks dipped and parted by a few feet.

Moriel grunted. "You don't know when to quit."

"Neither do you, pal," Akela called back.

The coasters neared each other and sped up the final peak.

Moriel kicked the bag, sending it flying out of Akela's hand. Akela ducked Moriel's second kick, but his eye stayed glued to the bag. Predicting its descent, he raced Moriel to the front car. He concentrated on his every step. *Right foot. Left foot. Right foot and...* The rollercoaster dived. *JUMP!*

Akela and Moriel leaped off. The bag seemed to float as their hands reached. Fighting the sprain, Akela willed his wings to flap once. He gained an ounce of momentum and snagged the prize. "Yes!" he cried.

Moriel fell, but grabbed his leg.

"No," Akela groaned. His sprained wing stung from trying to carry the extra weight. He swung his leg around but couldn't shake off Moriel who began climbing on him.

"Oh, that is *it*!" Akela shouted. He untied the drawstring.

Moriel got into Akela's face. He opened a fanged mouth, but didn't expect the fistful of pellets Akela jammed down his throat.

The demon stilled in frightened shock.

For a moment, nothing happened.

Moriel quivered. He choked a gurgle. Black smoke seeped from his nostrils. His eyes watered, then darkened to nothingness, and fermented sludge leaked from his lips.

Akela recoiled as more muck leaked in clumps down Moriel's chin then punched him in the nose.

The demon crashed into clustered trees.

Shuddering, Akela examined the bag. Noticing a slight gape in its mouth, he jerked the drawstring so tight not a flea could slip through and stuffed the loathsome thing in his satchel. "Blugh," he wretched. "I did *not* need to see that."

Returning to the Beijing train station, Akela got a good eyeful of the place. Crimson energy bathed the train yard. Comatose demons laid strewn all around Laszio and Eran's stained boots, and the two Privates stood slumped back to back. Akela smiled. Despite being weakened and outnumbered, the two pulled it off. God's minor miracles never ceased to amaze him.

Not paying attention, Akela misjudged the distance to the ground. He failed to slow and landed flat on his stomach. "Ugh... ow" he moaned.

"Akela?" Eran called. He approached and grabbed Akela's shoulders. Akela winced as he lifted him up. "Easy. Easy!"

Laszio, meanwhile, sat down, looking too tired to move. His sticks remained in his fists like they were stuck there.

Eran also seemed rather peaked but brushed off Akela's leather pads and asked, "Where's Moriel? Did you stop him?"

Eager to deliver good news, Akela dug into his satchel. "Took a while, but..." He revealed the bag of pellets.

"Oh, praise Him," Eran breathed. "Praise Him."

Laszio laid down, his back and wings flat. He stared expressionless at the clouds, then laid an arm to cover his eyes. "Yes," he said. "But what now?" He pounded a fist.

Wishing he had a suggestion, Akela found nothing to say.

A few minutes of nothing passed as Eran paced. There was a lostness in his eyes. They stirred in tight circles, clearly stressed by the sudden pressure to lead, but then he stood in place. His feathers glowed a burgeoning gold. "We're getting him back," he mumbled.

Laszio sat up. "What?"

Eran turned to him. "We're getting Jediah back."

"Hold up," Laszio said as he raised to a stand. "Captain ordered us to protect the Abyss."

"*If* they took his wings," Eran corrected. "But as far as we know, they haven't yet, and if we follow those tracks, we just might stop them before they do."

Laszio shook his head. "Even if we find the train, what if they're not there anymore? We won't know where they got off."

Taking pause, Eran rubbed his eyes in frustration. "Wait a sec. Akela, do you know where Nechum went?" he asked.

Thinking back, Akela's photogenic memory kicked into high gear. "Last I saw, he was chasing the train," he reported.

"Then there's a chance," Eran remarked, his face lighting up. "Nechum is smart. He'll find a way onto that train, and if he sticks close to them, I'm sure he can lead us straight to Jediah."

Laszio grimaced, saying, "There are a lot of holes in that plan."

"Then may God fill in the gaps," Eran responded. He turned to Jediah's sword that laid abandoned in the chalky dust. With solemn respect, he recovered it with careful hands and his plumed feathers wiped off the dirt in caressing strokes.

Something odd and yet familiar appeared in the corner of Akela's eye.

"Come on, Akela," Eran called, as he and Laszio turned to leave.

But Akela couldn't regard him, too enraptured by what he was seeing. A figure dressed in red shuffled and stumbled around behind a distant box car. Unsure what to think, Akela sprinted toward it. A raspy coughing grew louder in his ears. Akela slowed, turned the corner, and reeled back to what sat before him.

Hunched forward and clutching his stomach, Jediah hacked hard and loud.

Laszio and Eran, who followed, also sped around the box car. "Captain!" they all shouted in shocked delight.

Ready to dance and spin in circles, Akela slapped both hands to his forehead. "I don't believe it! This—This is incredible!" he exclaimed.

Jediah struggled to open one eye.

Laszio stuttered, "But wha—? Whe—? How did—?"

"How did you get away?" Eran interjected.

"Get away?" Jediah asked. "From what?"

Eran titled his head and queried, "Um, Yakum? Don't you remember the ransom?"

Jediah labored a swallow but managed a nod.

Noticing the strangeness in the circumstance, Akela's initial excitement dipped. "So how did you escape?" he asked. "Nechum chased Yakum's train because we all saw him leave... with... you."

Shaking himself, Jediah straightened and blinked twice.

Laszio leaned in. "You don't remember getting on the train?"

Mouth agape, Jediah gazed and answered, "No."

"But we *did* see you," Akela insisted. "*Everyone* saw you. You removed your sword. They chained you up, forced you on the train, and Nechum ran after them to get you out."

Hearing that, Jediah's hand patted his chest. His fingers didn't find his scabbard straps. Laszio stepped forward and offered him his blade. Jediah accepted it, but his careworn face continued to fall as if stricken. "Akela?" he said, "How many of us besides Nechum are here?"

"Um. Let's see," Akela started. "Myself. Laszio. Eran. And..." A frightening reality stole his wits, struck his core, and withered his voice. "Oh, no."

Jediah then asked the question they all were thinking, but dreaded to ask.

Where's Alameth?

Back in the Forbidden City, Elazar picked the lock and wrenched the shackle off his ankle. His hoarse throat drew growled breaths as he carved into the next demon guard who dared try to prevent his escape. Spotting one of Yakum's messengers on the run, he used a shield to drag the wretch back by the neck.

First Zivel. Now Yakum robbed Jediah from me.

"You!" Elazar bashed the messenger's head against the nearby pillar. "I've got a job for you. One. Simple. Fail-proof job. But if you *dare* double-cross me like your master did, I'll do far worse to you than what I've got in store for him."

"Y-yes, sir! Of course, sir!" the messenger babbled.

"Head to Hoia-Baciu Forest." Elazar instructed. "This message is for Lucifer alone."

Chapter 25

ALAMETH LAID AS STILL as possible. Reminders of his every affliction resurfaced at the barest move.

"On your knees, Captain."

Alameth grimaced.

"On your knees!"

Someone yanked the cuffs, and the hot throbbing in Alameth's wrists flared. They yanked again, dragging him. The marks that scored his legs reopened. Biting back a groan, Alameth spent what little energy he had left to lift his lower back, but his upper body and head sagged.

His disheveled hair fenced in his bowed face, but he didn't need to see who or what surrounded him. He pictured it already: the calloused thirst of blood-crazed eyes; the grinning hunger of slave drivers, murderers, and traffickers; and many burly hands practiced in the art of beating and maiming. He'd seen it all before, and yet... this time... Alameth hid a smile. For this time, there'd be no other victim than himself. This time, he wouldn't bear anyone's suffering but his own. Elazar's vengeance will be satisfied, and he'll protect a brother in the most honorable way any angel could ask for.

"Lord," Alameth prayed in silence. *"Thank you for this privilege to follow the example of Your Son for Jediah's sake. Impart to me Your peace, El Shaddai, and deliver the same to my brothers as You always have for Your rescued people—those You've blessed to bear Your Mark and Your name."*

A pungent vapor smothered the dank cave and broke Alameth's concentration. Yakum's presence lengthened the shadows. "Welcome, Captain," Yakum said. "We're sorry your old friend, Elazar, isn't here. But fret not. We'll hand you over... eventually."

Unwilling to give him the satisfaction of so much as a retort, Alameth kept his mouth shut. Long fingers seized his jaw. Yakum almost snapped his neck as he forced his chin up. He demanded something from him, but Alameth, determined not to listen, ignored every word no matter how sharp they rang in his ear.

Don't talk. Don't react. Don't talk. Don't react.

Yakum shook Alameth by the tunic, jostling his aching limbs, but Alameth bit his tongue to keep from moaning.

Don't talk. Don't react. Don't talk. Don't react.

Confusion crossed Yakum's face. Then he bore into Alameth with an all-consuming rage. He threw Alameth down. The hit rattled Alameth's head, and a new sprain stung his shoulder. Yakum screamed something at his guards, but the angel could only catch scant pieces of speech. Alameth's ears twitched to the sound of unsheathed knifes. Hundreds of red eyes, like an enclave of spiders, descended upon him.

Jediah raced the noonday shadows that stretched to the west, leaving the train station miles behind. The tracks led to a sea of close-knit mountains with silver rivers that coiled the spaces between them. Their rounded peaks were girthed in mist, but the only thing clothed in mist on Jediah's mind was Alameth, his brother, and whatever unspeakable things Elazar might do once he exposed him. Yakum might be fooled, but Elazar? Alameth's ruse didn't stand a chance.

Reaching the first train stop, he led Laszio, Eran, and Akela into the upper rafters of an outdoor loading pavilion. His eyes darted around and latched onto every useless thing that happened to be colored blue. "Does anyone see Nechum?" he asked.

"One sec." In two flashes, Akela left and returned. "No sign of Nechum, but I found this." He held a silver pin attached to a torn blue cloth.

Jediah's heart sank. It was a piece of Nechum's shawl.

Laszio took the clue from Akela and cupped it in his hands. "You don't suppose Yakum caught Nechum too, do you?"

Akela rocked on his heels and said, "Well, if they did, they did a pretty poor job hiding his crumb trail." He opened a second hand, revealing a second piece.

The ripped remains of Nechum's shawl were spread farther and farther apart the further the angels went, and Jediah saved every frayed rag. Never had he felt less worthy to lead. If his wingmen's injuries and Alameth's sacrifice weren't enough, now even Nechum suffered the loss of his cherished shawl—because of him. They didn't deserve this. None of them.

The successive parcels became smaller and smaller until threadbare strips were left—signs of Nechum's last ditch effort.

"Captain," Akela called. He plucked a blue piece no thicker than a string from a bramble. "It's the last one. I can't find anymore."

"Then maybe he's here," Jediah reasoned.

"He is," Nechum answered. He dropped from a tree, dressed in only his tunic and loose capris. He seemed smaller without his shawl, like part of his dignity had been stripped from him.

Too overjoyed for formalities, Akela wrapped Nechum in a hug.

The two hadn't separated yet when Laszio rushed to meet them. "Nechum, you're not gonna believe this, but Alameth—"

"Took our captain's place," Nechum finished. Pulling away from Akela, his eyes dipped down. "I finally figured it out after they dragged him off the train."

"Couldn't you break him out?" Eran asked.

Nechum shook his head. "I couldn't get past the barrier." He pointed toward the closest mountain.

Jediah took careful steps, sword in hand, and peeked through a gap between the leaves. No sentry. No guard. No lookout. But a red dome, a ministry demon's shield, covered the entire mountain from its peak to its foundations.

Jediah quaked. The possibility of Elazar's presence made him want to retreat, but his care for Alameth spurned him to push past all that. His original mission to capture Yakum also compelled him. Up till then, the reason he left the Abyss in the first place slipped away from him. Too many distractions crowded him. Elazar. Chloe. His guilt. His brothers. The tightening strain of it all corroded what level-headedness he had left.

Jediah rubbed his temples in his attempts to focus. He couldn't help anyone by splitting his attention in so many directions. Yakum didn't just threaten him and his brothers. He threatened all mankind. Ridding the earth of him benefitted everyone, and honoring God in obedience mattered more than his own personal agendas. If he followed God's will for him, Jediah reasoned, it would deliver Alameth. It would help Chloe. He and his brothers could then return to the status quo, and their current troubles would be over.

Spurred by the oaths of service he swore to his Lord, Jediah found the gumption to push his terror of Elazar aside. There was no room for it. He'd pierce the dark; cut all emotional ties if he must, but he wouldn't fail his Creator. Not again.

Examining the dome, Jediah noticed its lack of transparency. It was reinforced, multilayered by several shields from several demons. Frustration gnawed at him. If one shield wasn't invincible enough, two or three were impossible. "You're sure Yakum and Alameth are in there?" he asked Nechum.

Nechum's tired eyes stayed on the dome.

Eran's fingers tapped his belt. "Can we go under it?" he asked.

"No," Nechum said. "I've tried."

With an expression uncharacteristically solemn, Akela stared at the barrier as if sizing the whole thing up. His cobalt eyes acquired a slight white tint, almost ultraviolet, anxious yet filled with hope. Then, without a word, he threw off his satchel and stretched out his wings.

"Akela?" Jediah gripped his arm. "Akela, what are you doing?"

"Don't worry, Captain." A kind smile bloomed across Akela's face despite the tremor in his voice. It seemed what he was saying he also meant for himself. "I'll be back."

He gave no one the chance to respond.

Akela rocketed out of the hemisphere. The sky changed from blue to indigo, then indigo to black. Stars stretched into lines. The moon shrank to a period. Red dusted Mars; stormy Jupiter; ringed Saturn; and all other manner of celestial bodies morphed into one cosmic tapestry as he passed, and soon the entire solar system became just another glowing speck in the universe.

Beyond the galaxy's edge, Akela zipped into a nebulous cloud splashed in watercolor rainbows. He stopped and spun around. For a moment, he floated in the vacuum with his thoughts, his prayers, and the stars for company. As he stared back at the Milky Way, he set aside his cheery disposition. His idea was nuts. Logic couldn't justify it, but Akela found that fact gave him more hope than anything. God's great miracles were seldom logical.

"My Lord and King," Akela said. "I, your servant, have come to this Red Sea—the place where options run dry. Take myself into Your hand... and let what happens come to pass because of You and only You. May it be so. Amen."

He sucked in a breath. He waved his slim wings in gentle increments and gathered his nerves. "Okay. All or nothing."

New strength enlivened his system. The Holy fires of God's Shekinah glory took over. His golden uniform burst into beaming white, and his crystal wings ignited into a pair of burning comets. Akela flew in a grand loop. Then in a deafening clap, he launched at a velocity so high it stung his cheeks. Massive energy blasts boomed behind in his wake. Stars streaked brilliant reds, whites, yellows, and blues.

Akela grunted. He still wasn't fast enough. "Come on!" he hollered. "Drive me on, Lord! Drive me on!"

His wings buzzed louder, so loud it scared even himself.

The Milky Way's spirals enlarged. Its jeweled expanse encompassed his vision.

Akela gritted his teeth as a burning sensation ate his wingtips, then spread to the rest of him. His being began dissolving into electric particles, but he hunkered down, threw caution to the wind, and pushed harder. He stretched his hands out ahead of him, forming a spear. A resounding pow blasted his inner ears, and the extra thrust straightened his curls down to their ends.

Neck bent back, Jediah cast glances to the others. Something in him feared what was coming.

"Somebody knows what Akela's doing, right?" Laszio asked.

Nechum wrung his hands. "I have a hunch, but I don't like to think about it."

"Wait!" Laszio pointed at a falling star. "Is that him?"

Eran's eyes widened. "Tell me he's not."

Jediah jolted. "He is. Everybody duck!"

A golden comet pierced the atmosphere and bombed the barrier.

Ka-pow!

The shockwave rocked the spiritual atmosphere and reverberated many long seconds afterwards.

Jediah raised his head, as did the others, one by one. A yellow cloud descended and coated them in fine dust. He blinked through it to see the single puncture hole that smashed through the shield's surface. The cracks multiplied. The weakened dome caved inward like a lilting tent, then collapsed in a heap of fading red glass.

Stunned, Jediah remained stuck in place. He opened a palm to catch the golden rain. It collected softly in his cupped hand, and he rubbed a thumb over the sparkling, evaporating grains. A mournful sheer veiled him.

Akela wasn't returning any time soon.

Chapter 26

THE CAVERNS TREMBLED, but Alameth wasn't certain if he imagined it or not. The mind can play terrible tricks in this void he'd been trapped in—a cursed realm stuck in a maddening, repeating loop. He hoped his tormentors would have grown bored long by now. They didn't. They continued to help themselves to him. The gashes they gouged into his back, shoulders, and sides soaked his clothes with his energy. They traced their scalpels around the rims of his fake wing armor. They picked. They pried, but still Alameth wouldn't give up the 'key' they coveted. It remained the one thing he could do to retaliate.

Soon, the demons argued amongst themselves and turned their carving knives on each other. That is, until the tunnels shook. Their quarrel ceased into an eerie quiet.

The frigid floor cooled Alameth's thumping head. Chilled water trickled under his aching torso and kept the numbed parts of himself awake. He thanked the Lord for it. Fading out was a luxury he couldn't afford. He didn't know if his altered appearance could be sustained while unconscious, and too much relied on this charade.

Anxious from the minor quake, Yakum pointed and asked the nearest guard, "What was that? Was it Elazar?"

"I don't know, my lord," the guard replied. "It sounded like our shields failed."

"That's impossible. Find out what's really going on now! I can't risk anyone interfering!"

The demon bowed and hurried down the tunnel passage.

"And get *him* on his knees!" Yakum ordered.

A pitiful cry escaped Alameth's lips as they jerked him up. His stone-heavy head hung.

Yakum's spit speckled Alameth's neck as he spoke. "I grow tired of your stubborn silence, Jediah." He clamped a batch of Alameth's hair and shook him. "I've risked too much for you to deny me ultimate power now. Give me the key!"

A harsher shaking crackled Alameth's cramping neck. His vision darkened.

Nechum led Jediah, Eran, and Laszio through the underground. The winding tunnels were abundant, but his empathic sense stayed locked onto Alameth. The concentration of pain he felt from his brother mounted to the point where even he began to share in it.

Yakum lifted Alameth by the scruff of his neck. "Last chance, Jediah. Unfurl your wings."

Alameth took as deep a breath as his sore chest could.

Yakum's scowl subsided into indignant resignation. "Fine," he said. "Suit yourself. Open your wings once you're good and ready. But I do believe you'll be ready soon." Yakum opened a hand, and black mist collected and wound into a sphere. It was a writhing abomination of sputtering oil. Yakum nestled the vile thing in his palm, and Alameth recoiled as he inched it close to his nose.

Alameth squirmed as the pellet's putrid stench half choked him.

"It's rather thrilling for me really," Yakum taunted. "You're the first angel in centuries I've tested a toxin on. So then. How about we see what happens, huh?"

Gathering his courage, Alameth looked Yakum straight in the eye. "This... will not... end well for you."

"You mean, it won't end well for *you*," Yakum replied. He shoved the virus into Alameth's head and dropped him.

Alameth fell headfirst. Cold, sapping, killing cold, squeezed his head. A thousand thorns seemed to burrow themselves inside. Screams roared out of him he did not recognize. His legs kicked in seizures. His cuffed hands tore at their chains, desperate to break free and claw the thing out of his forehead, but the infection spread, creeping down his neck. He thrashed around as it consumed his chest and back. The quivering in his limbs wouldn't stop.

The world around him mutated.

Alameth blinked hard.

Stalactites and stalagmites became teeth. The cave's natural moisture turned to saliva.

Realizing he was hallucinating, Alameth twisted his neck back and forth. *It's not real. It's not real!* His attempts to shake off the madness failed. For the new visions replacing the old were twice as awful, yet the most frightening development was the ensuing dementia that thwarted his attempts to pray. He'd forget his words before they started.

Soon, his inner voice quieted altogether.

Alameth had forgotten why he was even there.

A sudden spark of remembrance broke through him, and Alameth fell into a panic. He was degrading, exactly like they wanted him to. The shame and horror of it shattered him. He hollered between gasps against both the toxin and Yakum, its maker.

Alameth raised a knee, but his leg couldn't bear his weight. He flopped to the floor, suddenly numb. He wanted to lift an arm. It wouldn't move. He tried to lift his head. It did nothing, and the all consuming paralysis soon trapped him inside his own growing insanity.

An awful screech echoed, and a prickling chill in Jediah's entire being froze him and everyone else in place. It seemed to last forever. Then a cacophony of ongoing cries and shrieks drowned out the first. The angels ducked their heads and clamped their ears after the first minute, just to get some relief from the racket. Then they stopped.

Laszio spun on his heel. "What was that?

A small rumble in the caverns grew into a quake. Crags cracked opened along the ceiling. Stones clattered and grounded into grime as entire sections of rock inched out of place in enormous blocks.

"Move!" Jediah shouted, as the first boulders thundered into a full-scale cave in. The avalanche chased them for several feet before settling.

Laszio stared back at the upturned earth. "What in the name of sense is Yakum trying to do?"

A pair of red eyes just behind caught Jediah's attention. He spun around. His blade rang out of the scabbard and slashed a black tendril. The severed chunk dissipated. "Yakum!"

The towering demon, dressed in ornamented robes, phased through the ground to float above. "Lost something, Captain? You are the *real* Captain, right?" Yakum queried.

Jediah's quills bristled and sharpened. "Where's Alameth?" he demanded.

Yakum narrowed his eyes and shrugged. "He's entertaining my troops, of course. You did what you wanted with my informant, Malkior. I consider the loss of one of yours as restitution. An angel for a demon. It's only fair."

"You're sick," Laszio interjected.

"I'm sorry," Yakum growled. "I didn't know you didn't know I wasn't talking to you." Their surroundings shook again. "You hear that, Captain?" the demon asked. "My troops are having a wild time with your little actor. But you can end it. Grant me the key. I'll call them off, and you get to take your body double home."

Jediah poised his sword with its blade close to his cheek. "I won't dishonor our brother's sacrifice by bending to you. I'm completing my mission, and you're going where you belong."

Yakum's eyes sizzled red. A mass of black amassed, and it poured out before him.

Acting fast, Jediah swept a wing behind him. The angled light knocked the other angels out of range before the dark fog could hem them in. "Find Alameth! Leave Yakum to me!" Jediah commanded.

The last spaces of air were pinched closed between himself and his muffled brothers' protests.

Jediah armored himself. "Yakum! The Lord rightly demands your freedom from you this day." He lit his sword. "You shall answer to Him for preying upon Adam's race and for desecrating our brothers." Wings bright and intense, Jediah torched the surrounding floor, and Yakum blinked against the sudden light.

With his senses still linked to Alameth's, Nechum continued to lead Laszio and Eran, but the closer they got to Alameth, the worse he felt. His heart had caught Alameth's malaise. It wearied him like a decomposing illness was eating him alive. After a while, Nechum stopped in his tracks as a draining sensation ran him through.

Laszio and Eran halted mid-sprint. "Okay, Nechum. Which way?" Laszio asked.

Nechum pointed left, but did so with hesitation. Something hollered at him, warning him not to take them any further.

"What's wrong?" asked Eran.

Stalled in his words, Nechum couldn't say anything. He felt like someone tore out his spirit and replaced it with a soulless doll.

Impatient, Laszio charged ahead. "There's no time," he said. "Alameth is—whoa!" His foot slipped out from under him, and he fell into something damp. A smelly, red puss coated his legs, a product of which Nechum dared not think.

"What the?" Laszio wiped it off in disgust.

Alarmed, Eran raised his wings in defense. He searched their surroundings, but the large cave seemed vacant. "Where is everyone?" he wondered aloud.

Bending over the goo, Nechum picked some of it up in his fingers. It felt warm. Shivering, he turned to see more red pools, and all color fled from his face. "U-um, brothers?" he began, but his next words froze on his tongue. Just above him, two demons hung from the ceiling with stalactites punctured through their chests and their lower halves melted off like wax.

Eran gaped at the sight of them. "W-what happened here?"

"I found him!" Laszio cried. Nechum and Eran watched him sprint to a lump that could have easily been mistaken for a grey rock. He slid to his knees beside the still form. "Alameth?" He rubbed his back. "Alameth, it's us." He leaned over him to see his face, but then recoiled, falling backwards in shock.

"Laszio! What is it?" Eran asked as he brandished his sticks.

Nechum shrank back. Grey mists raised a cuffed and chained Alameth up. It animated him like a puppet with its strings cut; his movements awkward and uncanny, but Nechum's heart dropped the farthest once he saw Alameth's eyes. They were neither green nor energized in white. They were black. Dead. Without sign of thought or conscience—demonized.

Laszio, who laid before him, fumbled to drag himself away. He called Alameth's name, but his voice hitched.

More fog loomed over Laszio at Alameth's bidding and splintered into a million needles.

Struggling against his own terror, Nechum stepped forward and offered an open hand. "Alameth, please. We know you. You wouldn't willfully attack your brothers."

Alameth looked at Nechum, but his fog lowered over Laszio.

"Alameth, stop," Nechum pleaded.

Suddenly, Eran, who had crept up from behind, rushed Alameth and pulled him away from Laszio.

"Eran, don't!" Nechum yelled. "You'll make things worse!"

Alameth slipped right out of Eran's arms, and his mist punched him right off his feet. Laszio intercepted Eran in midair. The two tumbled, then scrambled to escape Alameth's follow-up strikes.

An explosion of destructive cloud ravaged the cavern. Their grey plumes turned black and shrouded Alameth entirely. Blinded, the three angels huddled together behind a stone. Nechum crumbled. This was the worst nightmare he could have possibly imagined. Peeking toward the others, Nechum watched Laszio's fearful expression harden. His eyes turned pointed and set, as he pulled out his weapons.

"What are you doing?" Eran hollered in the tumult.

"What's it look like?" Laszio said as he harnessed a sphere. "I'm taking him down."

Eran shook his head and objected, "He's our brother, Laszio!"

"No, he's not!" Laszio argued. "This can't be Alameth!" He gestured to the swirling chaos around them. "Would Alameth act this way? Yakum isn't the only demon of death, Eran! I won't let this imposter disgrace our brother's image like this!"

Nechum pressed his hands against his temples. He couldn't believe what he was hearing or how this nightmare managed to become so much worse. His brothers were on the brink of attacking one another. Hoping to prevent conflict, Nechum started to speak, but before he could get a word in, smoke grabbed him. Laszio and Eran yelled his name as it then chucked him down the exit corridor. Knees torn and rubbing a sore arm, Nechum stared into the impenetrable fog that blocked the path inside.

Jediah battled a maelstrom of black as Yakum lingered on high, content to let his fog fight for him. Two, three, sometimes four mist prongs tried to spear Jediah, but his practiced sword arm slashed every one of them with pinpoint precision and accuracy. Unfortunately, for very tendril he spliced, another two replaced it.

One arm from the black mist stole Jediah's sword from behind, but Jediah clapped his wings, destroying the thieving appendage. He caught the falling blade, then plunged it into the floor. The flames that graced the sword's edges soaked into the ground and erupted into a towering ring of holy fire that consumed the black and extinguished it all in a puff of white. The inferno even reached the ceiling where Yakum spectated.

Yakum discarded his singed robe in annoyance.

Jediah's grip tightened on the hilt as he pulled his sword out of the ground. The steel steamed as it cooled, but before Jediah could charge Yakum, fresh mist flooded the floor. Its grainy particles ensnared Jediah's feet like tar and glued him down. It climbed his legs. Countless more strands whipped up to entangle him, but Jediah instinctively armored his wings before they could reach them.

Yakum descended as he spoke. "Impressive but not near impressive enough." He squinted. "Is that why you sent another in your place? Because you knew you're too weak to challenge me?"

Jediah lurched at him.

Yakum grinned. "Tell me. How long did it take to coach your imitator? Do your screams sound the same? Do you taste the same?" He licked his teeth, and Jediah didn't miss the gold specks between each tooth. "Guess there's only one way to find out."

Resisting the prodding mist, Jediah grunted. He had one shot to break free. He put all focus on the topmost quills that plated his collar. They glowed, bent at the tips, and shot Yakum square in the eyes.

With their master blinded, the darkness loosed. Jediah soared upward. Wrapping a wing over the sword hilt, Jediah channeled energy through his feathers and out the smooth metal strips. Floodlights swallowed the room in a complete whiteout.

The light dimmed into a lingering residue. Seeing Yakum sprawled on the floor, Jediah summoned the chains. *This was it. Mission complete.*

He swung. The chain arched as it whipped. Jediah tugged. The links strapped and tightened, but to his shock, Yakum wasn't ensnared. Black mist had snatched the opposite end.

Yakum opened his eyes of smoking red, and before Jediah could let go, the fog yanked him forward into a black pike. Jediah let out a ripping scream as his exposed left shoulder sank deep into its point.

Yakum approached with his hands behind his back. "Whoops," he crooned. "I missed." By mental command, he tipped the pike vertically, suspending Jediah like forked meat.

Jediah wriggled as he slid further down the shaft. Gold dripped out of him and smeared his hands, but to his greater terror, his vision warbled and narrowed. Examining the wound where he was skewered, Jediah watched black specks seep from the pike. They infected the wound and dyed his bleeding energy a shade darker.

Alameth wielded fog at the monster charging him, but the slobbering beast ducked and grabbed the chain that was still cuffed to his wrists. Alameth winced. The motion nearly yanked his arms out. The creature then called to its twin in a hideous, garbled speech that sounded wet and gluttonous. A white fireball grazed Alameth's shoulder seconds before the second monster launched itself into his side. Alameth hollered as they dragged him down. *They've imprisoned me! Beaten me! Tortured me! What more could they want from me?!?*

Enraged and desperate, Alameth poured more mist from his robes and smothered both beasts. The creatures tried to pull away, but Alameth willed his fog to throw the creatures to the ground and consume them whole. His mist's acidic stings leaked into their eyes and swarmed their mouths like bullet ants at the feast. He dared not let them go. Even as they wriggled like bugs being squashed under a slow, descending boot, he felt no pity.

One of them raised a claw for him. Alameth's chest squeezed itself in tighter. He locked his jaw. His breathes hastened and heated, and he doubled his efforts to annihilate them.

The monsters stilled. Victory came near, but then something changed. Alameth saw their drooling maws slip off their faces like masks, only to reveal his own face underneath. Gasping, Alameth stumbled backwards. Broken slabs cut his elbows, but that was nothing compared to the scathing glares coming from his own mirrored images.

Alameth's throat tightened. He lifted to his knees. These monsters *were* him, or maybe that's precisely what he was fast becoming. Scared, Alameth drew his arms in. *What was this vision?*

No sooner did he ask than a voice, as still and small as a whisper, replied from the recesses of his subconscious. It didn't sound like his own, but was more than familiar.

El Shaddai?

The name came to Alameth out of the blue. He didn't know from where or why, but it felt... right.

"I—," Alameth muttered. He didn't know what compelled him to answer.

The voice beckoned to him again, calling him from the pit he had fallen into.

A recognition of what he had done and what he was about to do rushed through Alameth's core. "I—I won't become them," he whispered. Lifting his face toward the heavens, his voice raised, firm and decided. "I won't be like them, Yahweh!" With that—aching, delirious, and broken—he settled himself into a divine peace he long missed.

Jediah's neck drooped as he panted against an increasing chill. Two hellish eyes, Yakum's eyes, filled his tunneling consciousness. He couldn't hear the demon's garbled scoffs, but he realized one thing: *He was close enough.*

Jediah kneed Yakum in the chin. Yakum fumbled and grabbed the pike for support, and seizing his chance, Jediah swatted with his razored wing. He pierced Yakum deep with sharp quills. Energy coursed hot through Jediah's feathers and ignited Yakum's side.

The demon screamed. After shearing himself away, he hunched over the spear. His smoldering side gleamed yellow as though dipped in molten ore.

With Yakum decommissioned, Jediah clenched his teeth and tore the spear up and out of his shoulder. He dropped, summoned the chains, and ensnared Yakum by the neck before they both thudded to the floor.

They laid silent.

Agony pulsed through Jediah's ruined shoulder and squelched all desires to move, but he knew move he must. His unfurling wings struggled to spread underneath him. The tips touched, and Yakum glowed beside him.

"Yakum," Jediah said. "On behalf of God the Father, God the Son, and God the Holy Ghost, I cast you into the void for your atrocities committed against the great I AM, His people, and His servants."

Yakum's lower legs fizzled. In seconds, chains clattered through the newly emptied air.

Curling in on his side, Jediah trembled, knowing he'd collapse if he tried to get up. As his hand covered his bleeding shoulder, his conflicting feelings collided. He did as God asked. He accomplished what He sent him out to do.

So why can't I rest?

Staring out into the whirling storm he created, Alameth spotted a figure covered in translucent armor. It broke through the grey curtain. Mist streamed in creamy ribbons around the figure's shin guards and arm braces. Wind batted his loose clothes.

Too tired to fight and unwilling to revert to his former rage, Alameth bowed his head and scrunched his eyes closed. *"Be still,"* he told himself. *"Be still and know that He is God."*

The stranger's padding feet stopped. Two hands touched Alameth's shoulders. He flinched, but the fingers weren't taloned or calloused. The hands were smooth and tender, soft as rose petals. They stroked soothing circles.

Then the stranger spoke in a gentle timbre he knew oh so well. "I know, brother... I know."

Memory dawned.

Nechum?

Alameth let the last of his mist slip into nothing. Lightheadedness took over. He swayed, but a pair of arms enveloped him and drew him close.

Chapter 27

NECHUM DISMISSED HIS force-fields, and the translucent plating protecting his head, arms, and torso dissolved. The full weight of his brother sank into his arms. Alameth felt so limp, so fragile, like powdered ash easily blown by the wind. Nothing like the strong, stalwart angel he knew he truly was.

Careful not to bother one scratch, Nechum set Alameth on his side. "Sorry it took us so long, brother," he said. Rough metal scuffed his fingers as he pried at the shackles. After no success, Nechum formed a shield the size of a toothpick and inserted it into the lock. "But we're all getting out of here. Jediah is handling Yakum. Akela is—" Nechum's hands stilled. "Coming. H-he'll be coming."

He rocked and tipped the pick against the tumblers. The lock clicked, and the second the cuffs slipped off, Nechum threw them as far as possible. With that, he turned his attention to Laszio and Eran. He called their names, but neither answered. They laid a foot away, unmoving.

Nechum's mouth went dry. He rushed to their sides. Alameth's handiwork had rendered their lower halves to mush. He brushed Eran's arm. Eran rolled over, and parts of him strung behind like spilt honey off a table.

Nechum's clammy palms cupped his mouth. Despite knowing they'd soon recover, to Nechum, anyone living through mutilation like this was worse for them than simply dying from it. There'd be no release. They'd have to suffer from beginning to end.

Alameth moaned. He curled in on himself and pressed his forehead hard into the stone floor.

"No, no, no, no," Nechum consoled, as he crawled back to him. "Stay still. Don't move." Crossing his legs, he supported Alameth's neck and nestled his head into his lap.

Alameth's pants hastened. His eyes, pitch as tar, darted around, not settling anywhere. Nechum's senses jittered to his trauma. He placed a firm palm over Alameth's eyes, encouraging them to close. "Lord?" he prayed. "I rely on You. Make clear to me the nature of this affliction that's befallen Alameth."

A gentle warmth churned inside of Nechum. Glory turned his clothes white. Its pure tides streamed down his sleeve and poured into Alameth's wounds, from the heavy slashes to the minor cuts. The brilliance filled Alameth as water fills a glass. It illuminated him and revealed a black blotch in his chest that swirled like mud caught under an ice sheet.

Without a second thought, Nechum fitted a pointed shield to his hand and punctured Alameth's chest. Alameth hollered. Putrid gases leaked, and a rubbery substance gushed out. Nechum seized the gunk with his bare hand. He pinned Alameth down with his free hand while he yanked with the other.

The stubborn slime stretched and stretched. Agitated, Nechum tightened his fist. Liquid fungus squiggled between his fingers, but as soon as he pulled it to a full arm's length, the black goo and all its roots snapped out of its host.

Nechum's heart jumped in his throat. He thought it'd be over, but instead of going limp, the substance wriggled around, latched to his wrist, and groped to consume his forearm. He yelped as a good portion of the blob wriggled free, but in a popping flash, a wave of glory engulfed Nechum's fist. It burned the blotch in purple bursts so rapidly that Nechum dropped it. Scattered sparks flitted, then puffed to nothing on the floor.

For a moment, Nechum sat stunned as his white clothes returned to blue, but then he noticed movement from Laszio. The half-awake soldier locked gazes with him—his brow creased in concern and remorse. Nechum read it all on his face. Laszio had heard and seen everything.

Alameth groaned, but the sound of it was quieter, less labored than before. He squinted. The original emerald hue of his irises peeked through, and to Nechum, they were as precious as gems once lost to desert sands.

Alameth grimaced as he swallowed.

Nechum cracked a weary smile. "Welcome back, brother."

As Alameth's eyes circled, they fixated on their surroundings. Soil leaked from the near collapsed ceiling. Fungus cultivated where sickly ooze had dried, feasting on the decomposed bacteria. Rodents wandered in, attracted by the bugs who also ate the rot.

Alameth's chest rose and fell faster. "Did I do this?" he asked.

Unable to be honest yet unwilling to lie, Nechum massaged Alameth's shoulders.

Pursing his lips, Alameth closed his eyes. Tears escaped their corners.

Nechum squeezed his hand and repeated, "It wasn't your fault."

At that moment, Eran stirred and tried to sit up. He opened his mouth as if to say something, but Laszio tapped his shoulder, pressed a finger to his lips, and gestured toward Alameth, who then had buried his face in Nechum's sleeve.

Footsteps echoed from the tunnel, but to Nechum's great relief, Jediah came into view. He was hunched. His right hand clutched an opened shoulder, but he still returned in one piece.

Jediah trudged to meet them, exhaustion in every breath.

"Is it over?" Nechum asked.

Jediah's watering eyes were glued to Laszio and Eran, who were trying to prop themselves up against larger rubble. "Yes," Jediah answered. "Our mission is over."

Nechum's chest tightened. The mission wasn't over. Whether anyone besides himself realized it, there remained a far greater purpose to this than the capture of two demons. A need—Jediah's need—had yet to be met, but Nechum didn't know how to proceed with it. What could an angel say or do for another angel such as him? One who was so bent on understanding what none of them could experience that he'd risk sending traceable letters to a sick child?

Rubbing his eyes, Nechum prayed. *"Alameth wasn't near as complicated as this, Lord. I can't even begin to approach. What do you expect me to do?"*

Jediah knelt beside Alameth and took his hand. "Alameth." His heartsick eyes darted everywhere as he searched for the words. A husked, restrained sob escaped him. "I don't know whether I should hug you or slap you."

An airy chuckle passed through Alameth's split lips.

Jediah rubbed his mouth and recollected himself. "Why? Why did you do that?"

Taking his time, Alameth grunted and lifted on one elbow. He raised his trembling hand over Jediah's good shoulder and took hold of Jediah's sword. His knuckles tightened. "We reflect God to everyone, right?" Their eyes connected. Then, just as his head lolled, Alameth's hand left the sword to slip down and touch Jediah's scarf—at the very spot where the stitched cross sat in the center of the Captain's crest.

Nechum watched the dark portions of Jediah's eyes lighten. A few of the creases that aged his face faded—if for a second.

"You're not looking so good, old friend," an ominous voice uttered.

The hope in Jediah's face dimmed. His posture went rigid.

Sensing Elazar's bitterness, Nechum frowned at the demon, who glared at Jediah's back. His hideous scar looked longer and fresher since the last he saw him in the Forbidden City.

Jediah's hands curled into fists.

Lengthening his back, Laszio shook a fist at Elazar. "Now you get out of here. Just get out of here! Can't you leave Jediah well enough alone?"

"Laszio," Jediah said in an almost hushed voice. He rose, turned around, and protected his shoulder wound with an extra layer of armored feathers.

"Weren't there six in your party?" Elazar asked. He swung Akela's satchel by the strap. "Never mind. I guessed he vaporized himself." He tossed the bag, and gold puffed from its leather. "And besides that, I found this in the tunnels." Between two fingers, he displayed a torn envelope. He tipped it forward, and a small braid flopped out. Its shape on the ground mimicked the body of a dead child.

Nechum sensed Jediah's building rage as Elazar began reading the letter he obviously already read. "Little miss Chloe, huh?" He shook his head. "Not such a noble deed to exploit girls to get what you want, Captain. Still, you seem to be in a bit of a quandary. You've got a message, but no messenger to send it. Shall I do you the favor?"

Jediah's hand snapped to his sword. "Don't bait me, demon!"

With a smirk, Elazar refolded the letter and stepped closer in challenge.

On protective instinct, Nechum clutched Jediah's arm to hold him back, but the steadiness in Jediah's darkened eyes urged him not to interfere. After an uncomfortable silence, Nechum stared at the ground, defeated and dreading the outcome.

Elazar and Jediah stepped closer and closer until they were an arm's length apart. Centuries of bitter tension between them spurned one's hatred and the other's grief.

Flaunting the letter, Elazar waved it in Jediah's face. "Ready to fight or bargain for it, Captain?" he asked.

At that, Jediah punched Elazar square in the nose and snatched the letter from his hand.

Nechum released a breath. *Was that really it? Was that all it took?*

Elazar sniffed, and he cupped his chin to catch the red energy that dripped from his nose. Yet he smiled. "Humph, knew you wouldn't." He raised a glowing hand. "Hence why I brought backup." A red shield broke the cragged ground under Jediah's feet, and heavy rocks battered him down into the pit.

Nechum got up as fast as he could to follow Jediah into the hole, but Elazar destroyed the ceiling, too. More rocks rushed in, filling the cavity like a waterfall in an empty river, and making it impossible for Nechum to know how much earth he'd have to phase through to reach Jediah.

Elazar reclaimed the letter and dusted it off. He smiled at the cataclysm he caused, then cast a grin at the angels. "Well, I did my part," he commented.

As he watched the wretched demon walk away, Nechum's neck heated. He didn't know yet what to do, but all he knew, and all that mattered, was that he just became the last line of defense between Elazar and Chloe. Nechum sprinted.

Hearing his footsteps, Elazar snapped around to raise a barrier, but in the split second before his shield manifested, Nechum leaped over its breech. He barrel rolled, stole the letter, and tucked it under his tunic. "I read the letter too, Elazar. We both know Jediah didn't disclose Chloe's location. You don't actually know where she lives."

"True," Elazar admitted. "But there's more than enough incriminating clues to go on." His hands glowed red. "Hand it over."

Nechum recognized Elazar's technique. He used energy shifting, the art of shifting one's focal energy point from one spot to another, to weaponize his shields. Akela used the same tactic on Io to speed them both to safety after his wings burned. Few angels or demons could do it with such flawless skill as Elazar showed, but Nechum steeled himself. It would hurt, but if he were to protect Chloe, he had to try.

Energy compounded and burned in Nechum's fingers as he forced most of it into his hands. Blue colors glowed in his palms as he stabilized the shift.

Elazar gave a lopsided smile. "Well, this ought to be interesting."

Nechum rushed in. Their hands of red and blue counteracted, repelling their opposite.

Chapter 28

JEDIAH SNAPPED AWAKE. Brown and white specks floated around him. A cold substance slinked along his limbs on every side, and he had the strangest feeling gravity had weakened. Confused as to where he was, he peered at a light that filtered through a clear, moving surface above. Only after standing up did he realize he was at the bottom of an underground pool. He reached up. His hand broke past the waterline, planted a firm hold on the surface and dragged himself out.

The cave walls around him formed a large bowl. Numerous tunnels leaked streams that fed the underground lake he stood upon, but before he could decide whether to pick a path or try phasing upward to reach his brothers, something stirred the atmosphere. Jediah grabbed his sword. The disturbance hummed in a low register like the rumbling of a greedy stomach.

"Well, well," a voice lulled. "A juicy morsel has entered my den."

Jediah's eyes widened. He flinched at the padding of hurried steps. A feline's eye-shine flashed and disappeared, startling him into slashing the air.

"You know, this scenario is strangely familiar to me," the voice crooned with a purr. Whoever stalked Jediah kept moving from place to place; his tonal inflections kept changing. "Now, where have I seen this before? Oh, yes. I remember. This is how they slew several of your precious saints before me. I believe it went something like this."

A lion roared, and the tunnels vibrated under Jediah's boots.

The stranger yawned. "But I'll admit, feeding the beasts got old for me after a while. Coliseum games could get boringly tedious."

Jediah glared to the right. "I know it's you, Lucifer!"

"Hm," the voice hummed from behind. "The sitting duck screams like an eagle."

Whipping around, Jediah scowled and shouted, "Mock all you want. You're still destined to lose. You and your ilk."

Clapping noises bounced around the arena. The audible clutter reverberated too loud to discern its source. "Bravo. Bravo. Got anymore speeches?"

A breath tickled Jediah's neck. The angel turned but again slashed empty air, and a mocking laughter resounded. Jediah released a single wing and shot light in the loudest direction. It hit nothing, and the shadows it cleared dipped back.

"You're wasting your time on me, and on Chloe," Lucifer hissed. "She can't help you anymore than you can help her. And you can't even touch me."

Jediah's wings flared, illuminating the place. "Begone, Lucifer! You're like the rest of your lot. Liars!"

"Like the rest, you say?" Lucifer commented. Foul saliva plopped on Jediah's forehead and smeared down his face. He looked up. The great demon himself shifted his chameleon colors and grinned down at him. "I assure you." His pupils tightened to slits. Fangs multiplied in his jaw. "None are like *me*."

Lucifer's face split to two, then four, then seven. Each head drew apart on sprouting necks. Their faces lengthened. Their toothed maws grew to sizes large enough to swallow cattle whole. Crimson scales glowed like cinders and spread across his body. Horned prongs crowned his heads, and his fingers and toes mutated bones large enough to support his growing muscles pound for pound.

Jediah hyperventilated. The sword shook in his hands.

The great dragon dropped from the ceiling. All fourteen blood coated eyes locked onto him, and all seven heads spoke in unison, "This game ends here."

Jediah barrel rolled from scythe-sized talons. He dove underwater, escaped chomping teeth, and emerged on the other side, flying for an open tunnel.

Satan's massive tail swatted him into the high wall. Ears ringing, Jediah flopped on a high ledge. His sword clattered two feet away. Fighting the vertigo, he crawled to reach it, but a huge hand pinned him down.

"That silly toothpick can't help you," Lucifer mocked. His fingers tightened, crushing Jediah and squeezing more energy out of his shoulder.

In a frantic burst, Jediah wriggled one arm free. He threw his hand out, nabbed his sword, and drove its sharp point up Lucifer's nail between the skin and cuticle. The Devil hollered. Huge red drops seeped down Jediah's blade as he wedged it in deeper.

Finally, Lucifer let go. Jediah gasped and clutched his bruising torso. He gripped the wall, pulling himself up, and looked down from his ledge.

One of Lucifer's heads ripped the sword from his finger and spat it out of reach into the pool.

Tangling with Elazar taxed Nechum's energy. The minutes wore on as they wrestled, and unlike himself, it seemed Elazar wasn't close to tired. Nechum's arms shook from weariness as Elazar leaned into their locked hands. In a spurt of desperation, Nechum leaned left, using Elazar's opposing strength to send him falling forward. Elazar stumbled. Nechum swept his leg, then conjured a force-field and caged him to the ground.

Victorious, Nechum released a relieved laugh. He couldn't believe he won, but then Elazar's eyes glowed. The demon pressed both palms into the ground, and his resulting shield broke the earth in all directions, throwing Nechum off his feet. Falling but aware of Elazar charging him, Nechum blocked his blow with a barrier.

The opponents panted and stared at each other through the azure veil. After an uneventful moment, Nechum wondered if Elazar might give up. After all, he had Chloe's letter and all the clues Elazar needed to track her down, but so long as he shielded himself, Elazar couldn't get to it. Nechum rued himself for not thinking of that sooner.

But then Elazar turned his eyes toward the others—toward his wounded brothers left exposed and in the open. Nechum paled as Elazar chuckled, "You can't protect them and yourself at the same time." The demon pulled out a dagger and threw it.

"No!" Nechum raised a shield that blocked the knife from hitting Eran, but just as he and Elazar already knew, very few of their kind could maintain two large shields at once.

Elazar's punch compressed Nechum's torso. Nechum clutched his throbbing stomach and coughed. The following blows battered his ears and cheeks and forced him to roll over. Pressing his forehead to the ground, Nechum covered his head to protect his face. Strong hands groped for his collar. They reached into his tunic, aimed to steal Jediah's letter, but Nechum flattened his chest against the floor, pinning the envelope firmly between himself and the stones.

Elazar grunted in frustration and pounded Nechum's neck, but the angel crossed his arms beneath his chest and locked them tight. Elazar would not get Chloe. Not if he could help it.

"Pest," Elazar spat.

In the corner of his eye, Nechum saw a long red cord, razor thin, form and extend from Elazar's palm. The whip cracked once, smacking the air. The next crack cut a slit in Nechum's tunic. "That was a warning," Elazar growled. "Hand over the letter."

Nechum regulated his breaths. He scrunched his eyes closed. "Mene, mene, tekel, parsin," he responded between gasps. "God has weighed you. God has measured you, and you will *forever* be in wanting."

Jediah sped down a tunnel too tight for the dragon to fit, but he knew better than to rest. Angry hisses cut the air. Serpent Lucifer slithered faster than Jediah could run and bowled him over.

Jediah twisted around. The green body coiled and fanned a skin hood. Lidless eyes rose high on a column of muscle, but once the snake struck, Jediah grabbed its fangs and kicked it in the eye. Lucifer recoiled, banging his head against the ceiling.

Jediah clapped his wings, but the Devil, as the monstrous lion, dismissed the wispy light like drops of rain. Lucifer's massive paws padded closer and exposed every yellowed claw. His shoulders rolled on one side then the other as he crouched on his haunches.

Jediah stumbled backwards, but his back hit a dead end. Stamina low and his shoulder wound taking its toll, he didn't have the energy needed to phase through the stones. He gasped his breaths, almost ready to collapse. A meaty paw swatted him into the opposite wall.

Everything in Jediah's being seemed to implode. Himself in a state of shock, he slid down onto compacted dirt. He opened a single eye—the one thing that didn't hurt to move. Lucifer the lion followed the gold streaks that led up to him, as does a hound to a wounded creature.

The lion rose on two legs, shed its mane, and walked. The bottom paws sprouted sandaled toes. Brown fur peeled off his face, and Lucifer's arms were then robed in purple and scarlet. His four wings expanded behind him as he crouched over Jediah and stroked his feathers. "Tis' a tragedy," he said. "You're gifted with immortality, yet somehow you waste it acting like you're as good as dead.... You don't even know the meaning of the word 'dead'.... Let me help you with that."

Lucifer squeezed Jediah's neck and wrapped his fingers around the base of his left wing.

Crack!

Jediah screamed without a voice as the sinews in his left wing snapped like thread. His feathers spasmed in mad protests.

Then Lucifer tore at the second.

Crunch!

Jediah laxed, senseless.

Both amputated wings were heaped together at the Devil's feet. Reaping them from the floor, the loathsome creature unhinged his jaw to an unnatural length. Fire leaped out, soldering the wings' bleeding ends closed. Then, while their roots still glowed, Lucifer gritted his teeth and pressed them hard into the middle of his back. Electrical reds and yellows sputtered and sparked. Jediah's golden feathers veined red, and Lucifer fanned the new pair of wings with his original four. "Thank you, Jediah, for your cooperation. Oh, and to ensure you don't regrow those too fast..." He reopened his fiery maw.

Gold stained Elazar's knuckles as he punched the back of Nechum's head for the seventeenth time. As frail as that ministry angel was, he was every bit as stubborn. No amount of whipping or pounding could get him to budge.

"Having trouble?"

Elazar stood up as Lucifer entered. His six wings waved in magnificence like they had always belonged together—except the middle set's muddied coloration didn't quite match. Lucifer tossed the roasted lump he was carrying. Jediah rolled unconscious with scalded burn marks across his bared back.

To Elazar's chagrin, Lucifer shoved him aside. "Here," he said. "Allow me." All six of his wings clapped. A wave of red and gold struck Nechum, knocking him far across the room into a smoking heap. In moments, Lucifer stooped over the angel, returned, and slapped Chloe's letter into Elazar's chest. "This is yours. And these," he motioned to Jediah's wings, "are mine." He walked toward the exit. "Come. It'll take time to muster our legions to seize the Abyss, and our old friends have waited for us long enough."

"You mean *your* old friends," Elazar countered.

Lucifer laughed and waved a dismissive hand. "Fine. Stay. I don't really care. We both got what we wanted."

Elazar stood in silence. He drank in the sight of Jediah, his enemy, beaten and stripped. It was just like he wanted, but as his anger began slipping away, Elazar encountered an emptiness. His fleeting wrath left a hole. After five millennia of obsessing for his justice, something yet remained unachieved.

Elazar heard someone growl from behind and looked back.

Several feet away, Laszio dragged himself with one arm. He winced and repressed gasps with every centimeter, but the storm in his eyes bore into Elazar. Eran, who laid beside him, restrained him with one hand. Their eyes locked together, and Elazar sensed a silent conversation play out between the two. Laszio's head bent down. His shoulder blades convulsed, and Eran, using his right wing, wrapped Laszio and drew him close to his side.

The scene fixated Elazar in place. There before him were Jediah's wingmen, yet instead of Laszio and Eran, he saw two very different angels... Jediah and himself... from another time and another place.

The rage Elazar missed rekindled. There was but one way to add devastating insult to Jediah's injury. He crinkled the letter and shook it in his fist. "You two tell Jediah I'll give Chloe *Jack's* regards."

Chapter 29

ERAN COULDN'T COUNT the hours underground, and not knowing how many had passed stressed him more. He massaged the tingling out of his regenerated legs. Laszio, who sat beside him, had his knees drawn to his chin and hadn't budged since Elazar left. They both just listened to a comatose Nechum's labored breaths. Nechum had yet to awaken, and Eran envied him for it. To be blissfully unaware of what had transpired would have been a kindness.

Jediah sat a distance away. Eran wanted to weep for the two soldered stumps on his back. His wings were gone. The Key was in enemy hands, and now Jediah counted on him and Laszio to protect the Abyss. Eran disdained the idea of abandoning their captain now, but he knew they must leave him behind and soon.

Eran tested the strength of his wings. Twinges peppered their joints, but they otherwise handled the air well. It wouldn't be long before they were fit for travel. Eran pressed his head into his hands. He didn't want to command. Never did. Jediah was captain and a gifted one. Who was he besides the lowest officer with the shakiest strategies and no plan?

"I don't remember ever feeling this low," Laszio murmured beside him. He seemed to have taken Eran's words right out of his mouth.

Eran raised his head and looked at his best friend. "To be honest, me neither."

Laszio's foot traced pointless circles in the dirt. "Can I confess something?" he whispered. "I'm ashamed to say it, but so many times... so many times I've asked the Lord 'why'. Why did He make me so weak?" He hugged his knees tighter. "There's so much I want to give, Eran. So much I want to do for Him. But even at my best, I fail. Why'd God make me like that? Why must I have the passion to conquer mountains yet incapable of placing a foothold on the smaller hills?"

Eran watched his friend sag like a dying tree, and he himself felt like dying with him.

Laszio licked his lips. "I love His people. I love my brothers. I love *Him*," his husked voice rushed. "So why does He hold me back?"

Eran bowed his head and admitted, "I've wondered the same things too, brother, but I don't know anymore than you do. God must have some reason."

"All I ever desired is to help Him," said Laszio. "Help God's good work in the world."

Hearing that, Eran paused. Something different, like another lens in his perception, took shape. "Help Him..." he repeated. "Help Him... Do we really help Him, Laszio?"

Laszio rolled his eyes and grunted, "No. All we do is mess up."

"No. I mean, not only us. I mean all of us. Does He really need any of our help?" After Laszio didn't respond, Eran pressed. "Well? Is He God or isn't He God?" A few seconds later, Eran sat up straighter. "I guess what we tend to forget, Laszio, is that whatever it is we do or have done, He could have done for Himself. Our worth can't be tied to what we can do for Him or how much we think He needs our help."

Dejected, Laszio turned toward him and asked, "Then why do we exist? Why create us to serve if we're not needed?"

"To show us the depths of His love," Eran answered. "He never needed us, but He's made us for Him to delight in. He's allowed us to be imperfect, so His unconditional grace can come to light. For what need is there for mercy when there's no fault? And..." Eran took a moment to reflect on his next words. For they mattered just as much to him as it did to Laszio. "God expressed how much He loves us by giving us the chance to do something we never could."

"And what is that?" asked Laszio.

Eran cleared his throat. "To become part of something far bigger than ourselves. Think of it, Laszio. God has invited us to share in the good work of bringing His message of love to those who need it. And last I checked," he planted a firm hand on his brother's shoulder as tears sprung from his eyes. "He uses His weakest for His greatest glories."

His arm and shoulder trembled. Removing his grip, Eran turned and stared ahead with a contented smile. "He created you to delight in you, Laszio. He created me to delight in me and to delight in all who love Him. And if we love Him, He gifts us with the means to express it in the exact unique way He designed us to... in whatever form that takes."

After a moment's silence, Laszio gave a tired chuckle, feeble yet sincere. "You always were the smart one, Eran."

"Well," said Eran. "One of us has to be."

Laszio laughed and gently elbowed Eran's side.

Gripping the tender spot, Eran smiled. "Easy. I'm gonna need that later."

"Mm."

Eran looked behind to find Nechum had opened a groggy eye. "Haven't we had enough fighting?"

"Hey," Laszio said. "How are you feeling?"

Nechum's cheek pressed against the stone. "Better... relatively."

Eran unfurled his restored wings. Laszio followed suit. Then, in unified consent, they made their feathers interlock. They glowed. The quills fluffed, and the two laid the new downy blanket over Nechum, enveloping him in soothing warmth. The tension in Nechum's shoulders dispelled.

A tall figure approached. Alameth, now able to stand, watched them with a kind sympathy Eran never expected to see from him ever. The second their eyes met, Alameth turned his gaze elsewhere and folded his hands. He frowned. His mouth opened and closed over and over, as though needing to speak but too ashamed to, but Eran knew exactly what he meant to say. "There's nothing to forgive..."

"... brother," Laszio finished.

Alameth's eyebrows raised. A strange gloss blanketed his eyes, and he smiled a smile that transfigured his entire being. No longer did he look like that aloof, unfeeling entity to Eran, nor that fearsome phantom that lingered close by. He was an angel—an angel who loved more deeply than he or Laszio knew and struggled with weaknesses and failings, just as they.

"Alameth," Nechum croaked.

Heeding Nechum's call, Alameth stooped down and sat beside him.

Nechum lifted a hand. "Help me up, please."

"What? No," Eran protested. "You need rest. You're not healed yet." He frowned at the wetted rips across Nechum's tunic where Elazar's lash had struck.

Instead of acknowledging Eran's concern, Nechum squeezed Alameth's hand and said, "Jediah needs you, Alameth. Go to him."

Alameth pursed his lips. He bowed his head, hiding his expression under his hood. "He doesn't need me. Why would he?" he asked.

"Believe me, brother," Nechum said. "He does."

Moving, even with Alameth's support, was near insufferable for Nechum. Every footstep equalled another stab to his legs, yet he trained his mind on Jediah. His empathic sense tasted a despair in him he only felt in the most broken of individuals.

Nechum's heel struck a protruding rock. He hissed as his entire ankle hummed.

"You want to go back?" Alameth whispered.

It occurred to Nechum Alameth wanted a way out, but as much as he disliked it, it was his turn to be firm. "No," he insisted. "We're doing this."

As they approached, Jediah cast a concerned look at Nechum's ragged appearance. He sighed, "You both should rest, brothers."

"Then may we rest with you?" Nechum asked.

Jediah turned his face away. "You need not ask my permission."

Nechum bit his tongue to keep from moaning as Alameth lowered him. His knees felt like snapping, but soon he sat with Alameth and Jediah on either side.

Nervous shivers ran all over Nechum as he watched Jediah pull off his scarf, the one that bared the captain's crest, and cast it aside. "That scarf looks better on you than on the ground, Captain," Nechum said.

Jediah stared at the cloth he threw away, now curled in its lonely pile. "What does it matter? I never deserved it anyway."

Nechum rested his hands in his lap. "But isn't that the point of God's grace, brother? Not deserving it?"

Jediah bent his neck, hiding his face further, and Nechum locked his jaw. His brother was slipping further away. "Jediah," Nechum flinched at first for addressing him informally, but realized this was the perfect time. They weren't officer and advisor right now. They were family. "I'm not going to pretend I have all the answers. I wish I did," he said.

Jediah didn't move.

Nechum swallowed. "But don't think for a second that you're alone. All of us have come up short. Many times and in many ways."

"I already know that, Nechum," Jediah replied.

"Yet," Nechum continued, "you don't know there are even those of us who've desperately longed for Christ's salvation for the same reasons you did." Taking a pause, Nechum turned to Alameth.

Alameth's green eyes shone from under his hood like a cat hiding in a box. He shrank back, uncertain about entering the conversation, but Nechum nodded to him with an encouraging smile. *It'll be okay, Alameth.*

Alameth sighed, then pulled back his hood to rest loosely on his shoulders. "He's referring to me, Captain."

Jediah's head snapped up to look at him.

Staring into his lap, Alameth rubbed his legs back and forth. "You've spent lifetimes suffering from guilt for wronging somebody, right?" he asked. "Thinking your foolish mistake not only hurt yourself but wounded someone close to you?"

The inner corners of Jediah's eyebrows raised at a slight angle. "Yeah," he said in a breathy whisper.

Alameth nodded and said, "I thought as much."

Jediah changed positions. "Who did you wrong?"

Alameth took a moment before starting. "It was about 2,000 years before the Son's Birth. God's promised people, the sons of Abraham, languished in Pharaoh's grip."

"Right before the Tabernacle Age," Jediah deduced.

"Yes," Alameth confirmed. "The length and breadth of Egypt's sins had reached its full measure. God determined then to punish their years of careless bloodshed and free the people of His prophecy. He hardened Pharaoh's heart and granted that power-hungry man the indomitable will he always wanted... We all know the price Pharaoh paid for his pride."

"The ten plagues." Jediah barely uttered those words, and Alameth lifted his head to reveal the most sorrowful eyes.

Realization caught up with Jediah. "The tenth plague... was you. You killed the firstborn." Jediah shook his head in disbelief.

Nechum rubbed Alameth's shoulder. He didn't know if he could continue. Already he sensed the past attacking Alameth's memories, cementing him in place.

Alameth's hair covered his face as he bowed his head. "And there will be a loud wailing throughout Egypt," he recited. "Worse than there has ever been or ever will be again."

"That must have been hard," Jediah consoled, bowing his head.

"Horrible," Alameth replied. "But not near as horrible as my response. For you see, Jediah... when God gave me that order... I yelled at Him."

Nechum didn't need his empathic sense to feel Jediah's shock. The soldier went ashen. His neck stretched upward, and his eyes bore into Alameth, confused and afraid.

Alameth beat back the trembling in his voice to continue speaking. "When God summoned me for the task, I remember thinking, 'How could He ask me this? To devastate generations all at once? He knew I hated dooming the lost. So why in heaven would He ask me?'" Alameth clutched his coat, wrinkling it with his fingers. "I forgot His providence. He knows the heart of every man. He knew that generation would become twice as evil as their stiff-necked parents and ancestors if not stopped. More importantly, His Messianic line, His seed to destroy the Curse, needed to leave Egypt. It depended on this disaster taking place. But I was so selfishly wrapped up in my own turmoil... I yelled... I screamed right in His presence. I first begged God not to make me do it. Then I outright refused do it."

Jediah gasped. Nechum too shivered. A refusal to God marked rebellion, the eternal death of the costliest sort.

Alameth's head raised. "Then, right when I almost walked away from the Throne forever," he shook his head. "I can't even describe the guilt that ran me through. It stopped me cold, and I realized the full gravity of what I had just done... I was directly opposing my Maker's ultimate plan to rescue *all* nations through Israel."

Alameth ran his hand through his hair. "My strength left me, and I fell prostate at His feet. I wept so loud—not just for His forgiveness, but for my weakness. Because I knew, even as I repented for my disrespect, I didn't have it in me to do what He asked. I could not obey."

Jediah scooted closer. "And then?"

"El Shaddai stepped down from His Throne." Alameth said. "And do you know what He said to me?" He smiled as the tears freely flowed.

Jediah shook his head, as his own tears sprang up, too.

Alameth continued, "He said to me, 'Your weakness is the very reason I've chosen you, Alameth. Consider whom I have called: Not many of them were wise; not many were powerful; not many were of noble birth. But I chose the foolish things of the world to shame the wise; I chose the weak things of the world to shame the strong. I chose the lowly and despised things of the world, and the things that are not, to nullify the things that are.' Then our Lord raised my head, saying, 'My grace is sufficient. For my power is made perfect through weakness. Remain in Me, and I will remain in you. Just as no branch can bear fruit by itself unless it remains in the vine, neither can you bear fruit unless you remain in Me.'"

Nechum couldn't contain himself either and cried quietly. Joy from knowing the goodness of their Lord was so strong, it couldn't be felt without breaking the heart.

"Then finally," Alameth recalled. "God helped me to my feet and said, 'Do not fear, Alameth. For I am with you; I will strengthen and uphold you in my right hand.'"

Jediah wiped the moisture dripping off his chin.

Alameth stood up and stepped closer to Jediah and kneeled. "Like you, Captain, I could have eaten myself alive for resisting Him as I did. But those four simple words He said to me continue to echo in my mind today and saved me, even calming me as I lifted the breath of life from millions... My grace is sufficient."

Jediah's gaze drifted aside.

"It's the point of belonging to God, brother," Alameth said. "Whether be we angels or the redeemed." Jediah's eyes returned to Alameth as he finished with, "Christ is sufficient. Through whatever harms, threats, or weaknesses, He's enough."

Jediah fell into a reverent silence, and Nechum's spirit rose to sense the change in him. Fire burgeoned in Jediah's sunset eyes until it dawned into a new morn. "He's enough," Jediah repeated to himself. He arose. His slouched and scorched back straightened, and despite the lack of wings, his nobility returned in his stance.

Nechum stood up and bowed in respect. "So what are your orders, Captain?"

Jediah opened his palm and looked at the frayed lock of braided hair he had kept. Cupping it, he gave it shelter in his pocket and turned on his heel for the tunnels.

"Sir?" Nechum called. "Where are you going?"

The reinvigorated warrior clenched both fists and put confidence in every stride. "I need my sword."

Chapter 30

PLASTIC LIDS BOUNCED as the nurse wheeled the food containers along. The cart's unfixed, gimpy wheel rattled despite the smooth floor, and she rescued another meal from tipping off its stack. It felt lukewarm in her hand. She sighed and wished the hospital upgraded their meal service, but food was food. Patients needed to eat. Room to room, she plastered on her practiced grin, repeated the same greeting, and left the platters. It was the same song and dance she played over fifty times a day.

She pulled the handle bar, stopping the cart's momentum. "Okay, room 602." She checked her clipboard, dragging a finger along the list. She picked a container from the top. "Poor thing. I hope she likes peas." Her knuckles tapped on the doorframe. "Chloe, it's dinnertime." She walked in. "Chloe? Are you up?" No sooner did she pass the half pulled curtain, the nurse's instincts kicked into high gear. She plopped the plastic container on the mini-table and hurried down the hall. "Hey, Philip! We need Dr. Boumont! Stat!"

The angels crammed around an old pay phone. Jediah concentrated hard and enabled his fingers to tap the metal box's numbers.

Nechum, meanwhile, knocked the phone off the receiver and, despite being in angelic form, shoved pocket change in its slot.

Certain he wouldn't have long to wait, Jediah began wrapping extra cloths around his palms. If he was going to protect Chloe while wingless, he needed to counteract Elazar's force-fields. The idea Eran gave him was unorthodox. It was risky, but if a wallop of Alameth's mist could do as much damage as they've just experienced, a smashed smoke pellet to Elazar's hands might do the trick.

"You sure you got the right number, Nechum?" Jediah asked as he secured the knots.

"Yes, I'm connecting you with the desk clerk." Nechum answered. "You sure you want to do this?"

Jediah nodded. "The phone lines are the surest and fastest way to Chloe."

"Merging your energy with human conduits will disorient you for a while," Nechum warned.

Jediah kept staring at the speaker where it swung. "It's a risk worth taking. The rest of you, follow Eran and Laszio's lead and stop Lucifer from freeing Apollyon."

"Captain," Laszio interjected.

Jediah expected objections such as 'Don't go alone' or 'Let us come with you'; all of which he prepared himself to dismiss.

But Laszio instead calmly placed a hand over his chest and bowed. "God be with you, brother." As he spoke, the rest of them all did the same.

Soaking in the sight, Jediah radiated with a loving pride and smiled. He returned their bows. Then, tightening the buckle that kept his sword strapped to his back, Jediah said, "Leading you all has been an honor. Laszio? Eran?"

His wingmen raised their chins and stood at attention.

"Be strong and courageous."

Their grey eyes alighted with swirling blues and greens and saluted. "Sir, yes, sir."

Nechum dialed the numbers and offered Jediah the phone. "Be careful, Captain."

It rang.

Touching the device, Jediah felt himself getting sucked into the speaker. Electrical currents smothered and stretched him thin. His head buzzed.

"Hello?" a voice boomed.

Jediah shot out of the desk clerk's phone, and all he could do was roll around to his hands and knees. Sounds were muffled in his ears. Everything around him swayed and was bathed in blues and reds. He raised a hand to feel his way around, but his fingers were numb.

"Jack?" a distant voice called.

He looked up. Random shapes materialize. They enlarged, forming what appeared to be a disfigured face. He scrunched his eyes, urging them to correct.

"Jack, you shouldn't be here."

Jediah threw up a hand in defense, but missed.

"Whoa, whoa, whoa. Easy. It's me, remember?" The rest of his supposed assailant took shape.

Blinking hard, Jediah stood up as the stranger came into focus. "Y-you're Chloe's ministry angel. The one from before."

The angel planted his hands on his hips. "And you're the angel who visited Chloe as a human a few days ago. Care to explain what's going on?"

Jediah fell forward and gripped the angel's clothes. "Where's Chloe? Where is she?"

"They're taking her upstate for emergency surgery," the angel replied.

Confused, Jediah tried looking around. Blue and red flashes intensified from the right hallway.

"Why are you here?" the angel demanded. "I don't know what's gotten into you, but I've gotta leave with her."

Jediah clung to him harder. "Take me with you."

"What?"

"Just do it!"

"Okay! Okay."

The angel guided him closer to the flashes. The pulsing lights strained Jediah's bleary eyes. They were mounted on a mammoth box with sharp-lined letters decorated on its side. By then, Jediah guessed it to be an emergency truck. Green clad workers attended to a wheeled bed and lifted it into the truck's cargo hold. Whether from instinct or logical deduction, Jediah knew it was Chloe.

The ministry angel sprinted Jediah forward, getting them both inside before the doors locked shut.

Jediah knelt by the bedside. There laid Chloe, more pale and frail than ever. A clear, nozzled mask attached her to a box. It seemed such a device would smother her, yet he could hear her breathing. Jediah found little reason to relax, however. Her Mark of the Trinity yet remained incomplete. Still, Jediah let out a breath. She was at least alive.

"You see, brother?" the ministry angel said. "She's fine."

"Yes," Jediah replied. "She *will* be." He unsheathed his sword and plunged it deep into the angel's chest. Glowing red stained the blade.

Astonishment and rage contorted the angel's face as he coughed up more red.

"Just like God said," Jediah said as he glared back. "Darkness can't comprehend the light."

Clenching his teeth, Elazar relinquished his disguise.

"You know me, *demon*," Jediah admitted. "But I know you too, and I knew you couldn't resist letting me near her just so I could watch her die."

Elazar sneered. His shaking hand gripped the blade, never minding the razor edge. "Well? You still came, didn't you? So let's get this over with." Elazar raised his other hand. Red colors raced up his arm, but Jediah smashed a grey smoke pellet into his fingers before the shield could materialize.

Elazar screamed. Acidic smoke ate his palm just as Jediah hoped it would, and the cloth he had strapped to his own palm protected his hand from similar damage.

Elazar ripped himself from Jediah's blade. "Curse you!" He raised the other hand, only for it to be ruined in the same way.

"There!" Jediah remarked while poising his sword. "Our odds are even!"

Elazar pulsed a brief shield from his chest, knocking the sword out of Jediah's hand. The two locked arms, tumbling and wrestling inside a tight box that traveled at eighty miles per hour.

Deep within the caves so familiar to them, Laszio and Eran scurried about in front of the Abyss's entry tunnel. Laszio added another log to a woodpile; one of many they've gathered on their way back. He had no idea why Eran insisted upon it at first. It seemed absurd and a waste of precious time. Even after his friend shared the full scope of his plan, it still sounded crazy. But Lucifer wouldn't expect it, which for Laszio actually gave credence to the old saying 'crazy enough to work.'

Laszio did worry, though, if they'd be able to set it all up in time. It required plenty of wood. Plus, they needed to inform the rest of Jediah's battalion about Lucifer's impending attack, as well as Eran's defense plan. Thankfully, with Nechum to brief the other soldiers and Alameth's ability to lift a forest's worth of timber, both tasks were swiftly met. Everything and everyone were in place.

Laszio lugged another branch and clunked it atop one of the stacks. "You sure this is enough?" he asked.

"It'll have to be." Eran replied. "We can't risk fetching more. It's miraculous enough Lucifer has taken this long as it is."

At that moment, a slight rattling caught their attention. The two angels looked at each other, and their eyes spelled out the same message: Lucifer had arrived. They plated their wings across their chests and faced uphill toward the other end of the corridor.

The clattering of steel echoed louder. Flickering shadows expanded and climbed the tunnel's throat until the rusted browns of the stones were consumed by black silhouettes. Lucifer's tall figure arose first. He loomed at the top of the hill, fanning all six wings. A second demon joined him. Then five. Then twenty. Then fifty. Hundreds more crawled along the walls like spiders or flocked in the air like crows. Their unanimous laughters and jeers were thunderous.

Lucifer raised a hand. The throng silenced, and he lingered there, sneering at Laszio and Eran like they were gnats.

Laszio's chest tightened. Not but twelve hours ago, this infamous demon thrashed their captain, and here they stood to try and take him down. Laszio leaned to Eran. "You think we can do this?" he whispered, sounding a tad more nervous than he wanted.

Eran's brow creased, but he looked Laszio square in the eye with a hint of a smile. "No."

Laszio laughed with a touch of apprehension. "Good. For a second I was worried."

They together whipped out their chorded sticks and tapped them against their energized wings. Light filled the sticks' etched patterns. The brilliance bled into their taut strings, and the strands burned golden flares, illuminating the angels' faces and their righteous anger.

Lucifer roared loud enough to cow a leviathan. "The battle has ended, little ones! Your captain has fallen, and the key is mine to bear."

"No," Laszio countered. He stepped forward to emphasize his point. "Let *me* tell *you* how this ends, Lucifer! With your humiliation! You will not fall to the mighty, oh fallen morning star—oh former son of the dawn! But to God's meekest and weakest! You hear me? The least of His shall crush your neck today!"

Raising his chin, Lucifer scoffed and led the charge. They all rushed as a single black swarm down the slope.

Laszio and Eran harnessed spheres to their strands and aimed toward a single point. For a few seconds, they waited. The thundering hoard advanced closer.

"Now," Eran signaled.

They snapped their strings. The spheres whizzed high and collided together in a loud 'pop.' The demon frontline paused, as the resulting white residue powdered them. They weren't impressed in the least. That is, until the floor broke.

A smoking fault line cracked open before them. Lucifer, who was undaunted by this, flew across the widening divide, but before the others could follow or retreat, the ground collapsed entirely, swallowing their first legion whole.

Laszio chuckled as Alameth's fog billowed from the increasing pit. Those demons were in for a horrible time. The demonic back line scrambled to escape the increasing cataclysm. Defiant shouts and terrified whines mounted as the angel of death rose to greet them atop the towering plumes, with eyes pulsing bright.

Some five hundred demons, however, weren't near as skittish about facing a Destroyer, and shot sparking arrows at Alameth. What they didn't expect was the thick curtain of light beams that erupted from the foggy pit below, snuffing out every shaft.

The demon army stared in confusion.

Alameth lifted the veil. A hundred wings flared like small bonfires, and Jediah's troops flew out. Though they were outnumbered, each angel waved and fanned their wings in fierce challenge.

Laszio and Eran shouted the soldier's war cry proudly with their comrades, as the two armies crashed into each other. "The Sword of the Lord we are!"

Unperturbed, Lucifer enlarged, sprouted seven heads, complete with dragon maws, and torched the closest angels. Jediah's battalion retaliated with their own light barrage. Lucifer, however, dismissed such feeble assaults.

Alameth amassed his mist, and Laszio held his breath. He wasn't sure how Alameth's attack would go, but he was the most powerful brother among them. If his assault didn't faze the Devil, he and Eran would have to resort to plan 'B'.

Alameth sent a tidal wave big enough to cover the highest of Lucifer's heads, but Lucifer rose high on his haunches. His wings, the size of sails, stirred a hurricane. The gales dissolved the fog and hurtled airborne angels to the ground.

"Guess it's Plan B!" Laszio shouted. He hurried with Eran to their positions behind the dragon.

A hellish glow grew in the back of all seven of Lucifer's throats. Orange flames lined in red poured out against the angelic forces, but a sudden, blue blockade turned the flames back on the fire breather himself. Only after the heat died did Lucifer see the glistening barrier that cut him off. The Devil spun around but released an angry roar to find that a whole dome had caged him in.

"Way to go, Nechum!" Laszio thought. He and Eran gave Nechum a thumbs up as he watched and maintained the shield from the outside.

"Watch it!" Eran pulled Laszio by the collar. They ducked out of the bellowing dragon's way. Breaking slab rumbled under his reptilian feet as he thrusted himself at Nechum. Having no luck, Lucifer scraped the shield like mad. His gigantic talons carved a slit and dug, chipping the slit wider.

Nechum recoiled, shocked and terrified, but just as Lucifer mounted up to smash the entire barrier, Nechum shot the Devil with the harshest scowl Laszio ever saw. He slapped both hands on the shield. The rippling azure thickened to an opaque aqua and resealed the hole.

Laszio and Eran cringed as Lucifer's claws screeched against the shield like knives on glass and his chomping fangs chipped at their tips. He carried on like that for a while. Then he calmed. All seven heads laughed, "You three really think you can trap me here?" Lucifer's massive tail swept the air above Laszio and Eran's heads as he faced them.

"We just did, sunshine," Laszio joked.

Lucifer roared, and a torrent blasted from his nostrils.

"Wings!" Eran ordered.

The heatwave they captured in their feathers propelled them straight up. Fire curved back. It ignited the surrounding wood piles and burned the great dragon, smelting his iron scales into a thinner layer of molten ore. Soot and smoke from the smoldering timber filled the dome, smothering everything inside in pitch black.

Jediah and Elazar's hands were blurs in their punches, blocks, and throws. Millennium's worth of combat experience burst from both of them with animalistic instinct—vicious and rapid, yet accurate and precise.

Elazar stabbed at Jediah. Jediah grappled his wrist and twisted it. The knife clanged to the floor. Jediah then spun Elazar around by the neck and slammed him against the window. Orange highway lights flashed as the ambulance sped along. "There's nothing left in you," Jediah remarked. "Nothing but hate!"

"It's all that's left of me," Elazar grunted. "You made me, after all."

"Oh, save it!" Jediah nearly tore Elazar's clothes from how hard he shook him. "You made your own choices! I spent centuries convicting myself for inciting your downfall while you played the victim. Well, guess what? I'm not playing your game anymore!"

Jediah grabbed Elazar's hair to bang his head, but Elazar phased right through the door. Left alone, for however briefly, Jediah picked up his sword and watched every angle. His eyes darted faster as the inactivity prolonged. He drew close to Chloe and held her small hand, hoping she'd somehow feel his presence.

On an inkling, Jediah spun around.

Elazar's eye glowed outside the front windshield. He seized the steering wheel, and veered the ambulance into a busy lane, terrifying the driver.

Jediah launched himself through the glass and knocked Elazar off the windshield. Car horns honked as the ambulance swerved back into its lane.

Elazar, who got a secure foothold on the ambulance grill, seized Jediah's tunic and repeatedly punched him in the jaw. Dizzy from the flurry of blows and emergency lights, Jediah thrust his head into Elazar's, stunning him. Jediah then broke free from his grip, flipped around, and kicked Elazar right off to be crushed under the tires. He heard thuds fade down the highway, but Jediah took no confidence in it. Elazar would journey to Hell if he were there.

Amidst the suffocating black, Laszio listened with Eran under the cover of ashen sparks. Heat wafted near as two of Lucifer's heads came close. In unison, the two soldiers flicked their feather darts and blinded all four eyes at once.

Lucifer's tail and legs thrashed in mad attempts to crush them. Laszio flew straight through the twisting necks as they writhed. His wings burned brighter and sliced small cuts across three throats as he passed. The necks clustered together. Then all seven jaws snapped in his direction. Laszio swerved left in a downward angle and heard the heads thud against the wall. Unfortunately, he misjudged his distance from the ground and scuffed his hands and knees in a near crash landing.

Lucifer stomped one of his feet. The resulting shockwave threw Laszio off and smacked him into the wall. His back numbed, he slumped near senseless.

"No. no. no," Eran repeated as he hoisted Laszio up. "Come on, brother. Stay with me."

Stretching his tingling back, Laszio grinned. "Always."

The black smoke lightened to a grey as the ash settled.

"Hang tight," Eran urged, as he pulled Laszio to a stand. "End of phase one. Prepare for phase two." He took off and flapped his wings as hard as ever, stirring the black flakes and re-stoking the fires.

Chapter 31

NECHUM FLINCHED AT every white pop as Laszio and Eran's spheres pinged off his dome's inner walls. Speeding faster, the lights teamed. Lucifer's roars grew deafening. Just as Eran had planned, by ricocheting countless orbs in the smoke cover, Lucifer wouldn't know which direction their spheres were coming from. He'd swing wildly and continue to miss the two angels as they peppered him with a meteor shower.

Nechum didn't know how much punishment the Devil could take, though, nor if his brothers might accidentally hit each other. "Lord, let this be over soon," he prayed.

Wack!

Nechum's ears rang, and his left temple hemorrhaged as he crashed to the floor. *"Stay awake,"* he pleaded to himself. *"Don't drop the shield. Stay awake."* He dared open an eye.

Three demons surrounded him. Their leader carried a hammer that dripped fresh gold. Grinning, he bent over Nechum, strangled him to pin him down, and aimed his hammer over his forehead. "X marks the spot," he taunted.

Nechum gagged and squirmed, but couldn't get loose. He imagined his forehead about to be split open.

The demon swung.

Mist whipped out, grabbed the hammer, and drove it multiple times into its owner's nose. The demon dropped cold, revealing Alameth standing right behind.

The grim angel shot a stark glare at the other demons, but the stubborn assailants jeered. They flanked Alameth, spitting their threats.

Alameth's eyes flickered in response. His fogs consumed the hammer. Its wood decayed to rot, and its iron rusted to fine powder.

The demons shrank back with second thoughts about picking a fight with a Destroyer.

The mist returned to Alameth's opened palm. He balled it in his fist, and it sputtered like an angry pet between his fingers. "Give me one... more... reason," he dared.

The demons fled like whipped dogs, and Nechum never thought he'd be so happy to see an angel of death in his life. Alameth's features softened as he bent to help him up. He dabbed energy off Nechum's temple with his sleeve. "Are you making it through this?" he asked.

"Trying to," Nechum jested through his rattled nerves. "Thanks."

More commotion raged overhead. Red and black uniforms from the opposing sides collided with each other in such dense pockets, it seemed a wonder the whole cave didn't tear itself apart.

Alameth pulled out his bow. He strung three arrows and the white shafts struck their mark. The meaty brute he targeted succumbed to paralysis and dropped heavy as a wheat sack. Alameth smiled. "Do you think I really needed to waste three shots on that one?"

Nechum shrugged. "I really wouldn't know."

Giving a thoughtful nod, Alameth lifted off for a better vantage point.

Nechum checked the dome. Despite his near lapse in consciousness moments ago, the shield remained intact. Still, he noticed things were oddly quiet in there. Lucifer didn't beat the walls. No pinging lights. No clear sign of defeat or victory yet.

Rain pelted the ambulance. Jediah remained poised on its roof and grew more and more wary. Elazar had likely delayed his next attack to throw him off on purpose.

The Seine River followed the busy road. Its waters blended with the night as an inky void, and only under the lamplight could one distinguish its irritated waves.

The ambulance turned left onto a bridge. Jediah frowned as the space shrank around the vehicle. *"No room for escape,"* he thought. *"Great place for an ambush."* He leaned far enough to check the waters below. The currents looked ravenous and eager to claim anyone that fell in.

The ambulance got halfway across the bridge, when an enormous truck pulled into the opposite lane. The behemoth's tires hissed and rumbled. Its horn blared louder than the emergency sirens. Then the truck's spotlights turned on the ambulance, and before Jediah could react, both vehicles collided.

Screeching rubber, shattering glass, and a cacophony of beeps and honks followed, as Jediah was thrown off onto the street. He screamed at the truck as it shoved the ambulance backwards. The bridge's concrete railing broke apart, and the back left tire of Chloe's vehicle hung over the edge. The truck stopped with its grill firmly smashed into the teetering ambulance.

Hearing the semi's engine rev again, Jediah dragged himself up, sprinted, and focused hard to seize the truck's tailgate before it could push the ambulance into the Seine. All eighteen wheels spun and smoked against him. They cast up buckets of rain water.

Jediah gritted his teeth—not from strain, but at how easily the physical wanted to slip from his metaphysical fingers. No matter how he adjusted his grip, it kept inching itself out.

He glared at the side-view mirror for the driver responsible only to see the trucker laying lifeless over his steering wheel. No doubt his foot was still stamped on the gas pedal. Jediah grunted and pulled harder, trying to drag the truck back. He checked the mirror again. Elazar exited the man he had possessed, who'm he used to ram the ambulance, and jumped out the driver's window. He eyed the ambulance where it sat precariously over the river.

"Elazar, don't!" Jediah shouted.

Elazar looked at him. He wouldn't smile—didn't so much as frown. "Her blood is on your head," he said, as he stepped toward the vehicle.

Desperate, Jediah prayed out loud. "I can't let go of this truck, Lord. I need help!"

The ambulance driver stumbled out and collapsed on the street. He laid there, shaken and bleeding.

"Get up," Jediah whispered, as he watched Elazar near the ambulance. "Come on. Please, get up."

The man fumbled to a stand. He hurried to the semi truck.

That's it. Almost there.

The man tugged the handle and threw the door open.

Jediah grunted. He couldn't hang onto the truck much longer. The rumbling engine shut off, and Jediah's pent up desperation unraveled so fast he sprinted, tackled Elazar, and tossed him off the bridge without registering exactly how he managed it.

As Elazar fell into the river, Jediah ran into the ambulance. The crunched windshield had caved into the warped dashboard. Metal shards had torn the polyester seats.

Weaving through debris, Jediah reached Chloe and found that the devices meant to lock her bed's wheels in place were compromised. It had already slid into the locked double doors.

Jediah placed a palm over her chest. Her lungs rose and fell. He sighed a prayer of relief. She was alive.

Thud!

Jediah unsheathed his sword.

Clang!

His hands firmed their grip.

Clank!

The ambulance doors swung open. Jediah grabbed, but his unfocused hands failed to stop the bed. In mortal panic, he dove after the girl, and the last thing he saw was her body, her soul, and spirit disappear into the swirling black.

The charred wood Laszio and Eran relied on died to embers, and the smoke thinned and steamed into a white grey. Disturbed by Lucifer's silence, Laszio ground his heel deeper in the powdered charcoal. This wasn't like the Devil. Either he was down and out or, more likely, biding his time. He and Eran had noticed something odd when their spheres stopped hitting Lucifer in his dragon form. The demonic cherub must have shape-shifted to a smaller size.

Laszio scanned the haze. Eran beside him also inched forward.

Then a silhouette revealed itself. Three bands of color that wrapped the figure alighted. Lucifer's four red wings crowned his head above and graced the floor at his feet. Jediah's stolen wings, on the other hand, twitched out of sync. They waved like the crooked appendages of a disgusting insect, and sported a muted gold, after intermingling with the demon's crimson for too long.

Laszio and Eran shot two spheres at his face. The Devil's wings knocked the lights aside. Laszio chilled. Their assault hadn't worn Lucifer down in the slightest.

The Devil sped forward, seized the two angels by their necks, and flung them into the air. Lucifer's six powerful wings clapped, and Laszio's vision filled with red and gold lighting.

Nechum gasped as the snapping thunder inside his dome vibrated. A barbed pain dug into him when his empathic sense connected with Laszio and Eran. *This was not good.*

Unnatural reds and golds then filled the cave's crevices. Both angel and demon armies froze and gawked as the light show traveled. Their mixed colors spread faster, leaving no space untouched.

Nechum's knees went weak. Whatever Lucifer was doing with Jediah's power would crush everyone. He yelled to anyone close enough to hear, "Find cover! Hurry!"

Shouts mounted as a quake beyond the Richter scale rattled even the air itself. Minerals on all sides split into pebbles. The ceiling crumbled, and stalactites plummeted, burying angel and demon alike.

Nechum searched for Alameth. He caught the glimpse of a grey coat within the densest of the sedimentary rain. Alameth stood tall. His fogs rammed and broke apart many large stones, but they were coming too fast. Bigger and bigger rocks pummeled him, and he soon dropped to his knees.

Coughing on dust, Nechum covered his mouth and raced to Alameth. He tried to raise a shield for them both, but a thousand pounds of dirt poured down. It bypassed the edges of his fledgling barrier. His field fizzled out. Nechum covered his head as the din blew him down. Rocks piled around him, and Nechum peeked past his elbow to watch the scant light dull, waver, then expire.

Chapter 32

JEDIAH'S HEAD BURST through the Seine River's surface. Foul bacterial water swept in his mouth, attempting to fill his human lungs. All the while, he hugged Chloe tight and kicked desperately to keep her face above water. He was thankful for the Seine's powerful current. Architectures and buildings flew past as it carried them both far from Elazar, but Jediah now feared a more present danger. The contaminated river's frigid grip stabbed his entire body. He dared not think of what it was doing to Chloe.

Desperate, Jediah nearly ran them both into a docked ferry boat in his struggle for the shore. The river soon narrowed into a thin channel. There were elevated sidewalks on each side, and Jediah noticed a bridge that stretched above, one capable of providing shelter from the dismal rain.

Stroking with one arm, he reached the rough wall and dragged himself and Chloe onto the solid concrete. He tasted copper as his physical body convulsed and evicted the water.

Chloe, however, didn't cough. Nor did she stir from the rain on her face.

Jediah hacked, but tucked her under his torso and rushed her under the bridge. Now sheltered from the storm, he plopped down, exhausted. The yellow street-lamps turned the deluge on either side of them into glinting curtains that cut them off from the rest of the world. He shivered terribly from the wet and wished his human form could activate his dormant energy. At least it would help his damp clothes dry, but a greater concern troubled him.

Jediah searched Chloe's face for signs of life, but her willowy body laid in his arms, cold and still. His body vibrated to his own catching breaths. He fought tears as he gently tried to dry her bare head with his soaked sleeve. "Come on, Chloe. No one's come for your breath of life yet. You're okay. Please, just open your eyes for me, sweetheart."

Her lips went from blue to purple. Her body became a waxen figure, and the incomplete Mark on her chest dimmed.

Jediah shook his head. He resisted it but began accepting the terrible reality. He was losing her. She'd be lost to the loving Father who loved her most. She'd be lost to a family she could have had but would never meet. Then—the ultimate death—she'd be lost to memory.

That final thought broke Jediah. The will to stay strong abandoned him. His neck and face heated. His lungs quaked as he shook and sobbed into her shoulder. The angel could do little else than hug her tighter, croaking his apologies for bringing this nightmare down upon her. "Not yet, Lord. Not yet. More time," he pleaded. "By Your merciful nature, Yahweh. Grant her more time."

An icy drop smacked the back of Jediah's neck. He jolted and angrily rubbed the spot where it stung. "Curse this physical form!" he spat.

Jediah froze. Caught in the moment, he became more aware of the dying cells all across his skin—the same strange sensation he, an angel, could never get used to. Jediah re-examined his hand and its sinews, veins, and tissues. Then it hit him. When he crossed into the first realm, his being adopted the temporal limits of that temporal realm.

My being adopted the realm!

A new hope skyrocketed within him. Jediah stared at Chloe's ghastly pallor. *Is it possible? Could I bring her into the second realm and outside time's reach?* Jediah wasn't sure what might happen with such an audacious plan. No living mortal had entered their realm—at least, not since Apostle John of the Patmos Isle was drawn into the spiritual plain to write the Scripture's final pages. However, if it be God's will, Jediah knew, it could very well preserve her life. It had to.

Pressing a palm to Chloe's forehead, Jediah focused. He remembered how energy shifting worked. He wasn't sure if his present physical form could withstand the process, but Chloe's ebbing life couldn't wait. It was now or never.

Jediah gritted his teeth. By a God given miracle, his angelic energy awakened, but as he suspected, his human body wasn't designed to handle it. His organs twisted in cramped knots, as energy moved from his back to his arm. Sweat beaded his forehead. It rippled up his muscles and ate his delicate flesh alive until his energy reached his hand. His rigid fingers shook and burned, but he forged through the needling pain. Energy seeped out of his fingertips to soak through her skin, and the portions of energy he shared with her reached her soul. Chloe was ready to be drawn into his world.

"Lord," Jediah prayed, "be glorified in this." He shed his mortal shell, and she began to change along with him.

Laszio's eyes fluttered. He felt a sticky substance drying on his brow. The shambles surrounding him formed a burrow with a single hole big enough to crawl through just ahead of him. His mind whirred to piece his memories together. Lucifer had blasted them at point blank range. He laid waste to the caves. No doubt he had reached the Abyss's center by now or was about to.

Laszio lifted himself on sore arms. His tender knees screamed. Raising his stick in his hand, he discovered a broken cord with a frayed end attached to it and the opposite stick missing. He cast the useless weapon aside, and a sudden throbbing in his back flared. Laszio checked over his shoulder. A stump remained where his right wing used to be. Worried for Eran, he called out for him.

Eran mumbled in response. He laid just behind Laszio, and his remaining right wing twitched as he tried to unfurl it.

"Let's go, brother," Laszio said. "Our work's not done yet." Chips bit Laszio's hands as he crawled. Meeting a slope, he dragged himself up on bleeding elbows and emerged from the mess. Realizing there were no sounds behind him, he twisted around. Eran hadn't moved. His face still laid in the dirt.

Laszio slid back down the slope and offered a hand. "Hey. Did you hear me, Eran? We've got work to do. Get up."

Eran lifted weary eyes.

Unnerved by his friend's lost expression, Laszio scooted in closer. "Look. So Lucifer used the key and got the best of us. It's still not over."

"How can it not be over?" Eran said as he punched the dirt. "Our brothers are completely crushed. They trusted me. They put their faith in me, and I got them buried in gravel."

"Hey, *we* failed," Laszio corrected. "And so what? Jediah makes tough calls like that all the time. He's not always right either. Besides, there are two things I noticed that made goading Lucifer into trashing the cave a fantastically good thing. One, God is still on the Throne. Ain't nothin' changing that. And two, I'm willing to bet that smart-aleck just wiped out his entire army along with ours with that stunt."

At that, Eran's back shot up, straight as a rod. "Really?"

"Wouldn't surprise me a bit," Laszio said with a grin. "It helps that I listened for once to a brilliant genius who told me, 'God uses His weakest for His greatest glories.'" Laszio again offered his hand.

Jediah cradled Chloe close. As much of a feather weight as she always was, she weighed even less in the spiritual realm. It still rained in the first realm, but the weather had little sway in the second.

Jediah wandered the damp Paris streets, anxious to return her to her family, but he hit a major problem. He had no clue where to take Chloe or who to leave her with. The crash site was out of the question so long as Elazar was at large. The only human guardian he'd recognize was her grandfather. Chloe's guardian angel was another he'd like to find, but since Elazar had impersonated him, Jediah hated to think about what he might have done to the real one. No option remained besides 'keep moving'. She was safest so long as they didn't linger in one spot.

Careful to support her neck, Jediah propped Chloe up with his arm, and she subconsciously snuggled into his shoulder. It had taken mere seconds for the spiritual realm to affect her. Her furrowed brow had smoothed. The tired bags under her eyes were erased, and she rested in contented sleep. A formerly lost vitality returned to the edges of her smile and glowed in her skin. Nothing could have comforted Jediah more. He even wondered, if she stayed there long enough, would it cure her illness and regrow her hair? His smile broadened. Though yet unsaved, Christ's abounding love still showed her a measure of His grace and mercy.

A different kind of protective drive suddenly consumed Jediah, and he pondered if this was what fathers felt when holding their daughters. Though her future was a mystery and her eternity yet uncertain to him, visions of her fully grown and walking with the Lord played in Jediah's mind. He saw her bloom. He envisioned her wedding, her children, and the family Christ might grant her.

Moved by this hope, Jediah sang. He kept his voice low and the ballad tender so as not to disturb her. His ancient melody, sung in the Celestial tongue, recounted God's deeds through the ages, and every once in a while, he could almost swear she was awake and listening.

Minutes passed. Jediah entered a dreary garden. The miserable weather spoiled its budding flowers, and bending trees sagged from soaked bark. The walkway weaved through the weeping willows, and at the first curve, a bench came into view.

Jediah paused. Just past a curtain of leaves, Elazar sat there, staring off toward the Seine where he himself must have washed up.

Jediah wanted to bolt at first but knew losing visual on Elazar was riskier. Elazar's empathic sense would have picked up his and Chloe's presence already.

Hugging Chloe close, Jediah neared the bench.

Elazar didn't turn his head as he spoke. "Foolish of you to bring her here. Much less into our realm."

"I had no choice," Jediah said in a tired monotone.

Elazar stood up from his seat. He walked toward Jediah, but his steps faltered, weaker than usual. Jediah realized he had a hand pressed over the wet, gaping wound in his chest—the one when he first ran him through in the ambulance.

Elazar tossed Jediah's sword at his feet. "You dropped that," he stated, as he raised his half-healed palms, both still scarred from Alameth's acidic pellets. "Come. Let's finish this."

"And when exactly *is* it finished, Elazar?" Jediah shot back. "When will you ever be finished? Do oceans need to dry and the moon to bleed?"

"My vengeance isn't complete until you're broken. Fight me!"

Jediah stared Elazar down. He stroked Chloe's thin arm. "I have more important things to do than to indulge your petty grudge."

Elazar clenched his teeth. The horrid scar glowed bright crimson. "You said it yourself," he said. "There's nothing left in me but hate. I'm your worst enemy, so what are you waiting for? Finish what you started!"

"Is one scar truly what all this is about?" Jediah barked. "One careless scratch merits war?"

"You hate me!" Elazar screamed. "You acted like you cared about me! Acted like you trusted me! Then you lash me like an animal!" To Jediah's bitter shock, Elazar's mood turned on a dime. He quivered as he devolved into an emotional wreck. "You called me radical! Called me traitor! I put my faith in you... And it turned out you never cared about me to begin with."

Taken aback, Jediah shook his head and countered in a matter-of-fact tone, "I never hated you, Elazar."

"Stop lying to me! I orchestrated the slaughter of millions. I tormented you and you brothers. I stole your wings and your dignity. You can't possibly not hate me." Elazar shuddered during his rant, and tears streamed from his good eye.

Suddenly, Jediah's eyes were opened to the leftover speck that remained of the former Elazar's shriveled heart—the last surviving piece. Jediah's voice warbled as he spoke, "You mourned our friendship too, didn't you. You're a cold creature, Elazar. There is no saving you... yet even an unrepentant heart like yours can weep for what's lost. I didn't consider it before, but it's clear to me now. After all this time, you suffered from guilt just as much and just long as I have."

"I'm not guilty, you idiot," Elazar retorted. "I'm ashamed of nothing. Nothing!"

"No," Jediah countered. "You're not. And you know it." Moistening his lips, he looked Elazar square in the eye. "Even now, you're still scraping to wipe the guilt clean."

Elazar dipped his chin. The angle added a sinister slant to his glare. "Shut. Up."

"Why else hadn't your revenge satisfied you?" Jediah asked. "You've so convinced yourself payback would restore your happiness, that you've blinded yourself from what you need."

"I said shut up!" Elazar yelled.

Jediah shook his head. "And yet you refuse what you need."

"What? God's *forgiveness*?" the demon spat.

Jediah stared at the pavement. "You don't want forgiveness, Elazar. You want justification. You want my genuine hate to prove you were in your rights to break your vows to God. Is that not so? If I ever do hate you, you'd get your justification... you'd win." Jediah looked up. "I see right through you. This revenge is your attempt to clear your conscious."

Elazar reached for his dagger. "I tire of your lies," he growled. "Admit the truth."

Demon and angel shared the silence.

Closing his eyes, Jediah answered in as tranquil a voice as he could. "Then hear me now, Elazar, and may God deal with me, be it ever so severely, if what I say bears any falsehood... Elazar, whether you accept it or not—" Jediah struggled against his thickening voice. "You were my brother. I loved you. I still love you, and I'll continue to love you. And loving you, despite what you've become, agonizes me more than anything under heaven. Surely, that's enough revenge to satisfy you."

Elazar's mouth gaped. His grip on the dagger faltered, and his eyebrows raised in what appeared to be relief. His eye danced around, lost and unsure, but then his countenance hardened. He raised his dagger. Jediah stepped back as he pointed it at Chloe. "Sure. Go on. Keep lying," Elazar motioned a cut across his throat. "But let's see if you keep saying that after I kill your little princess."

The furnace in Jediah's depths rekindled. "You're. Not. Touching. Her."

Elazar scoffed. He raised his half-scalded palms, and flickering shields stretched into two long blades.

Jediah laid Chloe down on the bench. He gripped her hand. "Fear not. You're safe."

"Ha," Elazar mocked. "She'll never know safety again."

Planting himself between her and Elazar, Jediah picked up his sword and raised it to his foe's chin level. Their blades touched and scraped slowly. Pressure between their weapons mounted as the strength in their arms met and matched the other.

Laszio's boots skidded to a halt in the Abyss's center. Eran followed close behind.

Lucifer had passed the prison pools and now fanned his wings, showing off the extra pair for the prisoners' adulation. "My subjects, your warden is finished, and your deliverer has come!"

Walls rumbled as demons drummed victory chants inside their cells.

Lucifer's grand robes of blue, purple, and scarlet flowed as he walked. He set himself before Apollyon's mountainous gates and raised his hands. "Apollyon! Your master commands you. Come forth—"

The cave echoed to a rhythmic thumping. Laszio used his single wing to bat the ground, splashing white light from its quills.

Lucifer dropped his arms and peeked over his shoulder.

"Lucifer!" Laszio called. "I demand the right of single combat! Accept my challenge or forfeit!"

Pivoting around, Lucifer grinned at him and Eran—two battered, flightless, and unarmed soldiers. "Look at you two," he crooned. "I don't know whether to laugh or cry."

"You're never opening that gate, demon," Eran retorted. He fanned his single wing and gave the same traditional challenge Laszio had given. "Fight us or surrender!"

Lucifer rolled his eyes. He turned to the cell. "I'll accept both your challenges in a moment."

"Don't try it," Laszio warned.

Lucifer curled Jediah's wings in. Red light charged in their roots, and the feathers vibrated so that the quills split apart in messy angles. The crimson colors climbed. Demonic shouts thundered, but then Lucifer flinched. The crowd silenced.

The Devil contorted as one of Jediah's feathers popped and sputtered thick red. Then another five quills spewed open and caught fire. Lucifer shrieked as a hundred more of Jediah's feathers joined the nuclear meltdown, dowsing him in the burning winepress of God's wrath.

"Now, Eran!" Laszio sprinted forward. Eran's feet matched his, stride for stride, but then Lucifer's red eyes locked onto them. His remaining four wings drew him up.

Lucifer's being gained mass, as he mutated into a twisted amalgamation of monsters yet unseen. His hundred arms and legs filled the Abyss. Barbed fur sprouted between slimed scales. Purple poison seeped from his pores. His shadow leeched the color from whatever it touched, and atop a mountain of bulbous eyes sat his grinning head and its four faces, each one set in a cardinal direction.

Laszio stiffened and stumbled backwards. He looked to Eran for encouragement, but Eran shared the same terrified gaze. Still, they clasped hands and refused to run. "*Anytime you want, Lord,*" Laszio prayed. "*Anytime.*"

The seconds ticked against them. Lucifer's five hundred tentacles and paws wrecked the cells. Prisoners escaped with his every step, and the freed demon cherubs sprouted their claws, legs, and scorpion tails to follow him.

Shuddering, Laszio raised his fists and wrapped his single wing to protect his chest.

With acid leaking from his many mouths, Lucifer opened one of his largest four. He arched his neck and hacked up the vomit that pooled in his maw.

Pop!

A comet burst in and detonated a mist bomb between the front set of Lucifer's eyes. Lucifer toppled, squashing some of his cherubs.

Laszio could have leapt for joy at the lightning that streaked across the ceiling. He pumped Eran's shoulder. "He made it!"

Akela circled back, shouting, "Hey, Lucifer! How rude to check in early! Your room's not ready yet!" He landed with a thunderclap next to his comrades. His golden wings buzzed so fast the bouncing ends of his curls crackled static. He beamed at his brothers and waved the note Eran had left for him in his satchel. "Hey. Got your message."

Laszio clapped Akela's shoulder. "And not a second too soon, brother."

"We're here too!" Nechum declared, as he and Alameth ran in. Nechum's eyes widened at Lucifer, the lumbering monstrosity. "Um, brothers?" More black and green junk spewed from one of Lucifer's mouths, and Nechum raised a protective shield. The gunk smothered thickly over the barrier.

Careful not to break his own sword with a direct clash, Jediah deflected Elazar's blade but suffered another cut to his side.

"It's your fault, you know!" Elazar said, as he sliced a third gash across Jediah's brow. "She wouldn't be on my radar if it weren't for you." He swiped again, but Jediah ducked. "You know, I never tasted what the human's call the 'joys of the flesh.'"

Jediah froze.

Elazar grinned, knowing he struck a nerve. "Maybe, after you're out of commission, I'll try it out on her!"

Enraged, Jediah carved into Elazar's thigh. Then, using his spare energy, he opened a dimensional rift and tackled Elazar right through it into the third spiritual plain. At least Elazar would be that much farther away from Chloe there.

They plopped together in a field of blue-tinted grass. Elazar kicked Jediah off. He lunged, dagger in hand, and sliced a slow cut along Jediah's jaw. Jediah grabbed Elazar's wrist, and his arm shook as he tried to redirect the knife. Elazar leaned in and twisted it back. The point pricked the corner of Jediah's eye and threatened to gouge it out.

Gritting his teeth, Jediah kneed Elazar in the torso. The dagger dropped. Then, after throwing Elazar off, Jediah retrieved his sword and shortened the blade.

Elazar charged.

Jediah threw his sword.

As expected, Elazar's reflexes kicked in, and he caught it in his bare hands. "That trick won't save you," he mocked. His finger touched the hilt. The button triggered, and the sword ran him through; right in the exact spot of the first wound. A look of shock tore through Elazar as he fell backwards into the soft grass.

Sobered by the sight of him, Jediah didn't withdraw the sword right away.

Elazar, glaring with wide eyes, puffed hisses through his clenched teeth.

Jediah slowly took the hilt, and despite his waning strength, his trembling hand pulled the sword out.

"Now," Laszio and Eran commanded.

Nechum split open the shield. Lucifer's muck slopped on either side. God's unfiltered glory consumed all five angels, and their eyes and robes of burning white cast golden beams that contested Lucifer's shadow.

Opening his hands, Alameth flooded the Abyss in fog just as planned. Their torrents subdued every escapee, chucked them back in their cells, and trapped them inside.

Lucifer howled in frustration. His poisons oozed faster, and their ink bled into Alameth's mist. Infecting, consuming, and spreading towards Alameth.

Alameth stiffened. He grunted as he got his mist to resist the black disease to a standstill. "Whatever you're going to do, do it quickly," he pleaded.

Nechum jumped on Akela's back and interlocked his legs.

Akela's wings hummed. "Buckled in?" he asked.

Gripping Akela's shoulders, Nechum shoved out a breath, then covered them under a pointed shield.

"Alrighty then!" Akela grinned. "Let's do this!"

Laszio watched them strike Lucifer's chin first. This was the best idea Eran had yet. Nechum's invincible shield, paired with Akela's powerhouse speed, gave Lucifer a run for his money. The Devil stumbled backwards, but before he could even react, Akela and Nechum had already burst from the opposite wall, plowing a massive chunk off his biggest cheek. Lucifer's arms swatted the air in futile circles. Then the blue-laced golden comet tore off a limb.

Laszio couldn't imagine Akela and Nechum getting any faster, but Akela somehow split the seconds into milliseconds, then milliseconds into microseconds until his light trails became semi-solid bands. Blinding megavolts sheered away Lucifer's hide.

Returning, Akela grounded to a halt. Nechum fumbled off his back, dizzy but otherwise okay.

Lucifer growled at the leaking holes they peppered him with. "You think this will stop-"

Akela zoomed in and chucked a bag down his gullet.

Lucifer paused mid-sentence. Bewildered and dreading what he swallowed, he stared at the messenger.

Akela grinned. "You talk too much."

Lucifer gripped his throat as Yakum's black mist vapored and leaked out all of his nostrils, ears, and lips. Even his hundred eyes smoked.

Akela flew back, chipper as ever. "Needed to get rid of that," he commented.

"Alameth, strap him down!" Eran ordered.

Alameth clenched his quivering hands. Mist entombed all but Lucifer's massive, four-faced head. The Abyss rumbled as the Devil dropped to one knee.

Laszio and Eran wrapped an arm around each other. They pulled their sides together and stretched out their single wings as if they were one complete set.

"Lord," they both prayed. "This victory is Yours."

They flapped in perfect sync; then gave another unison flap that rocketed them up towards Lucifer's lower chin. They sensed God Himself overtaking them. Movement ceased to be their own. Then, without thought, their free arms recoiled. Their diamond-hard feathers wrapped, forming fisted gauntlets. Then came the punch.

Their fists hit their mark. Laszio felt his wing shattering in slow motion. Each feather rang loud before cracking and falling away, yet he felt no pain.

The resulting, shockwave rocked the Abyss's walls and upturned chunks of stone.

The dust cleared, and Laszio and Eran—panting, wingless, and radiating the Glory of God—planted their feet on the neck of Evil Incarnate.

The wet tip of Jediah's sword hovered close to Elazar's neck. He considered lopping his head off his shoulders.

"What are you waiting for?" Elazar asked. "Do it."

Jediah swung back, but reminding himself of what Elazar wanted—justification for his hatred—he hesitated. Seconds passed. A minute. Jediah lowered his sword. "I won't. I won't give you more fuel for your fire."

Elazar swept Jediah's feet out from under him. Jediah landed hard, and his sword thudded out of reach. Elazar stalked Jediah as he struggled to crawl back. "You're pathetic. All those angels call you noble, yet you've cowered in shame behind their backs." He kicked Jediah's chest. "You've always been guilty." Elazar struck again. "You'll forever be guilty." Jediah coughed up energy as Elazar stomped on his throat. "And there's nothing you can do about it!" Shields gloved Elazar's hands as he brought them down.

Stars flashed in Jediah's head.

Jediah awoke on his side. Elazar's boots were but a few feet away from him, but far beyond, he saw a vision of Chloe—in the arms of His Lord. Those pierced hands had drawn her close to His heartbeat. His smile shone upon her, both overjoyed to see her, yet saddened by a deep longing for her.

Then His Lord's luminous eyes turned toward him, bidding the angel to rise.

Jediah forgot his injuries. He forgot Elazar, and a deeper will, one that he recognized not to be his own, moved his arms for him. As he lifted to his hands and knees, silver and gold lined his red clothes, and the tears mended themselves.

"You're right, Elazar." Jediah said. "I can't escape my weaknesses or my guilt," He raised a knee and lifted his eyes. "But God never said I had to. And I imagine... it's the same for His redeemed people too. My weakness becomes His strength and my guilt an example of His Grace. For He does in me, what I cannot do for myself." Stronger golds and silvers wafted over Jediah like ocean tides, and glimmering white colored his sleeves.

A rhythm like the resounding music of the seraphs revived Jediah's spirit. Its drum became the new passion that fueled his heart. Suddenly, the ends of his reddish brown hair came to life as tongues of purple flame. His clothes were adorned in a purity so overpowering, its hidden rainbows were hidden no more. Colors of all spectrums, even those never before seen, imbued each thread.

Lightning cracked around Jediah's eyes. Excess energy beaconed from his being. Jediah could be described right then as nothing less than a supernova—wondrous and terrible.

Elazar stumbled back.

"Jesus is Lord!" Jediah declared. "He is enough, and *He's* my answer to problems and beings like you!"

For a moment, Elazar balked. He formed a spear, but God's glory that clothed Jediah evaporated the projectile. Elazar then punched the air, sending a firestorm of red. Jediah opened an iridescent palm and blasted them to nothing. The boom knocked Elazar down. Still, Elazar's stubbornness wouldn't wane. Try after try, his attacks were dashed in aftershocks equal to atom bombs.

Jediah turned his pearled face to the third realm's sky. "Lord! King of Heaven and Earth! Of the visible and invisible! I cannot deal with Elazar myself. So I leave him to Your hands and to Your judgment!"

Crystal rivers swept in. Glory expanded overhead as a pure cloud, and soon power to fill the earth entered and humbled everything into silence. Then with resounding hallelujahs and a heralding maelstrom, the Triune God revealed Himself to them in full, wrapped in the cosmos of His splendor.

Jediah fell prostrate. He dared not look directly at God's holy face, but lifted his head enough to see His very righteousness materialize in a visible shape. It sucked him and Elazar into its endless vacuum. Jediah's vision filled with such blinding colors that if infinite space in all its spectral stars and nebulas compacted into one jewel, it could not match one speck of it. God's mysteries given form were an unfathomable web of interlinking, sparkling strands. Not even Jediah, an angel, could comprehend its reach, nor its length, nor its height, nor its depth. It outlasted time. It out-spanned distance. It perceived beyond thought. It outmatched all wickedness—physical, spiritual, outside and within.

Eyes brimming with tears, Jediah's core trembled, and he bowed lower in worship.

The Abyss awoke. Thunder roared and snapped as the red stones vibrated white. Laszio and Eran stepped away from Lucifer, alarmed, but then they recognized the familiar, all-encompassing presence. They were all being caught up in God's very being.

The Lord swept Lucifer far off in His inter-dimensional current. The Abyss's cells and its prisons came to life in His presence, and the destruction reassembled, resealing the prisoners more securely than before.

Awed and speechless, Laszio along with Eran, Akela, Nechum, and Alameth bowed together in full reverence before All Mighty God—the Great I AM.

A new crag for a new prison cell broke open next to Apollyon's. Laszio cringed for amid the tumult, a terrified screaming could be barely heard, and he caught sight of Elazar's dissolving face being thrown inside.

The new gate slammed shut.

It barred.

Then silence.

God's power held time in stasis. Then Laszio beheld Elazar's cell doors fade, then disappear—lost forever.

The white glory in his clothes subsided, but Laszio's gladdened heart continued to offer thankfulness after thankfulness to El Shaddai long after.

It was finished.

Chapter 33

ALONG THE ABYSS'S WALLS lingered a residual holiness from the Father of Lights. It coated every surface in diamonds, turning the cave into one dazzling geode.

Nechum set his tired self down. He drank in his new memories—the battles, the victories, the struggles—all pieces of a narrative God had orchestrated and would continue to compose. Releasing a sigh, he laid back, folded peaceful hands, and reveled in thoughts of a long overdue nap.

Laszio and Eran knelt on either side of him. They sported new pairs of wings, larger and grander than before.

Laszio rubbed Nechum's shoulder. "Eager to return to your village?" he asked.

Nechum laughed, "Yeah. I think I've had enough excitement to last me a few hundred years."

Eran shook his head. "What are you talking about? Excitement is, as humans say, our bread and bagel."

Nechum rolled his eyes. "You mean 'bread and butter', and don't apply terms you don't understand."

"We *are* gonna miss you, though," said Laszio, as his eyebrows dipped.

"Yeah," Nechum replied. "I'll miss you too."

"Oof!"

Nechum turned his head to see Akela bear hugging Alameth, and Alameth straining for balance. "You didn't have to do that," Alameth coughed, as he patted Akela with a demure smile.

Akela released Alameth and brushed an unruly curl behind his ear. "I know. My hugs are rough. It's just, the last time I saw you, you were...and I, um..."

Alameth chuckled. In quiet strength, he wrapped an arm around Akela's shoulders and pulled him into a gentler hug. "Thank you. For everything."

Nechum relaxed contented. No hurts soured the moment. No unwarranted suspicions or fears tainted the relief. Everyone's hearts brimmed with thrilling joy, and their eyes shone hues richer than their first day together.

Closing his eyes, Nechum broke away from the present. The mission was now truly complete. As he set his hands down, Nechum's fingers hit metal. His brow furrowed. He turned his head and brushed dirt off the mystery object, revealing a familiar sword.

"Wait a minute," Akela remarked. He patted his sides and spun around as he searched the floor. "Hey, has anybody seen my satchel?"

Jediah raised his head and found himself back in the Paris garden. Akela's satchel leaned against him. Its flap had been left open, and he recognized the torn pieces of Nechum's shawl inside. It confused him to discover Akela's belongings here. Still, he snapped the clasp closed and pulled the satchel strap over his head.

The rain had stopped. The clouds cleared, and resting on the park bench where Jediah's last fight began, laid Chloe with her head cradled in the lap of Jesus Himself.

Jediah arose and knelt before the Messiah.

"Well done, my good and faithful, servant," Jesus said. "Well done."

Jediah heard rustling fabric. Then a small strip of crimson adorned his shoulders. Confused, he fingered the cloth and recognized the stitched pattern. It was his scarf, and it bore the captain's crest.

Then Christ's palm, calloused from carpenter's wood, touched Jediah's sore back. A healing warmth grew beneath those tender fingers, and Jediah could feel new feathers blooming like seeds. They expanded, voluminous and strong, and soon Jediah could once again see his beloved wings, fully restored. Too joyful to think, Jediah forgot formal etiquette and grabbed the hem of Christ's robe and kissed it.

To hear the Son of God's laughter was soothing music. "Do not cling to me," Jesus said. "Arise."

Rising to a stand, Jediah wiped off his moist cheeks.

Jesus, who had scooped little Chloe in His arms, passed her to Jediah. "I now send you to deliver her to her family."

Unable to speak. Jediah nodded. He turned to go on his way, but then stalled. He stared at the Mark not yet complete on Chloe's chest. "Lord?" he asked. "Will she be saved?"

Jesus tipped His head. His eyes brimmed with an understanding kindness, yet He said not a word.

"Right," Jediah relented. "Only You will know."

Nodding, Jesus ushered him on his way.

Cameras and news anchors scrambled to get the story. Tow trucks hissed as they pulled the wrecked ambulance away from the edge. Police officers spoke through the static of their radios while their chiefs barked orders, and crowds circled the site of the incident.

Kenneth struggled with his ill stomach as he stood beside the bridge rail, watching motor boats dredge the rough waters. Little hope remained of finding Chloe's body. The grief of outliving his own granddaughter, the worst tragedy he hoped to never endure, consumed him. He wanted to die.

He couldn't bear it anymore. His growing sobs caused him to cave over the cement rail, and his tears joined the Seine. He opened his wrinkled hands toward heaven. "Heavenly Father. My faithful Father. Long have You carried me through the trials of my life, but this...this," Ken leaned harder against the rail as his arthritis attacked his knees. "I have agonized and agonized over my granddaughter, Lord. You have heard me lift her up in prayer so many times for her heart to open and for You to send her others besides myself to minister to her. Maybe even one of your holy angels."

Kenneth raised and lowered a fist. The veins protruded through the thinned skin. "You know the plans You have for us. Plans to prosper us, to give us a hope and a future through the gift of Your Son's blood which can save us from our sins. But Chloe never yet sought Your Son." He blinked back more tears. "But You hold power over the grave... So I humbly ask again, Lord, for that ministering spirit. Please... please, Lord, send Your best angel to bring her back to us."

As Ken finished his prayer, his anxiety calmed. The Holy Spirit moved within him, teaching his heart to let faith keep hope's candle alive.

A car door opened and shut.

Perplexed, Ken turned around to check on his vehicle. No one was there, except a little round head that poked just above the window's edge.

It moved.

Struggling with disbelief, Ken ignored his arthritis and swung the door open. Chloe laid asleep, looking somehow healthier than before.

"Chloe?" Ken almost feared his aging mind, thinking dementia might have finally caught up with him, but then two bright eyes opened.

"Grandpa?"

Sobbing freely, Ken wrapped his granddaughter in his arms and rocked her back and forth. "Thank you. Thank you, Father God." He pulled back and studied her. "Are you okay, Chloe?"

Chloe squinted. She looked around as if searching for something. "Where'd he go?"

"He?" Ken asked. "Who are you talking about, sweetheart?"

"The nice man who sang to me."

Adrenaline coursed through Ken's body, and an awed realization forced him to sit down on the car floor. He gripped her hand. "What did this man look like?" Noticing a lump in her fist, Ken opened her hand and discovered a braided lock of reddish-brown hair—just like the ones Chloe braided in that odd man's hair.

Chloe drifted back into slumber, yet she smiled as though returning to a beautiful dream. "He was real shiny, Grandpa."

A knowing smile etched itself upon Ken's face as he nodded. "I'm sure he was, sweetheart. I'm sure he was."

Jediah watched the scene from a distant rooftop. He almost laughed to watch Chloe's family drown the poor girl in kisses amidst the claps, whistles, and astonished faces of the crowds. He then noticed a ministry angel, Chloe's guardian, limping his way to them. Even from afar, Jediah could see the angel's thrilled reaction to Chloe's return.

The night trudged on. The throng dispersed. Police and medical crews vacated. The news media packed their equipment, and the one section of broken bridge, now fenced in by traffic cones, remained the sole clue that any accident ever happened.

As Jediah continued his vigil over the resumed parade of coming and going cars, for the first time, in the longest time, he felt unhindered peace. No more guilt. No more anxiety.

He searched Akela's satchel. His hand withdrew the soft pieces of blue fabric. He smiled to himself. *One last mission.*

The task, though tedious, never became a chore. Jediah assembled the torn shawl beside himself. Certain of their pattern, he set two pieces at a time on his lap and stroked the frayed threads. Popped stitches mended, and bit by bit, through hours of careful work, the restored shawl draped Jediah's legs like a cashmere blanket. He folded the fabric, then placed the silver cross pin in its center.

He heard footsteps.

Jediah turned his head, and Nechum was already there, carrying his sword in both hands. The battered blade had been recently polished. Not a scratch remained. Nechum smiled as he offered it back. "I believe you lost this, brother."

Jediah chuckled and presented the shawl. "Care to trade?" He drew up to a stand. "Besides, I think this suits you better." Draping the shawl over Nechum's narrow shoulders, he filled with joy to see it returned to its compassionate owner. The angelic crest pin reflected its tiny glow off Nechum's face.

Nechum smiled, and as he handed Jediah his sword, their eyes locked. They nodded in unspoken appreciation. Then Jediah slid it back in his scabbard.

Nechum folded his arms in thought. "It's amazing, isn't it? We angels enjoy God's grace, but hopelessly lost, rebellious humans get to experience all of His righteousness in full measure."

The feathers across Jediah's sides and back warmed. Their soft down buzzed with the thrill at the thought. *Christians: the ultimate manifestation of His love—Bearers of His Complete Image.*

Nechum stared at the blue haze in the east and sighed, "A new day is coming."

"Indeed it is," Jediah whispered.

Silent moments passed as they awaited the sunrise. Blue warmed to pink. Pink turned to gold. Then the first rays of the sun's crown peeked. A few sparrows chirped in the waking world, and Nechum sang with them—a song which Jediah joined in perfect harmony.

Praise God from whom all blessings flow...
Praise Him all creatures here below...
Praise Him above ye heavenly hosts...
Praise Father, Son, and Holy Ghost...

Epilogue

THE CARE HOME STAFF lessened as they traded workers for the night shift. Amidst the dwindling voices, Alameth hummed his lullaby. Fog followed his feet down the hall. He stopped before a shut room.

Jediah approached close behind him. His fingers trembled as he adjusted his scarf. "After you, old friend," he offered.

Rolling his eyes, Alameth chuckled, "We're all the same age, remember?"

"It was a joke," Jediah said in a resigned tone.

Alameth shook his head. "Let's leave the jokes to Nechum, sir. At least, *he's* funny."

A dimensional rift opened, and Nechum stepped in. "Am I late?" he asked.

"No, you're just in time," Jediah answered.

Akela, Laszio, and Eran exited the same portal. "Phew," Akela remarked to the others. "Told you we were going the right way."

Sergeants Laszio and Eran checked the hallways. Their braids swung around as their heads moved in diligent vigil. After a minute, they nodded to each other, faced Jediah, and saluted. "All clear, Captain." Their serious expressions quickly gave way to relaxed smiles, as their postures turned casual.

Alameth considered their brief security check unnecessary, but he recognized their actions for what they were—their way of showing support.

Akela fiddled his fingers. "Well, can't keep everyone waiting."

Alameth felt odd at first when Jediah waited for him to lead, but realized Jediah needed him to. He and Jediah's forms dissolved through the wood and reassembled on the other side.

Upon sighting the bed, Alameth removed his hood.

Sunset doused the blank walls in orange. The breeze that slipped in brushed gauze curtains. Heart monitors beeped, and the mechanical clicks from a machine controlled the old woman's breaths. Her hands, worn and wrinkled by toils and cares, were held tight by younger, mournful visitors.

Alameth watched Jediah wander to the dresser. His fingers traced the rows of picture frames, each set in meticulous order. A proud graduate displayed a certificate. A groom kissed his radiant bride. A child cuddled in his young mother's arms. Vacations, portraits, and parties and a baptism. Then Alameth noticed Jediah's chin quiver to see what sat on the end. A worn Bible, its pages wrinkled and kinked, laid open, and its bookmark was a single yellowed letter with a familiar signature.

Alameth gave Jediah a few minutes before he turned his attention to the sleeping woman. Her Mark of the Trinity cast heaven's glow, and Alameth heard the Holy Spirit within her beckon him. Singing in a low register, the angel of death touched her brow. She trembled. Her lungs stilled. The rims of her lips purpled. Her skin paled into a blue, grey tint, and as Alameth's hand dissolved into her mouth, she sank into the mattress. The wispy hairs of her head disappeared into her pillow.

The Mark shimmered bright.

The monitor emitted a single tone, and Alameth called Jediah over. "It's time."

Jediah inched toward the bedside. The Mark stretched open and consumed her body. Entering the spiritual realm, Chloe opened her spiritual eyes for the first time. Gone were the wrinkles. Her hair sprouted thick and long. Eternity's wonders were now hers to cherish, and Jediah would be her first sight.

She shielded her face at first, trembling before the angel who gleamed as of welded bronze—whose wings glistened like a golden sea and whose eyes were vibrant stars.

Jediah leaned over and touched her shoulder. "Fear not, Chloe. Your Lord has sent His servants to take you home."

Chloe gasped at his voice. She peeked at the stranger again, this time slack-jawed.

Jediah's shining smile stretched from cheek to cheek.

Chloe looked him over again. "You... You were—" Sitting up, she touched his tear-stained cheek. "Jack?"

"Well, actually," the angel laughed. "God calls me Jediah."

Chloe shook her head in elated disbelief, and before another word could be said, she threw herself into his arms. Her embrace tightened as Jediah buried his face into her hair.

Alameth could have watched their reunion for hours and by the looks of Laszio, Eran, Akela, and Nechum, they could have too.

Jediah pulled back. "Come," he said to her. "The King has requested His daughter to enter His courts."

Crying, Chloe seized his palm with a sure hold. "Take me to Him."

Jediah picked up where Alameth's song left off and led her out of the room.

The other angels let them pass, drinking in and sharing in their rapturous joy.

A new path to God's country opened. As Alameth watched Chloe and his brothers cross the dimensional plain, he could make out Jesus, standing on the pearled shore.

Chloe released Jediah's hand and rushed into the Son's arms with nary a look back and bawled in her Savior's robes. He stroked her head, weeping for joy over one of millions He gave His very life for.

Alameth smiled. "Worth it," he said to himself. "Always worth it."

THE END

"Though you have not seen Him, you love Him. Though you do not now see Him, you believe in Him and rejoice with joy that is inexpressible and filled with glory, obtaining the outcome of your faith, the salvation of your souls. Concerning this salvation, the prophets who prophesied about the grace that was to be yours searched and inquired carefully, inquiring what person or time the Spirit of Christ in them was indicating when he predicted the sufferings of Christ and the subsequent glories. It was revealed to them that they were serving not themselves but you, in the things that have now been announced to you through those who preached the good news to you by the Holy Spirit sent from heaven...
<u>*things into which angels long to look.*</u>*" 1 Peter 1:8-12 (ESV)*

Character Glossary

JEDIAH
NAME MEANING: GOD KNOWS; GOD PROTECTS
  ANGELIC TYPE: SOLDIER
  WEAPON OF CHOICE: SWORD

Dubbed Apollyon's Bane for his valor in the Scorpion Wars, Captain Jediah had become one of the most respected warriors in God's army. Steadfast, occasionally stern, yet compassionate, he's adamant about doing things right in the right way. As Keeper of the Abyss, it's his primary mission to keep its demons imprisoned until the end of the age.

NECHUM
NAME MEANING: RELIEVER OF ANXIETY
  ANGELIC TYPE: MINISTRY

Kindhearted Nechum has been the primary guardian of a small town in the British countryside for decades. He tries to deal patiently with others, even when they slightly annoy him. You can't depend on Nechum to throw a strong punch, but you can be confident he'll always have a listening ear and a gentle hand.

ALAMETH

NAME MEANING: SHROUDED, HIDDEN, COVERED
ANGELIC TYPE: ANGEL OF DEATH

Few know what goes on in Alameth's head. Tall, quiet, and stoic, he often keeps to himself and naturally intimidates those around him. Still, the angels that work closest with him know he's one of the most earnest there is. Knowing whether he actually feels anything, though, is another matter...

AKELA

NAME MEANING: HAPPY
ANGELIC TYPE: MESSENGER

Ever joyful, Akela passionately lives up to his God given name. His insatiable curiosity drives him to see, experience, and learn about every little thing God created. In Akela's eyes, God's love, glory, and purpose can be seen in everything—be it place, person, thing, animal, or angel. (He has yet to make a smooth landing.)

ERAN
NAME MEANING: WATCHFUL, AWAKE
ANGELIC TYPE: SOLDIER
WEAPON OF CHOICE: CHINESE YO-YO

Private Eran is one of Captain Jediah's most loyal wingmen and is battle partners with his best friend, Private Laszio. His knack for thinking outside the box makes him quite the strategist, yet his tendency to second guess often undermines his potential.

LASZIO
NAME MEANING: GOD IS MY HELP
ANGELIC TYPE: SOLDIER
WEAPON OF CHOICE: CHINESE YO-YO

Private Laszio is the second of Captain Jediah's most loyal wingmen, and he's Private Eran's best friend and battle partner. He's the smallest member of Jediah's barracks. It doesn't help that he's the weakest too, but his firecracker personality and tireless desire to improve his skills far outweighs his meager size.

Angel Glossary

WARRIOR ANGEL

UNIFORM COLOR: RED
NUMBER OF WINGS: TWO

To protect and defend. That's every soldier's duty in God's army. These stalwart angels adapted to the front-lines quickly after the Sin Curse and are well known for their bravery, fortitude, and resourcefulness. God designed them with massive wings that are well suited for strength, along with feathers that they can harden into diamond armor at will. Soldiers can also shoot devastating waves of pure light with every swish and clap of their wings.

MESSENGER ANGEL

UNIFORM COLOR: YELLOW
NUMBER OF WINGS: TWO

The very word 'angel' means 'messenger' in the human tongue, and the angels specified as messengers take their work seriously. If it's a message to be sent, it's a message that will be delivered safely and swiftly. They're the most agile flyers and can slip through most war zones with little trouble. It helps that their skinny wings can reach ridiculously high speeds too.

MINISTRY ANGEL
UNIFORM COLOR: BLUE
NUMBER OF WINGS: NONE

The modern world may have grown more and more complex, but that hasn't stopped ministry angels from ducking in and out of human society on a regular basis. Encamped across the globe, these angels safeguard Christians and watch over humanity on an up close and personal level. They may lack wings, but God has granted them two unique gifts: spiritual force-fields and the emotionally insightful empathic sense.

WORSHIP ANGEL
UNIFORM COLOR: PURPLE
NUMBER OF WINGS: (CHERUB) FOUR ; (SERAPH) SIX

Worship is the beating heart of God's creation, and the worship angels understand its significance the most. Forever encircling the Throne of God, they lead all other angels in praise, worship, and service to their King. Whether near or far, their continual dances and songs provide a universal reminder to everything in all realms exactly who the source of love and life is. Worship angels come in two kinds: the four winged cherubs (the powerful animal shape-shifters); and the six winged seraphs (the graceful burning ones).

NATURE ANGEL
UNIFORM COLOR: GREEN
NUMBER OF WINGS: NONE

Since the Sin Curse, planet earth has decayed at a steady rate. It's only through God and His empowerment of His nature angels that the world hadn't already ripped itself apart. These wingless beings are the rarest among their brethren, and their kind are split into four sub-groups: Wind-class, Earth-class, Water-class, and Fire-class. With limited authority over their assigned elements, each nature angel carries a grave responsibility. Whether it means to maintain order or to inflict disaster, the elements will proclaim God's name to Adam's sons.

ANGEL OF DEATH (DESTROYER)
UNIFORM COLOR: GREY
NUMBER OF WINGS: NONE

Don't be fooled. These ominous denizens of pestilence and plague value life more than you could ever know. Shrouded under their hoods, angels of death emit a thick fog that reacts to their will and emotions like an extension of themselves. Everything that breathes has good reason to be wary in their presence. They're God's judgment arm, and they're not called Destroyers for nothing.

About the Author

A born again Christian, Hannah Mae uses her wide variety of interests to show how a saving relationship with Jesus is no limiter to creativity, fun, and wonder. She's a dance studio owner, runs FlyingFaith.org, and is a 1st place recipient of the ACFW "First Impressions" Award. From her love of Marvel movies to studying Scripture, Hannah absolutely cherishes all Jesus gave her and eagerly awaits her eternal life with Him to come.

Read more at https://www.flyingfaith.org/.

Made in the USA
Monee, IL
22 June 2024